ROUGH TRADE

ROUGH TRADE

A Boo & Junior Gig

Todd Robinson

Copyright © 2016 by Todd Robinson
Cover and jacket design by 2Faced Design
Interior designed and formatted by E.M. Tippetts Book Designs

ISBN 978-1-943818-00-6
eISBN: 978-1-943818-15-0
Library of Congress Control Number: 2016939203

First hardcover edition August 2016 by Polis Books, LLC
1201 Hudson Street
Hoboken, NJ 07030
www.PolisBooks.com

POLIS BOOKS

Also by Todd Robinson

Dirty Words
The Hard Bounce

FOURTEEN YEARS AGO

We were bored as fuck.

Let me tell you something about monotony and summertime in a group home. The combination was dangerous. Overheat a bunch of teenage boys whose balls just kicked into overdrive and don't give them a whole hell of a lot to do.

You see where I'm going here?

"Aw, the damn cue ball is gone again." Ollie had his skinny arm elbow-deep into the corner pocket of the pool table in St. Gabe's rec center, hoping the ball was merely jammed.

"It's gone, Ollie," I said. In the week and a half since somebody donated the old table to St. Gabriel's Home for Boys, six of the balls had wandered off into the general population. Not to mention the two cue sticks that had disappeared.

Why the social workers thought billiards would be a good activity for a hundred or so locked up juveniles was beyond me. All it did was give us another means by which to arm ourselves. And they just kept replacing the goddamn balls.

"Can't you make us something?" Junior went back to dipping his sewing needle into the ink sleeve of a black Bic pen, then popping the ink into the skin of his forearm. He thought he could be a tattoo artist once he got out of The Home. He was working on his own self-inflicted piece—his first tattoo.

Ollie scratched at the wispy peach fuzz that he was trying to cultivate on his upper lip. "I dunno. Maybe if I could get my hands on some resin."

Junior rolled his eyes. "Oh, for fuck's sake."

"What?" Ollie asked, sliding his ridiculously oversize State-provided glasses back into his nose.

"I was kidding."

Ollie shrugged. "I wasn't." Ollie was the kid who, in his spare time, wrote letters to the producers of *MacGyver* to point out technical inaccuracies he'd catch on the re-runs. The subtleties of sarcasm whipped by him most of the time.

And Junior was about as subtle as a moustache on the prom queen.

Me? I was the guy who was terrible with metaphors.

Where were we?

Oh yeah.

We were trying to alleviate the tedium and boredom of life in a State home without resorting to violence or watching the Red Sox.

Junior dipped the needle back into the plastic ink tube, then jabbed himself a couple more times with tiny intakes of pained breath. He claimed the tattoo was going to be a skull, but it looked like a chipmunk head with human teeth.

I went back to re-reading the first ten pages of *The Girl in the Plain Brown Wrapper*. It was the fourth time I'd read the tattered paperback. Library options were limited at The Home.

Ever the power-nerd, Ollie began waving the pool cue around, making the *ggggzzzzz* sounds of a light saber.

"Please stop that," I said.

"You dare speak against the Jedi, OBoo-Wan?"

"Christ on a crutch, I can practically smell our reps drifting away," I said. I was making a joke, but there was no overstating the importance of reputation at St. Gabe's. Having a rep meant you got tested, or you didn't. It meant you spent your days defending your turf, or lived with a reasonable amount of comfort until somebody grew the balls to challenge the throne.

My crew, The Avengers (thanks again, Ollie), had managed to hang on to a certain respectful distance from the other caged animals despite the occasional prancing Jedi.

But that shit could change in an instant.

Ollie froze mid-*ggggzzzzz*, his hands white-knuckling the pool cue between his fingers. Only two things made Ollie freak out like that. The first one was sharks.

The second was the newest predator in our pressure cooker of a zoo.

Something locked in my chest and I turned, hoping to God that a great white had somehow made its way the forty miles inland to The Home.

Instead, I found the face of Zach Bingham. He blocked most of the doorway as he stood in it, flexing his huge hands. Six feet four and two hundred and eighty pounds of mad dog.

A sixteen-year-old mad dog.

Zach took his time giving each and every one of us a solid glower.

The shark's eyes would have been warmer.

"What?" Junior challenged Zach's stare. As it stood, we had safety in numbers at The Home. Zach didn't. All the crews at St. Gabe's figured it was safer to keep Zach on the outside, despite him making one hell of a fuck-you-guy.

And if the rumors were true, that fuck-you-guy could very quickly turn into guy-fucking-you.

For that reason alone, the fear of being bottom-bitch to a gorilla, everybody tended to stay on the outskirts of Zach's pathways.

Almost everybody.

There was one member of our crew who was running late for our failed billiards meet-up. The one member of our crew who even Zach knew better than to toy with.

Twitch.

Twitch pushed his miniscule body through and under Zach's armpit. "Move it or lose it, Lumpy." It was an easy bridge for the tiny pale psycho, who just so happened to be the tiny pale psycho on our side of the issues.

Zach took a step back, allowing for Twitch's entrance. Apparently, crazy recognized crazy.

Twitch stood right in front of Zach, craning his neck up to look at his ugly puss.

Zach had to nearly touch his chin to his chest to meet Twitch's eyes.

"What's up?" was all Twitch said.

With a smile.

Ollie kept his hands on the stick.

Junior was as tense as a violin string, his eyes flicking over to me, then back to Zach. Under the table, he pointed at me, then pointed up.

That meant *hit 'em high*.

That also meant Junior was ready to hit him low.

The next move was Zach's.

Instead, he looked us over one more time and growled, "Later."

He said it like a deadline.

Twitch picked up a pool cue and smiled. "I got next game." His namesake eyebrow jiggled with excitement.

I looked at Junior. "Gonna be a long two years." That was how long we had before Zach was legally unleashed back onto society. Junior and I still had three each, give or take.

Junior hadn't taken his eyes off the doorway. "We're gonna need a bigger boat," he said, wiping the pinpricks of blood and ink off his forearm with a paper towel.

Twitch looked over the table. "Oh, *man*. Where's the cue ball?"

"There's no cue," said Ollie

"Screw it." Twitch pocketed the five ball and left.

CHAPTER 1

"Tommy, the goddamn band isn't my problem right now." I stood in the middle of a blizzard while Tommy Sheralt, the owner of The Cellar, read me the riot act. You'd figure that Tommy would be a wee bit more sympathetic since he'd worked as a bouncer at the bar thirty years before, back when it was a jazz club and not the rock and roll shit-magnet that it was today.

Normally, in my role as bouncer, the riot act went through me like poop through a goose. But in this case, the entire world had turned to a static-filled television screen and I was trying to make some semblance of order out of the eighty jackasses lined up outside for the show. Now Tommy also wanted me to keep tabs on the prima donna lead singer of The Kingly. Even if Jason St. John and his band were the darlings of the Boston music scene that week, he was still a grade-A douchebag.

"If that little prick is too doped up to play, it's gonna be on you." The swirling snow stuck in Tommy's white moustache. Most people thought he looked like a deranged Santa Claus. Unfortunately, the only thing he was delivering to me was pains in my ass.

"How the hell is it on me? You're the one who booked the asshole."

"And you run my security. Secure that dipshit."

"I don't know what you want me to do, Tommy."

"Boo?" Junior called me from the doorway.

A hipster dork in a Berkeley sweatshirt huddled in the cold. "What time do The Kingly go on? Open the downstairs, already. We're freezing our balls off." The whine in his voice set my teeth grinding.

"Shut it!" I yelled at him. My balls were also in icy peril, but that didn't stop the world from busting them.

Tommy took another swig from his Heineken, easily already a half case in. "Send Junior to follow Jason. I don't want him shooting up, popping pills, or whatever he does between sets."

"You can't be genuinely asking me to send staff off on a mouse hunt. Not tonight." We were already dangerously understaffed for the show, and he wanted me to give up Junior? Two of our weekend swing staff had come down with some hardcore flu. Who knew that repeated transitions from the doorway on a freezing Boston night into overheated crowds stuffed into The Cellar's bacteria factory would be bad for your health?

"I'm not asking." With that, he walked back in to the awfully warm-looking bar.

"Boo!" Junior called with more urgency, waving his arms in the doorway to catch my eye but unwilling to step outside into the snownado to get it.

"What?" I snapped back as I marched into the bar's foyer.

"Jesus fuck. No more coffee for you."

"Sorry. I'm cold as hell and Tommy is in my ass." I stomped my feet, trying to move warm blood into my toes. At that point, however, I didn't think there was any warm blood left in my body to move around. Five more minutes and I was going to be singing songs from *Frozen*.

Yeah, I know songs from *Frozen*.

Blow me.

Junior sniffed at me, his sinuses clear and unimpeded from being inside and away from the Arctic wasteland that Boston was becoming. "Yeah, well, you don't have to snap at me. Here I was trying to be humanistical and shit."

"Sorry, honey. You want to switch off?"

"Well, I was going to offer, but then you were a dick."

"I'll be your best friend."

"You already are."

"Then I'll add a cookie."

"No raisins." Junior put his coat and mittens on. I could have made fun of the mittens, but I really, really wanted to warm myself up. Besides, he at least had mittens. All I had was my continued badass status and impending frostbite.

"Wait a minute..." I said. Over twenty years of friendship and a decade of working together, and Junior had never before offered to switch out on a cold winter night. Mostly because he was pissy about me making fun of his mittens.

"What?" Junior said with all the innocence of a fox with feathers stuck between its teeth.

"What's happening?"

"Why does something have to be happening?"

"We got a problem?"

"Brewing," Junior said, busted.

"Goddammit. What the hell is going on now?" Junior wasn't one to shy away from a situation in the bar. If anything, the opposite was the norm. I was missing something.

Junior lifted his chin to indicate where the problem was. Even in the packed bar, I could see the issue at hand. Waves of tension were flowing forward from where two guys sat at the end of the bar.

Kissing.

Great. On top of everything else, I'd have to play Dick Police too.

Junior didn't bother hiding his disgust at their show. Personally, I didn't like seeing *anybody* dry humping at the bar.

And the couple on hand was going for broke. Even at the other end of the bar, I could see their tongues dancing like a pink pair of tangoing eels.

"Those two are heading into Painsville. Population: them," Junior said, shaking his head.

Like I said, I didn't give a damn who was trading fluid. But I could see that the chromosomal match of the two was making Junior's skin crawl.

And Junior wasn't alone. Some dangerous looks were shooting the lovebirds' way from the surrounding crowd.

The Cellar happens to be the biggest scumbag bar in Boston, complete with a high level of tolerance for behavior that would be frowned upon in polite society. Cursing. Fighting. Drinking until you puked. All of those were pretty common. We didn't encourage the latter two, but they happened.

A couple furiously making out at the end of the bar wasn't unacceptable.

But when you were two dudes?

And that bar was The Cellar?

It was suicidal.

"We're gonna have to do something," I said.

"All yours," Junior said with finality.

"Rock-paper-scissors?"

"No fuckin' way. Frankly, I'm inclined to let the lions have 'em." He lifted his chin toward the mob of non-progressives forming by the pinball machine.

Junior had never been much of a humanitarian.

It was like watching a Discovery Channel show. The predators slowly gathered around the prey. Three different factions of skinhead, normally divided on the principals of who to hate the most, were milling behind the couple. The discussion over how to most successfully beat the crap out of the lovers had apparently unified them.

Jesus.

"Fine." I walked through the tight crowd, keeping my eyes on the action soon to be at hand if I didn't hustle. If the situation went fubar, people were going to get knocked over.

I stood close enough where the lovebirds should have noticed me. If they did, they didn't let it interfere with their making out. "Excuse me," I yelled, so as to be heard over the blaring jukebox.

The two stopped mashing on each other to slowly turn their gazes on me, burning with attitude. "Is there a problem?" the smaller one asked. He was wearing a muscle shirt and had more gel in his hair than most boy bands.

"Guys...seriously," I stammered. "You're gonna have to cut it out."

The other guy had on a clean-cut suit and looked mildly embarrassed, but the blaze of self-righteousness burned white-hot in the smaller one. He was a guy used to having things his way. "You have a problem with us? Is that it?"

"No," I sort of lied. "But this isn't the place."

"C'mon, Alex. Let's go." The Suit took Alex by the hand and stood up from his barstool. I allowed myself some hope that they would leave of their own accord, and that would be the end of it. At least Suit seemed to know what time it was. And that time was to go.

Alex was having none of it. "What? This isn't the *place*?" He stood, but only so he could waggle his finger closer to my nose. "We need a *place*? You want to put us in our own *place*? *Jawohl, mein Fuhrer.*"

Oh, for fuck's sake.

I desperately wanted to grab Alex's finger and twist it until he cried, but I could feel the heat of the mob's hatred burning behind me, rising in equal measure to Alex's indignation.

"Alex, this is ridiculous." The Suit had picked up on the vibe. He grabbed Alex's arm.

Alex violently tore himself away. "No! No. I want to hear this."

I breathed deeply through my nose and tried to keep my temper and my voice even. "Listen to your buddy, Alex. You're opening yourself up to a world of trouble right now."

Alex laughed right in my face. "What, from you, tough guy? Do you know who I am?"

Oh, that old chestnut.

Under other circumstances, I'd choke the laugh from his throat. He knew it too. He savored waving the meat in front of the chained pit bull.

Enough.

I'd had enough.

"No," I said. "But I'm sure I'll read in the newspapers who you used to be."

All it took was a step back and a turn around.

The hooligans knew what that meant.

All hell was about to break loose. And I'd just signaled the go-ahead by giving the lovebirds my back.

Before I took step one, the sound of a pint glass shattering hit my ears. Some girl to my left screamed.

Alex screamed.

I turned back to see The Suit bleeding from a half dozen places where the glass had cut him. Alex's scream was cut short by the right fist of a Nazi skin burying itself deeply into his stomach. As he dropped to the floor on his knees, a boot from a punk rocker caught him right in the jaw.

"Call the fucking cops," I yelled to Audrey behind the bar.

It was an all-out donnybrook. I grabbed at shirts willy-nilly and shoved them toward the door. Junior met them halfway and both he and G.G. ejected the fighters into the Square. The Suit tried to run. As he turned out the door, I saw two more skins tackle him to the ground, out of my line of sight.

I grabbed Alex and lifted him off the hardwood. He had an awful big mouth for a guy who couldn't have weighed more than a buck ten.

"Please," he pleaded. Tears ran down his terrified face, mingling with the blood and snot running down his nose. "Help us."

"I tried, you stupid prick." I hauled him through the bloodthirsty crowd, half of which didn't even know why they were swinging fists.

Welcome to The Cellar.

When we hit the doorway, I pulled his ear close to my mouth and said, "You better run your legs faster than you do your mouth." I then chucked him into Kenmore Square, trying to throw him behind the hate-filled mob that was beating on his boyfriend.

To his credit, Alex didn't run.

He tried to help his partner, pulling him out from under the fists raining down.

He got him stood up, at which point they tried to escape their attackers together.

They didn't get far. Suit went down in the snow again. Then Alex hit the ground next to his boyfriend and rolled into a ball as the boots rained down.

Behind me came a sound of fist-on-flesh. Another skin flew through the air and out the door as G.G. followed. "That's the last of the brawlers." The big man was wild-eyed and panting from the adrenaline rush. "What was that about?"

Junior spat onto the sidewalk. "Fuck 'em. It's a lesson that needed learning, right, Boo?"

I felt sick as the mob tired itself out beating the helpless men and scattered like roaches as sirens roared into the square. I could see blood dotting the snow around their unconscious bodies.

I'd had the option of at least protecting Alex. I'd had his salvation in my hands. I could have easily dragged him up the back stairs and locked him in the office until the free-for-all had died out. I could have saved him the beating rather than tossing him.

I wasn't all that sure I would have done any of it.

And it didn't make me feel good when I realized that.

"YOU GOTTA BE kidding me." Junior was righteously put-off by his tagalong assignment on Jason St. John, lead singer of The Kingly. The band had finally gotten on stage for their first set, Jason well into his rock star douchebag routine, and I was trying to both placate Junior and dodge the line of questioning from the cop with the notebook.

"Excuse me, can that wait a minute?" The young cop was trying to sort out how two semi-conscious homosexuals wound up ten feet from the door of the club. "So you're saying that the fight was outside."

"I'm not saying it was a fight at all. The two who got taken away in the ambulance got the unholy fuck beaten out of them."

The cop leveled his glare at me. "But they were inside the club. That's where it started."

"I'm saying that those two were deliberately inciting a dangerous element that was inside the club. I told them to cut it out or leave. They were followed outside." Sometimes it disturbed me how practiced I was at telling the cops only as much truth as they needed to hear. Since part of my job was to keep the club out of danger from lawsuits and legal issues, I had to walk a delicate balance when you considered that the *rest* of what I did opened up the club to lawsuits and legal issues.

The Tightrope of Bullshit, Junior calls it.

"Are any of their attackers still inside?"

"No."

"Do you know where they went?"

"Nope." I knew the names of some of the brawlers, but I wasn't getting myself or The Cellar involved any more than I had to. Playing dumb was the best way to accomplish that.

I play dumb *real* well.

The cop handed me a card with the precinct information on it. "If you see any of them, give us a call."

"Sure." Just for shits and giggles, I took the card. The cops were going to have better luck calling the Madame Vesuvia Gypsy Fortune Hotline for information.

The cop left and I sat on the barstool by the door. I could feel Junior seething behind me. "Say it."

"It's bullshit."

"Bullshit or not, Tommy wants one of us to go." I rubbed my sore leg. The cold seeping through my clothes jammed dull rods of pain into the place where a piece of my leg used to be. The place where a bullet made a beeline through my thigh less than a year before. I kneaded the area above my knee to indicate to Junior why I wasn't the best candidate to be tailing anybody through a goddamn nor'easter.

Junior's face pinched up as the sense within my words stung him. During the same timeframe of my unfortunate run-in with a bullet, Junior had played chicken with a midsized sedan and lost. Lost badly. As much as my injury hadn't healed entirely, Junior was left in tougher shape. He'd recovered all right, but had dropped a lot of muscle during his recuperation, making him the most expendable staff member and he knew it. He was still a bruiser, but he was now a good fifteen pounds lighter than me and had two good legs on him to boot.

Almost on cue, Tommy came off the main floor and walked over to us. "You're gonna follow Jason, right?" he asked Junior directly.

"I got him," I said quickly, "but I don't know what I'm supposed to do."

Junior's eyebrows went up, but he didn't say anything. In the split-second that Tommy asked the question, I decided it would serve the night better to give Junior a bit of his tough-guy dignity back and fuck my discomfort. Besides, most of the crowd that remained post-brawl were just fans of The Kingly. And they were more of a chai latte than coffee and whiskey crew.

Tommy looked back to me. He didn't give a good goddamn who went, so long as somebody stayed close to his Friday night investment. "Just make sure he's back here a half hour after they finish the first set."

Historically, Jason St. John had a bad tendency to get doped up between sets. In times past, Jason had disappeared between sets for unacceptable amounts of time that would piss off the audience. Sometimes, he didn't return at all, like he did last summer at The Middle East—at which point, the club's owners had to return the ten-dollar cover to the crowd of over six hundred. As a rule, club owners aren't keen on handing back six grand that they already had in their pockets.

A pissed off crowd was also not what a club wanted.

The Kingly had a bad rep at all the venues as a result, but they still put asses in seats.

"You sure?" Junior said after Tommy walked downstairs. "How's your leg?" he asked, a little ashamed.

"It's fine," I lied. I really needed to rest it, but Junior needed the show of confidence more.

"It's still bullshit," Junior said, cracking his knuckles.

"Part of the job, my man," I said.

Sadly, it was.

The music in the basement built to a crescendo, the crowd's energy matching the rise. The song stopped suddenly and the audience erupted. I put on my black fleece hat and walked down the stairs. G.G. stood at the bottom, huge arms folded, watching the crowd for misbehavior.

"Damn, Boo. These white boys ain't half bad," he said.

"Why do you have to bring white into it?"

"Because they'll never be half as good as Earth, Wind & Fire."

"Fair enough." I scanned the crowd for Jason. I couldn't find him in the milling mass. "You see Jason?" I figured G.G. might have a better vantage point, being six inches taller than me.

"Who's Jason?"

"The skinny jerkoff who just finished singing."

"He left the stage and went up the back stairs before the last note ended."

Dammit. I limped my way through the audience, hampered by my size and gimpy leg. I found a pocket of space and went up the back stairs fast as I could. In my delusion, I'd hoped that the nor'easter might deter Jason from leaving between sets. No such luck. I opened the metal back door and saw him trudging over a drift at the north end of the municipal parking lot behind the bar.

I guess "neither snow nor rain nor heat nor gloom of night" applied to junkies as well as to the post office.

Tailing someone isn't as easy as you'd think, even aided as I was by the blinding snow—note the word "blinding." The flakes stuck in thick clumps to my eyelids and icy water stung my eyes as they melted. Tommy was damned sure going to give me a hazard bonus after this crap.

I followed Jason onto the ass-end of Newbury Street, where he made a right going to Brookline Ave. He never looked back once, the needs of his mission giving him something else to worry about. He would have spotted me in a heartbeat, the two of us being the only pedestrians on that length of real estate. On Brookline, he made a left. If I was a betting man, I'd have laid money that his destination would be on the stretch of clubs off Lansdowne. I'd have been right too.

While it was easier to lose myself in the small masses of people on Lansdowne, it was also easier for him to blend in. Why couldn't this asshole be four inches taller? For that matter, why couldn't I?

As I was about to lose him for good, I saw the top of his greasy hairdo walk into Raja, one of the many trendy lounges that had been infesting my Boston for the last ten years. Lounges that liked keeping guys like me off the premises by charging twelve bucks for a whiskey.

I followed him into the spacious bar, incense punching holes in my cold-stuffed nose. The place was done up in bold crimsons and dark wood, blood-hued curtains hanging off the walls, Mediterranean style. Groups of expensively dressed patrons reclined on oversized gold silk pillows. Stuffed with baby seal fur, no doubt. The Raja was a startling contrast to the lead-paint nouveaux style of The Cellar.

Jason was beelining for Ian Summerfield, who sat at the bar he owned—Raja only one of the few he supposedly had a piece of. The British ex-pat sat resplendent in a suit that I might have been able to afford if I took a second mortgage out on the house I didn't own. Without any evidence other than the gossip that floated bar-to-bar, I knew Ian had supposedly bankrolled his bar investments with the massive amount of narcotics that he funneled through them.

Seeing that he and Jason knew each other—the twenty-something hipster rocker douche and the middle-aged poseur bar impresario—leant some weight to the gossip.

Ian had an obscenely filled cognac glass in his hand and was conversing with another nattily dressed individual. (I only used the words "resplendent" and "nattily" where Ian and his cohorts were concerned.) His eyes caught Jason moving across the floor, and I thought I could detect a slightly disgusted eye roll from the Englishman.

He leaned to the other side and spoke into the ear of a bar bimbo in a scoop-backed dress. She nodded and stood, her pink martini lifted off the bar as she moved away from the upcoming conversation that, no doubt, Ian didn't want her to hear.

She turned and nodded to him, a half smile on her ruby lips.

My insides turned as cold as my outsides when I recognized both the smile and the lips it played across.

CHAPTER 2

A LOT OF things suck in my world. For the most part, my top three have been the New York Yankees, tartar sauce, and catching my dick in my zipper.

But goddamn, I had a new number one with a bullet…and I can't even put a name to it. It was the feeling that donkey-punched my soul when I realized that the bar bimbo hanging off the arm of Boston's biggest—rumored—peddler of fancy-pants pharmaceuticals was somebody I gave a lot of fucks about at one point.

The bar bimbo was my ex-girlfriend, Kelly.

Well, technically, she wasn't my *girl*friend.

It's complicated.

Most would say we'd merely spent some time touching each other's naughty bits. It was a little more than that.

At least I thought it was.

For me it was.

Like I said…

Complicated.

Either way, holy bouncing Buddha on a pogo stick.

In that moment of chest-seizing shock, blackness swarmed in from my left. For a second I thought I'd fainted, until I realized that the blackness was solid.

"Hey, Boo." Marcus Beauchamp stood right in my line of vision.

"Hey, Marcus," I said through teeth clenched tight enough to press a diamond. "Didn't know IronClad was taking contracts at drug dens now."

The big boss and chief of IronClad Security folded his thick arms. IronClad was one of the main competitors to my and Junior's own 4DC Security. And by competition, I meant like The New England Patriots were competitors with the Kippy's Diner Pop Warner team. IronClad did security for hoity-toity rich people clubs, visiting heads of state, and major corporations.

4DC? We followed two-bit junkies around in a fucking blizzard.

At least our name was cooler, even though we ripped off "Dirty Deeds Done Dirt Cheap" from AC/DC.

So, nanny, nanny boo-boo on them.

Marcus sniffed and ran his finger along the lapels of his own natty suit. Christ, was everyone natty? What the hell did natty mean, anyway? "You still working in that flea-infested rock club, or you here to bother my patrons for some loose change?"

I went to step around him. "Excuse me," I said, not really giving a flying fuck if I was excused or not.

In case you haven't figured it yet, we didn't like each other very much.

He placed a thick hand flat on my chest. The excusing didn't look like it was going to happen any time soon.

I looked past Marcus's shoulder to Kelly. Ian's hand trailed dangerously low on her hip as she walked to a banquette on the end of the bar. The edges around the room were starting to flare red. I wasn't the jealous type, but if that hand had touched ass…

Marcus saw me looking and pulled one of the curtains down over the doorway. "Unh-uh. No peeking. Why don't you hit the pavement before somebody in here thinks we're operating a homeless shelter." He swept a gesture toward my clothes.

I looked down at the worn sweatshirt and jeans I'd purchased late in the last millennium. At least my Army-Navy pea coat was pretty new. And my fleece hat was straight-up Tar-Jay, bitches. "I'm keeping an eye on Jason over there. He's playing at The Cellar tonight and we don't need him skagged out on your boss's products."

"I don't give two shits if you're keeping an eye on your mother's fat ass while she sucks my dick."

The crimson edges to my vision flared a little sharper. Right around Marcus's head.

"Watch your mouth, Marcus. I'm warning—"

Marcus laughed. "This isn't your house, Malone. It's mine. Besides you falling depths below our dress code, we have instructions to keep you, specifically, out of here."

What? "Huh?"

"You heard me." Marcus rolled his shoulders, readying for me to make a move that wasn't verbal.

"You want me out, you're going to have to do better than that, Marcus. ." I let the challenge hang on my words. I walked past him and grabbed a handful of hanging curtain.

Marcus's hand closed around my neck and shoved me back. When I hit the wall, the blood rushed into my head and the world went red. I braced my back against the wall and slammed my knee into Marcus's sternum. When he doubled over, I brought the knee back up into his skull, pressing his head down to amplify the impact. Something went crunch and Marcus dropped sideways, his grasping hand pulling down the whole kit and caboodle of curtain on top of him. The room gasped and there I was. As grand an entrance as a fuckwit could make. I took a step forward, ready to grab Jason by the scruff of his neck and drag him back to The Cellar by force.

Instead, I pitched forward and belly-flopped onto the floor.

Note to any tough guys: Don't knee somebody twice with your bad leg. All the motivational rage in the world won't make a bad leg behave.

I crashed down face-to-face with Marcus. Blood gushed satisfyingly from his smashed nose and his eyes were slightly crossed. "You shouldn't talk about my mother."

It was the best I had.

Two more nattily suited mooses—meese?—broke through the initial paralysis that accompanied sudden violence and launched themselves toward us. A quick assessment of the situation told me they weren't coming to take my drink order. Favoring my newly re-injured getaway stick, I hopped furiously toward the exit. The better part of valor, and all. As I burst out the door, I stole a glance back and caught Kelly's eyes.

I wished I hadn't. Beyond the obvious surprise and curiosity, I saw a sea of sadness in them, even at a hundred feet. And a good dose of pity.

Even outside, I wasn't safe from Marcus's stampeding goons. If somebody had gotten the drop on Junior inside The Cellar like I did with their homie, they wouldn't have been in the clear until I couldn't chase them anymore—which, in my current state, amounted to about six feet.

A cab pulled up in front of Raja, the door opening. I hobbled around the other side and jumped into the open door before the exiting passenger shut it. One of Marcus's moose—meese?—spotted me in the cab, yelled for his buddy.

"Kenmore Square, please," I said. Always room for politeness.

The cab driver turned and looked at me. "Are you kidding me here? Kenmore's around the corner."

"What are you, Magellan? Drive." My two pursuers burst out the door. "Drive. *Drive!*"

The first moose yanked the door handle of the cab, pulling hard enough to rock the car noticeably.

Joke was on them. I'd locked the door. Clever man.

Then he opened the passenger door on the front, swinging a huge fist wrapped in a pair of chromed brass knuckles at the partition. The plexi held, but boomed as the meaty fist ricocheted off.

Calmly, I slid open the partition, reached through the window, and grabbed the moose's wrist. "Kenmore Square, please," I said a second time, a lot louder.

"Holy Jesus!" the cabbie yelled, flooring the pedal just as another moose was running around to the passenger side with a piece of rebar in his mitts.

The cab sprayed dirty snow into the face of the second moose as we dragged his partner down Lansdown.

Halfway down the street, I let go of my attacker's wrist and watched as he hit the slush-filled curb. The cab gave a slight *buh-bump* as it rolled over his ankle.

As I looked back, the guy sat in the dirty snow, clutching his foot and screaming like a death metal singer who'd stepped on a Lego. Looked like I'd made one more successful assault on IronClad, via cab-on-tootsie.

Score one for the good guy.

I barely had enough time to breathe a sigh of relief at my own survival as the cab made the two short lefts and pulled up in front of The Cellar. I figured I'd have the rest of the night to breathe all the sighs I needed.

Except I opened the door onto anarchy.

All freaking hell was breaking loose at my own club. A milling crowd drifted in front, yelling and hooting, a surefire indication of a brawl. I tossed a five through the partition and got out as quickly as I could.

Fuck, fuck, fuck…

Junior was on his back on a patch of ice. Some hipster fucko was raining shots down into his face as Junior clutched at the guy's lapels. Before I could get there, G.G. grabbed Junior's assailant by the back of his coat and launched him up and over both the snowdrift and the railing behind it. When the guy saw that the odds had changed, he bolted.

I chased him the aforementioned six feet before the inferno in my leg took hold again.

When he saw that my attempted pursuit had run its course, he turned and yelled back at me. "You tell that cunt that I'll be back later." He spat onto the sidewalk, then disappeared down the stairs of the Kenmore T station.

I didn't respond, since I had no idea who the supposed cunt was, nor the context for who the mystery cunt may have been.

I turned back to Junior. G.G. held him up under the arms as he regained his senses. Blood dribbled between his mashed lips. "That guy call me a cunt?"

"Not sure, buddy. Definitely in the realm of possibility."

"That's not nice." Junior straightened himself up and brushed some of the snow from his shirtfront. Groggily, he looked around for the reason he'd just been owned. "I slipped," he mumbled. "I had the asshole and I slipped on the ice. I went down under him. I fucking had him."

I took a handful of snow and handed it to him. "Here. Hold this against your mouth."

"Thanks." That made three people who had gotten stomped in less than two hours. And the night wasn't over yet. The snow in front of the bar had so much blood smeared into it, it looked like somebody had lost a fight with a cherry Slushee machine. Junior's eyes cleared a bit when the snow came in contact with his swelling face. "How was your field trip?"

"Good. Good." I rolled the leg of my Dickies over my knee and applied a handful of snow to my own injury. "Think I may have got us into a war with Ian Summerfield and, by proxy, IronClad."

Junior nodded, impressed. "IronClad? Marcus there?"

"Yep."

"At least tell me you got to tag that cock-knocker."

"Broke his nose, I think."

"Good on ya. Can we go back in? I'm freezing balls."

"Sure."

Junior looked around. "Where's Jason?"

FUCK!

I knew I was forgetting something.

THE BAR HAD a dangerous energy to it when we walked in. Most of the crowd had witnessed Junior getting dropped.

One thing about the bouncing biz and life amidst the wildlife: never let the animals see that the zookeeper is vulnerable.

The noise level dropped suddenly, as if everyone in the room had a solid shit-talk running and all shut their yaps at once so we wouldn't hear it. As we passed the jukebox, I did catch one snippet, a Townie in a Bruins cap muttering to his buddy, "Nice fucking bouncing, tough guy."

I didn't say anything. I took the cap off his head and held it over his eyes for a second.

In the first half of that second, he said, "Hey!"

The second half was occupied by my fist colliding right onto the embroidered yellow B.

His head snapped back and he fell against the juke. His buddy yelped when G.G. lifted him under his arms and bopped him hard off the doorjamb, then out into the snow.

I cracked the Townie twice more in the mouth, until I felt wetness under my knuckles. Then I spun him around, grabbed a handful of the back of his jeans, and launched him right behind his buddy.

The room was a lot quieter after that.

But not quiet enough.

I yanked the jukebox cord from the socket right in the middle of "Back In Black" and the room fell silent as a morgue. I looked around the room, stopping to catch any faces that might have decided to give me the stink-eye. There wasn't a one. Even Tommy wasn't looking at me.

"Anybody got a comment?" I roared.

Nobody did.

"Nobody? Everybody sure? 'Cause now's the time, bitches." Adrenaline surged through me, my rage barely checked.

Silence.

I plugged the jukebox back in.

The animals knew who was in charge again.

CHAPTER 3

WE WENT INTO high alert.

Tommy was having a hissy fit about me losing Jason, the crowd was getting restless, and I was beginning to lose my various patiences.

Junior was no help. "Did you ever think that this might not be the best time to make a stand against the drug trade? I mean, we're not in top form, Batman."

"Marcus grabbed me. Talked some shit. I reacted."

I didn't mention Kelly. It wasn't that I was afraid Junior would think less of me for letting it get to me, it was that *I* was thinking less of me for letting it get to me.

Junior shook his head. We weren't used to being helpless.

Okay, we weren't helpless, but we were not the threats we had been a year ago. And even in our top form, we couldn't have gone head to head with Summerfield and IronClad.

"Where the hell is Jason?" Tommy hollered at me for the fifth time in fifteen minutes.

I bit my lip and fought the urge to put my fist into his. "I told you, Tommy.

He went to Raja and I got tossed. I warned you about that asshat."

Tommy spat some more curses in my direction, but knew I was right. No amount of money was worth the trouble Jason St. John brought down on the house. Not on this night, at least.

"What the hell happened with the guy outside?" I asked Junior.

Junior's ears went red with embarrassment. "I had him. Then I went down on the ice and he got on top of me." The story already had taken on the quality of rote, Junior convincing himself that it was all the ice's fault. It wasn't the first brawl Junior had lost, but it was probably the first since he was fourteen.

"I got that much already. Why did you toss him?"

"I don't know what happened. I heard a crash and saw him shaking Ginny by the shoulders."

I could understand that. Ginny had been waiting tables at The Cellar for almost four years and had sharpened her tongue to a point where she could cut drywall with it. Many a customer had their tempers flared by a few words from Ginny. It didn't excuse the manhandling, but it was understandable.

"Yo, Boo!" G.G. yelled up the stairs.

"What's up?"

"Jason's back."

I hobbled down the stairs two at a time, ready to strangle him with his own skinny jeans. I quickly scanned the room, but couldn't spot him. "Where is he?"

"He's in the back." G.G. pointed toward the small room to the left of the stage that band members lounged in between sets.

"Thanks." I started pushing my way through the crowd, clenching my fists.

Reading my mind, G.G. yelled to my back. "Don't hurt him too bad, Boo. Tommy will have your ass if he can't play the last set."

I shoved the door to the back hard enough to make it bang like a shotgun. Jason jumped up, startled. Unluckily for him, it also startled the shirtless girl who was blowing him. Jason shrieked in pain and doubled over on the dirty concrete floor.

"Ohmygod," the girl wailed. "Are you all right?"

Jason squealed and rolled around on the floor in response.

"Get the fuck out," I snarled.

"I can't! I can't stand up," Jason mewled.

"Not you, shithead."

The girl grabbed her top and jacket and bolted from the room. Hoots and cheers erupted behind me as I slammed the door shut after her. I propped a folding chair under the doorknob to keep any other interested parties at bay.

"Oh Christ," he squealed at me. "Is it still on? Please tell me that bitch didn't bite my cock off."

"You're fine. Stand up."

"Check. I can't look."

I had no intention of checking. I grabbed two handfuls of his denim shirt and slammed him against the wall. "Stop your whining and answer my questions."

Under the haze of whatever pharmaceuticals he'd bought and dropped at Raja, his unfocused eyes tried looking into mine but instead skittered around like two fried eggs on a skillet. "What the fuck's your problem? Where's Tommy? You almost got my junk bit off."

I bounced his head off the grafitti. Decades-old paint flakes crackled down into his greasy hair. "Tommy's no happier with you right now than I am. What did Summerfield say to you?"

"Ow, man. Take a pill." I bounced his head again, then threw him onto the ratty couch right where I knew there was a sharp spring poking up. Jason bucked and grabbed his ass. "Dammit!" His flaccid dick wobbled at me as he hopped up.

I checked my gag reflex and decided to give him a moment. "Pick your pants up."

"Up your ass," he said. Jason yanked up his underwear and leather pants, wincing. That's what rock stars get for wearing such tight pants.

"I'm not asking again without loosening your teeth, got it? Now, what did Summerfield say to you?"

"Where the fuck is Tommy? This is your last night on the job, dickhole."

I slapped him hard. The back of my brain reminded me that I may have been pissed at Jason but not as much as I was with the rest of the situation. It was hard not to take it out on him. "Last chance."

"Are you going to hit me again if I tell you you've got an anger management problem, dude?"

"You're not the first one to say it."

"Wait a minute. You were at Raja. The hell was that all about?"

"You tell me."

"I'm not the one who started the Royal Rumble in there. I was just there to—"

"I know why you were there. Everybody knows how you roll, Trippy. I was following you to make sure you didn't forget to make your way back here for the second set."

He didn't seem ashamed that everybody knew he was popping. If anything, he seemed pleased. Maybe he thought that his cavalier drug use enhanced his rock star creds. "Hey, man. Like Kiss said, 'I wanna rock all night and party...'"

Bad enough he hit me with butchered lyrics, but then he followed up by making the devil horns with his fingers at me.

I grabbed his pinkie and twisted, if only out of respect to Ronnie James Dio. "Last chance, Jason. What did Summerfield say? You either answer me, or I take this finger with me and we end your musical career right now."

"*Owowowowowow!*" Jason squealed and went to his knees. "Whaddaya mean, what did he say? About you?"

"No, about Kiss, dicktard. Yes, me." I let go of his finger.

Jason pulled his hand back and cradled it under his arm. "Not much. Just said, 'Oh dear' after you left."

"He actually said, 'Oh dear'?" Fucking douche.

"Yeah. For the record, the guy didn't seem half as concerned about you as you seem to be about him. His girl was more upset than he was."

His girl.

His girl.

Some small animal with very sharp teeth began gnawing inside my chest. "What did she say?"

"Not much. She got all freaked out and said she had to go."

"Did she?"

"Yeah. Summerfield was pissed. Maybe pissed isn't the word—maybe irritated. Guy's a cucumber. Anyhow, he kissed her and she left. That was it." Jason flexed his fingers and lifted his chin at me, a smug smile on his face. "That's what this is about, isn't it?"

The animal chomped harder.

I glared at him, but didn't take the bait.

The crowd was starting to chant *King-Ly! King-Ly! King-Ly!* There were three hundred strong ready to tear the place down if this dickhead didn't take the stage.

"I want you on stage in five minutes. Finish your set and get the fuck gone." I turned to walk out.

"He said one other thing after she left."

"What?"

"I don't know if it was about you or not, but he said it to the guy whose nose you busted."

"What was it?" At least that confirmed Marcus's nose got broke.

"He said that they were gonna have to take care of the problem."

"Was I the problem?"

"What do you think?"

Well, wasn't that just ducky?

THE KINGLY GOT onstage and started their second set. I went back to the door with Junior, grinding my teeth over the new pile of fecal matter I'd managed to get us into. I stood just outside the entrance, puffing furiously away at the third straight cigarette I was chaining.

"You think they'll hit us here?" he asked, the frayed end of a cocktail straw twirling between his lips.

"Wouldn't you?"

"Tonight?"

"Abso-fucking-lutely. They know we're busted up. There's no better time to come at us." I immediately lit another cigarette, ignoring the creeping ache in my lungs. I needed to keep my hands busy. "So what are you thinking?"

"I'm thinking you're an asshole."

"You always think that."

"True, but the feeling is particularly strong tonight. What do you wanna do? We could call in some backup."

I shook my head. "The rest of the boys who aren't puking their guts out with the flu are out in Cambridge working the Slapshot show. No way they're getting back here by the time we close in this weather."

I gave it some thought, then raised an eyebrow at Junior.

He knew where that eyebrow was heading, other than to the middle of my forehead. "Aw, hell no. Don't be thinking what I think you're thinking. That's going to make it worse."

"Can it get worse?"

"Don't say that!"

"I think we have to."

"Fuck." Junior frowned, making the bulldog face that I knew only accompanied his darkest moods and imaginings. "If you think so."

"What do you think?"

"You don't wanna know what I think."

I ground out my smoke into a pink pile of bloodied snow, a reminder of what had already gone down that night. And what might be coming.

I went upstairs.

To call Twitch.

CHAPTER 4

2:15 IN THE a.m.

The bar had been closed for fifteen minutes and the last stragglers were getting the heave-ho.

No sign of Twitch. I'd left a voicemail message, but wasn't sure he'd gotten it. Twitch wasn't the kind of guy who regularly checked messages. If I had to guess, he didn't get all that many he had to check.

One could assume he was home, since Twitch also wasn't a "night out on the town" kind of guy. He was more of a "sit at home on Saturday night cleaning his guns and watching Fox News" type. Hence the few and far between messages from the few and far between friends he had.

Like I was one to talk.

"Maybe they're not showing," Junior said hopefully.

I wasn't as hopeful. "We would."

"I know, but maybe they're not showing tonight. The blizzard's kicked up again."

"It'll be tonight."

"I'm just saying, they have to know we're expecting them. Maybe they'll wait and nail us with the element of surprise. Catch us when we're not expecting it."

The soreness in my leg reminded me of the storm's presence with every step. Its status was "fuck you."

"It'll be tonight." The IronClad crew weren't element-of-surprise type guys.

G.G. walked up the back stairs. "Downstairs is locked up. All out."

"You can take off, then," I said.

"You're kidding, right?" G.G. curled his lip at me. "You think I ain't got your back?"

"I'm not saying that. I'm saying this isn't your fight."

"Whatever part of that might be true, fuck you for saying that. I ain't going nowhere."

I had to admit that having G.G. behind us made me feel better, but I'd have laid money on IronClad showing up with at least six guys. We were still going to be outnumbered by double. "Thanks, man," I mumbled.

"And fuck you for thinking that you have to thank me."

I walked to the porthole in the thick wooden front door. All I saw was snow. Then I saw the cut of halogen lights moving down Comm Ave. Halogen lights that were on the front of a black SUV that stopped in front of The Cellar.

IronClad had arrived.

"They're he—" I started to say. Then another SUV pulled up behind the first. Then a third cut around in front and backed alongside a snowdrift.

"What?" Junior pocketed a roll of quarters and handed G.G. a pool cue. G.G. snapped the cue over his knee and handed the bottom half to Junior.

I counted the first six as they climbed out of the cars on the side that I could see. Then another seven walked around from the other side. Each one the size of a small African nation.

Boy, was my estimate off.

"Boy, are they ever here."

Boy, oh boy, oh boy.

"Last chance," I said to Junior and G.G.

"Fuck you," they said in unison.

Then Junior added, "Sundance."

I could have done without the Sundance.

I opened the door and walked out into the snow, my two-man crew behind me. Marcus stood front and center, his arms behind his back, his baker's dozen-strong wrecking crew behind him. However, I was pleased to see his nose was taped tight against his face. At least I had that, considering that the three of us were probably ending our night with most of ourselves taped to the rest of us. Maybe some staples.

"Hey, Marcus," I said cheerily. "You bring enough guys with you?"

"Gonna sucker punch me now, Malone?" He brought his hands around and slapped a Louisville Slugger into his right palm.

And so the dance began...

"Well, if I remember the incident correctly, I believe you put your hands on me first."

"And I'm gonna put them on you last too."

I counted his crew. "Sure doesn't look like you planned on that."

"What's that supposed to mean?"

"I dunno," Junior said, scratching his chin. "Thirteen guys? You knew we were only gonna be here with three or four. It kinda makes you look like a pussy, dude."

Nyah-nyah.

If we could goad him into a one-on-one, he might not release his dogs on us. To do that, he'd lose a lot of the respect with his crew. If I beat him, same thing, so I'd decided to let him get some licks in and take a dive to protect us all. It was the only way we were going to walk away with all our bones on the right side of our skin. Marcus was a big bully, but like all bullies he was a coward at heart. He'd already tasted my capacity for inflicting bodily harm once that night. Even banged-up, I liked my chances against the moron. I'd deal with Summerfield myself, later.

Marcus looked to his crew, who stared back at him with as much challenge as we did. Any one of them was willing to see him go down and take his spot in their food chain. They may have been his crew, but I could suss out immediately that not a one of them was his friend.

I went on. "So why don't you stop being such a vadge, put the bat down, and let's do this. Me and you." Out of the corner of my eye, I saw the car door on the front SUV open and somebody get out. Fourteen guys? Really?

I didn't take my eyes off of Marcus, though.

Marcus snorted. "Yeah. I'll put the bat down. On top of your fuckin' head." He raised the bat high and charged me. I crouched and crossed my arms in an X over my head. I was most likely going to have both my forearms snapped by the blow, but at least it wasn't going to be my skull. And I'd have my legs loose to punt his nuts into Southie.

Phup, phup, phup.

Three short bursts of sound—like someone punching a pillow—and the bat exploded into splinters in Marcus's hands.

Twitch.

Marcus's swing came short by about a foot, since the part that was intended to Humpty Dumpty my skull had been vaporized.

That meant my Plan A was still valid.

I blasted him square on the sack with the top of my size-thirteen wides, making sure it was with my good leg. I was both intentionally and unintentionally damaging quite the number of male genitalia that night.

Marcus shrieked and fell to his knees onto the snow.

Aw, crap.

I'd accidentally won the fight, despite myself.

The IronClad boys all frantically looked around for the source of the shots. I wanted to figure it out myself, but didn't want to give away my own ignorance toward the sudden turn of events.

"Hey, guys," came Twitch's voice, swirling in the driving snow, seemingly coming from everywhere at once and nowhere in particular. A chill wracked my body, and it wasn't from the cold.

"Hold your fire, buddy!" I yelled to the air, hoping that he would. With Twitch, one could never be too sure.

Marcus rolled over, screaming at me, albeit in a higher voice than when he'd arrived. "A gun? Who's a fucking pussy now, Malone?"

He had a point. In our world, bringing a gun into a fistfight was the ultimate puss-out. But this was neither a fistfight nor remotely fair from the get-go.

All this "who's a pussy" business was very delicate.

"Hey, Marcus," called Twitch from nowhere. "Nice to see you, bitch."

"Fuck you, freak. Why don't you stand down here with the rest of your boyfriends?" I didn't know that Marcus and Twitch knew each other. But that was the power of reputation in what we do. In whatever capacity they knew of one another, Marcus knew enough about Twitch to call him a freak. Twitch knew enough about Marcus to call him a bitch. Both were kinda right.

"What's the matter, Marcus?" said G.G., leaning over Marcus's prone body. "Don't like it when the playing field's even?"

"Even or not, the quarrel is between the two of us, wouldn't you agree, Mr. Malone?" Stepping into the forefront was number fourteen himself.

Ian Fucking Summerfield.

I balled my fists and locked eyes with him. "I'd say so."

"Then does your offer of a one-on-one stand? Because I think if we're to settle this amongst aggrieved parties, you and I are the ones who should be engaging the other."

"I'm your huckleberry."

Summerfield shook his head like he hadn't heard me right. "I'm sorry, is that an affirmative?"

Guess he skipped on *Tombstone* to watch *Downton Abbey*.

"Let's step." I dropped my foot back and got ready to dance with the fucker—who frankly had to be out of his goddamn mind, or at least sampling his own pills, to think this fight was ending any way he'd enjoy.

Summerfield smiled as he removed his topcoat and handed it to the tower of meat to his left. "You gentlemen are to stand down until this is ended.

Understood?"

"Yes, Mr. Summerfield," the collected ton and a half of meat said together, like the world's biggest collection of grade-schoolers answering their principal.

Summerfield waved his hand into the air and lifted his eyebrows at me expectantly.

"Don't shoot him, Twitch," I yelled to the wind.

"Awww," the wind complained back.

We slowly circled each other. Was this guy out of his freakin' mind? I'd already wiped the floor with his frontman two times that night. Besides, to work my leg back into shape, I'd been taking some Muai Thai kickboxing classes at the Allston YMCA. I planned on showing Mr. Fancy Accent how we did it during the Revolution. I guessed his height at about six feet three, which put him a couple above me, but his weight was all wire. I easily had forty pounds on his Benedict Cumber-ass.

He wasn't going to outmuscle me, the best he could hope to be was—

—faster.

Funny.

I'd just noticed that he held his weight in an odd way, leaning into his front foot, when that same foot shot out like a tree snake and nailed me.

Right on my bad knee.

"I couldn't help but notice that you're favoring that leg a bit, Mr. Malone."

Blasting pain shot right up to my hip and I staggered back, clutching at the magnesium flare that had ignited inside my knee.

The snow burst into blood-red hues as my rage, my comfortable fury, rushed through me.

The beast was out, motherfucker.

I snarled and charged him, swinging a haymaker for the fences.

Summerfield casually turned to his left and my thunderous fist collided with nothing but snowflakes. He spun back, under my shoulder, and drove his fingertips deep into my armpit. My shoulder exploded in pain and my entire arm went numb. I knew enough martial arts to recognize a knife-hand into a nerve cluster. I also knew enough martial arts to recognize that I knew just enough martial arts to get my ass handed to me by someone who knew what they were doing.

Ian Summerfield had evidently been taking more than a couple of classes at the Y.

All of this came together in my head the same time that a really expensive shoe came together with the point of my jaw, snapping my head back.

By the grace of God and the iron railing that flanked the perimeter of the bar, I looped over but didn't go down. My dead arm curled over the top rail.

Summerfield straightened out the pleats of his pants. "I think it would be prudent if you stayed away from my property in the future."

Sucker. I wasn't down, therefore, I wasn't out. I threw myself forward and grabbed the shoulders of his suit jacket, intending to yank his head into my knee the same way I'd done Marcus. I even had my tough guy comment ready about Kelly not being his fucking property. But I was dropping this prick off at the depot for Painsville first.

I drove my fists down, and was smart enough to bring up my good knee this time. I started my devastatingly pointed statement as my knee impacted viciously into the fabric of the coat.

Thing was, Ian wasn't in it at that moment.

Goddamn it.

I didn't even get the first word out. Only a feeble "shhh" as he floated out of the jacket a half second after my fingers touched camel hair. He turned with a backhand that whacked me on the temple. A bright flash bloomed inside my right eye and I slipped backward again.

Yeah. The guy was faster than my ability to produce a vowel.

Summerfield moved in on me. He palmed me square on the nose. Blood instantly began filling my sinuses.

"Don't enter any of my nightclubs again, Mr. Malone, even to use the pisser." A sweeping side kick to the inside of my thigh threw me off-balance.

I gritted my teeth against the instant cramping of my groin muscle under the kick. "You and your douchebag clubs can suck my—"

Then the same foot whipped up and kicked my chest, driving my back into the railing, pinning me without even letting me finish my retort. Who knew the Brits were so rude?

Then the son of a bitch held me flat against the railing with his piston of a goddamn leg like a bug on posterboard. "I hope we're clear," he said.

Then he dropped his foot off my nipple and took his suit jacket from my hand, which I hadn't even realized I was still hanging on to.

Then...

Was he turning his back to me?

Nope.

He was spinning.

The heel of the other expensive shoe smashed into the spot where my jaw connected to the rest of my face, and I was flipping skyward over the top rail. I landed hard, splayed face-first in the snow.

Now I was down...

...and fucking *ow*.

He crouched on the other side of the railing. "Next time, I will be forced to hurt you." He stood up, dusted the snow from the front of his coat, and walked back to the waiting SUV.

Good thing he didn't hurt me this time.

The car drove off, spitting dirty snow on the back of my head as a final insult as the driver executed a U-turn.

Junior stood over me. "You got whupped."

I tried to lift my head. "Yes. Yes, I did."

"By a guy named Summerfield."

"You're not going to let me live that down, are you?"

"Think I'll have some ammo until I get beat down by some guy named Percy Flowerpot or some shit like that."

"Seems fair."

"You need help getting up there, Sundance?"

"Nah," I said. "I think I'm just gonna lie here in the snow for a while, Butch."

"Suit yourself." Junior and G.G. went back into the warmth of the bar, leaving me in my frozen humiliation.

I really did need help getting up.

Jerk completely missed my sarcasm.

Fuck it. Lying in the snow felt good against my injured most of me.

Another day, another dollar, another quart of blood spilled onto Kenmore Square.

CHAPTER 5

EVERYTHING HURT. MY pride. My body. My spirit.

I limped back into The Cellar. Junior and G.G. were racking up a pool game like nothing at all had gone down. I guess nothing had. To them.

"You want winner?" asked Junior.

"No, thanks." My right arm still didn't have full feeling back yet. A tingling numbness working its way through my shoulder to my fingertips was all I had. I walked behind the bar and pulled the pourer off the full bottle of Beam and took three long pulls. Seemed like a "fuck glasses" kind of night. Tommy could blow himself. I'd replace the bottle later in the week. "Any of you guys see Twitch?"

"Nah, man," said G.G. "Those were some freaky Jedi moves your boy pulled there."

Freaky wasn't the half of it. Twitch was the master of urban camouflage. It was the most finely tuned survival tactic he'd learned back at St. Gabe's. Granted, he was already a near-albino hiding in a snowstorm, but Twitch could make himself invisible standing on second base at Fenway during a playoff game.

Junior scratched the eight on his first shot. "Dammit."

Twitch walked in from the back as the ball dropped. "Anybody got next?"

"You do," Junior said, disgusted at his play. Then he froze when he got a look at Twitch's getup.

Twitch was rocking some kind of dirty-white military snowsuit that, god knows, he must have bought in the kids' section of the Army/Navy. The cold had lowered his normal skin tone from a creepy pink hue to a zombie gray. No wonder we couldn't spot him.

"Wassup, little brother. Thanks for the backup." G.G. low-fived Twitch, who smiled broadly across his boyish face. Twenty-seven years old and he could still be carded at Chuck E. Cheese. His pure white next to G.G.'s all black made the two of them look like a lopsided yin-yang of racial harmony.

"Where the hell were you?" Junior asked from behind the bar.

"On the roof."

"How the hell did you get onto the roof?" I asked.

"The stairs," he said.

Ask a stupid question...

"You want anything?" Junior asked him. The box of Chablis gurgled as he poured himself another glass of the grape-flavored toxic waste The Cellar called wine.

"Nah." Twitch racked the pool balls. He was unusually casual for someone who'd only moments earlier fired sniper shots from a rooftop.

"Where's the gun?" I fed a buck into the jukebox and dropped some Clutch into the air. The blood that had frozen in my upper lip stubble started to melt and drip into my mouth. I chased it with some more bourbon. Not bad. It's a wonder that whisky and plasma isn't a more popular cocktail.

"What gun?" Twitch smiled innocently. "I don't see a gun." Then he looked to G.G. "You see a gun?"

"I don't see a damn thing. I never do."

I heard footfalls coming down the back stairs from the office. Ginny was still arranging the night's receipts in her hands when she almost walked into

Twitch. "Gah!" she startled. "What the fuck is that?"

"That's a Twitch," I said, quietly thanking the gods that Twitch no longer had the gun.

"Looks like a Gollum," she said, giving him the once-over. "No offense."

Twitch shrugged. "You'd be surprised how often I get that." Some color went back into his face as he blushed. Only Twitch could hear a comparison to a fish-gut-sucking goblin and take it as a flirtation. Poor guy. It was probably the closest he ever got to one.

Ginny looked like she had something to say. Thank god "Binge and Purge" started blaring from the speakers at a teeth-rattling level. I was in no mood for her commentary. I pointed to my ears and shrugged.

Ginny rolled her eyes and marched over to me. She tiptoed up and yelled into my ear, "I need to talk to you!"

"About what?"

Up close, she got a better look at the damage that had temporarily re-structured my face. "Are you bleeding?"

"No," I yelled. "Old family tradition. I come from a long line of white trash squirrels. I like to store ketchup in my nostrils for the winter."

"I can't talk to you while you're bleeding," she said. She walked to the bar and scooped some ice into a bar rag.

The song cut out, and I caught a piece conversation between G.G. and Twitch.

"...the hell did you shoot that moving bat out of his hands? In a damn blizzard?" G.G. asked.

Twitch shrugged. "I was aiming for his head."

The next track clicked on a second too late. I'd have really felt better off not knowing how that sentence ended.

Ginny handed me some napkins and the makeshift ice pack. I rolled up two napkins and shoved them in my nostrils. "That's...that's not better," Ginny said, grabbing my bottle and taking a gulp. "Did Byron kick your ass too?"

Maybe it was my underlying anger about my ex banging the drug lord who'd just handed my ass to me, or maybe it was simply the punches to the head I'd sustained, but any woman drinking straight from a whiskey bottle is pretty hot.

"Who the fuck is Byron?" I said, taking the bottle back and matching her intake. I could feel the whiskey beelining to my brain, possibly aided by the probable concussion, or the blood loss, or the concussion.

Then again, it might have been the concussion.

"Byron was the guy who got all grabby with me before." It was the middle of winter, but Ginny dressed to bar-impress. She wore an old Rathskeller half shirt and jeans tight around her curves. I guess I'd assumed the guy's Russian hands and Roman fingers were merely the end result of a few too many four-dollar pints and a run-of-the-mill dickhead's lack of self-control.

"Who?"

Ginny sighed. "The guy who Junior danced with earlier."

"*Haaaaaaaaaaaaaaaahahahahaaaaa!*" I pointed right at Junior.

"What?" he said.

"Byron!"

"Huh?"

"The guy who kicked your ass was named Byron."

"Ah, dammit," Junior said as he realized that the years of mockery he had ahead of him had been stripped from him. "At least my guy didn't talk with a Mary Poppins accent."

"His name is Byron!" I said gleefully. "*Byyyyyyyyron.*"

"Shut up," Junior said, pouting.

Ginny blinked rapidly as she looked back and forth between the two of us. "You're both retarded," she said, grabbing the bottle back.

Yes, my brain decided, *whiskey-chugging Nova Scotian broads were indeed hot.* I wasn't in any kind of place to argue with her, but again—concussion. "No. Junior and I suffered completely different ass kickings."

"You guys are terrible at this."

A tiny bit of humiliation crept in again, even as I remembered Byron's parting words.

He wanted me to tell the cunt he'd be back.

Unfortunately, my mouth ran before my brain even knew there was a race. "You're the cunt!" I said.

"Excuse me?" Ginny's eyes went wide. Her gorgeous blue, blue eyes...

Hold on. Concussion. Back to the point. "Wait, you know that asshole?"

"What did you just call me?"

"Byron called you that. Outside."

"Yeah, I'm sure he did. You guys want another shot at him?"

SIXTEEN YEARS AGO

"GREAT. ON TOP of being the size of a Panzer tank, he bats for the Yankees?" asked Twitch.

"That's the word," Junior said. The forty-pound iron barbells clanked as he lifted them off the rack.

Word had spread around The Home that Zach Bingham had "got" a couple of guys. The last thing you wanted at The Home was to get "got," since what you "got" was a twelve-gauge poopchute for your troubles.

"I haven't heard anything yet," said Twitch, straining his scrawny arms with the fifteen-pounders.

"You seen Delgado lately?" I asked.

"No."

"Exactly." I had seen Delgado, if only for the briefest of glimpses. He'd made himself invisible since Tuesday last, when Zach supposedly caught him alone in the food storage room. It wasn't like Delgado was hiding, per se, he just turned into a shadow. A ghost that walked the halls of St. Gabe's. A ghost that has started walking kind of funny.

That was the main reason we'd all assembled into crews like we did. Rectal self-preservation. Some crews assembled for the opposite reason. It was a lot easier to take out your sexual frustration when you had a couple of like-minded guys to hold down your fuck puppet. The counselors loved it when we worked as a team on projects, but there were only so many things you can build out of Popsicle sticks.

You were a cobra or you were a mongoose. Offense or defense, both sides evenly matched until one managed an advantage.

Zach Bingham was a goddamn six-hundred-pound gorilla in a room full of cobras and mongooses. The natural order was disturbed by that psycho's presence. And our six-hundred-pound gorilla didn't only sit wherever he wanted, apparently he stuck his tallywhacker into whoever he wanted to.

"I—heard he—fucked Sherwood—too." Junior said between grunts. Before Zach arrived, Junior had owned the biggest biceps at The Home. He'd been working out viciously ever since. Being in second place pissed him off. Junior and I both took pride that we already had the workout-honed bodies of grown men before we were even halfway through our teens, but there were limitations to what we could achieve against Bingham's base genetics.

"No shit?" I said. Sherwood was the alpha dog of one of the more powerful rape gangs. I couldn't help but smile at the idea. As disturbed as I was by Zach's presence, the idea of Sherwood getting a taste of his own medicine tickled me eight shades of pink.

"Nope. Kinda poetic, ain't it?"

"Yeah. The guy should be laureate."

"He should be a lasso?" Junior put the weights back and flexed, obviously pleased with his development. "What the fuck does that mean?"

"That's a lariat."

"Isn't that what you said?"

"Never mind." I picked up the weights he'd deposited and started doing my own reps. "The point is that I'm not going to lose any sleep about the guy so long as he's banging the bangers. Fair play, I say."

"Delgado wasn't a banger," said Junior.

"I say we take the motherfucker out." Twitch's eyelid jumped a couple times in emphasis.

"What, for some light dinner and dancing?"

"I'm not joking, Boo."

I knew he wasn't. I looked him right in his beady pink-tinted eyes. "But we don't make a move until he does. He doesn't bother us, we got no beef." I had to admit, as much as the guy made my skin crawl, he hadn't aggressed on us at all.

"What do we do if he does?" asked Junior. "I hate to agree with Twitch—"

"Thanks," said Twitch without a trace of sarcasm. Usually nobody agreed with him.

"—*but*, this guy needs to be taken care of before and not after he decides to use our asses for pussy practice."

And like the summoning of some mythological beast, the door opened and Zach walked into the weight room. Slowly, he moved his eyes over each of us.

We watched him watching us. The staredown was a standoff at three to one. Then I looked at Twitch's rigid posture. I knew he wanted to say something.

Zach smiled at us as he picked the forty-five pound plates up off the floor. He scraped them slowly onto the thirty pound bar, wincing pleasurably as he did. It didn't take Freud to figure out the subtext there.

Twitch slowly turned back to us, his face a mask of murderous rage. "Now's our window, guys."

He slid two more forty-fives onto the bench. Two hundred and ten pounds.

"We can end this here, Boo," Junior whispered toward the floor. "I'm tired of looking over my shoulder for this guy."

"Yeah." A dangerous gleam danced behind Twitch's eyes. "All we gotta do is grab a side of the bar and push…"

The last two forty-fives. Three hundred pounds.

The air in the room crackled around us. "No," I said softly.

Zach bookended the bench with two twenty-fives. Three fifty total. He lay down on the bench and lifted the weight easily. Sweet peanut butter and Jesus.

"Boo…"

"No!" I whispered hard, and turned on Junior. "You want to be those guys? 'Cause we can turn that corner right now, if that's the call you wanna make." He knew what I meant. We weren't killers. We didn't execute people. In St. Gabe's, despite all the tough-guy posturing, all the violence that we were ready to distribute—we both knew we had lines we had chosen not to cross.

Junior, jaw set tight, said, "No."

We never said it, but despite it all, we wanted to be good guys. St. Gabe's didn't have too many. We were still between the ages of adult reality and the childish notions that the myth of the superhero was one to be aspired to.

"I'm okay with it," Twitch said.

"No," I said to him one more time.

I didn't know if Twitch heard my words at all. His eyes were locked on the immense weight on Zach's bench press.

He took a step.

I put my hand out to his tiny bird-like chest.

Twitch charged.

I roped him around the waist and lifted him up off the floor.

"Let me go," Twitch said flatly and without emotion.

"He's got a lot of weight on that bar already," I said. "Maybe gravity will take care of him for us. Let's go."

The weight clanged as Zach placed the bar back onto the bench and sat up. He was smiling at our impromptu wrestling match on the other side of the workout room.

I dropped Twitch and shoved him through the doorway. I turned back as Junior passed by me and then met eyes with Zach's.

He was still smiling. The pink tip of his tongue flicked to the corner of his mouth.

I shut the door behind me, unease pulling at my more violent instincts.

There's not a lot of times that I think back on and wish we'd been "those guys."

But there are a couple.

CHAPTER 6

"WHAT ARE YOU talking about?" I passed the bottle back to Ginny. She took another swig, and I tried not to think nasty thoughts about my co-worker as the whiskey moistened both her plump lips and my libido.

"Byron. Byron Walsh. He's my roommate's asshole jazz musician ex. He's been stalking Dana ever since they broke up. He left his stuff in our apartment when he went on tour and he wants it back."

"Define 'stuff'?" I pulled out my Parliaments and lit one.

"May I?" Ginny asked. I offered her the lit cigarette from my mouth. She winced. "Can I get one without nose blood on it?"

I held the open pack to her. She took out a blood-free cigarette and leaned forward for me to light it, the deep opening of her cut T-shirt falling forward slightly. I tried not to peek at the cleavage. I failed.

"What stuff?" I said again.

"I have no idea. Dana says that Byron borrowed money that he never paid back, so Byron's shit stays put until then."

"Does he?"

"Does it matter?" Ginny flipped a lock of blonde hair out of her eyes and put her hands on her hips.

"Yeah. It does if Byron's beef is righteous, and your girl Dana is playing some 'woman scorned' bullshit on all our asses."

Ginny smiled quickly at something I couldn't see the humor behind. "Listen, Boo. Dana and I talked about this and we want you guys to scare him off. The guy is a serious dickweed. He's been harassing—"

"You didn't answer my question."

"Maybe. I don't know. Whatever it is, it's between him and Dana."

"Then I'm perfectly fine leaving it that way. Junior and I have no intention of getting in the middle of some boyfriend-girlfriend drama."

"Believe me, you won't be. If it makes you feel better, think of it as me giving you five hundred bucks to keep that asshole away from *me*. He was here tonight trying to get to Dana through *me*. He said he was coming back tomorrow. He's already tried to break into our apartment once."

"What?"

"There are gouges around the lock on our door. Luckily, we got a good lock. Then he keyed Dana's car, he smashed our window—"

"Not interested."

"C'mon, Boo..."

"No."

Junior, seeing the intensity of the conversation that he wasn't a part of, felt the immediate need to butt in. "Hey, what's going on?"

Ginny smiled at me again, then turned to Junior. "Boo won't take my five hundred bucks to go toe-to-toe with Byron again."

Junior wrinkled his nose in distaste at me. When you've had your nose broken as many times as Junior, that's a lot of wrinkling. "Shee-yit. For five hundred bucks, I'll go toe-to-toe with Brock Lesnar."

"Glad one of you isn't a pussy," she said.

I glared at Ginny. She knew where my buttons were. She knew how to push them. "We don't have the time for this. In case you hadn't noticed, Junior, we've got problems of our own right now."

Junior held up a finger. "Yeah, but in case you hadn't noticed, *your* problems ain't paying me five hundred bucks."

True that.

"Fine." I threw my hands up in the air. "You want it, it's yours."

"Oh c'mon. You know it's only a matter of time before your Knight In Shining Armor dysfunction kicks in. Damsels! In distress! You live for this shit," Junior said.

"I would really appreciate it," Ginny said.

Junior waved his hands between me and Ginny. "Go on," he said to her. "Bat your eyelashes. He'll show up tomorrow on a fucking white horse."

"I am not batting my eyelashes," Ginny said.

I glared at Junior. Mostly because he was right. The first pangs of guilt had already started eating at me for dismissing Ginny's need for us. Even though every rational instinct told me it was a *bad* idea. The whole deal had more red flags than the Chinese Army on parade. "Fine. If I agree to this, will you shut up?"

"Maybe."

"I'll settle for maybe," I said.

"Hot diggidy." Junior clapped and rubbed his hands together. "Who's Byron again?"

Looked like Junior and I both suffered concussions that night.

Ginny thumbed toward the door. "You kidding me? Byron's the guy who owned you about three hours ago."

"Hey," Junior said. "First of all, nobody owned me. I slipped and—"

"And he's a jazz musician, tough guy."

"I got taken down by a jazz musician named Byron?" Junior looked like he wanted to hurl.

Ginny sat at a table and motioned for us to sit with her. "He and Dana broke up about three weeks ago." Ginny took another swig from my bottle. I took it back and took a bigger swig. "He's been harassing us ever since for his shit, saying he'll give Dana the money once he gets his stuff. Dana saying to pay up first, then he gets his stuff. Back and forth, back and forth. I guess he got tired of waiting and decided to go all aggro about it."

"Done and done," said Junior. "Tell us where we can find the prick."

Ginny shook her head. "I don't know. I don't think Dana knows either. Soon as he and his band came back from Europe is when all this crap began. He was staying with us for a couple weeks before he left, so I don't even know if he has a place."

"Oh, that old chestnut. What do you call a musician without a girlfriend?"

"Homeless," Junior and Ginny said at the same time.

"He said something about being back tomorrow," I said. "Was he talking about here or your place?"

Ginny shook her head again. The smoke-diffused light caught in her wheat-colored hair. I wondered what it smelled like. "He knows I don't work tomorrow."

"How does he know your schedule?"

"Dana's my roommate. He used to date Dana. When you live with roommates, you tend to use the alone time whenever you can get it in the apartment." She explained it in a tone normally used to speak to five-year-olds.

"Ah," said Junior, a couple seconds later than he should have.

"So he'll be back at your place tomorrow?"

"Either that or he'll try something at the roller rink tomorrow afternoon." Ginny played roller derby on Sunday afternoons. I wasn't sure if "played" was the right word for it, but I didn't have another. "We have to leave by eleven. Byron knows the derby schedule too, so if he's going to try a smash-and-grab, I'm going to guess that it'll be when we're at the rink." She handed me half of a blank bar check with her address on the back.

"So we'll have to split up the watches." I looked at the half-empty bottle in my hand. Had I drank that much already?

"So you guys will take care of this for me?"

I clapped my hand onto her thigh. Damn if roller derby didn't tighten up

Ginny's legs. "For you, Ginny, anything."

Ginny peeled my hand off her leg like it was a large insect of questionable motive. She looked at Junior. "Is he tanked?"

"Getting there," Junior said.

"I am not," I lied. "Can't a man..." I couldn't figure out how to phrase the rest of my question.

"No, he can't," Ginny said as she stood, buttoning her coat. Then, back to Junior, "Has he been bitching about that Kelly chick again?"

Junior tapped his nose.

Ginny smacked me on the back of the head. "Get over it. Night, boys," she called out to Twitch and G.G.

"Night, Ginny." G.G. held up his beer.

Twitch was too busy focusing on lining up the eight ball. With a sharp crack, he sank it coming off a hard angle into the side pocket.

"Damn, little man," said G.G. "You're a shark."

Twitch smiled and shrugged. "I'm gifted."

I supposed that was one way of looking at it.

They both moved to our table. "I should've known better than to play pool against a dude who shoots a moving bat in a snowstorm."

Twitch held up his hands innocently. "Again, I have no idea what you guys are talking about. And, again, I was aiming for his head."

Yup. Still wished I hadn't heard it the first time. More so the second time.

"Well, I'm out," said G.G.

"You mind putting in some early work tomorrow?"

"You payin' me?"

"Sure."

"Then I'm there."

I handed him the paper with the address. "Ginny's got a guy who's been trying to get in. Her roommate's ex-boyfriend."

"Uh-oh. You sure we want to get in the middle of a lovers' brawl?"

"No, but it's a favor for Ginny. Can you be there by eleven?"

"In the morning?" G.G. looked at his watch. "It's cruel, but I can do it. She got cable?"

"I dunno," I said.

"She better. I ain't missing the Patriots game."

"We'll relieve you before kickoff."

"I'll see you tomorrow, then." He grabbed his backpack and was gone.

Twitch looked to the two of us.

"No," I said firmly.

"What?"

"We don't need you for this job."

"Well, fuck *you* very much."

"It's a brawn, not brains or bullets kinda situation, brother. No offense." Junior put it better than I could, considering my current state.

That explanation seemed to placate Twitch. "If you need me, ring me." He mimed a receiver to his ear as he backed out the door. The snow was still swirling behind him. I couldn't help but wonder where he'd stashed the gun.

"I'm taking off in a minute before this is completely un-driveable." Junior's '79 Buick, Miss Kitty, could drive through a Himalayan mountain, but the last time the heater worked, people still thought Nickleback was cool. "You need a ride?"

"Nah. I'm gonna crash out here, if we gotta be at the rink early. Just pick me up here."

"You sure?" Junior's bulldog face wasn't able to express much concern, but it was there, nevertheless.

"Yeah. See you in the morning."

"Mañana. And, Boo?"

"Yeah?"

Junior raised an eyebrow at me. "You could've told me that Kelly had a little sumthin' sumthin' to do with tonight."

"She really didn't," I lied.

"You're lying, brother. Don't even know if you know it, but you are."

"Actually, I am well aware of my own delusions."

"Well, quit it." He zipped up his coat and flipped me off before he put his mittens on. "You know better than to think you have to lie to me. And you also have to know better than to think that I'm not gonna call you out on it."

"Does it make it better that I'm mostly lying to myself?"

"Nope. Later, dick."

"Later, fucko."

Alone in the bar, I listened to the hum of the ice machine in the kitchen and the demons in my brain. Being alone with the demons made me realize what a wallop it was seeing Kelly again. I hadn't laid eyes on her since I gave her the heave-ho. I decided to make a big dent in what remained of the whiskey to shut the demons up before they started.

It's all your fault, the demons whispered.

Should have known better. All the whiskey in Kentucky couldn't shut those pricks up. Not only that, but the goddamn demons weren't even specific enough to let me know what exactly was my fault. Discourteous bastards, those demons.

Didn't matter. Whatever they wanted to throw my way, I could find enough evidence of blame to hold myself accountable.

Why the hell couldn't I let this one go?

I was self-aware enough to recognize the circumstances of my own infatuation. I lived a pretty guarded life, for good reasons. Despite my years of honing sharp edges to keep the world at bay, to keep anybody from getting close, Kelly had cut through my defenses like a light saber through jello.

Old wounds had been re-opened by her boss, Jack Donnelly, when he wanted me and Junior to track down his daughter. Memories of my own lost years, my own lost family, were bled out of me slowly and oh so painfully. Things I thought lost to me forever were floating in front of my face like ghosts.

But that's the thing about ghosts.

They're dead.

They just don't know it sometimes.

And sometimes we forget too.

That was the flaw when building psychological walls to defend yourself from the outside world. You never realized how weak that wall was from the inside. It may look good and sturdy, but when the walls cracked, then came tumbling down, it was because I was still that naked, trembling, and hurt little boy behind those walls.

Maybe he wanted out.

I couldn't handle him being out.

Keeping him inside those walls was how I'd been able to live my life for the last couple decades. Vulnerability was for suckers.

Then all of a sudden, oopsie-dasie, there I was. Vulnerable as a motherfucker.

And I did not fucking jive that. Not one bit.

It was one of the reasons I'd pushed Kelly away and begun building walls back up again as fast as my mental bricklayer could erect them.

Even worse was, I thought I might have loved her.

You can't love anything, my demons whispered.

I thought she loved me.

The demons laughed.

Who the hell knew?

We do, the demons said. *And so do you.*

I did know.

Say it.

No.

Say it. What happens to the women you love, Boo? What happens every time?

They die. That was the other reason I sent Kelly packing.

Paranoid?

Sure.

Superstitious and self-destructive?

Yup and yup.

Didn't make any of it less true historically.

Say it.

"The women I love die," I whispered to no one.

"You say somethin', Mr. Boo?"

I yelled something akin to *"Ba-gackin!"* and jumped backward. Which sucked, because I was sitting on a bar stool and toppled backward onto the floor. When I opened my eyes, Luke's kind, grandfatherly face was peering over me.

"Mr. Boo, you all right?" His brown face was creased with age and now worry. "Oh dear. You bleeding?" He gave a finger twirl to the general region of my face.

"Only for about an hour."

"Another night in paradise, huh?" he said with a gentle chuckle.

"The usual." I was glad I'd instinctively made a sound like an electrocuted chicken, rather than let loose the string of curse words that expressed everything I was feeling then. You didn't curse in front of Luke. House law for the eternity and a half that he'd been cleanup man at The Cellar. "Man, you scared me. Didn't think you'd be able to make it in tonight."

Luke grinned. "Ain't missed a day yet. Don't plan on missing one ever. The blizzard of '78 didn't stop me, this dusting ain't gonna." He offered me his hand. I grabbed his grip, strong and dry, and he helped me stand.

"Wish I could say the same. I think I'm gonna take some Z's in the office." My knees wobbled, but I grabbed the bar before I made with a whiskeyed forward roll. Hoo-daddy, I was drunker than I thought.

Luke unwrapped the thick scarf from his skinny neck before he spoke. "Don't want to be too presumptuous here, Mr. Boo, but I saw the way you were staring at the miserable, old reflection of yourself."

"What did you see there, Luke?"

Luke gave a sly smile. "You got a woman-trouble face, Mr. Boo, you don't mind me sayin'…"

"How could you tell?"

"Youngblood like you? Half a bottle of whiskey empty on the bar? When a man's your age, drinking like that, staring into a sad ol' abyss? I'm just playing the odds."

"That easy, huh?"

Luke winked at me, pressing an arthritic knuckle to his grin. "Shhhh. Don't tell anybody. I don't wanna ruin my reputation as a Magical Old Negro."

Despite my roiling inner emotions, a surprised laugh burst out of me. "Really, Luke?"

"Some of you boys seen too many Morgan Freeman movies." Luke opened the utility closet and pulled out his mop and bucket.

"You may be right there."

"But while I'm not Bagger Vance, I have been around quite a few blocks. Anything I can help you with?"

"Maybe…" I thought about how exactly to phrase the question I'd been trying to avoid thinking about. "Why do you think some women like…bad men?"

Luke pondered my question, leaning on his mop handle and sucking his teeth. "Mmm. Never really thought on it too hard. Lots of women do like the outlaw types though, don't they?"

"Why you think that is?"

"Can't say, Mr. Boo. Sometimes, some women develop a taste for the darkness, if that makes any sense."

"Yeah. It does." I cracked a bottle of water and could still taste blood in my mouth.

"And I hope you realize that when I say 'the darkness,' that it isn't magical Negro code for 'Once you go black…'"

Thank God I was standing next to the slop sink, because that sip of water came shooting out, half of it painfully through my swollen nose. It took an effort, but I swallowed the curse that would have normally followed a choking spit-take. Through a wheeze, I said, "Never crossed my mind."

"You worried about some girl?"

"Starting to."

Luke shook his head. "You ain't a bad man, Mr. Boo. Most girls should be so lucky."

"Nice of you to say, Luke."

"And hear me when I say it. I've known some bad men in my time." Something changed in Luke's eyes for a moment, a piece of his own past caught behind his irises. Something told me not to ask.

"Thanks, Luke. Magical advice or not, thanks."

As quickly as it appeared, that flicker of memory was extinguished behind Luke's bright grin.

"Get yourself some sleep. You want me to wake you up before I go?"

"No thanks, Luke. Junior's going to pick me up in the morning."

"Night, then, Mr. Boo."

"Night, Bagger Vance."

"Wisenheimer." Luke turned on his tiny transistor, a gospel ballad warbling tinnily from the speaker. Luke hummed along.

As I walked up the stairs to the office, the seeds of an idea began sprouting. Each step made the notion seem like a good one. My better instincts, and not my drunken ones, tried to tell me otherwise.

My fingers drifted over the pocket with my wallet in it.

The demons said, *"Do it..."*

Jim Beam agreed with them.

Fueled by my anger and my overall sadness, the idea lingered as I stretched out as far as I could on the small loveseat that we'd found on the street. Anything bigger wouldn't fit in the cramped space we called an office. One desk in a liquor storage room does not an office make, but the loveseat helped. I lay my head on the side that smelled the least like cat pee and closed my eyes.

I considered Luke's words. It was nice that he didn't think me a bad guy, even if the rest of the world seemed to disagree. Although I wasn't speaking about myself in particular, Luke had hit a different nail on the head. I may not have been the current darkness, but I might have been the initial taste.

Conveniently for my demons and whiskied brain, my wallet was digging into my ass, so I took it out of my pocket. Before placing it on the desk, I opened it, thumbed through the few bills in it, my Coffee Haus club card, the old, beginning-to-fade business card.

Kelly's business card.

Boo's drunk and concussed brain decided something had to be said.

I wasn't even sure her number was the same after everything that had gone down last summer.

But I picked up the phone anyway.

CHAPTER 7

"WAKEY-WAKEY. EGGS AND bakey, bitch." My first thought was that I was being awakened with a faceful of Columbian tear gas, but it was just Junior holding a steaming cup of his lethal coffee under my nose.

My eyes burst open like two kernels of popcorn as the whiskey bum-rushed from my stomach back to my throat.

Junior recognized the expression. "Bathroom, bathroom!" he yelled, taking a huge step away from me in the event I didn't make it.

I made it. Barely.

After a few good seconds assuring myself that all of my organs remained on the inside, I caught a look in the mirror at my busted-up self. Bloodshot eyes? Check. Blood crusted nose? Check. Breath of a walrus with cirrhosis? Oh yeah.

Then the memory hit me along with another wave of sick that I couldn't blame on the whiskey.

What.

The.

Fuck.

Did.

I.

DO?

I muttered, "Nonononono," as snippets of my drunk-dial to Kelly came back to me.

Me: *What the hell are you doing?*

Kelly: *Boo? What happened? Why—*

Me: *You're banging a drug dealer now?*

Oh sweet Jeebus.

I actually said it.

Then the memory mercifully shut itself off. Junior's mitten roped through the doorway, coffee in hand. "Drink this. Wake the hell up."

I took a sip of Junior's home brew and felt my tongue cramp. Good stuff. "Uggg. What time is it?"

"Ten thirty."

"Jesus, how do people live like this?" I stumbled from the staff lavatory and back to the office, flopping onto the loveseat and burying my face in my hand.

"Savages, all." Junior placed the Styrofoam cup on the desk blotter I'd slept on, next to the wide drool stain. "Drink it. I got a Thermos in the car." Junior picked the disconnected phone off the desk and put it back onto the cradle. "I tried to call and wake you up, but you left the damn phone off the..." Junior looked at me like I'd sharted my Sunday pants right in the middle of Communion.

"What?"

"Please, brudda..." Junior held Kelly's card between his index and middle finger.

"Don't."

"Tell me you didn't."

"I might have."

Another flash of conversation.

Kelly: *You can't be serious.*

Junior threw the card into the trash can. Something I should have done months ago. "You're gonna get all wrapped up again…"

"No. I'm not. I feel bad enough as is."

"No. I don't think you do. We got enough shit to deal with without you getting all goddamn moony over a broad *you* dumped months ago."

Another flash. Kelly had made a similar point.

Kelly: *You cut me loose without so much as a goodbye, and this is how you're going to try to reintroduce yourself into my life? Drunk at four o'clock in the morning? And you have the gall to tell me off about the people I'm associating with? Where do you find the nerve?*

In the bottom of a bottle, apparently.

Every remembered word poked a small hole in my gut, because every word she'd said to me was right on the money.

Ugh. I wasn't a drunk-dial guy. I really wasn't. I felt like thirty-two flavors of shit, and only half of that was the hangover.

"Think I should call and apologize?"

"What? No!" Junior choked on his mouthful of coffee. He wiped the front of his shirt with the back of his mitten. "Let it go! You—forget it. Your stupid ass ain't to be trusted." Junior reached into the garbage can and took the business card back out. He tore it into four pieces and shoved them into his mouth, making a scene of chewing them up and swallowing.

Then the taste hit.

"*Blugh…*"

I took the coffee and swigged another inhuman mouthful, emptying the Styrofoam. "While I admire the lengths to which you are going to prevent me from making a further ass of myself, keep in mind that paper has been in my wallet, soaking up all my back-pocket sweat for months. Bon appétit, dumbass."

Junior gagged, a line of drool sputtering from between his lips. He went to chase it with his coffee, which was one of the few flavors on earth that might have overpowered my butt gravy, but his cup was empty.

He grabbed mine, also empty.

Beads of sweat popped out on his thick brow, and he turned a sickly pale of green.

"Bathroom, bathroom!" I yelled.

He made it.

Barely.

We had to drive out to Lynn for the derby. Junior turned Miss Kitty onto the McClellan Highway going north. We ate cold sausage and egg sandwiches as we drove slowly on the icy roads.

"What do you think I should do?" I asked.

"'Bout what?" Junior slurped loudly from his Thermos and put it back into the cup holder. The steam from the coffee fogged up the windshield. I wiped him a clear spot with a napkin. "Thanks, honey."

"Anytime, pookie. About Kelly."

Junior snorted. "I think you should leave well enough alone. Wasn't one dance with Kwai Chang Caine enough for you?"

I didn't say anything. Junior knew it wasn't and wouldn't be.

"You cut her loose, brother. That was your choice. You ain't got any say in what she does from that point on."

"But what if she doesn't know?"

"Know what?"

"What Summerfield does with his little backdoor import-export business. Maybe she thinks he's just some cat with a fancy accent and a club."

Junior bobbed his head. "If she doesn't, what makes it your fuckin' duty to be the snitch?" Junior turned onto Mass 1-A at the Beach Street exit. "And what if she does know? You ever think that maybe she doesn't give a damn?"

Huh. Hadn't thought of that.

Then Junior rolled his neck. "Christ. You told her, didn't ya?"

"Maybe."

"Why?"

"What?"

"Why?" Junior gulped another mouthful of coffee, sloshing another dribble onto his black pea coat. "Dammit."

"What do you mean, why? I don't like my ex..." I trailed off, but it was too late.

"Wait, wait, wait a minute. Did you almost call the girl you banged for maybe two weeks your ex-girlfriend?"

My ears burned red. Junior wasn't wrong, but I had a hard time with the whole "experiencing nice emotions" and whatnot. Despite the short time Kelly and I had been an item, I had allowed those sentiments to seep in. They'd made me lose an edge that had nearly got us all fitted for coffinwear. I'd cut her loose to save her.

Frankly, I was embarrassed to have to explain to Junior that those feelings hadn't entirely gone away despite my efforts. I carefully thought out how to word my response.

"Shut the fuck up," I said.

Junior snorted. "*You* shut the fuck up."

"YOU shut the fuck up."

"Shut the fuck up! Snitches get stitches."

And so on...

Eventually, we made it to Lynn.

JUNIOR AND I took our seats for The Boston Bruisettes versus the Brighton Beatdowns. Ginny rolled for the Beatdowns under the name of Rhoda Ruder. Junior and I took our seats right in the center of the aluminum bleachers as the girls on the Bruisettes were being introduced.

A tiny dude in what I could only describe as a Liberace-in-his-prime outfit and a curly moustache that looked like it took up way too much of his day strolled to the center of the rink. With a grandiose gesture, he said into a wireless mike, "Ladies and gentlemen! Welcome to the Boston Roller Derby League!"

The audience whooped and hollered.

"Our first team tonight of wild, wicked, whip-yo-ass women…The Boston Bruisettes! Give it up for *Annabelle Lecter*!" Annabelle, a heavily tattooed punk chick took her lap around the rink, then raised her skirt to show the word "kicker" ironed on her backside. Ass kicker. Cute.

"I'm in love," said Junior.

"With Liberace over there?"

"You know I hate sequins."

"Hell, he may be the most feminine one in the ring." I kept my eyes on the audience. I only had a vague recollection of what Byron looked like, but watched for anyone who looked like he wasn't here for the bout. Ginny had said once she was introduced she'd scan the crowd and point at him when she passed us.

"*Rita Haymaker!*" Rita, a curvy beauty in a schoolgirl outfit, zipped around the rink, alternating wiggling her ass and shimmying her ample boobs. It was a miracle the girl could suspend her top-heaviness on eight tiny wheels.

"I'm in love," said Junior.

"Are you going to do this all afternoon?"

"Don't deny me my love."

"It would help if you looked for Byron. You did get more of a look at him than I did."

"What's that supposed to mean?"

"It means you got a better look at him than I did." Junior was still way oversensitive about being on the low end of his fistfight with Byron.

"Well, soooo-rry."

I got the feeling he wasn't, though. Maybe it was the five syllables he used in the word "sorry." I had to admit being more than a little distracted myself. Especially by Barbi Bender. Barbi didn't showboat. She just casually took her lap. Some things don't need an exclamation point. "I wonder which one's Dana."

"Doesn't matter to me. I'd guard the body of any of these chicks anytime."

"Is she even a skater?"

"Hm. I dunno. Didn't think to ask."

I looked over the cheering mass again, this time for a woman's face. Surprisingly, there were a number of women mixed in with the hormonally overloading hipster men. Half the crowd looked like trust fund jag-offs who spent a lot of money to look like they just finished a shift in the coal mines. The air was thick with irony and badly groomed facial hair. All were shouting and whooping it up. I recognized a few patrons from the bar, but nobody looked like Byron, per se.

"*Rhoda Ruder!*"

The crowd hollered their loudest for Ginny. Apparently, she was a fan favorite. She took her loop, shaking her fist high, but I could see her eyes moving person to person. Once she passed us, she shook her head.

Junior's phone beeped. "G.G. texted me. All quiet at the house. He's going a little nuts. Apparently, they do not, in fact, have cable, and the Patriots game is starting in a half hour."

We'd left G.G. back at Ginny's place, in case Byron tried a smash-and-grab while Ginny and Dana were at the roller derby. We said we'd relieve him after the match, since it was his shift at the bar. Even though Junior knew he had his best chance at putting his knuckles to Byron's face back at Ginny's place, you try to keep him from a bunch of barely clad chicks beating the crap out of each other.

"Tell him we'll relieve him by the start of the third."

The derby started and the two teams went at it. I couldn't claim to fully understand the rules, but from what I could tell, it was half a race and half a hockey brawl. I managed to figure out that each team had a girl with a red cardboard arrow glued to her helmet. The other girls had to either help or hinder her progress through the cluster.

Ginny was hell on wheels, pun intended. When she had the arrow, she was fluid and fast. When she was a blocker, she leveled the other girls brutally. It wasn't hard to see why the fans dug her. Whatever got your motor running, roller derby-wise, Ginny was an ace.

The buzzer sounded, marking halftime of the game. The Beatdowns were up twenty-seven to sixteen, but I'd be damned if I had any idea how the scoring system came to that amount.

Junior and I worked our way toward the locker room. If Byron was going to try to start a problem, he'd be an idiot to do it with this many witnesses. The danger for Ginny and Dana would have been on their way to the rink or on their way home.

"Imagine the possibilities," said Junior in a way that made me a bit ill.

"What are you talking about?"

"Dude! A girls' locker room. A girls' *roller derby* locker room."

I didn't know why the sport made the difference, but was afraid to ask. "What the hell do you think is going on in there?"

"Tickle fights."

A skinny security guard in a Boston Derby T-shirt stood at the door, bony arms folded in a rough approximation of toughness.

"Can I help you guys?" he asked.

"Yeah," I said. "We have to talk to Ginny or Dana."

"I don't know who you're talking about."

I rolled my eyes. "Rhoda Ruder."

The guard snorted. "Sure, buddy. You have any idea how many guys want to talk to her?"

"Listen, pencil-neck," said Junior. "You call on that little walkie you got strapped on your belt and get us in there or get her out here. Tell whoever's on that other end that Boo and Junior need to talk to her."

He narrowed his eyes at us suspiciously, then turned his back to us and covered the mouthpiece so we couldn't hear what he was saying.

A voice on the other end squawked, "I'll be right there."

Skinny smiled smugly. "He'll be right here," he said.

Who the hell was "he"?

That question was answered quickly as I spotted a shock of white hair moving a good six inches above the tallest person in the room. "Boo Malone! Well, I'll be goddamned."

"Mitch." I extended my hand to him, a smile stretching across my face at seeing the old-timer. Mitch Young took my hand in his and shook it warmly, then pulled me into a hug.

"Junior!" Mitch gave him the same shake-hug. "Great to see you boys. Christ, you both look like shit."

"And you look old."

"Yeah, well. That's the goddamn passage of time for you." Mitch twirled the frayed toothpick between his teeth. He'd been chewing the same toothpicks for ten years, trying to give up his beloved menthols.

Skinny hooked his thumbs into his belt. "You know these guys, Mitch?"

Mitch sighed. "Walter, why don't you go check the restrooms and make sure that nobody's smoking a reefer."

Gotta love a guy who still calls it reefer.

After Walter skulked off, Mitch looked at us sheepishly. "Goddamn nephew. Hard to believe we share biological stock, huh?"

"Hey, brudda," Junior said. "Sometimes those apples drop off the family tree, then roll a long way down a big friggin' hill."

"True that." Mitch was a local legend in the Boston security business, with a reputation that bordered on mythological. One of my personal favorites was the story of him denying Elvis Costello entrance into The Rat in '79, telling him, "I don't care if you're Abbott and Costello, you don't get in without an ID." True story. Or true legend. Either way.

"Nice to see some real security on this gig. The girls look like they can rile a crowd up."

Mitch laughed, a deep rumble that started in his belly and put a smile on the face of everyone in earshot. "You have no idea."

"You working anywhere else?"

Mitch's ears went red. "Actually, the rink is my gig."

I swallowed my embarrassment for him. Mitch Young being reduced to roller rink security was like Bruce Lee being forced to teach a Zumba class.

"Hey," I said, clapping a hand on his still-solid shoulder. "A gig is a gig is a gig, right?"

"Damn right," he said, his attempt to salvage some dignity both obvious and painful to watch. "Old bouncers don't retire, they just work at goddamn roller rinks. So, Walter said you needed to speak to Rhoda?"

"Yeah."

Mitch opened the locker door a crack and yelled in, "Ladies?"

"*Hiiiii, Mitch,*" came a sweetly unison reply, like a class of second-graders addressing the principal.

"You all decent? We got visitors for Rhoda."

"Whenever you're around, my thoughts are never decent, Mitch," a husky voice that rang of a young Kathleen Turner called out. The girls all whooped, and Mitch went three shades redder. I wondered if he was conscious of the fact that he was rubbing his wedding ring with the thumb on the same hand.

The door opened and Ginny poked her head out. "Hey, guys. I didn't see him, did you?" She was dabbing at her sweaty cleavage with a towel. I took a quick look over at Junior to make sure he hadn't fainted.

"Nope."

Mitch looked at us. "Who are you looking for?"

"Guy named Byron. He's been harassing Ginny—sorry, Rhoda, and her roommate. We're actually kinda on the clock."

"Well, goddamn, you point him out when you see him and I'll toss his ass in the dumpster."

The dumpster toss was one of my favorites as well. Another chapter in the legendary Book of Mitch was that he was the first one to make it a practice at The Cellar. Today, a dumpster toss was almost a rite of passage at the club. "We're gonna go trade spots with G.G. Would you mind making sure she gets to her car unmolested?"

"I'd consider it an honor."

"Thanks, my man. We gotta boogie." Junior and I turned to go.

Behind us, I heard Ginny say, "Thank you, Mitch."

Then the chorus from within. "*Thaaaank you, Mitch.*"

The last thing I heard, almost sub-audibly, was Mitch. "Till death do I part..."

As we walked out of the rink, Mitch's words echoed in my ears and added to the sourness in my stomach that started with the hangover.

Old bouncers don't retire.

I couldn't help but feel I'd gotten a peek into my own future and I didn't like the look of it. Junior's mouth was also turned down at the corners. "That ain't right."

"I hear ya."

"Not one goddamn tickle fight."

Same planet. Different worlds.

CHAPTER 8

"HOLD UP HERE," I said to Junior as we approached Ginny's street in Jamaica Plain.

"Why?"

I pointed at a car sitting by itself, plumes of exhaust condensing in the frigidity. "There."

"Maybe somebody's warming their car up."

"Maybe. Let's wait a minute and see if he pulls out." I never would have been suspicious if it hadn't been so goddamn cold out. If it was Byron, he'd have had to keep the engine running or freeze to death.

"He's not going anywhere," Junior said, squinting.

"I was thinking, what if Byron's watching the house? Maybe he saw G.G. going in. If we go in the back and G.G. goes out the front, we can lure him in."

"Why don't we just bum rush the car? Yank him out and throw a boot party."

My teeth chattered in the chill of Miss Kitty's interior. I found myself envious of Byron's car—if it was, in fact, Byron's car. "One, we don't know it's him in there."

Junior shrugged and rolled his neck, visibly jonesing to engage Byron for a second round. "Dragging him out the window is one way of finding out."

"Two, if we beat his ass on the street, he can call the cops on us and file for assault. And he'd be right. If we catch him in Ginny's…well, we got him dead bang. If he wants to call the cops, he'd be confessing to breaking and entering too."

"Fucking pussy." In our world, you never called the cops on somebody. Ever. If you could dole out the lumps, you better be able to take them too. Our whole scene was one big fight club. If anyone got his ass kicked and went to the cops, he'd never live it down.

"I'm just saying, is all. We don't know how Byron rolls. I don't know about you, but I don't need to get locked up over this jag-off."

"I was calling you a pussy, not Byron."

"Fair enough. Allow me then to finish up with point three."

"Shoot."

"Let's assume that it is Byron in there, okay?"

"Okay."

"He's in an idling car."

"Yeah, so?"

"You and me, we're not exactly cat burglars. What if he sees us and jumps the car into gear? Let's assume he realizes we're not creeping up on him to wish him a happy Kwanzaa."

Junior frowned. "Are you anywhere near a point?"

"Say he goes with flight instead of fight. If I recall events correctly, you didn't do so well the last time you played chicken with one of Detroit's finest automotive products."

"Let's go in the back."

Unfortunately, "the back" was connected in the rear by somebody's yard and an eight-foot-high picket fence. The good news was nobody would be able to see us from either street.

Stealth wasn't exactly our forte, so we went with casual. We opened the gate to the backyard and walked in like we belonged.

"Who's going over first?" Both of us needed assistance to get over the wall, but I figured whoever did it first would be able to manage it with the most dignity intact.

"Like we always do?" Junior placed his fist into his open palm, ready for yet another bout in our lifelong game of rock-paper-scissors. "On three?"

"On three," I said.

"One…two…*HOLY FUCKBALLS!*"

Furious barking erupted from the back door of the house. Big barking. We both jumped in tandem and got ready to bolt. I looked at the rear of the house for any sign of a doggy door. From the sound of the barks, the animal would need a garage door to fit through.

Junior was crouched in a ready position. "Jesus, I almost pissed my Fruit of the Looms."

"Let's go again and get the hell inside." My skin was flushed from the adrenaline rush, but my lip stubble was starting to develop icicles.

"*Onetwothree*—shoot!"

Paper.

Junior threw rock.

"Shit." Junior locked his fingers together and bent low at the knees. The snarling dog was loud, but I could still hear Junior mumble something about a "tubby bastard" as he hoisted me up.

My first leg was over, then found purchase on a chain-link fence that rimmed the pickets on Ginny's side. Hell, it might not be that tough after—

Then the back door opened. A miniature old lady in matching blue slippers, robe, and hair stood to the side to let the dog by. "Awright, Pickles. Cawm down."

Pickles?

Pickles was a Rottweiler that looked to be pushing Junior's weight. Except he was fast. Pickles shot across the small yard like a furry Armageddon. The old lady shut the door behind herself, oblivious to both our presence and the trauma that Pickles was about to inflict on us.

Junior screamed. "Hey, HEY, *HAAAYYYY! Get me up! Get me up!*"

I grabbed the shoulders of his pea coat and heaved myself backward, trying to leverage his weight. Precariously, my toes clung to the top bar of the fence. Junior made it most of the way over before he stopped.

Junior's face was a mask of fear as he howled. "Pickles got me! *Pickles got me!*"

With one last lurch, I threw my weight backward. Pickles' snout peeked up over the fence, clamped to Junior's foot, then separated. I quickly prayed that the separation didn't include Junior's foot and ankle.

We landed in a tangle on Ginny's side of the fence. Junior's thick mass drove right into my sternum, knocking the wind out of me. As I lay wheezing, Junior scrambled off, clutching his foot. Saints be praised, he still had a foot to clutch, but his sneaker was gone.

G.G. came busting out Ginny's back door with a tire iron in his hands. He lowered his arm when he recognized us. "What the hell is wrong with you two?"

I was still struggling to get air into my compressed lungs, but managed to wheeze, "We're…being…stealthy. Pickles…" I pointed back to the gap between the fence slats where Pickles gnashed his jaws, trying to work his way through to us.

"Five," Junior said, counting the toes on his right foot for the second time as he hopped into the back door and into Ginny's kitchen.

"You're lucky you got a foot to count it on," said G.G., looking into the neighbor's yard from his perch on the back steps. "Pickles don't look like he's playing."

From the kitchen window, I could see Pickles making a day of it with Junior's sneaker. Pickles tore the nylon tongue clean off and swallowed it. I swallowed too. Rock-paper-scissors had saved me. I was wearing work boots, which might not have popped off my foot so easily. If I hadn't gone over the fence first, Pickles would be making the same meal of my leg below the knee.

"Goddamn eighty-dollar pair of Reeboks," Junior grumbled. He flung his soaking wet sock into the garbage can. "Now I gotta hop around in this?" Junior waved his hand in the general direction of the accumulated world.

"Am I good to go?" G.G. asked. "Been listening to the goddamn game on the radio like a peasant."

"Yeah, but when you do, just walk out like you were alone. We think Byron's casing the joint and we don't want him to know we're here. Pretend to lock the door."

"Got ya. Later, Boo."

"Later."

"See ya, Hopalong." The big man snorfled a little at his own joke.

"Bite me," Junior grumbled.

"Careful what you wish for," I said.

"Oh, *hyuk-hyuk-hyuk*. You two are a riot."

Junior and I sat in the living room. Ginny and Dana may not have had cable, but they did have a huge selection of DVDs.

"Holy Christ," Junior said as he flipped through the titles. "Goddamn broads."

"Whatcha got?"

"*Pretty Woman. Les Misérables . . .*" Pronounced Less Miserables, natch. "Sweet Mother of Mercy…"

"Please tell me they have something with Batman."

"*Brokeback* fuckin' *Mountain*."

I shrugged. "Won best director."

Junior gave me a look that could have cracked granite. "Don't even kid."

"Got the Joker in it. Kind of…"

Then something thumped off the door. Hard. Junior ran at the door before I could even stand from the chair. He yanked the door open onto a very surprised Byron as I rounded the hallway bend. Byron froze in the spot he was in, crowbar in the jamb of the doorway that was now wide open, to his surprise.

"Hiya, Byron." Junior drilled him right in the mouth with a straight right.

Byron tumbled backward down the porch steps, the crowbar falling soundlessly onto a snow drift.

Junior was on top of him before he could even put his hands up.

I calmly followed and picked up the crowbar, out and away from Byron's reach. This dance was all Junior's.

Kneeling on his chest, Junior laid shot after shot into Byron's mug. All the while yelling, "How's your face? How's your face?" between blows, with the odd "cocksucker" and "bitch" thrown in to add flavoring.

"That's enough, Junior."

"*How's your face, faggot?*"

"Junior!"

Junior raised his hand up once more, then lowered it. Thankfully for Byron, it wasn't lowered into his puss again. Instead, Junior pulled out thick plastic ties from his back pocket.

Byron was nearly unconscious and bleeding freely from his busted mouth, but alive. I helped Junior turn him over and we fastened his hands behind him. It was over so fast, it was nearly unsatisfying. We each grabbed a shoulder on his jacket and dragged him back inside Ginny's before any neighbors came walking by.

We dropped Byron on the floor of the hallway. Junior sat on the floor and groaned as he massaged the blood back into his bare foot, which had turned light blue with purply splotches.

"You okay?" I asked.

"Peachy." He reached into his pocket and tossed me his car keys. "Go get Miss Kitty, will ya? I don't feel like walking a block with no shoe on."

I lifted my chin toward Byron. "You done with him?"

"Yeah. I've had my fun. I am gonna take his shoes, though."

"Fair enough." I walked outside, and for the second time in twenty-four hours, I saw blood splattered in the snow. I was glad none of it was ours this time. I kicked some fresh powder over it with the side of my boot.

WE DEBATED WHICH trunk to stuff Byron into. While Junior didn't like the thought of bloodying up Miss Kitty's boot, we'd be able to get him in and out of the Buick much easier than the Neon he was driving.

Byron stirred a bit and groaned as we deposited him into Miss Kitty's smelly trunk. Junior popped him again on the jaw. Byron groaned and went limp once more.

Across the street, I saw curtains move behind the window of one of the tenements. A hand that looked like it was holding a phone. "C'mon, man," I said. "Natives are starting to get nosy."

Junior slammed the lid down heavily and climbed into the driver's seat.

I followed Miss Kitty onto the Mass Pike heading east. Junior hadn't told me where we were going and I hadn't asked. It seemed like he had a plan. Either way, I was glad to be in a car that had a working goddamn heating system. Off the Pike, we got onto I-95 North, then US-1A heading into Revere. Then I got the clue. We got off the parkway and I followed Junior onto Revere Beach Road.

He pulled over and stopped. I turned into the spot behind him. The beach was empty, and the ocean looked murderously bitter. I got all New England nostalgic when I looked at the Atlantic in the winter. It was then that I sensed in my bones the freezing death that claimed generation after generation of fishing boats coming down from Gloucester and New Bedford. It ain't all foliage and clam chowder.

My mother and I lived for a couple years in a tiny apartment out in Gloucester, one of the many that she, my sister, and I resided in during our short-stay existence. I was always fascinated by the memorials, the names of those the sea had claimed. I could stare at the statue of the Man at the Wheel for hours.

As the memory of my own lost family surfaced, I had an epiphany, a little one. When I was a kid, I used to love the statues in Boston too. The Aquarium dolphins, all the pieces in the public garden. All of a sudden, I realized why I did. Something inside of me wanted to feel what the stability, the permanence of a statue felt like within a life that was nothing but transitory. The constant movement of the ocean reminded me of the beauty of constant movement as well. The statues reminded me of my mother. The ocean reminded me of my sister. Both were just memories now.

The old familiar sadness washed over me as I closed my eyes and inhaled the cold, cold, salty breeze and allowed myself to feel the emotions I normally buried.

But my wistful New Englander musings disappeared right quick as I remembered we still had a shoeless bleeding guy in Miss Kitty's trunk.

Junior shut the engine on Miss Kitty and emerged from the car, baseball bat in hand. He walked over to my driver's side window. "Kill the engine and pop the hood."

I did so, curious as to where this was going. I wasn't about to join him outside yet, since I planned on enjoying the toasty interior as long as I could before returning to the icebox of Junior's car.

Although I couldn't see what Junior was up to under the hood, I heard the sounds of his angry tinkering through the vents. A minute later, Junior slammed the hood down, the Neon's car battery in his hands. Calmly, he walked the short length of beach down to the break of water, and shot-put the battery into the ocean. He waved me out of the car. I lifted my collar over my neck and grudgingly joined him. For good measure, he ripped the passenger-side mirror off. It resisted for a second, but came apart from the car, a short tangle of wires protruding from the base.

"Fuckin' technology," said Junior. "Electric mirror's gonna cost him three hundo more to fix than if he had a regular goddamn mirror."

I was feeling a little bad about leaving Byron on a frozen beach with a busted car, but we were close enough to civilization where he wouldn't freeze to death as long as he was willing to sacrifice a little dignity.

And I still wasn't entirely sure about how wrong he was in the situation with Ginny and her roommate. Sure, he could have been less of a dick about it…but that was where my guilt ended.

Fuck him. He was being a dick.

"Shall we let our prisoner out?"

"Sure." He handed the bat to me and pulled out his cell. "You want the honors?"

"What are you doing?"

"I wanna take a video of this jackhole."

"Why?"

Junior shrugged. "It'll make me happy?"

"Think that it might not be in our best interests to document the crime we're committing?"

"Are we?"

"Are we what?"

"Committing a crime?"

"Pretty much."

"Really? I mean, the guy is a douche and a bully."

"Still doesn't make it legal to beat him up, kidnap him, and wreck his car."

"Huh." Junior seemed genuinely surprised that our excursion might be looked at differently from a legal standpoint. "Can I just keep the video for a day? I'll delete it tomorrow. Promise." Junior held up crossed fingers.

"You're showing me crossed fingers, moron."

"What? No. This is scout's honor."

"No. You're telling me that…fuck it. Let's get this over with. I'm fucking cold. No video."

Junior shut off the camera on his phone, grumbling about the lack of fun inherent in my personality. He handed me the bat and twisted the key in the trunk lock. The lid popped open a crack and Byron's arm snaked across the opening. Junior yelped and jumped back, clutching his hip, cell phone spinning out of his grip. "Sonofabitch cut me!" He pointed at the blindly swiping hand. Somehow, inside the trunk, Byron had gotten his hands on a box cutter, which would explain both how he got loose and how he injured Junior.

"That your box cutter?"

Junior glared at me. "The fuck you waiting for, Boo? A goddamn invitation?"

In my surprise, I'd forgotten the bat in my hands. Byron was halfway out of the trunk, his own phone in his other hand, videotaping us.

I swung the bat down as Byron was stepping out. The bat collided with the trunk, slamming it down on Byron's head, instead of knocking the cutter from his grip as I'd hoped. He did drop his recording device, however.

"My car!" Junior screamed at me, more pissed at the damage to Miss Kitty than the gash on his thigh. He grabbed my arms to prevent a second assault on his beloved.

In the meantime, a stunned and bleeding Byron rolled out of the trunk, onto the sand-and-snow-blown street. He was still slashing at the air with the box cutter as he grabbed his phone. "*Fuck you!*" he shrieked, holding the phone in a shaking hand, waving the box cutter with the other. "I'm taping you sonsabitches. You come near me again, and…and…"

Twin smears of thick white powder streaked down his upper lip and across his cheek. Guess he'd also had a bit of blow on him, which he'd decided to partake in during his downtime in the trunk.

Junior and I stopped wrestling with the bat and stared at him.

"Who said we wanted to come near you again?" I asked. "You just—"

Byron took the beginning of my sentence to mean something else entirely. "Fuck you! You're not killing me! Fuck you!"

"The fuck are you talking about?" Junior said, as much to the air as to either Byron or me.

"I know who you work for, you bastards." Byron's breaths were deep and ragged in his panic. His bloodshot eyes bulged from the sockets, either from pure fear or the blow, or both. He had enough powder on his face to blast off the entire defensive line of the '77 Bruins. Between the coke and the crusted blood, he looked like the world's looniest Kabuki dancer. "You're not killing me!"

"We're not—"

"My shit is inside the house you threw me out of, you dumb pricks!"

"Look, man," I said. "We don't have the slightest idea what the fuck you're talking about. Leave the girls alone."

Byron's face twisted up into a mask of cocaine-infused confusion. "What girls?"

"Whaddaya mean, 'what girls'?" Junior asked.

We all fell silent, the wind and trickling waves the lone sounds as we looked back and forth to each other, hoping somebody could fill the humongous gaps in our broadly differing narratives.

"I—" was all I got out.

Byron turned and sprinted down the beach, screaming the whole way. Junior and I stood there, silent and stunned as we watched Byron's lopsided escape. After all, he did only have one of Junior's shoes on.

As he further distanced himself, I asked Junior, "You took the time to put your shoe on him?"

"I took his. Seemed fair."

"Seems odd that you made the effort to put one shoe on him though. How they fitting you?"

Junior shrugged and wiggled the brown boot on his left foot. "Not too bad. I think they'd be tight if I had socks on. Think the asshole got the message?"

I cupped my hands around a cigarette and lit it in the strong beach gusts. Who says I have no life skills? "Hey," I yelled toward the nearly disappeared Byron as I puffed on the filter. "Leave Dana and Ginny alone. *Hey!*"

I didn't think he could hear me with the wind and distance, but I figured I had to say *some*thing in order to feel I'd done my due diligence.

I watched the frantic dot in the distance run down the beach fifty more yards before he cut a quick left and darted between the rows of houses. I gave it another minute, then stubbed out my butt in the sand.

Junior and I stood there listening to the ocean for a few more moments before either of us spoke again.

Junior cleared his throat. "Well, *that* was fuckin' weird."

"Owww!" Junior winced as he dabbed at his wound with a wet napkin. It was a shallow cut, but long and painful-looking. His cries would have been embarrassing, had the diner had anyone but us and the waitress to hear it. Nevertheless, the elderly waitress in the hairnet stared at us unhappily. Probably because Junior's pants were halfway off so he could clean the cut on his hip, just above the thigh.

"Couldn't you do that in the bathroom?"

"In a diner? No friggin' way. You know how many germs there are in a diner bathroom?"

The waitress narrowed her eyes. The cook added his glare to the mix over his fry station.

"He's kidding," I said with a smile. "You have a wonderful and clean establishment." I would have added a wave, but my hands were stuck to the table. "You mind keeping it down?" I whispered to Junior. "I'd rather not get my burger with spit in it." I smiled at the cook again. The way the place looked, spit might very well have been what they cleaned the table with.

"Hey, you keep quiet. You're not the one who got pig-stuck. Another three inches and he would have cut my hog off."

"Well, maybe if you'd taken that goddamn box cutter out of your trunk..."

Junior aped the tonality of my sentence in a whiny singsong, using only the word "*myenh*."

I rolled my eyes. "Speaking of changing the subject, what the hell do you think Byron was talking about?"

Junior shrugged. "He knew we were working for the girls. So what?"

I tried to tap my fork in thought on the table, but it was stuck too. "I dunno. He really thought we were going to kill him. Why would he think that?"

"Well, gee. Maybe because we beat the crap out of him, dumped him in my trunk, and drove him out to the beach?"

"Maybe."

"And maybe he was a little bit coked off his nut too."

"True."

"It has been known to make a person paranoid."

"Also true. I can't help but feel that he thought we were somebody else."

"Who?" Junior dabbed the cut again. "Fuckin' *ow!*"

I didn't look, but felt the staff's glares again. "Damned if I know."

"Then don't worry about it. Jackass like him has to have all sorts looking to kick his ass. We did what we wanted to do. I don't think he'll be bugging the girls again."

"I would be surprised if he did."

The waitress came over with our burgers. She dropped the hard plastic plates on the table from enough height to make her point about how much she valued our business. "Enjoy," she said. I didn't feel like she meant it.

I checked my burger for loogies.

My beeper sounded. "Lemme use your cell. It's Ginny."

Junior rolled his eyes, taking a huge bite out of his burger. "You gotta get a phone, man."

"I have a phone." After the escapades that had nearly killed us last summer, Twitch had made the whole crew run-packs, which included burner phones we were under strict instructions to keep charged.

Just in case.

Along with the phones that had all of our phone numbers programmed in them, the run-packs came complete with homemade lead-knuckled sap gloves—Twitch's very own design—CharlieCards, a change of clothes, protein bars, and an empty money belt that he suggested we put twenty bucks a week in. Mine had eleven dollars.

"You need to carry that shit, not leave it in the closet," Junior said, splattering his burger with ketchup.

"You gonna let me use your phone or not?" My Luddite ways were a constant source of griping for Junior. I wasn't paranoid, I'd just seen *Terminator* too many times to live without suspicion that technology might try to kill me someday.

Fine. I'm paranoid.

Junior took his iPhone out of his pocket, grimacing. "Still got goddamn sand in it." He blew a couple of grains off the screen and out of the headphone jack, then slid it across the table.

I slid my finger across the screen. "What's your passcode?"

"I don't have a passcode."

"Then why is this phone asking me for a passcode?"

Junior grabbed the phone out of my hands. "Goddammit."

"What?"

"This isn't my phone."

"Well, hell. Byron must have picked up your phone after you two clowns decided to play *Candid Camera* with each other."

"Fuuuuuck."

I shook my head and walked over to the glaring waitress. "I'm sorry. Do you have a payphone anywhere?"

With a completely straight face, she said, "Yeah. Go out front. There's a time machine. Set it for 1989…"

I actually had to hand it to her. That was a solid response. I would have asked to use the diner's phone, but I didn't think my ego could handle another razor slice from Flo's stiletto wit.

I walked back to the table.

Junior popped a pickle slice into his mouth. "Think I should call my phone? Arrange a swap?"

"Yeah. I'm sure he'll be real enthusiastic about that exchange."

"Well, his shit's still at Ginny's. I'm sure he still wants it. We call, tell him that he ponies up the money, we give him back his stuff."

"He did seem pretty desperate. He thinks somebody, namely us, is going to kill him for it."

Junior's face dropped. "Aw, crap. You think he doubled back?"

"If he did, we just gave him enough time to arm himself with something more than a box cutter."

"Let's move."

We each tossed a twenty on the table and hauled ass out to the parking lot.

FOURTEEN YEARS AGO

I DIDN'T SEE the shot coming. Hell, I didn't even remember getting hit, so I couldn't say until later what it was that clobbered me. I was getting in the shower; then my next memory was of waking up, water running up my nose, choking, weight between my shoulder blades and on my hips. I heard the giggling of Zach Bingham's two cronies as they sat on my back, pinning me down on the slick tiles stinking of mildew.

The cronies, two recent additions to The Home, joined up right quick with the guy who was clearly the biggest threat. Once he got himself a crew, Zach saw an opportunity to take a shot at us.

And he was taking it right then and there.

I held my head up and saw Junior through the thick steam, also down, propped up on one elbow as he struggled to hang on to consciousness. A wide gash across his hairline bled openly down his face, swirling in the waters from the community shower at St. Gabe's.

Emerging from the steam behind Junior—Zach. The giant was naked, and sporting a proportional erection.

Which meant it was pretty goddamn huge. And it was pointing right at Junior's butthole.

Junior's head wobbled woozily on his neck as he tried to pull himself away. "Junior...*JUNIOR!*" I yelled.

Zach looked at me with those predator's eyes. "I want quiet," was all he said. Immediately, one of the cronies stuffed a washcloth into my mouth. I gagged as the wet terrycloth hit the back of my throat.

"Ain't gonna happen, Zach," Junior said, his words as glazed as his expression. But if Zach wanted to do what it seriously appeared he wanted to do, well, Junior would have to come to terms real fast with being a sausage casing.

Zach replied to Junior's defiance by tugging firmly on his own balls once, twice, then positioning himself behind my friend, pushing Junior's legs wide with his own knees.

Junior whipped a weak elbow into Zach's chest. Zach grabbed a handful of Junior's red hair and slammed his face into the tile.

I heard something crack loudly. I hoped it was the cheap tile, and not my best friend's skull.

Junior went limp. Zach smiled and spit into his palm.

CHAPTER 9

WE HAULED ASS back to JP, Junior bitching the entire time about his missing iPhone. Odds were, even with the time we'd taken to eat and get back to Ginny's, Byron wouldn't have been able to get back to her place, outside of calling a cab. Even then, cabs didn't normally roll the streets of Revere, so he'd have a good wait before a gypsy cab could get him. And even then, I'd have laid odds that any cabbie worth his salt would get one look at the blood-and-cocaine covered Byron and keep on driving.

I kept telling myself these things as we skidded to a halt in the snow in front of Ginny's apartment.

Junior and I ran up the steps and banged on the door. We were both out of breath by the time we hit the top step. Christ, we were out of shape.

The door opened. "Ginny…" I wheezed. The rest of the sentence was caught in surprise when I saw that the door had been opened by the guy from the roller derby match—the one in the Liberace getup and the complicated moustache.

Junior shook his head. "The fuck are you doing here?"

"Excuse me?"

Ginny popped into the doorway between us and Liberace. "Hey, guys," she said, a rigid grin nervously plastered on her face. "Everything okay?"

"Uh, yeah. All's good. Wanted to make sure you were all right."

The stage smile stretched wider. "Okay, good. I'll see you guys at work." She went to close the door right in our faces.

I stopped the door with my palm. "Hey, hey! Listen! If Byron shows up again—"

Ginny's eyes went wide. "You found him?"

"He came here," I said.

From around Ginny, Liberace grabbed the door and pulled it back open. "Byron? What about Byron?"

"Dana..." Ginny said.

"We kicked his ass, dumped him on Revere Beach," Junior said. "So you tell Dana that he won't be—"

Fury lit behind Liberace's eyes. "Why don't you tell me yourself."

"I'm sorry. The fuck are you again?" I asked.

"I'm fucking Dana!"

What?

It sank in. Ginny pursed her lips and squeezed her eyes shut. I glared at her.

"'Scuse me," Junior said. "How are you fucking Dana? Is that why Byron was so pissed?"

Dana's jaw dropped.

"Junior..."

"No offense, but if my girl was messing around with this guy? Frankly, I been thinking you were on the fruity side this whole time. Again, no offense."

Sweet, bleeding eyes of Jesus.

Ginny's jaw dropped.

My jaw stayed where it was, since I've known Junior for over twenty years.

We all stood in the doorway for a couple seconds, be it in shock, horror, confusion. Take your pick.

Then...

Junior's jaw dropped. "Wait tha—*WHOA!*"

He got it.

"This is fucked up, Ginny," I said. "You didn't tell us we were…"

"That you were what, Boo? That you were helping a guy with his boyfriend?"

"No! You didn't say that. That is precisely a thing that you did not say."

"You we're also helping *me*, Boo. Does that part matter?"

Dana stepped in between us, fury blazing in his eyes. "What did you do, Ginny?"

"I took care of the problem, Dana."

"What did you *do*?"

"We discussed this," Ginny said.

"We discussed scaring him off, but you never said anything about hiring goons."

I wanted to protest, but the goon shoe kinda fit. Pretty comfortably, actually.

"What did you think I was going to do, wear a scary mask?" Ginny said, her voice rising.

Junior pulled my sleeve. "Let's bounce, dude. This ain't gonna get any less fucked up the longer we stand here."

Dana stormed out and grabbed the sleeve of Junior's coat. "No! You're staying right here and telling me what you did to Byron."

In a flash, Junior's eyes were ablaze in a fury that surprised even me. He swatted Dana's wrist with enough force to smack it painfully across the doorjamb.

"Get your faggot hands offa me, you hear?" Junior snarled, pulling his fist back. Now my jaw dropped.

Dana flinched and took a step back.

Ginny yelled, "No!" and stepped in between the two of them, her arms splayed back protectively across the doorway.

Junior opened his fist and stormed down the steps toward Miss Kitty.

Junior's sudden turn to aggressiveness had thrown me. And there wasn't a lot that could surprise me where Junior was concerned.

That reaction? That surprised me. But I still had to have his back. I turned to Ginny. "You should have told us what we were in the middle of."

"Should it matter, Boo?"

I waved a hand toward Junior. "Yeah, apparently it does."

"Then how the fuck *could* I have told you? Assholes." She slammed the door in my face. Immediately, I could hear her and Dana yelling at each other.

Miss Kitty's engine roared to life. "Boo! Let's go!"

So, my inner voice said. *Looks like we're done here.*

I trotted down the stairs and climbed into the car.

Junior seethed quietly until we turned onto Huntington. "The fuck was that?"

"My sentiments exactly."

"Goddamn it. I do not appreciate not knowing the depths of the shit I'm sticking my head into, Boo. Am I wrong?"

I opened my mouth to answer, then caught myself. I wanted to say, "no," but Junior's reaction was way uncalled for. Even though I was incredibly irate at Ginny for the little game she played us with, Junior took it to a whole 'nother dimension.

Junior wasn't wrong to be put-off, but I had to question his full reasons why.

I wasn't wrong to feel pissed off at how the whole shebang unfolded.

But something was wrong. Felt wrong.

Gay, straight, that part shouldn't matter, right? Especially when it came down to who deservesd a good smack in the head. Byron was a royal fucktrumpet either way.

So why was that little detail bugging me?

Maybe I wasn't as open-minded as I liked to think…

Shit, the guy got over on Junior. And a half-capacity Junior was still a force to be reckoned with under most circumstances. Byron could hold his own.

But the good ol' Massachusetts liberal in me kept *tsk-tsk*ing me for beating up a gay guy. Like that alone made our actions wrong—whether or not the guy had earned the hell out of it.

That little voice in my head kept yelling that beating up a gay guy was no better than beating up a woman, as if being gay automatically equated weakness.

Meanwhile, the fading bruises on Junior's face indicated otherwise.

Years of sensitivity conditioning, most of which I'd happily spent my life ignoring, were in a mighty conflict with my current reality.

And it was giving me a real-world headache.

Junior slammed his palms on the steering wheel, shocking me out of my liberal guilt. "Lookit, my fucking hands." Junior held up his scarred knuckles, a couple of them now raw, one split open from his enthusiastic application of them to Byron's face. "Guy bled all over me."

"So?"

"What if that motherfucker has AIDS?"

"That's messed up," I said.

"I know!"

I wasn't agreeing with him.

But I wasn't about to disagree with him either.

Junior pulled Miss Kitty hard to the right and stomped the brakes into a squealing stop in front of a Store 24. He stomped into the convenience store. I didn't have any idea what the hell was happening anymore. I cracked the window and lit a smoke, trying to wrap my mind around the issue and how to handle it on all sides. For fuck's sake, we all still had to work together.

That said, Ginny wasn't wrong to question whether or not we would have stepped in with as much gusto.

I already had that answer.

We wouldn't have.

So she was wrong too.

And she wasn't.

Goddammit.

It wasn't like there was a man code written down anywhere, but there was an unspoken rule: a man handled his own. There were exceptions, like with any rule. But if you were having girl trouble? Handle that shit. Like any battle a man has to take on, you take your lumps, be they bruises on your face or on your heart, and you move on. And if you were capable, you gave some back along the way.

But this…this was new territory.

The current situation was wayyyyy-hey-hey outside the handbook, written code or unspoken. And I was having a bad time processing it. Man code should apply to all men, right? No matter what orifice got your rocks off. Right?

Right?

Or was a bully always a bully?

Who the fuck was I asking?

Junior stormed back out, dumping a mini bottle of hand sanitizer on each hand, vigorously rubbing his hands together like an OCD nutjob.

Try not to judge Junior too hard. Everybody hated somebody for one reason or another. And we feared others for sometimes the same reasons.

Most people who get called homophobes weren't suffering any kind of phobia at all. They were just assholes. Junior, on the other hand, had a real, deep-seated paranoia. And it was one that, even though I couldn't condone it…I knew where it came from.

We drove the rest of the way back to my apartment in silence, me chain-smoking to have something to do other than converse with my friend, who no doubt had more nasty words in reserve to toss my way.

My face still hurt from having a foot planted off it the night before, and muscle soreness was settling in from the cold, a lack of sleep, and the other events from the past twenty-four. I just wanted my bed for a couple hours before I had to head in for the night shift.

Junior pulled into my driveway. I went to give him the old bro-smack-handshake farewell. (I don't know what the fuck it's called. Do you?) But Junior held his hand up. "Nah, man. I don't know what's on these hands."

"Other than a gallon of Purell? I'm gonna guess ketchup and possibly a booger."

"Shit ain't funny, man."

"It's a little funny."

Junior glared at me. One of the cornerstones of our friendship was our ability to bust each other's balls when we were being stupid. And Junior was being stooooopid. However, he was in a stupid place that was too deep for me to even throw a rope into.

So I just rolled my eyes. "Movie tomorrow?"

"Yeah. Can we see something with tits?"

"I think John Goodman's in something."

"Again. Not funny."

"I'll call you tomorrow." I shut the door and walked in front of the car.

"Yeah. Have fun with that shift tonight."

Aw hell. It was Sunday. I was working with Ginny. Junior stomped on the gas, spinning the wheels, spraying me with slush and gravel.

It was going to be a long night.

And if I'd had any idea how long that night was going to be, I might not have gotten out of bed.

I almost forgot to disable the booby traps that Twitch had installed for a security system after a surprise visitor had shot me in the leg last summer. Sometimes it was good to have equally paranoid sociopaths in your inner circle of friends. Except for the first time I forgot which direction I needed to turn the key to disable rather than arm. One face-full of foam chemical mace later and I wasn't about to forget again.

Burrito, the world's fattest Chihuahua, was yapping up a storm a good ten feet from the door. The night I took a chemical facial, Burrito decided to lap up the mace that hit the floor while I screamed and tried to pull my eyes out.

Since then, he'd learned to stand back when I walked through the door. He was also less likely to nosh on whatever fell off my face, be it an escaping buffalo wing or foamed mace.

I lay down on my bed, needing the rest, but with a brain that was a fitful ball of swirling, conflicted emotions. Anger at being deceived. Feeling foolish because I wasn't sure that I had been. Yeah, we'd been played, but only because Ginny needed us.

And would we have stepped in otherwise? Would we have given her the help she needed?

Byron had tipped our hand. *My* hand, at least. I could only speak for myself when I said that I would have gladly taken the second shot at the guy for any number of reasons—taking down Junior being one. For me, it was about Ginny, about stepping into a situation that homegirl had found herself in the middle of. My White Knight instinct overrode my common sense. I knew it…I somehow fucking *knew* that we needed to keep our noses clear of the situation.

But once again, I ignored the same senses that I prided myself on having in my capacity as a bouncer.

It may have looked like a pile of shit, but all I smelled was perfume.

And as messed up and baffled as the situation had left me, I could only imagine what bugfuck chipmunk was tearing sharp-clawed laps inside Junior's brain.

Family could be fucked in the head sometimes. Other people had an uncle who spent his day on Facebook re-posting Tea Party pictures of Obama as a witch doctor, or a sweet Nana who'd tell anybody who'd listen about how that Mexican maid kept taking her jewelry. As much as I didn't like to come to terms with reality, my brother was a straight-up homophobe.

Part of me understood where Junior was coming from, what he felt deep down from the way-back days.

There was a part of me that felt the exact same way.

I understood.

The difference was, I wasn't comfortable with the cards fate had dealt me as a kid, the opinions and observations that were branded into my mind from those years back at St. Gabe's. I still felt them. But I fought them.

Sometimes I won.

Sometimes I didn't.

But Junior? He wore those scars as badges. All of them. He stubbornly held on to those marks, loud and proud. To try to get rid of them would be to lessen their significance. To Junior, those hard-earned scars were the proof that he had survived.

And who was I to try to take that victory, his very survival, away from him?

I was his brother.

I didn't always agree with the things he felt, thought, or said.

Even when I understood them.

But I wasn't the one to tell him he was wrong.

Finally I was able to drift off with that comforting self-assuring horseshit inside my mind. I was at Junior's back. I was always going to be at Junior's back. Period.

Some days he made it harder than others.

But I had his back.

THE INSISTENT CHIRPING of my beeper woke me. Immediately after I thumbed the button to make it stop, a heavy knock sounded at my front door. Burrito lost his goddamn Chihuahua mind, yapping up and down the hallway.

I didn't like visitors. Not since the last unannounced one put a bullet just above my knee.

I jumped out of bed, shivering in the cold. I threw a dirty sweatshirt over my head, pulled the jeans on fast. Shoes on, no time for socks.

The knock sounded again. I turned down the hallway, saw two gigantic shadows in the glass. Really large shadows…

Fuck. Had to be Summerfield's boys. Two more of Marcus's IronClad goons coming for round two. Either that, or the Jehovah's Witnesses had been hitting the HGH hard lately.

Well, the jokers were going to be in for one hell of a surprise when I rained down Twitch's booby-trapped hell on them.

That was what I thought, before the one on the left kicked the door off the hinges, brand new locks and all.

I was still three feet away from the panic buttons.

Shit.

The two roided-out monstrosities charged at me down the hallway. One of them, a black dude with long cornrows, got to me first, hit me low, and pulled my legs out from under me. I came down hard, the back of my skull slamming off the hardwood. My head filled with stars even before the huge fist slammed into my cheek.

My head snapped to the right—just in time for Burrito to enter the fray. Bad news was, he started biting *me* on the ear instead of sticking his little razor teeth into the guys trying to end the person who kept him in kibble.

Cornrows stood up and grabbed a leg. The other dude could have easily been a defensive lineman for the Pats. He grabbed my other leg. I knew what was coming, and covered my balls. The Lineman's gigantic boot came down on my hands. It hurt like hell, but I was thankful my hands took more damage than my balls. The two started dragging me down the hallway to the door, intent on bringing me somewhere with them.

I had no intention of going anywhere.

Some days, I thank God I'm a lazy housekeeper.

As I slid by my toolbox, I reached into the top and gratefully wrapped my fingers around the handle of my hammer. I slammed it down onto the inside of Cornrows' ankle. He screamed as the knobby bone made a satisfying cracking sound. He dropped to his ass and clutched his leg.

Burrito finally got the hint on who the real enemy was, and with a snarl that would have impressed the Chihuahua version of Cerberus, he chomped onto Lineman's hand.

Lineman squeaked in pain, a strange sound to come out of a physical specimen of his size. He flung Burrito into the living room, where the dog skidded along the floor, coming to a stop under the coffee table.

But he'd done enough. My legs were free.

I jumped up and hit the comically large Staples EASY button. The two cans of mace attached on opposite sides of the door at eye level sprayed right into

Lineman's neck.

Sadly, eye level isn't the same for all of us.

The dispersion caught him off guard, but didn't exactly have the crippling effect I'd hoped for. The thick froth layered across his throat and collarbone, all of it foaming a good five inches under his eyes.

So I improvised. I grabbed both sides of his neck, rubbed my hands vigorously in the chemicals, and jammed them right into the fucker's eyes.

That did the trick.

Lineman screamed and toppled backward down my icy front steps. Cornrows was already hobbling down the street toward their car.

Really?

Was he getting into a fucking Prius?

He was.

Lineman, half-blinded, staggered a serpentine path toward the car as well.

I threw my hammer at the back of their car, but missed by a good four feet.

I took a good breath to holler a victory taunt at my assailants, but instead took in two good lungfuls of the chemical mace suspended in the air. My lungs weren't fans and closed up shop. Gagging and choking, I sat down on the stairs and wiped the sweat from my eyes, forgetting that I'd slathered them in the mace on Lineman's neck.

I wanted to scream, but my throat was still raw from the dose I'd inhaled. Instead, I made a few sounds in my throat akin to Burrito's squeaky toys and jammed fistfuls of snow onto my face

Speaking of my guard dog, at that exact moment, Burrito found the inch-and-a-half of ass crack sticking out the back of my jeans and figured it was as good a time and place to sink his teeth as any.

NOSE RE-BLOODIED.

Eyelids poofy.

Fat lip re-fattened.

Taking damage inventory in the dirty mirror, I could say I'd gotten off easy considering the size, if not the talent, of the two meatheads Summerfield had sent my way. Most of the damage was lumped onto what Summerfield had already done to me the night before. After a vigorous rinsing, my eyes finally stopped feeling like I'd mistaken a bottle of Tabasco for Visine.

Any time you could dish as well as you got and walk away, especially when the odds leaned definitively in favor of getting an ass kicking—that could be filed away as a win. And, hell, after the previous night, I was willing to take the win any way I could.

Then an intermittent buzzing started in my left ear. I stuck a finger in there and wiggled it, hoping somehow my magic pinky could cure it. I pulled my finger out and it started up again. It took me a second before I realized the buzzing wasn't from inside my oft-rattled skull, but vibrating on the connected wall to my bedroom closet.

There were only two things in that closet. One was my clothes in various degrees of unwash. The other was bad news. I jammed some more toilet paper up my nose to stem the new bleeding and ran to the closet. Underneath dirty laundry and the several shirts that had gotten a little too snug after months of not working out post lead-in-leg, sat the duffel bag that had been a gift from Twitch to go along with my semi-effective security measures.

Equally useful in the event of going to the mattress or the zombie apocalypse, in Twitch's words. Junior had the same bag. Ollie had the same. Twitch had the same.

We were on strict orders not to use the phone unless it was an emergency, and even then, we were to use a set of code words that Ollie had come up with in his infinite nerdiness.

I looked at the display and saw the last words I wanted to see.

Avengers Assemble.

In other words: Code Blue. It was sent from Junior's phone.

The message meant *run*.

Apparently, I wasn't alone on Summerfield's revenge list.

I grabbed the run-pack and my jacket and bolted out the door for our safe house.

FOURTEEN YEARS AGO

WE WERE ABOUT to get raped. Period. We were beaten, outnumbered, barely conscious.

Zach leaned over Junior, lubricating his junk with spit.

We were almost out of fight.

I put my face against the filthy tile and closed my eyes. I didn't want to see what was going to happen next. I gritted my teeth when I heard the scream.

Then I realized the scream wasn't Junior's…

…it was Zach's.

As suddenly as we'd been attacked, the hands that were holding me down were gone. I heard feet slapping on tile as Zach's cronies ran away from the fight once the dynamic had shifted.

I raised my head and saw two things I hadn't expected. One was Ollie on Zach's back, a pillowcase over the rape machine's head. Ollie's feet were dug into Zach's lower back, both hands pulling back from the mouth of the pillowcase. He hung onto Zach like a champion bull rider.

But that wasn't why Zach was howling.

Twitch sat on his foot like a kid going for a ride, arms wrapped around his knee, legs crisscrossed over his ankles...and Twitch's teeth were sunk deep into the meaty flesh of Zach's thigh. Blood flowed from between Twitch's clamped jaws. But for the pillowcase, there wasn't a shred of clothing on anybody.

Zach didn't know which attacker to fend off first. It looked like a pictorial I'd seen in an old *National Geographic* of hyenas taking down a water buffalo. The thickness of Zach's musculature kept his flailing arms from reaching behind to get Ollie off his back.

But that didn't keep him from trying. He backed into the wall, crushing Ollie between his bulk and the tile. Ollie *whoofed* as the air got knocked out of him, but held on.

Zach kicked out the leg that had Twitch along for the ride, but that wasn't enough to shake him off. Like a pink police baton, Zach's fully erect penis kept slapping Twitch on the top of his head.

Junior lifted his head and pushed himself into a sitting position against the shower wall.

I tried to stand and offer my assistance, but a wave of concussed nausea overwhelmed me, and I doubled over.

However...

In their panicked exit, Zach's partners had left us a gift.

As my eyes cleared, I saw what they'd clobbered me with. I grabbed the piece of rope that had been tightly bound with duct tape along its length. At the business end they'd attached our missing cue ball.

"Junior!" I yelled.

Woozily, Junior looked toward me.

I skidded the homemade bludgeon across the floor to him. Junior grabbed the rope end, and with a surprisingly fluid motion, came up swinging. The cue ball caught Zach right under the chin with a sound like he'd bitten into an ice cube. The horsepower behind the blow almost sent Junior back to the shower floor.

Blood blossomed immediately into the rough white fabric of the pillowcase.

Zach's arms came down as he dropped to his knees. He let out a low moan through a mouth that sounded shattered.

Junior brought the bludgeon back around a second time, the cue ball striking Zach square on the back of the head. The behemoth pitched forward. Twitch rolled out of the way before he got crushed, but Ollie rode him all the way down, adding extra weight to the landing.

Zach's face met the shower floor with one more sickening crunch.

Ollie finally let go of the pillowcase. A pair of shattered teeth fell from the open end and rattled into the drain.

Junior bellowed a primal howl and raised his arm high to bring down the cue ball for a final time. If Zach was still breathing—and I wasn't sure he was— that last shot would make it a surety that the breath in his lungs would be his last.

I got myself up halfway and let gravity and momentum do their jobs. I tackled Junior around the waist, but his arm still came down with murderous force. The cue ball shattered the tile two inches to the left of Zach's skull, then fell from Junior's grip.

Junior was still screaming, "*Fuck you!*" at the fallen Zach as Ollie and I dragged him from the showers.

Twitch picked up Zach's teeth as a souvenir, then followed us out before the workers at The Home came to investigate.

We watched the EMTs wheel the still-unconscious Zach out the front a half hour later. I don't know if he lived or not. I didn't give a fuck either way, but I was sure we would have heard if he'd died, even as a hushed rumor.

We never heard anything.

We never saw Zach at St. Gabe's again.

We'd not only defended ourselves against the threat, we'd removed it.

And Zach removed any and all chance of Junior enjoying a rerun of *Will & Grace.*

CHAPTER 10

It took me way too long under the circumstances to get to The Cellar. This was
life without a car. The weekend Green Line was like riding in a metal turtle—
especially since it felt like I had a target on my back. The moment I got to the
stop, a pair of cruisers went up my street. It was safe to assume that one of the
neighbors had seen or heard my little kerfuffle and called it in. After the events
of last year, I was pretty sure I was on the unfriendly list of a number of Boston
cops who would love to bust my ass for something. Anything.

I got the train without taking a baseball bat to the back of the head, so
I considered myself lucky. Even so, I felt the eyes of every other passenger.
This shit was making me even more paranoid than my normal walking-around
paranoid. And as I've explained, that shit ain't insignificant.

I took the stairs at the Kenmore stop two at a time and burst into the bar
with enough force to make Audrey jiggle spastically—the fruit knife she was
cutting limes with jumped off the board, nearly taking one of her fingers with it.
The Cellar was full of Sunday drinkers and stragglers who still held an interest
in the early evening football game on the two box TVs that had made their way

into the bar after falling straight off the back of a truck in 1992.

"Goddamn it, Boo!" Calming herself from my dramatic entrance, Audrey took a big gulp from her ever-present Jack and water.

I quickly scanned the bar for any possible threat, but other than the snack mix, nothing appeared to be an immediate hazard to my health.

"Sorry. Anybody else here?"

"Who would be here? You're two hours early."

"Junior. Twitch. Ollie. The boys?"

"No, but Brendan called twice looking for you."

"Underdog called?"

Audrey scrunched her face at me in disapproval of the nickname we'd all used for the last half decade for Boston police officer/regular customer/former junkie/possibly the world's worst undercover vice officer Brendan Miller.

"What did Under—what did Brendan want?"

"He just said for you to call him as soon as you got here."

Cops at my house, maybe. Cops calling me at work. This was shaping into one hell of an evening.

"He calls again, tell him I'm here. In the meantime, the boys are on their way. Send them up to the office."

As I went down the rear hallway to the stairs, she called out, "He was really serious, Boo!"

I'm sure he was, I thought. But answering a possible disturbing the peace call, or whatever he wanted to ask me about, was going to have to wait.

I walked up to the office and stopped when I saw the padlock hanging off. Tentatively, quietly, I tried the door. The deadbolt was still engaged. Luke most likely just forgot the padlock after he re-stocked the bars. I unlocked the bolt and then nearly shat myself when there was somebody already inside.

"I wasn't jerking it!" said Twitch, watching porn on his tablet.

"Jesus Christ, Twitch. How did you get in here?"

He shrugged. "Like I do."

Like he did. It wasn't enough that he'd gotten by Audrey, but he'd somehow picked both locks. I was actually a little surprised he hadn't figured out a way to close the padlock from the inside.

Twitch closed the browser on the two flexible lesbians. "The fuck is going on?"

"Two goons hit me at my house."

Twitch's face lit up. "Did you engage my security measures? Did they work?"

"Yes and kinda. I guess they tried Junior's too."

Twitch's forehead creased with a slight twitching action along the eye. "What do you mean they 'kinda' worked?"

Immediately, the old familiar stress headache bunched up in the middle of my face. I pinched the bridge of my nose. "Can we discuss this later? It worked fine."

"Why can't we discuss this now?"

A timid knock that could only have been Ollie sounded on the door.

I opened the door and saw the one member of our crew who operated in the world that other, more normal human beings did. Ollie stood there in a too-big red parka, clutching his own run-pack, his thick glasses fogged from the cold he'd just come out of. "What's going on? Why did Junior send the alert?"

"I dunno. He's not here yet."

"Should we be worried?" Ollie asked.

"Again, I do not know. He sent the alert, so I'm gonna assume he took no more damage than I did." My tongue pressed against the thickened part of my lip.

"What happened to you?"

"I got jumped at my house. More than likely members of the IronClad crew."

Ollie raised his hand. "I'm sorry. I don't know who the IronClad crew is."

Christ. What was Ollie even doing here? Yes, he was a part of our gang, our family, but this fresh hell we'd gotten ourselves into didn't involve him in the least. The guy was a citizen. And an upstanding one, if you could ignore the company he kept.

"IronClad is another security company. They mostly do work for Ian Summerfield's clubs."

"And he is…"

"Possibly the biggest pill runner in Boston," Twitch said.

"Oh Christ," Ollie said. He took off his glasses and began nervously polishing them on his shirt. "What the hell are we mixed up in now?"

I could see the remnants of our previous shenanigans dancing in Ollie's subconscious. We had needed his expertise with all things technical in the past. As a result, he'd seen things that would make most tough guys pee in their Dickies.

Ollie was one of us.

But he would never be one of us.

"Ollie," I said. "This doesn't involve you. You should probably go home."

"What are you talking about? It involves all of us. How does it include him, then?" He pointed at Twitch, who had re-opened the video of the lesbians.

Twitch raised his hand without taking his eyes off the action. "I shot at them last night."

"You did what?"

"They… We called Twitch for some backup. We had a situation."

"And you didn't call me? Why?"

I pinched my nose again. There was no way around it now. Ollie was getting his feelings hurt. Truth was, Ollie was more than useful with what he was good at. And none of those things was in a brawl. In a stand-down fight, Ollie was about as useful as tits on a bull.

"I get it," Ollie said, nodding his head. "You guys think I'm a pussy."

"No, Ollie…"

Twitch raised his hand. "I do, no offense."

Ollie's face went red, and his voice went up a notch. "No offense? How is that supposed to be not offensive?"

"Because it's true."

"Up your ass, Twitch. Do any of you remember how 'useless' I was with Zach Bingham back in the day?"

That fucking name again. All the old ghosts were having a surprise party in my life that week. One ghost at a goddamn time. I put my hand on Ollie's shoulder. "Ollie, listen…"

He shook my hand off, his eyes red. "No! Fuck you both, then. You want to play your tough guy games? You don't need me? Fine. I'm out." He slammed the door open and almost bounced off Underdog, whose hand was poised to knock on the door.

"Jesus Christ, Ollie!" Underdog held his hands up, stepping back from the rampaging nerdling.

Ollie stormed down the stairs and was gone before I could even formulate an apology. And even if he'd earned his stripes in one scrap back in the Home, he didn't need to be involved in our bullshit. He was much better off out of it.

Underdog stepped into the room. "Boo, where's Junior?"

Subtly, and without taking full notice of Underdog, Twitch nudged his own run-pack under the desk. I could only imagine what was in it that he didn't want the police officer to see.

"The fuck, Underdog? I don't know where Junior is."

"Then you better find him." There was a cop authority in the tone that I didn't like. A tone that had only recently appeared in Underdog's recovery from years of drug abuse. It was the voice of the cop Brendan Miller, and not Underdog's. Not the voice of my friend.

Then it dawned on me that I'd thought Dog wanted to talk to me about the fight on my stoop, not that he'd be looking for Junior. "Why are you looking for Junior?"

"A lot of cops are looking for him, Boo. You too."

"The frig for?"

"The name Byron Walsh mean anything to you?"

Fuuuuuuuuuck. The prick went to the cops after we beat his ass. I hadn't seen that coming, considering the drugs and all. The realization came crashing down on me that Byron—much like Ollie—didn't live in the same plane of existence as we did in our mostly imaginary tough-guy world. Even though he'd jammed himself into that world in the worst way possible, he'd reacted like any normal person would. We beat his ass, he went to the cops. Plain and simple.

"Yeah," I said softly.

"Well, he's fucking dead, Boo."

CHAPTER 11

My STOMACH DROPPED into my shoes. So I said the first thing that came to mind, which was pretty stupid. "What do you mean?"

"What do I mean? I mean he's dead. They found him in Revere."

Right where we'd left him.

Underdog's gaze was gone, replaced by the cold metal stare of the police officer named Brendan Miller. "What did you guys do, Boo?"

"I…" I was shell-shocked. We'd given the guy a righteous beating, sure enough, but enough to kill him? "Maybe the guy had a latent aneurism, a heart defect, something."

"You even know what a latent aneurism is?" Dog asked in a tone I didn't like.

"I used to watch *House.*"

Dog didn't think that was funny.

In all fairness, neither did I. Nor did I know what the hell I was talking about. Panic was settling in.

We couldn't have killed him.

Could we?

Because if we did, we were fucked. Dead bang.

I was so wrapped up in the possibility that I didn't even have the right questions. "Why do you think we had anything to do with this?"

"I can't help you if you don't talk to me, Boo."

"I dunno," Twitch said. "Doesn't sound like you wanna help to me."

"Twitch," Dog said, slowly turning toward him, "I'm going to suggest that you shut your mouth and get gone. There might be a lot of cops here really soon. They might search the place, and this office. And in this office right now is you and that bag you think I didn't see you kick under the desk."

I saw the debate dancing in Twitch's eyes. He was never someone to back down from a challenge. And this was a big one, from a big authority. If I didn't step in, this could erupt into something really bad, really fast.

"Dog is right, Twitch."

"What?"

"This isn't your conversation. You should take off. Lay low, I'll call you tonight."

Twitch stood slowly, picking up his bag. He walked by Underdog, the mad dog stare never leaving his eyes. For a second, I thought he might spit on the floor, maybe on Underdog's shoes.

"It's okay, Twitch."

"Yeah. We'll see," he said.

The room remained silent but for Twitch's footfalls down the stairs. Once they'd stopped, I said, "You here to arrest me, Dog?"

"I'm here to talk to you."

"Tell me what you got first."

"Did you do it?"

"I don't know what 'it' is."

"Goddammit, Boo. There's a dead body with Junior's phone in his pocket. We got a call from several people in JP who saw two guys—two guys with very similar descriptions to two guys I know—stuff what was possibly the body of

Byron Walsh into the trunk of a brown Buick that was at least a couple decades old. Those same witnesses then saw the two men drive off, one of them in the Buick, the other in a car meeting the description of one owned by the deceased. Any of this ringing bells?"

"So far." I pulled a fresh bottle of Jim Beam off the liquor shelf. I poured a few belts into a coffee cup that had been turning into penicillin for a week. At that point, I didn't care. "You want any?"

"You know I'm not drinking."

I took two big gulps. "Oh yeah. You're clean now. Little Underdog's not a puppy any more. He's all grown up. Not even a drop of the brown stuff." I was feeling a hostility toward Dog that I knew was ill-focused, even in the moment. Junior and I were going back into cages. My back was against the wall, so I was tumbling into default mode: drinking and aggression, my old familiar amigos.

"This the tone you're honestly going to take right now?" Underdog said.

"What tone would you like? You're the one who came strolling into my office accusing me and Junior of murder."

"I'm not accusing you of anything yet. I'm asking you what happened."

"Gimme some of that whiskey, I'm freezing my balls off," Junior said.

Underdog and I both jumped at the ghostly-pale and tattooed apparition that was shrouded in the doorway. What was up with everybody making like Batman?

And why the fuck was Junior only wearing boxer shorts and wrapped in a thin comforter?

Junior took the bottle from me with a frozen and shaking hand. Hard liquor wasn't normally his thing, but under the circumstances, he seemed willing to forego preferences. "The hell is going on? Where are the boys? Hey, Dog…" His shivering turned to a shudder, making him the living embodiment of screwed, blued, and tattooed.

"You're gonna make us ask, aren't you?" I said.

Junior swigged the bourbon, then coughed and wiped his mouth. "What? The ensemble? I was going to bed. A ton of cops were banging at my door, so

I grabbed the emergency bag and jumped out the window. I got behind my neighbors' garage before the cops thought to check the back."

"Why do think the cops were at your door, Junior?" Underdog said with an incredulous tone.

Junior curled his mouth down. "I dunno. Took it to be nothing good, so I figured we'd group up and figure this shit out. Was gonna call you next, Dog. See if you could give an answer to the whys of it."

"That's why I'm here in the first place."

"Huh...perfect. The fuck is going on, Dog?" Junior opened the short metal file cabinet where we stored extra clothes (if you've ever worked in a bar, you'd understand) and some emergency blunt weaponry (if you've ever worked at a bar like The Cellar, you'd understand).

"You tell me. You want to explain why we got a body in Revere with his head staved in? A body that has your cell phone on it?"

"See? I told you we must have grabbed each other's phones. Man, I shoulda put a password on that piece of shit. If that butt pirate called a sex line, I'm... wait...the fuck you say?"

I stood up. "We didn't stave anybody's head in, Dog."

"Seriously," Junior said. "And I don't even know what 'staved in' means."

Underdog shook his head in wonder. "It means that somebody bashed in Byron Walsh's head."

Junior frowned. "Sucks to be Byron." Junior took another long swig, then made a sound in his throat like he'd downed a shot filled with thumbtacks. "Don't know how you enjoy this shit, Malone." Then, to Underdog, "Yeah. Anyway, we didn't stove in shit. We beat his ass, but we didn't do no stoving. No way, no how. So what's the problem?"

"To the cops, it sure looks like we did," I said.

"There's more," Underdog said, a sick expression on his face.

Shit... "What?"

"The neighbors reported that you were yelling homophobic slurs as you guys were...doing whatever you did in the first place."

"Yeah," Junior said. "But I didn't know that the guy was a faggot when I called him a faggot."

Underdog threw his hands up. "Well, I hope you say exactly that to the jury."

"Say what to what jury? We didn't do shit. Well, we did shit, but we didn't stove. How many times we gotta tell you that?" Junior fluffed out his T-shirt and Pogue Mahone sweatshirt, then, to my relief, began dressing himself.

"You know that there's a change of clothes in the run-pack, right?" I said. "You could've dressed yourself on the way, rather than freezing your ass off and subjecting us to your nudity."

"Shit," Junior said, pulling the sweatshirt over his head. "I wore those in August when I forgot to pick up my laundry."

"You ate the protein bars too, didn't you?"

"You didn't?"

Underdog loudly cleared his throat. "Can we get back to the much bigger problem at hand than Junior's lack of self-control?"

"Sure," I said, not wanting to hear any more. But I supposed if we were sinking in shit, we might as well know how deep the septic tank was.

"The DA wants to prosecute this as a hate crime."

That was a deep septic tank.

"You guys understand how grim this is looking, right?" Dog said, a pleading note in his voice.

"That was an accident," I said.

Underdog's face dropped when he thought that I was breaking open the confession.

"No, no, no," I said. "We…uh…accidentally called him those names. Still didn't kill him."

"You accidentally beat on a homosexual man while calling him a faggot?"

"I think I might have called him a cocksucker too," Junior said, pulling on a pair of black Dickies. "But like I said, I had no idea the guy was a weenie enthusiast at the time, so bingo bango bongo—no hate crime. Am I right?"

"That's not going to help, Junior!" Dog said, his voice squeaking. A tiny, tiny bit of our friend was peeking out from under the face of Officer Brendan Miller. Underdog was honestly concerned at the level of trouble we were looking at.

"Hey, just coming clean."

"The hate crime part was an accident," I said. "That was an accident. We didn't know that we were actually committing one when we said the things we said."

"But you meant the beating part."

"Hells yeah," Junior said. "The douchebag was stalking Ginny and his ex-boyfriend."

"Wait, wait, wait…" Underdog cut in. "You knew he had a boyfriend, but didn't know he was gay?"

"That was all after-the-fact information. We didn't know it at the time," I said.

"Yeah," Junior said. "We were there to provide motivation for him to cut the shit with Ginny."

Underdog slumped against the wall and rubbed his face vigorously, trying to wipe off the stupid that Junior and I had verbally smeared him with. When his hands came down, the cop was gone. All that was left was our buddy Underdog. He glanced at the bottle of booze with a hunger that I was uncomfortable seeing in him after his months of sobriety.

"Hey," I said, sliding myself between his gaze and the bottle. "My first question is this, Dog. Do you believe us?"

Underdog took a deep breath. "Yeah. I do. Is there anyone who can back your side?"

I thought about Ginny, about her terror at Junior's second anti-gay outburst of the day. I didn't think her testimony would be in our favor at that moment. "Maybe."

"Well, try to make that a definitely. What else?"

"Anybody looking into Byron?" I asked. "Seeing who else maybe wanted the guy dead?"

Underdog shook his head. "No need to right now. Everything points at you two."

"To be fair," Junior said, "the guy *was* a cocksucker."

"Really?" I said.

"What? That was a…what d'ya call it? A metaphor." Junior beamed, pleased that he'd not only used a metaphor but managed to correctly name it.

"Stop using metaphors. Please," I said.

Underdog looked at the two of us, no small amount of bewilderment in his expression. He shook his head. "I really don't know, guys. This all looks really, really bad."

That much was becoming clearer by the moment. "So now what?" I asked.

"You gotta come in with me, Junior," Underdog said.

Junior zipped up his Dickies, then stopped. "What?"

Dog held his hands up. "For questioning. It's going to happen one way or the other, but it's going to look better from the onset if you come in with me willingly. Right now, every trail points to you guys and you guys only."

The idea of Junior being questioned terrified me. "But those trails stop short of killing the guy, Dog," I said.

"Doesn't matter. They follow a timeline. Motive. Opportunity. You guys have both. And Homicide already thinks they have enough to call the case. They're not going to look any further into this when there's already enough to bury you both deep. And, honestly, you're next, Boo."

"Bring me in, then," I said. I didn't want that, but after talking to my not-so-eloquent partner, the cops would throw away the key on both of us, maybe even find reason to charge us with the Brinks heist as well.

"They're not looking at you specifically, Boo," Dog said. "Yet. All they have points at Junior, what with the cell phone. It's not going to take too much to make you as the second, but right now, they don't have any reason to sweat you."

"So what do we do, Dog? You haven't said a word on that end," Junior said, his face bunched up into the bulldog mug that only accompanied his most acute angers and stresses.

Dog looked to me. "You need to find another direction for us to look in, Boo."

"Me? Isn't that your fucking job?"

Dog's face went red in anger. "I'm already risking my fucking job even talking to you two. And, frankly, you *did* put a beating on the victim. You *did* drive him out to Revere in the trunk of your fucking car, and you *did* run from the police."

He had us there.

"And I'm going to be working double time to keep them off your ass so you can do this in the meantime. You know details that I don't, and, frankly, I'm better off not knowing until either you bring me some new information or you get your own ass thrown in a cell next to Junior."

It wouldn't be the first time. But we'd spent our entire adult lives trying to not repeat that particular era in our history.

Junior pulled Byron's cell phone out of his bag. "So…should I bring this?"

Underdog and I gaped at him.

"What is that?" Underdog asked.

Junior shrugged. "Byron's phone."

"Why are you still carrying that?" I asked.

"Forgot it wasn't mine. In my hasty escape, I just grabbed it off my nightstand."

"Oh…my God…" Dog said, covering his face. "Leave it here. That makes it look much worse."

"Hey!" I said. "Maybe there's something on the phone that might hint at who caved in Byron's skull."

"Did you look in it?"

"It's got a passcode," Junior said.

"One thing at a time," Underdog said. "Like I said, there's no interest at all in secondary suspects. When the time comes, you need to give that to a defense lawyer, let them try to figure something out."

"Defense—this is really that bad?"

The authoritative voice that boomed up the stairwell answered that question for us. "*Darrell McCullough?*" We all looked to each other. Though it was Junior's given name, I didn't know if he'd heard it spoken aloud in twenty years.

Junior's entire body tensed up. His eyes flicked to the bolted door next to the vodka shelf that connected to the karate studio that had closed its doors three years ago. The studio that led to another stairwell. Another way out.

Dog couldn't read Junior's mind as easily as I could, but Brendan Miller the cop could recognize a runner when he saw one. "Don't. Don't make this worse, Junior. If you didn't do anything, don't give us more reason to think you did."

"Us?" I said.

"Fuck yourself, Boo." Brendan Miller fired a look at me that Underdog wouldn't have been capable of a year ago. If I hadn't been the target, I might have been proud of my probably now-former buddy.

A tentative footfall squeaked on the old wooden stairs. "Shit," a voice echoed softly from the same spot halfway up the stairs.

Junior's shoulders relaxed. His face took on a beaten expression I'd never seen before. Underdog saw it too.

Underdog reached into his back pocket and pulled out his ID. He stuck the badge out the door. "This is Officer Brendan Miller. I am up here with the suspect. He is cooperating and complying. He will be coming in with me. Stand down."

A long silence.

"Your call, Officer Miller. We'll be outside."

Junior held out his wrists. "Put 'em on, Officer."

"Don't have to, Junior. This is just for questioning. You cooperating is going to help."

Junior threw his thick keychain onto the desk. He looked at me. "You take care of my girl, Boo." He was talking about Miss Kitty. "And don't you fucking leave me in there."

I stood to follow them both out the door, but Underdog placed a gentle hand on my chest, whispering, "Stay here. Stay off their radar as long as you can."

They walked out, and I sat at the desk in silence. Audrey would have enough questions when I headed back downstairs. I poured another drink and sat in the quiet for a while after my two friends left for the station. I dropped the white cap off the bottle and it rolled under the desk. I reached under to grab it...

That was when I saw The Boy huddled under the desk. I stared at him. He stared back sadly. A tiny hand touched his nose, then his lip. My own hand followed suit, touching my sore lip and my recently bleeding nose.

Junior's alert had nothing to do with what I thought it did. He was alerting us to the police possibly crashing down our doors. Those sure as hell weren't cops that came to my doorstep looking to bleed me.

Who were they, then?

Were they somehow tied into said staving of Byron's skull? They certainly seemed capable of staving. They sure tried to do some staving on me.

No. They had to be sent by Summerfield.

And I needed to stop using the word "staving."

"What the hell?" I muttered to The Boy under the desk.

Oh yeah. Did I mention that at times of extreme mental stress, I have hallucinations of my eight-year-old self? The eight-year-old self that's locked in time inside the moment when the man who killed my mother shot me in the chest?

The Boy never talks, but he's there. I see him.

Yeah. I'm pretty fucked in the head.

CHAPTER 12

I WENT DOWN the stairs to find a visibly shaken Audrey pouring herself another glass of Tennessee nerve tonic with trembling hands. I couldn't help but notice that several of the bar's shadier element had made themselves scarce once Boston's Finest arrived in force. "Willy!" she said when I came out the back. "What happened? Why were those detectives here? Why did Junior leave with Brendan?"

She wasn't being nosy. She was being the bar mama. Seeing Junior walk out with Underdog after the cops showed up looking for him had set off her alarms. Audrey had a daughter around our age that we'd never met, but there were dropped defenses, loose phrases over the years that led me to believe she'd been a world of trouble for our Big Mama growing up. She'd married well and lived in Arizona now, but Audrey still chose to wrap her thick arms around all of The Cellar's orphans.

I could hear heartbreak in her questions, a heartbreak I was sure her daughter had walked her through over the years.

"I can't really talk about it right now, darlin.'"

"Willie, you have to tell me something. What happened?"

I took her rough hand in mine. "Teensy misunderstanding."

"I'm not stupid. The cops don't show up like that over teensy misunderstandings."

"Okay, really, really big misunderstanding. We're gonna clear it up."

She took in a big shuddering breath and blew it out. "Okay...okay."

Clearly, she only sorta believed me, but I could see her finding comfort in my lies. I wasn't even at the halfway mark believing my own words. We were fucked, as far as I was concerned. I just didn't want Audrey to see it.

I felt all eyes on me, every ear straining for the story. I looked around at the remaining customers and saw a few heads turn quickly. Then I saw, exiting the kitchen, one of the nameless and interchangeable waitresses who came in and out of the staff during the winters when all the colleges were in session. Guess Ginny had decided to call in.

The waitress gave me a half wave in front of a suspicious gaze. Guess she'd seen the whole boys-in-blue display. Great. Now we were getting shady looks from staff whose names I couldn't be bothered to learn.

"Are you working tonight?" Audrey asked.

Crap. I was on the clock in less than three hours. I couldn't good and well work an eight-hour shift with this hanging over my head. "I gotta clear this up. Lemme see if G.G. can cover."

I grabbed the bar phone and dialed G.G. It rang four times before his groggy voice came over the line. "This better be good."

Without my asking, Audrey placed a large shot of whiskey for me next to the phone. "G.G.—sorry, homie. Were you asleep?"

"Nah, man. I had to get up anyway to answer a phone call from some white boy who casually refers to me as 'homie' after I worked all night."

I lifted my shot to Audrey and downed it. "Is there any way you can cover for me tonight?"

"You shitting me, right Boo? I worked three in a row. April Fools ain't for another couple months."

"You know I wouldn't ask if it wasn't an emergency."

He sighed. "You killing me, man."

"It gets worse." As I said it, I realized I had another responsibility and another problem.

"I ain't hearing that."

"I might need you for a few nights." I grabbed a bar napkin and a pen. On it, I wrote, *Can you feed Burrito tonight when you get off?* I slid it to Audrey. If I planned on laying low from the cops, it was more than likely for the best that I stayed away from my residence for a while.

"Come on, Boo. Kendra's already pissed at me for working too much."

Audrey nodded and smiled through her puffy red eyes that looked like they might start spilling tears at any moment. She loved Burrito like he was the grandson she'd never been blessed with, and she was the only human the malevolent little bastard never tried to bite a chunk off of. "Christmas is coming. Tell her you need the extra money to lavish her with gifts."

He paused. "That might actually work."

"Can you do it?" I slid my house keys off the chain and handed them to Audrey.

Another sigh. "Yes. But last time you bubbleheads needed extensive shift coverage, you both got taken to the cleaners pretty bad. You wanna 411 me on this one, or am I better off not knowing?"

"Junior's being questioned for murder."

Another pause. "I ain't hearing that. Tell Audrey I'll be in by nine."

Click.

JUNIOR FORGOT TO tell me where he parked, so I had to lap the block to find Miss Kitty. Once I got behind the wheel, I stopped and froze. Other than my little jaunt in Byron's Neon out to the beach, I hadn't driven a car in almost six years. And when I did, it certainly wasn't the boat that Miss Kitty was. After three attempts, and a blaring horn from the Nissan that nearly clipped me, I got the car onto Comm Ave.

Before I really thought about it, I was turned toward Jamaica Plain and Ginny's apartment. I had to start somewhere, and the only connection I had to Byron and his killer were Ginny and Dana. I should have called her from the bar phone, but lacked the forethought. I was winging it. Safe to say they were going to be none too happy to see my ass after this morning. I hoped she'd cooled off since then.

Fifteen minutes later, I pulled up on McBride Street and sat. I scanned the street up and down for a police presence. Even though Underdog had told me I wasn't on their radar yet, I had no idea when I would be. In the meantime, I was going to keep my head low.

I walked up the street, wary of any eyes that might be on me, either neighbors recognizing me from the day before, my mystery attackers, or— Christ. Being paranoid really started to suck when you knew you had every reason to be paranoid.

I knocked on Ginny's door and waited, shivering.

"Who is it?"

"It's Boo, Ginny."

"Go away, you pricks!"

"Ginny, I'm alone. I can't apologize for the things Junior said earlier. I…we both know he has issues. I really need to talk to Dana. And it's cold as balls out here. Can you please open the door?"

"Dana's not here. He went to work. We will have this discussion tonight."

"Hey, I already know you called in. You can't just avoid me. We're going to share a shift sooner than later. I understand you're pissed. You have reasons to be. So do I. In the meantime—"

"In the meantime, why don't you two go eat a bag of dicks?"

"I'm alone. Junior is—"

"Actually…" came a voice from directly behind me.

I spun, my heart seizing. I skidded on the icy steps before I realized I was neither getting arrested nor taking a pipe to the head.

Twitch stood there, an impish smile on his face. "S'up?"

"The fuck are you doing here, Twitch?"

"I'm helping."

"How—" Before I finished my question, I realized that, with many things Twitch, I was probably better off without the answer.

"I been here the whole time. I can't go home right now, what with Summerfield's boys on the prowl for us. Maybe."

"What?"

"I was lying on the floor of the back seat."

Jesus. "Why didn't you say anything?"

"I dunno. Thought I might need the element of surprise."

"For what?"

"For whatever."

Fair enough. I knocked on the door again. "Ginny? You still there?"

Nothing. Then, "Yes."

"Listen. Junior's been taken into custody. No matter what you think about our sociological belief systems, this has gotten *way* out of control. I need to talk to Dana and I need to do it now."

I heard the deadbolt click back. Then the door opened a slit. "What has he been taken into custody for?"

Did she not know yet? "Have the cops been here?"

"No. Why would they be? What did you do, Boo?"

Shitshitshit. "Byron is dead. The cops think me and Junior did it."

"Oh God," came a soft voice from behind the door.

Dana's voice.

Then just about the worst thing that could have happened, happened. My anxiety and temper caught up with me. All the lies, the deceit, the confusion and my desperation boiled over. The world snapped red.

And I lost my temper.

I pressed my weight against the door, pushing Ginny back. "Hey…HEY!" she protested as I moved into the doorway.

"Enough," I said. "Dana, we need to talk right now."

I saw a fearful look on Dana's face as he saw mine, which I could only imagine wasn't at its friendliest.

He bolted to my left, into the kitchen. As I pressed Ginny into the wall behind the door, I heard a phone drop to the floor. Dana screamed, "I'm calling the police."

"No, you're not," I said, double-timing my step.

Dana was picking a wall unit phone from the floor, his face absolutely terrified. I grabbed the cord and yanked it out of the wall. "For fuck's sake," I yelled. "Do none of you people know what a goddamn conversation is?"

"Get out of my apartment!" Ginny yelled, shoving me hard from behind.

I lurched toward Dana, who screamed and grabbed a cutting board from the counter and swung it at my skull. The scarred wood whistled a hair from my temple.

On the backswing, I caught Dana's wrist and squeezed the bones together. He squealed and dropped the board.

"I just want to talk, you dumb shit!"

"Let him go!" Ginny screamed, raising a George Forman grill over her head.

Then the unmistakable slide of an automatic having a round chambered froze the room.

"What's wrong with you people?" Twitch said.

I didn't even want to turn and look at him. "Twitch? What are you doing?"

"Taking control of this ridiculous situation."

True that.

He went on. "Now, Boo? Let go of that guy's arm."

I did.

"Ginny? Put down George Forman and step away from George Forman."

She did.

"Now, can we all have a conversation in the living room?"

I slowly turned toward my armed friend. "Give me the gun, Twitch," I said.

"Why?"

"I need to prove a point."

Twitch re-set the chamber, removing the bullet from the breech. "Everybody calm?"

Dana and Ginny nodded, although the terror never left their eyes.

Twitch handed me the gun.

I placed the gun on the counter next to Dana's hand and stepped back.

"We just want to talk. We didn't kill Byron. If you don't believe me, well, you can shoot me."

Ginny yelped as Twitch bent over and whipped out another gun, a smaller one, from an ankle holster. "The fuck, Boo?" he said. "How do we know he wasn't the one who iced his boyfriend in the first place?"

Shit. We didn't.

"This is a faith-based conversation, Twitch. I'm asking them to believe me. Dana?"

"Yeah?" Dana still hadn't taken the gun off the counter. Trembling, he stared at it like the gun itself was a life-or-death situation.

"Did you kill Byron?"

"No." His eyes stayed on the gun.

"Look me in the eyes and say it."

His eyes flicked up from the gun and into my own hard gaze.

"No."

I waited. I waited for my fine-tuned bullshit detector to go off. It didn't. I believed him. I'd looked into the eyes of killers before, and Dana's weren't those.

"Twitch, you got any more guns on you?" I asked.

"Hell, I didn't think I was gonna need more than two today."

"Please give the other gun to Ginny."

The electricity in the room amped up a notch.

Twitch's shoulders slumped like a kid who was getting his Xbox taken away. "Man. I don't know how good your math is, but that equals two guns to none." Twitch's eye started fluttering like the intro to "Hot For Teacher."

I looked at Ginny. "We need them to trust us right now."

Twitch stared hard at me, but handed the gun to Ginny.

Ginny didn't reach for Twitch's offering. She took a deep breath, then said, "I believe you, Boo. I don't need the gun."

"Excellent," Twitch said, placing his gun back into his ankle holster. "Anybody want me to run to the store for beer?"

"I DON'T KNOW anyone who would want Byron dead," Dana said, his eyes locked onto the bottle of Sam Adams that Twitch handed to him. We'd all sat down in the living room, leaving all firearms and cooking-related bludgeons in the kitchen as a show of good faith.

"How long were you two seeing each other?"

"About three months. It wasn't very long."

"Before he ran off, he snorted a load of coke inside Junior's trunk. Did he owe anybody money?"

"He owed me money."

"How much?"

"About two thousand."

"For what?"

"I lent him some money. Charged a trip for him to the Netherlands. His combo booked some dates in Europe, and he didn't have the money up front to foot the trip."

"His combo?"

"Jazz combo."

Fucking jazz. Why couldn't they just call themselves a band like everybody else?

Dana went on. "He plays…played the trumpet in an old-school torch singer combo called Ellie Confidential and the Brass Balls Band."

Clever name. Had to give him that much. "Why the break-up?"

"He came back from tour. My bills came due. He didn't have any money, he said. Kept blowing me off. Started acting erratic and weird."

"When was this?"

"He came back about two weeks ago. Last week, we changed the locks and I told him not to come back without the money he owed me."

"You said he was starting to act erratically. How?"

"Paranoid. Every sound made him jump."

Well, I sure as shit knew those feels.

"He was acting strung-out," Ginny added.

"Okay. Well, when Junior and I . . .did our thing, he seemed to think we were working for someone else."

"Who?" Dana asked.

"That was what I was hoping you could tell me."

Dana shook his head and looked at Ginny, who said, "No idea."

"He also seemed to think that whoever Junior and I were working for was after something in your house, probably with his stuff."

"Again," Dana said, "not a clue."

"So, you mind giving me a clearer definition of exactly what items of his you've been keeping here and let me decide for myself?"

Ginny and Dana exchanged guilty looks.

Over his bottle, Twitch's eyes darted to mine.

"What?" I said.

"Mostly clothes," Dana said. "He tended to live out of a bag."

"Mostly clothes is not entirely clothes," I said.

"Something else too," Dana said.

"Please tell me you're joking."

The expressions they again shot one another along with the silence told me they weren't. And if they suddenly revealed to me that they'd been sitting on six kilos of heroin, I...I didn't have an answer for what I was going to do.

I gave Dana a minute to continue. Instead, he and Ginny looked at each other again.

"What other stuff?" Twitch finally asked.

"We…" Ginny started.

"We held on to his trumpet," Dana said.

"Figured it was only fair," said Ginny with a tilt of her beer.

That was not the answer I expected.

"Seriously?"

They nodded.

I sighed. "While heisting the means of a man's income while insisting he give you the money he owes you is certainly both a dick move and one that makes no sense whatsoever—"

"But—" Ginny stammered.

"I am *not* fucking finished!" I said loud enough to not only make the gruesome twosome flinch but finally shut them up. "A trumpet isn't quite the item that requires a third party to send a hit squad after the owner. Think harder," I said through gritted teeth.

"That's all we have," Ginny said softly.

"How much is that kind of thing worth?" I asked, grasping at straws.

Dana shrugged. "I have no idea."

Twitch raised his hand. "The range is pretty extreme. Anywhere from a couple hundred dollars to a few thousand. Again, assuming there's no Stradivarius variation on a trumpet. Some shit that Beethoven played would be more valuable."

"How in sweet fuck all do you know that?" I asked.

"Ollie's got a nice trumpet."

"Ollie plays the trumpet?"

"No. He stuffs it with old rags and fucks it like a Fleshlight. It's a very specific fetish. Yes, he plays the trumpet."

The hell? I'd known the guy for over half my life and had no idea he played an instrument. I had only a half second to think upon the idea that people, no matter how well you think you know them, can still surprise you. And the flitter of sadness that he never shared that with me.

Then I remembered we had a dead jazz musician on our hands and my best friend was being questioned under police custody.

"So," I said, turning back to Dana and Ginny, "you took away a guy's living when he didn't pay you back the money he owed you, effectively giving him no way to earn the money back to pay you what was owed."

Ginny leveled her eyes at me. "Well, when you put it that way."

"Just saying."

My ineffective line of questioning was abruptly cut short by three hard knocks on Ginny's door.

Twitch's eyes went wide. "That's a cop."

It sure as hell sounded like a cop's knock. Ginny and Dana looked at me. I looked at the door. Then I looked at Twitch.

Who, somehow, was no longer there.

Goddamn it.

I hoped he'd disappeared his ass back to the kitchen to get rid of the two guns we'd left sitting on the counter.

I poked my head round the corner. Based on the strangely headed outline in the pebbled glass, I narrowed down the possible visitors to a cop in his peaked cap or a town crier.

"Uhh..." I whispered. "Is anybody going to answer the door?"

"Is he looking for you?" asked Ginny.

Fuuuuuuuck. That might be the case.

"Maybe," was all I said as I opened the slatted door of the hall coat closet and hid myself behind their coats.

"Boo. *Boo!*" Ginny whispered hoarsely. "God damn you." She walked to the door, where my line of vision ended.

I heard her paste on the ignorance. "Hello, Officer. Can I help you?"

"Yeah," a male voice said. "There was an incident in the neighborhood yesterday. We're questioning anyone who might have seen anything."

I held my breath as the uniform passed in front of the closet. As he removed his hat, I could see a blond flattop and a fairly large frame, but that was about it.

I hadn't heard Ginny invite him in. But he was in, nevertheless.

"What kind of incident?" Dana asked, his voice quavering.

"We're looking into the disappearance of Byron Walsh."

Disappearance?

Leaning forward, I could angle my vision through the slats a little better and see most of the living room. Something was off. The cop stood over Dana in his chair opposite the couch and the coffee table. Standing too close, intimidating him with his size. As the cop turned, I saw the curtain over the kitchen doorway part just the slightest bit; then a small shadow moved soundlessly behind the couch.

What the fuck was Twitch up to?

Why was he back in the room?

Something was definitely off. I took a deep breath through my nose and immediately regretted it. I didn't know exactly where the truckload of potpourri had been dumped in that closet, but my nasal cavity sure did.

I clamped my hand over my mouth and nose and clenched tightly.

Fun fact: Junior once described my sneezing as comparable to a howler monkey having his balls electroshocked. If the sneeze got loose, the jig was up. Like most things in my life, I hadn't really thought through this line of action and raced to think how I was going to explain my presence.

I had nothing.

Through my watering eyes, I saw a tiny pale hand creep out from under the coffee table and pull a throw pillow off the couch behind the cop.

"You seem upset, Mr…" the cop said to Dana.

Dana looked up at the looming officer. Over the distance and through the slats, I could see the tears in his eyes. He was losing it. "Campbell. Dana Campbell."

The cop didn't write it down.

Ginny's eyes kept darting between her roommate and the officer.

"Is there anything you'd like to tell me?" The cop's hand moved toward his notebook, then slid to the holster, gently popping the safety strap off his cannon of a revolver.

This was going somewhere bad.

Dana turned his head as the tears started rolling down his *faWAAAA-CHTUUUUUUUUUUUUUUU!*

That, by the way, was what my sneeze sounded like.

My head was too close to the door and smacked into the slats, knocking three loose, my face poking out like a poor man's version of Jack Nicholson in *The Shining.*

Before I could even consider following up with a *"Heeeeeere's JOHNNIE,"* the cop drew his gun in one swift motion and was arcing it up toward my face.

Twitch popped up behind him, rolling out from underneath the coffee table.

As the cop's gun was leveling at my nose, Twitch pressed the cushion against the back of the cop's head, then pressed a gun into the pillow.

The cop's eyes went wide for a fraction of a second.

The fraction before Twitch pulled the trigger.

Bang.

CHAPTER 13

I'M EIGHT YEARS old in my mother's kitchen.

The cop's forehead popped outward like a piece of squeezed bubble wrap, but didn't burst. His right eye crossed up and to the center, as if trying to see what just happened to his brain. The left eye stayed on me.

The bullet hits my chest and I fall, fall, fall.

A thick gush of blood cascaded out his nose.

Another shot and my mother falls to the cracked linoleum.

Then the life winked out of both eyes. The cop crumpled onto the area rug, lifeless.

Ginny fell to the floor in a dead faint.

The Boy opens his mouth to scream.

Dana opened his mouth to scream.

"Don't scream," said Twitch. *He doesn't belong here, in my mother's kitchen.*

Dana smartly listened to the man with the gun.

The Boy can't scream.

I am The Boy.

I am in my mother's kitchen.

My brother Twitch just shot a cop. In the head.

My mother's boyfriend just killed her. Just killed me.

I was in Ginny's living room, and there was now a dead cop on the floor. More blood.

The Boy is here.

Boo.

Boo.

"Huh?" I felt the cold of shock seeping in through my fingertips.

Every instinct told me to hide. To run. I was frozen, my body as lifeless as the cop. As my mother.

"Boo!" Twitch was kneeling over the dead officer, pulling the cop's gun out of his hand with no more concern in his voice or demeanor than if he were pulling a Hot Pocket out of the microwave. "This isn't a cop, Boo."

"Huh?"

Twitch held up the hand cannon like an auctioneer. It was a nasty-looking silver snub-nosed revolver. "This is a .44 Ruger. Boston PD don't carry these."

"That's it? That was why you shot this guy in the head?" I said quietly. I was afraid that if I said it much louder, it would come out a shriek.

"They're not allowed to carry these, Boo. BPD all carry Glock model 22 or 23 which are .40 caliber semi-automatics. SWAT teams carry .45 caliber either Sig Sauers or Smith & Wessons."

None of that meant a goddamn thing to me. Whenever Twitch turned into Tom Clancy, the part of my brain that processed math shut down.

I ran to the door. I opened it half expecting a few boys in blue to open fire, but only encountered the cold air. I looked up and down the street. No black-and-whites anywhere.

My blood pressure dropped a notch. I had a hard time believing that a beat cop in JP would be strolling the neighborhood in this weather, canvassing a murder.

Wait a minute…

Pieces started to fall.

The "cop" said he was investigating a disappearance, not a murder.

And I was pretty goddamn sure that Byron's murder had long progressed past the point of canvassing uniforms and into the hands of detectives.

Twitch was right.

But we still had a fucking corpse on the living room floor.

When I walked back into the living room, Dana had Ginny off the floor and was moving her toward the bathroom. She was conscious, but her lips were blue with shock.

"He's not a cop," I said feebly. It seemed even to me a small comfort for the carnage in their home.

Twitch had Fake Cop's wallet open. He looked at me with grateful tears in his eyes. "You believe me?"

And all of a sudden, he was the kid at St. Gabe's again. The kid who was desperate for acceptance, to impress the big kids. To be believed when he told you that he'd done the right thing. He wanted me to tell him he'd done a good thing.

This touching moment when I saw Twitch for the boy he was deep inside was slightly knocked off-rail when a chunk of brain fell out of the hole on the back of Fake Cop's head. It landed on Ginny's ruined Oriental rug with a wet plop.

It also snapped me back to the horrible, horrible reality I was currently facing. I breathed deeply through my nose, trying not to hyperventilate. The stench of gunpowder, blood, and evacuated bowels filled my senses.

I felt like storming, grabbing the situation by the balls and squeezing hard. I really did. My legs and knees, however, were still weak from the execution I'd stood three feet away from. As I wobbled over to the bathroom, the sounds of vomit hitting toilet water hit my ears. I knocked stormish-ly on the door.

"We gotta talk, guys." And yes, that sounded just as stupid to me.

The door opened a crack. Dana's red-rimmed eyes looked back at me. His lips were also pale underneath his wobbling moustache. Christ, if both he and

Ginny dropped from shock, this shitshow was would turn into a full-blown Emmy-winning six-seasons-and-a-movie shit-com.

Ginny yanked the door all the way open. She'd regained some of her color the way a solid vomiting could do for you. "What are we gonna do? What are we gonna do, Boo?" Her face was a mask of barely contained panic, hair a pulled-back tangle. "Is he dead? Maybe…maybe he's not dead."

The chunk o'brain plop echoed back into my mind. "Um…no. He's dead. He's…really dead."

Ginny's face scrunched up and went beet red as she cried, "Ohmygod. There's a fucking dead guy on my carpet."

"Pretty sure he was intent on killing all of us." I wasn't, but I figured the suspicion was as good as surety when there was a corpse on the floor.

"What aren't you telling me, Dana?"

"What?"

"That guy wasn't here for me."

Dana's lower lip started trembling. "I don't know anything."

"Well, somebody was ready to kill the both of you for whatever it is you don't know."

"What are we going to do here, Boo?" Twitch called from the living room.

How the fuck did I know? Why was he asking me? Did his plan stop just short of having a goddamn body to handle?

And everyone was looking to me for an answer.

"You guys have to go," I said to Ginny and Dana.

"What?" Ginny said, snapping out of her stupor.

"Grab a bag and get the hell gone. Don't tell me where. Do it now."

"Where are we supposed to go?" she said.

"Go back to Nova-fucking-Scotia, for all I care! Let me handle this." Man, I sure could talk a talk. For a second, even I believed me. Then I remembered that I knew me. Knew me well. Very goddamn suddenly, the situation had spun out of any league I was qualified to play in.

I went back to Twitch while Dana and Ginny scootched off to grab whatever they could carry.

Twitch was doing his best to roll the body up into the carpet. A dead arm flopped out of the fold. Twitch had a sheen of sweat on his already pasty face and his bird-like chest heaved with exertion. The physical labor part of what to do with a body was plainly not in his wheelhouse.

Then the idea hit me, along with the nausea that was going to accompany my call.

Damn.

"You gotta go, Twitch."

"What?"

"You gotta get out of here, too. I'll take care of this."

"I'm not—"

"You're getting the fuck gone!" I used a tone I hadn't used with Twitch since we were kids, when Junior and I ran our crew at St. Gabe's. It was my boss voice. My bouncer tone. If everyone had decided I was the point man on this disaster, then I was sure as hell going to be one.

Twitch's body immediately went rigid, his eyes popped wide. His shoulders slumped forward, his posture that of the little brother not only being bossed by but accepting the bossing from big brother.

"Where am I supposed to go?"

"Stick with Ginny and Dana. Keep their heads down."

"We're not going anywhere with that psycho," came Ginny's voice from behind me. Her eyes were fiery, but there was a legitimate fear of Twitch behind them: fear of what he was capable of.

If she only knew.

Ginny slung a red backpack over her shoulder. Dana put a calming hand on her back that she shrugged off.

"Do what the fuck you want, Ginny," I said. "I'm trying to keep you alive right now. And, very probably, the reason you might get killed is because of the goddamn lies you handed to me and Junior in the first place." I could feel my own rage building. The whole shebang rumbled through my head, boiled down into its simplest terms.

It wasn't fair.

And I fucking told her so.

"All of this. None of it would have happened if you'd been straight with us at the start."

"You're right, Boo. It wouldn't," she said, nodding. "Because you wouldn't have helped us at all. You and Junior, with the macho bullshit you two strut around with…you wouldn't have helped us at all if you knew Dana was a man and that he was gay."

"You don't know that, because you didn't tell us the whole story. So you don't get to judge us. Not now. Not when we're neck deep in the mess that you shoveled all over us in the first place."

"We needed you. I needed your help."

"And you're still not telling me everything."

Twitch held up a finger. "Um, guys?"

But I was on a roll. "I'm talking to you, Dana. You seem awfully fucking quiet for the person at the epicenter of this shitquake."

"I don't know anything." His voice quavered as he spoke. "I don't know anything. Shouldn't we be calling the police or something?"

With that suggestion, Ginny seemed to forget her righteous indignation at my machismo and remembered the concrete fact that there was a carcass in a police uniform rolled up in her carpet. Her face broke into tears. "And there's a body on my fucking floor."

"No cops," Twitch said, a dangerous tone undercutting his words. The little brother was gone. The dangerous person who just shot a suspected fake-cop-cum-possible-killer in the head was back.

This was turning ugly. Fast.

"Look. You two get yourselves gone. You want to do it alone? Do it alone. I got enough crap to wash off of me and Junior now, thanks to you two. I'm perfectly fine losing your goddamn problems the moment this body is gone."

"Are you listening to yourself?" Ginny said.

"I got this," I said with a firmness that belied the fact that I was lying my ass off.

It might have been the biggest lie of my life. And I'd spent a lifetime telling whoppers to myself.

We all stood there for a moment. Then Ginny and Dana started for the door. The only words spoken as they left us were Dana's.

"I don't know anything," he said once more for good measure, almost mantra-like.

And goddammit, I believed him.

Which left us as screwed as we were when we showed up.

Except we were much, much worse off now.

You know. With a fucking corpse.

Fuuuuuuck.

"Give me the gun," I said to Twitch.

"What?"

"The gun you…used. That's gotta go too."

"I can—"

I held out my hand.

He didn't say anything, just handed me the ugly piece of metal. I slipped it into the back of my pants, the cold barrel icing my spine as it nestled between my butt cheeks. "Now get out of here."

"But…"

"If this shit goes south, I need someone on the outside. I don't need you caught up in this anymore."

"Uh, Boo? I don't know what you define as 'caught up,' but I already killed a guy."

I had no answer to that.

Twitch hung his head, hurt emanating off his tiny body. As completely cuckoo as it sounds, it hurt me to send him off like that. Twitch spent his time with me trying to please. Fucked up as it was, killing the guy was just Twitch trying to help. And far as I was concerned, he may have saved us all.

Fake Cop was pulling his piece on me. That much was a stone cold fact.

Maybe it was an instinctive response to a two hundred and forty pound man bursting out of closet and sneezing like a Yeti with a sinus infection.

But maybe, just maybe, he was going to shoot us all either way.

I didn't know what would have happened; I just now had to deal with what did.

Because heaven help us if Twitch was wrong, and that was an honest-to-God real cop that wasn't breathing anymore because of us.

With the posture of a beaten dog in retreat, Twitch left too. Leaving me with only my thoughts and the recently departed.

I sat on Ginny's couch and put my face in my hands.

How the hell did we end up here?

At least Junior wouldn't be facing possible charges for *this* murder. Instead, he was facing charges for the one that we didn't do. Ain't that some shit?

Kind of amazing, if you really thought about it.

Was there a lesson so far?

I was sure there was one in there. Somewhere.

But I'd be damned if I could tell you what it was.

I pulled my burner phone out to make the call. If this all turned worse than it already was, I decided I was going to eat it. The whole turd sandwich. I didn't know how much of the fall I could take, but I had every intention of taking it all.

I needed to minimize the impact. If stepping in front of the bullets kept Junior and Twitch out of the same cell I would wind up in, then I had to do it. Like Mr. Spock said, "The needs of the many outweigh the needs of the few."

Holy shit. Did I just quote *Star Trek*?

Ollie would be proud.

Twitch would call me a nerd.

Junior would just call me out for my martyr complex. And he would be right.

But Junior wasn't there, now was he?

I had to take care of my family, one way or the other.

I didn't know any prayers, so I just looked up at the ceiling and spoke to Ginny's fan.

"Give me a fucking break here, will you?"

The ceiling fan didn't answer me, so I dialed the phone number I thought I'd never call.

The phone rang twice before a woman's voice picked up, a pleasant Irish lilt inflecting the greeting. "Conor's Publick. How can I help you today?"

I almost laughed. If only she knew the answer.

"Frankie Cade, please. Tell him Boo Malone needs a favor."

THE CALL WAS made.

I sat on the easy chair next to the dead man.

What the fuck had I landed in the middle of?

Why was this dude even here?

If the guy was a dirty cop and was there to cause traumatic bodily harm to Dana and Ginny, he sure as shit wouldn't do so with his service piece. But "dirty" wasn't the important word in that sentence. "Cop" was.

Who the frig was he?

I was missing some ridiculously huge pieces in the narrative I was in the middle of, and had no idea how to figure out where the gaps were.

The possibly fake cop was looking for something. I think.

Dana said he was holding Byron's possessions after his trip abroad.

Somebody put Byron on the wrong side of the grass.

What I had wasn't too bad. My pieces fit together well. All I was literally missing were the who, the what, the where, the when, and the why.

Shit.

I decided to start with the 'what'. Once I knew the particulars of the item Byron was—maybe—killed over, it could lead me to the rest.

I opened the first bedroom door to what I quickly figured for Ginny's room. Bright and tidy, a Helmut Newton poster hung on the wall over the bed, a black and white of some guy with a tire slung over his shoulder, more abs than I'd ever see in a lifetime. I subconsciously sucked in my gut as I closed the door.

The second bedroom was an unholy mess. A pile of dirty laundry sat behind the door. The black bedspread was in a heap at the foot of the bed, a framed, signed T-shirt from Tool leaned against the wall on top of a dresser piled with makeup and empty Diet Coke cans.

Huh. Tool was Ginny's favorite band. Call me ignorant, but I was impressed that the tiny gay dude would be a Tool fan. Maybe Ginny had turned him on to them. Goes to show you what running with the stereotype will get you.

How was I ever going to find Byron's mess in this junkyard? And how was I going to do it without contracting Hep C?

Wait…makeup?

I glanced back at the pile of laundry. Half a bra was sticking out of the pile.

Looked like I was in was Ginny's room after all.

Should have stuck with the gay dudes being fastidious rather than the girls being fastidious stereotype. Or maybe I could try to stop stereotyping at all. Wouldn't that be something? So would flying cars. Neither one was likely in my lifetime.

I went back to Dana's room and opened the closet. There was a suitcase with a piece of paper taped to it that read BYRON'S CRAP.

I shit you not.

I pulled out the big suitcase and opened it. A couple of suits. A shaving kit. Stuff you'd pack for an extended trip abroad. I felt around the lined material. Nothing I could feel squirreled between the layers.

Wait. Dana said he'd taken Byron's trumpet as well.

I reached up to the shelf and moved a couple of boxes of old photographs and a vacuum bag of what looked like summer clothes. Still couldn't see what, if anything, was behind them. I felt around and my fingertips brushed a plastic handle. I grabbed it and slid whatever that handle was attached to toward me.

And lo-and-behold, I had me a trumpet case.

I had a strong feeling that there wasn't going to be an instrument inside there. I popped the first hasp and held my breath.

I'd seen enough television and gangster movies to know that musical cases were only used to carry actual musical instruments maybe one out of ten times.

Okay, television might have skewed the numbers in my head a little bit.

I popped the second hasp and slowly opened the case…

It was a goddamn trumpet.

Somebody knocked at the door, and my heart tried to karate chop its way out of my ribcage.

It was him.

I closed the case and shoved it back onto the shelf.

He knocked again more insistently.

"Keep your fucking pants on," I said, heading down the hallway.

I quietly opened the door to face the curled smile and blind eye of one Louis Blanc. "Evening, boyo," he said. "Were you plannin' on letting hypothermia take me?"

The first time I opened a door to him, he shot me in the leg.

The last time I'd seen him, he was flat on his back on The Cellar's floor, with me on top of him, pressing a broken bottle neck into his throat.

All in all, we had a unique relationship.

He'd shown up at The Cellar that day to let me know that his boss, Frankie "The Mick" Cade, was in my debt after I'd passed some sensitive information his way. He let me know all this after I decided not to open his throat on the dirty barroom floor.

Fuck that debt.

I'd had no intention of calling that favor in. Ever.

Funny how circumstances could make a person reconsider their own personal codes of morality, wasn't it?

To be fair, even straddling my tallest high-horse, I hadn't been able to see far enough into the distance to catch the slightest glimpse of this particular situation.

I was calling that card.

He strolled past me like he was coming over to watch a hockey game. "In a bit of trouble, are we?" A half-smoked Gauloise cigarette poked out between his teeth. He winked at me with his milky-white blind eye. The long scar arching back from the eyelid wiggled when he did. He clapped me on the shoulder.

I wanted to knock the smugness out of his words with a right cross, but I had to keep in mind the trouble I was in. That Junior and I were in. "You could say that."

Obviously, I couldn't go into detail on the phone.

I hadn't talked directly to Cade. The girl on the phone asked me the nature of my problem. I said major and immediate.

She said I'd get a call back.

Thirty seconds later, Ginny's phone rang, and a deep voice simply said, "Give me the address. Nothing more."

"Let's sit down and discuss exactly..." The fancy cigarette dropped from between Blanc's lips as he entered the living room. His eyes were laser-beam focused on the arm sticking out of the half-rolled carpet. "Is that a body?"

"Yep."

"Is that a sleeve to a Boston Police officer's uniform?"

"Yes, I—"

Blanc spun around, a small silver gun appearing in his hand like a magician's trick—and pointing right at my forehead. "Have you lost your fucking mind, lad?"

I held my hands straight up, palms open, and stared into the barrel, strangely wondering if it was the same gun he'd shot me with the last time. I hated guns. Had since one killed my mother when I was eight. Hated having them pointed at me even more. Everything stood out in sharp contrast, with the gun dead-center of my focus. I could even see the eyebrow over Blanc's one good eye bristling.

"I know what you're thinking..." I said

"Oh, boyo. You have no clue what I'm thinking right now. And let me tell you, if you did, you sure as hell wouldn't be keen on it. Where's your boyfriend?"

"What?"

"His monstrosity of an automobile is parked outside. Where is he? Don't need him popping out and irritating my already itchy finger."

"He's currently with the police, being questioned."

"About what? It wouldn't have anything to do with this, would it?"

"Something else."

"No rest for the wicked, eh?" He waved the gun up and down my frame. "I'm kindly going to ask you to disrobe."

"What?"

"Your clothes," he said. "Can't be too careful, as I'm still not entirely sure how fond of me you are, *etcetera*. I'm sure you understand."

If he only knew precisely how fond of him I'd be if he helped me out of the mess I was currently in. A little burlesque would be worth it. I quickly stripped off my sweatshirt. The waist snagged for a second on the gun I'd forgotten was tucked into my pants. "Um, I have a gun?"

"That sounded like a question."

I supposed it did. I cleared my throat. "I have a gun. In the back of my pants."

"Turn around and remove it. Do it with two fingers and do it slower than you'd even imagine I'd like."

Because things could never go smoothly, the tiny sight on the barrel snagged on my belt. "It's stuck."

"I can see that. Undo your belt with the other hand."

I put my other hand onto the buckle. A bit too quickly, apparently.

"Slow it down." A smile played out on his lips, his dead eye somehow filled with more mirth than his functioning eyeball. "That didn't come out as I intended."

"No problem," I said as I unbuckled my pants. "If you have a Poison CD to put on while I do this, it might help."

"Funny. Place the gun on the floor and step back."

I did.

Blanc gestured to the gun with his own. "That the gun that did the deed?"

"Yes."

"You do the deed?"

I stayed silent. I tried to give him a steely look right in the eyes, but my gaze kept flicking over to the chalky orb instead of the one that was looking at me. Instead of steely, I landed on shifty.

"Very well, then," he said. "Resume."

I kicked my Timberlands off and dropped my pants. I rubbed a hand over the long scar above my knee that he'd given me less than a year earlier.

"Looks to be healing nicely, that."

Instead of taking the bait, I just opened my arms wide and turned. "Satisfied?"

"Keep going."

"You can't be serious."

"Keep going."

Fun fact about me: I dropped my boxers with less shame than that which I removed my undershirt with. Not that I have a dick that any former sack-bunnies of mine would blog about, more along the lines of...

"Sweet Jesus," Blanc said.

Yeah. That.

"You've got quite a tapestry upon you, lad." He sounded almost impressed by the latticework of scars along my torso.

"We done?"

"Almost. Bend over and spread 'em."

"Now, wait a goddamn minute..."

"Just kidding. Cover yourself." Blanc picked up Twitch's gun off the floor, emptied the bullets from the clip, then handed it back to me.

I had half my clothes restored when I noticed he still hadn't stopped with the pointing of his own gun. "Think you can put that away now?" I said as I shoved my useless unloaded weapon back between my butt cleavage.

"Soon." With his free hand, he plucked a fresh cigarette from the golden case inside his jacket pocket and lit it with his equally expensive-looking lighter.

Instinctively, I wanted to tell him to put it out, to be courteous toward my friend's home. Then I remembered what Twitch had done to it. All things considered, I had the low-ground, morally.

"Starting at the beginning, you want to tell me who the departed member of the Metropolitan Police force is?"

"I don't know who he is."

"This does not help."

"Why does it fucking matter? I'm calling in the favor that was promised to me."

"Let's be clear." Blanc ashed his cigarette into an empty beer bottle on the coffee table. "During the last bout of unpleasantness that brought us together, Mr. Cade wanted me to pass to you the message that he was in your debt. How this came to be interpreted as a favor, specifically, seems to be something that you have decided."

Well, shit.

He went on. "That said, Mr. Cade decided to send me along to see what exactly you could have meant by the aforementioned 'favor.' A favor is Green Monster tickets on opening day. A favor is a last-minute reservation at Menton on Valentine's Day. This…" he waved the cigarette in the direction of the corpse, "…this is something that is far, far larger than a favor, wouldn't you say?"

I clenched my jaw. "Admittedly, it is a large favor."

"Let me ask you again, keeping in mind that I don't like repeating myself. Who is this rolled up in the carpet in what appears to be a Bee Pee Dee uniform?"

"Someone who came here to hurt and or kill the residents. I was here. I… intervened. That's all I know. He's not a cop." I hoped I sounded surer than I felt.

"I'm only asking, since, you know, if it is, in fact, a proper police officer, I'm putting a bullet into your head." Blanc held up his gun. "Then I shall be tossing my favorite gun here into the Charles River and leaving you here with your sins."

It was then I noticed that he'd never taken his gloves off. The man was ready to end me, if it came to that. "Good to know."

"So, why don't you roll up your sleeves, and unroll that carpet?"

I blew out a long breath and went to the body. I slid my fingers under the rough fabric, tried to remember a prayer, and flipped the body. I tensed up and closed my eyes in case a bullet was about to put me out of my misery.

I waited, misery intact.

I waited.

And waited…

"Well, well, well," said Blanc, a hint of amusement in his voice.

"Are you going to shoot me?"

"Not right now, but the night is young."

I chanced a look at Blanc, who holstered the gun underneath his sports coat as he walked to me. He leaned in close, inspecting what was left of the dead man's face. "Farewell and adieu to you, Mr. Shaughness."

"You know him?"

"Galal Shaughness."

"Really? Galal Shaughness?"

"His father was Irish."

"And his mother?"

"Wasn't."

Fair enough.

"Who is he?"

"Muscle. Works primarily out of New York. Third generation West Side. The Irish boys in the Apple don't have as much structure as the old days. Primarily they hire out nowadays. I suppose I should be curious what you and your cohorts have been up to that would warrant such attention, but I'm afraid that my curiosity pales in comparison with the issue at hand." He flipped open his cell phone case. "Now, let's see how Mr. Cade would like to proceed."

Blanc held the phone to his ear. I held my breath.

"*Dia duit, boss. Forbairt suimiúil…*" He turned his back to me, as though having the entire conversation in Gaelic wasn't going to be enough to exclude me. The only words I recognized in the entire conversation were the names Malone and Galal Shaughness. At one point, I could hear Cade laughing uproariously through the earpiece, which brought a raspy chuckle out of the normally impassive Blanc.

"*Fuair sé. Feicfidh mé* é a láimhseáil ó anseo." With that, he put the phone back into his pocket and withdrew a smaller phone from his jacket. "Today is your lucky day, Mr. Malone." He pressd a few buttons on the phone, snapped the cheap flip phone in half, then walked to the kitchen and dropped the pieces into a saucepan.

"Now what?"

"Now we wait." He filled the saucepan with water, then set it over a high flame on the stovetop. "Anything to drink in this fine establishment?"

WITHOUT MUCH SCROUNGING, I found a half bottle of whipped cream-flavored vodka under the kitchen sink. I wasn't going to speculate as to whom it belonged.

We both winced at the first sip of the cloying alcohol, but bore the sickly brunt. Blanc carefully folded his sportscoat over his arm and sat on the lounge chair. I sat on the couch and almost put my feet up on the re-rolled up corpse rug. Instead, I awkwardly rolled around on my ass, balanced on one cheek for a moment, remembered that I had a gun in the back of my pants, almost drove it into my anus, then re-balanced myself with all of the grace that the previous actions allowed.

I didn't want to look at the body anymore. I didn't want to look at Blanc either, that Mona Lisa smile of his displaying his enjoyment at the predicament I'd found myself in.

I didn't know what to do with my hands, so I clasped the glass of diabetes-inducing vodka and tried to will it into Jim Beam like the Jesus of Jamaica Plain.

After a few minutes of silence, Blanc placed his glass on the end table and said, "Why do I get the feeling that this both is and isn't your first?"

I didn't know what he meant by that. I had the feeling he wasn't just talking about the killing. I looked up at him.

Right into that goddamn smile.

An image of my mother flashed within my mind along with the piles of other bodies left behind in in my life's wake. Some deserving, most of them simply caught in the maelstrom of fatality that my swirled around me.

I used to think, when half a bottle into the periodic pity-parties, that my sphere of detruction only applied to the people I loved—that my proximity got them hurt. Got them killed.

But in that moment, looking at Blanc, I saw it for what it was.

I was like a black cat walking under a ladder, breaking a mirror and knocking salt over when I did. And my bad luck touched everyone and everything around me. Maybe I could be more sensible and maybe take into account some of my life choices, but fuck that.

I continued my silence.

Blanc leaned forward, adjusted the cuff of his suit pants. "Do you remember when you called me a murderer?"

I remembered. It was when I was on top of him, ready to open his neck with a broken bottle. Kind of hard to forget.

I nodded.

"I told you then that I wasn't. That there was a difference between a murderer and a killer. If I remember correctly, I also said that I thought you knew the difference."

With a croak in my throat, I said, "I remember."

"I'm not so sure I was right."

"Meaning?"

"I'm not sure you knew the difference then."

The doorbell rang and my skin creeped icily over my bones.

Blanc stood, tugging at the cuffs of his shirt. "But I think you do now, boyo, doncha?" The Mona Lisa blossomed into a full-blown smile this time. The first time I'd ever seen one on Blanc's face. The glee almost reached his dead eye as he strolled to answer the door. "Cleanup crew is here."

"Should I go?"

"Now *you're* kidding, right?"

I wasn't, but I didn't know what I was supposed to do. I felt as fidgety as a four-year-old in church.

Blanc walked back in with two large Hispanic men in mover's jumpsuits. They walked with a jail-yard swagger. Behind them was an older dark-skinned woman who, under other circumstances, could have been mistaken for their mother. The woman toted bags of cleaning supplies and a squeegee mop.

The motherly woman looked around the room, taking stock of the mess. "No too bad," she said in a thick accent, smiling sunnily.

Really?

Blanc held a hand out to me. "Car keys."

"What?"

"The body goes into the monstrosity your life-partner calls a car. You, my friend, are driving the car."

Shit.

The two movers rolled out a blue tarp and slid the body, carpet and all, onto the plastic. Some blood had seeped thickly onto the hardwood, but otherwise left less a mess than *Dateline* would lead you to believe. All said and done, it was as easy a job as the cleanup crew could have expected.

"I'm going to pull the car around. Be a mate and hold the door for these fine gents?" Blanc said as he buttoned up his wool coat.

I opened the door to the frigid night and waited. I lit a smoke and noted the panel truck that had parked in the perfect position to blind the neighbors to anything coming in or out of Ginny's front door. *Claddagh Moving Co.* was painted in huge letters on the side of the truck. Underneath, *Ireland's Relocation Associates.*

IRA.

Who said the Irish mob didn't have a sense of humor?

Blanc pulled Miss Kitty around the front of the panel van, again blocking any lookie-loos. I felt the strangest sensation seeing Blanc behind the wheel of Junior's beloved car, like I was watching my best friend's girlfriend being molested publicly by the biggest douchebag at the bar.

Huh.

Felt kind of like seeing Summerfield's hand on Kelly's ass.

Ugh.

Then...

Blanc popped the trunk.

And drew his gun.

Followed immediately by a small arm extending another gun from the depths of Miss Kitty's cavernous boot.

Twitch was in the goddamn trunk.

Despite my best instincts to keep the corpse disposal on the down low, I yelled out, "No!"

The two gunslingers stood there in their best John Woo mutual-destruction poses.

"Mr. Malone?" Blanc said. "Please keep your voice down."

I looked around at the neighboring houses, remembering that it was one of those nosy motherfuckers who'd dropped the dime on Junior and me in the first place.

Behind me, I heard a loud thump, much like a body wrapped in a rug and then wrapped in plastic would make when dropped suddenly. I turned back to see the "movers" unzipping their jumpsuits. Wild-eyed, they reached inside. Gentle smile gone, the old lady was beelining for something in her cleaning bag.

I held my hands up. "Wait, wait, wait!" I said to them in an Irish whisper. Christ, I hoped they spoke English.

They glared at me, but kept their hands where they were.

I was frozen, caught between keeping the cleanup crew from adding more weaponry into the mix and a firefight in the middle of the street.

"Mr. Malone?" Blanc said in a tight, angry voice. His gaze remained along his extended shooting arm, never breaking eye contact with Twitch. "Will you kindly come down here and explain this situation?"

I looked back at the cleanup crew. Both movers kept their hands inside their jumpsuits. The old lady stood stone-still, a dead expression on her face and a small snub-nosed revolver in each hand.

I made the double-handed open-palm motion for them to stay where they were. I thought back to my tenth grade Spanish. "*Espera, espera!*"

The guy with the ponytail scrunched up his face. "The fuck you saying, homes?"

Well, that answered that.

"Just hold up one minute. We have a misunderstanding happening."

The *abuela* shifted the black pinpricks that replaced her eyeballs to me. "No a good time for meesunderstanding."

No shit.

"Now, Mr. Malone," Blanc said, a bit louder from outside. I didn't like that he was abandoning his own volume control.

I approached the car slowly. Up the block, I saw headlights turn at the top of the street. "Guys, there's a car coming, so I strongly suggest that you both put your dicks back into your pants."

"Him first," Twitch said, a fear on his countenance that I had never, ever seen in the lifetime of knowing him. This was really not good. Both of his eyelids were spasming like two moths had landed on his face and were having simultaneous epileptic fits.

Twitch was a tiny pink man who made his way through life knowing he could make people fear him when he needed to. Especially those who initially underestimated what he was capable of.

Which was not the man on the end of his gun that night.

Not Louis Blanc.

"You're joking," Blanc said to Twitch. I saw a muscle jumping with tension under Blanc's dead eye, right under the thick scar. I was pretty sure even Blanc had never come across a Twitch before.

Two psychopaths, their eye muscles doing Cirque du Soleil, juggling their newborn emotions in the middle of the street.

With guns.

And I fucking hated guns.

I repressed the screaming of such sentiment. I really did.

I looked back up the street. The car was five houses down. "Put the gun down, Twitch." I reached back into our history and used as much of my senior authority as I could draw on.

The headlights reflected off the panel van. Six cars away.

Twitch's whole head twitched.

Blanc's arm tensed.

Two cars.

Twitch lowered the gun into the car.

Blanc moved his hand inside his coat.

The car passed. The face of a little boy, maybe five years old, was pressed against the passenger side window. The driver didn't even look over. The kid waved. I gave him a little wave back.

Blanc said, "You want to tell me who this is and why in sweet fuck all he was hiding in your trunk?"

"I didn't know he was in there."

"He didn't," Twitch said.

Blanc looked at us, back and forth. "There's no answer that either one of you is going to give me that isn't going to sound utterly ridiculous, is there?"

"Nope," I said.

Blanc shook his head and blew out a deep breath. "Let's make strides to end this evening, then, shall we?"

Twitch and I sat in the car as the movers efficiently hustled the remains of Galal Shaughness into Miss Kitty's trunk.

"I'm sorry, Boo."

I didn't reply. I didn't know what to do with him anymore. He'd more than likely saved the lives of Ginny, Dana, and me. Then he'd almost gotten the both of us killed less than an hour later.

I needed Junior.

My crew had always been an assemblage of misfits, each bringing an enriching quality to the mix, a quality that sometimes made them outcasts in the first place. Together, we were formidable. Broken down into parts, we were a flying mess of dysfunction.

But Junior and I were the core—the yin and yang at the center. I needed his sometimes idiotic common sense the same way he needed my pragmatism. Ollie brought the smarts, Twitch brought the…efficiency?

We were all broken pieces.

Together, we were a reasonably functional human being. But sometimes… the wrong two pieces in the wrong situation…

Ollie once called our family unit "ReVoltron." I didn't know what that meant, but it made Twitch laugh like hell..

Blanc rapped his knuckles on my window. I rolled it down, and he handed me the keys. "Follow my car. The apartment should be ready and sparkling by the morning."

"Gimme five minutes," I said, turning the key. Miss Kitty's old engine coughed up a few hairballs, then roared to life. "It's an old car. Gotta let her warm up."

Blanc stared at me, I'm pretty sure wondering whether or not Miss Kitty had it in her to not break down on the ride. I wasn't sure how much more he was willing to take before he cut his losses by putting bullets into us and ending his night. Truth be told, I was surprised he hadn't already.

"Mr. Blanc?" Twitch said.

"What?"

"Pleasure to meet you. Big fan."

I wished I could say that Twitch's declaration of fandom for the hired killer surprised me, but my surprise glands had been emptied out and had shriveled up and died at that point.

Blanc walked back to his car, muttering in great puffs of frozen breath.

"You're staying here," I said to Twitch.

"But…"

"I need you to stay here and watch the apartment while this crew cleans up your mess."

Twitch sank a small amount into himself at that. I could easily have said *our* mess, but didn't. I also could have said that I didn't mean it that way.

I didn't do that either.

But I knew Twitch well enough to know what worked. I needed to give him purpose. "Watch them. Make sure they don't walk out with anything that's not theirs."

Twitch pepped back up again. "I can do that." Eager to please his big brother. It felt dirty. It felt manipulative.

But I also knew that it was what I had to do. The first part of which was untethering myself from Twitch. And I had to do so leaving him no opportunity to pull his ninja routine on me again. I didn't need him popping out of the goddamn glove compartment when I least expected it.

Part of him no doubt knew I was giving him the royal blow-off, but the greater part of him, the part that needed the task, needed to be of use, overrode the obvious.

Blanc pulled his black sedan up to the window as Twitch climbed out.

"Where's he going?"

I held my hand up until Twitch was out of earshot. "He wants to make sure that they don't miss anything. Shall we?"

Blanc believed my lie about as much as Twitch did, but in the greater interest of ending the debacle of a night, he simply rolled up his tinted window with a whirr.

Oh hell, I'd forgotten something. "One sec," I said, holding up a finger.

"Fer fook's seck," I heard Blanc say through the window as he slammed his car back into park. I noticed that the more frustrated he got, the heavier his accent became. A little more effort on my end, and Blanc would be spouting about green clovers and blue diamonds.

Trotting back into the house, I waved at the crew, who gave me looks like they were still hoping to get a chance to shoot me. Twitch was in the kitchen, his head in the fridge. His tiny pink face popped up as I passed. "You okay, Boo?" he said through whatever it was he was already chewing on.

"All good," I said as I ran back into Dana's room, opened the closet, and retrieved the trumpet. I still had a feeling it was all connected to the damn trumpet, since it was the only thing that Dana had kept of Byron's that wasn't underpants, skinny jeans, and brightly colored polo shirts.

Worst-case scenario, I'd give the damned thing to Ollie as an apology and call it a day.

I almost slipped down the icy steps in my haste, and could see Blanc shaking his head in disbelief. He rolled the tinted window down a crack. "May we please move on now?" His gaze, even through the small window opening, very noticeably moved to the case in my hand.

"Yep," I said. "Don't want to forget my trumpet."

"You don't strike me as a musical sort," Blanc said.

"Huge fan of John Coltrane," I said, fumbling in the cold with the car keys and frozen fingers.

"Really?"

"Oh yeah. Since I was a kid." I opened the door.

"Well, then, why do you play the trumpet?"

"Huh?"

"Coltrane played the saxophone."

"Milo Davis?" I only knew two names of jazz musicians. I'd officially used them both.

"Closer. *Miles* Davis played the trumpet."

Okay. Guess I only knew one. "What I meant. My lips are icing over."

Blanc reached over and opened the passenger door. When the interior light turned on, he made a point of removing his gun from his jacket once again. He didn't point it at me, but that didn't mean he wasn't going to. He just placed it on the seat and laid his hand over it. "Mr. Malone. Is there something in that case I need to know about? That I might possibly have to shoot you over?"

I guess Blanc watched the same TV shows I did. Slowly, I opened the case and showed him the trumpet. "We good?" I asked.

"As good as we're going to be, I suppose." He reached over the seat and pulled the door shut.

I tossed the trumpet onto the back seat, climbed into Miss Kitty, and followed him away from Ginny's house.

Blanc drove down to Centre Street, popped into the traffic circle, and hopped onto Arborway, then Parkman Drive. Wherever our destination was, I was glad we weren't cutting through the city proper.

After a good stretch of suburbia, I was beginning to relax. By relax, I mean I was finally able to unclench my anus without fear of soiling myself at the idea of driving a corpse around town.

A couple more turns and we were on MA-9. By the time we jumped on and off the turnpike, I wondered just where the fuck we were heading. I didn't think we'd be pulling over in the middle of the Tobin and tossing the departed into the Charles, but I sincerely hoped we weren't going to drive into New Hampshire to dig a shallow grave in a field outside Nashua. My already shot nerves weren't up to the road trip.

Once we pulled off outside Billerica, I started allowing myself to believe that we might get out of this.

And then came the flashing red and blue lights.

Not a hundred yards off the exit, and the cops crawled out of a side street and hit me with a *woop-woop*.

Anus clench re-engaged.

There was no way Blanc didn't see the lights or hear the siren. He didn't pull over.

So I didn't either.

We kept driving.

My mind raced, bordering on panic.

Goddamn it.

God*dammit*.

We didn't speed up.

We didn't slow down.

We just kept on keeping on.

Despite the barely above-freezing temperatures in the car, a greasy sheen of sweat popped out on my forehead and across the back of my neck. I was glad I didn't have Twitch in the car. Behind me was a real cop. And I wasn't sure that, things being what they were, Twitch wouldn't have blasted him too.

I needed to get out of this without another goddamn body.

And if I could swing it, I wanted to apply that stratagem to the rest of my life. Which I would be spending in a cell if I couldn't figure the best way out of my current predicament.

"Pull over the Buick," barked from the loudspeaker on top of the black-and-white.

Blanc didn't pull over.

Neither did I.

The siren *woop-woop*ed again. The officer repeated himself with more force. "In the Buick. Pull over to the right and shut off your engine."

Blanc put on his right turn signal.

So did I. It seemed we were pulling over after all.

Sour bile jumped up from my empty stomach, coating my throat and mouth.

But Blanc didn't pull over. He made a right turn.

And gunned it.

Fuck it.

So did I.

Miss Kitty's beautiful powerhouse of an engine roared like an enraged primeval beast and spat gravel under her wide tires as I cornered hard. I let loose a blaze-o'-glory howl that rattled the windows. Fuck it. Fuck it all!

The police car blazed to life, full sirens and lights as it slipped the corner behind me. My eyes flicked to the rearview and I wondered about the ramming power of Miss Kitty.

I almost shot past Blanc before I noticed he had, in fact, pulled over in a wide driveway-cum-parking lot blocked from the road by a tall fence rimmed with razor wire.

I slammed my foot on the brakes and turned into the lot, skidding only inches short from smashing into the flank of Blanc's car.

The police car screeched alongside us, blocking me from turning back onto the road, should that option be one I had under consideration.

But to be honest?

I had nothing.

My mind was a clean slate of panic.

Both doors of the police car flew open, two officers erupted from the vehicle with their guns drawn out low and screaming at me.

"Put your hands high, palms up!"

I placed my palms flat on the interior roof and stared straight ahead, afraid to so much as gently blink.

The lead officer came to my driver's side. The second officer, a female cop, nervously moved both her gun and her gaze back and forth from my hands to Blanc's car.

The lead officer, older than his partner by at least a decade, tried opening my door, and found it locked. "Open the door."

I made the slightest movement of my hands to do exactly that when Officer Two shrieked, "Keep your hands where I can see them!" Her gun moved toward my head so fast the sight tapped the window.

I didn't shit myself, so that was something, but I did let out an impressively forceful fart.

Even in my peripheral vision, I could see how badly her hands were shaking. I was guessing the two didn't see too many situations like the one I'd put them in the middle of out here in the boonies. It looked like it was a night of firsts for a lot of people.

Trying to keep my voice even, I said, "I can't do both, guys."

Before they could figure out what to do next, a loud clank struck the air and the driveway gate started grinding its way slowly open.

Emerging from between the gates, walking two thick-necked pit bulls on inch-and a-half chains came a…troll?

The guy was barely five feet tall with an inch or two for spare change, but walked with the swagger of a man twice his size. "Put the guns away, R.J.," he said casually, scratching a beard with more hair than remained on his pate.

"What's going on here, Bray?" said the older cop. Presumably R.J.

"They're here to see me."

The lady cop said, "We got an APB…"

Uh oh…

"Don't care if you got an XYZ. They're here to see me. Lou?"

Blanc stepped out of his car. "Officers." His sly smile was back on, but there was something underneath it. Something deadly. "Bray."

"Be with you in a moment, Lou," Bray said, turning his attention back to R.J. "Would you mind stepping to the side with me so we can discuss this? The bitch can stay in the car."

"Hey," the female officer said, but with more hurt than anger or authority.

R.J.'s graying moustache wiggled ominously, but he holstered his piece. "Listen to the man, Stephanie."

Steph, while unhappy with the new orders, if not being stripped of her opportunity to shoot me, also put her gun away.

The two pit bulls in Bray's grasp snarled and chuffed, but didn't bark. White foam rimmed their wide jaws as they looked over the assemblage, no doubt wondering which of us they'd like to digest chunks of the most.

Laconically, Bray spat out the frayed toothpick from between his teeth. He gave a short, sharp whistle through his wet lips and said, "Stand down."

Both dogs immediately plopped their haunches onto the gravel and sat at a stiff attention that would have impressed the hardest drill sergeant.

"What's the story here, Bray?" R.J. said, walking toward the side of the car. Even though Bray had the dogs heeled, the old cop kept his eyes on the two, his hand only a short distance from his gun.

"Just a misunderstanding. These boys are dropping off a car for me."

"The Buick?"

"Yeah. You didn't call it in yet, did ya?" Something dangerous flared in Bray's eyes as he stroked his beard.

"Not yet. Figured that since we were this close to your place, we'd wait and see where it was headed."

"You did right, R.J. Walk with me."

Their quick exchange rattled me deep. The way the old cop was laying things out made it sound like they were looking for Miss Kitty. Specifically.

The cop and the troll walked back through the tall gates. As they progressed up the lane, motion detectors flared up arc lights illuminating the gravel path. Motion detectors that must have been disabled when Bray made his way to us in the darkness. Not that that was fucking creepy or anything…

"In for a penny, eh?" Blanc said, lighting a cigarette. The flame from his gold lighter reflected off his milky eye. He took a deep drag and blew twin streams of smoke through his nostrils. "Think we're well past a point where this can safely be called a 'favor,' boyo?"

I had to agree with him, but stayed silent. The problem with this particular act in my little drama was that it was collapsing underneath the weight of my own overactive sense of debt.

Balance had shifted big time.

After tonight, I was going to owe Blanc and Cade.

And I really, really hated that I would.

After a few minutes, the path lights blazed on again, marking the approach of Bray and R.J. As they passed under the gate, R.J.'s voice carried on the frosty air. "All I'm saying is—"

Bray cut him off sharply. "What you're saying it that you're unhappy with the amount I regularly add to your paycheck?"

"No, no. That's not what I'm saying—"

"So what are you saying, R.J.?"

"I'm saying that staying out of your business is one thing. Ignoring an All Points Bulletin on a vehicle is another." Officer R.J. stuck his thumbs in his gun belt, trying to lean Bray into his way of thinking by being all cop-like.

"And staying out of your business is yet another," Bray said with a smile, popping another toothpick between his wet lips.

"What's that supposed to mean?"

"What I mean is, if I can ignore the fact that you're fucking Officer Stephanie behind the Sunoco, then I think you can ignore this tidbit."

Silence.

Whoops.

Officer R.J. began thumbing the wedding ring on his left hand.

"Good night, R.J."

"Night, Bray," Officer R.J. said softly. He even tipped his hat at Blanc and me as he passed us on the way to his car, tail between his legs.

As R.J. opened the police sedan's door, I heard Officer Steph say, "What the hell is—"

"Shut up, Steph," R.J. said. The police car pulled into a three-point turn and slowly drove back the way we came.

I let out the huge breath I didn't even know I was holding in.

Bray grinned and flipped the toothpick between his teeth, frayed end out. "Well, might as well pull the cars around back."

I followed Blanc once more up the long path to a large trailer with a sheet metal shack built onto the side. A hand-painted sign read *Porter's Pawn and Wreck.*

Miss Kitty's headlights passed over several dilapidated cars, a few smashed in well beyond repair. Other, less identifiable hunks of garbage and twisted metal rimmed the road all the way up to the lowered trailer.

I parked Miss Kitty and followed Blanc and Bray into the mobile home. Inside, the place smelled like someone had recently pooped in a bag of Cheetos, and I wasn't too sure if it was the dogs or Bray. The walls were lined with smoke-browned centerfolds and tourism posters for Disneyland.

Seeing the two side by side skeeved me out more than I'd have thought possible.

The left half of the trailer was fenced off in chain link and Plexiglas, a short glass counter filled with jewelry, watches, and other bric-a-brac. The wall behind held a couple of guitars, an old TV, a signed Drew Bledsoe jersey, and a saxophone. Guess that was the pawnshop part of the trailer.

I tried to stay in the background when the back of my legs hit something at thigh-level directly behind me. A loud snarl told me what it was and I almost added to the shit smell in the trailer.

The dogs were crated to one side of the office. Both still sat with a military rigidity, but their jowls trembled with fury as they stared me down.

They won.

I yelped and jumped my butt off the cage.

"Don't lean on that unless you want to get an ass full of teeth," Bray said.

Yeah. Thanks, dick.

Bray carefully moved several old copies of *Swank* and a number of *Paris Reviews* off a console and started flipping switches. The yard lit up brightly, and I could see more clearly what was in his backyard.

Oh *hell* no.

Bray said we were bringing him the Buick. Not like he was going to tell the cops that we were bringing him a body, but he was being more specific than I'd realized.

With a nightmarish rumble, the enormous car crusher turned on.

Oh *fuck* no.

"Keys," Bray said, opening his hand toward me.

I reached into my pocket and placed Junior's Motörhead fob into Bray's grease-rimmed fingers. It felt like I was signing a death warrant.

"Gonna give it a quick strip and get it done for you before the sun comes up. Anything you need to get out of the car, do it now."

"Gun?" Blanc said to me, opening and closing his fingers.

I handed him the empty pistol.

The three of us walked back out to the yard. Blanc opened Miss Kitty's passenger door and tossed the gun onto the seat.

"That thing unloaded? Bray asked. "Don't need it popping off rounds mid-crush."

Blanc nodded.

Bray handed me another set of keys. "First car at the bottom of the lane on the left. Got about a half tank. Enjoy." He said it with an amused smile that I didn't enjoy.

"What is it?" Blanc asked.

"A red '90 Dodge Omni." Bray laughed in a manner befitting his name. I wasn't a car guy, so I had no idea what was so funny.

It was bad enough simply hearing Blanc chuckle earlier. I was soundly filled with dread when Bray's statement made him guffaw outright.

"Well, then, I'm off," Blanc said. "I'll drive you to your new steed."

"I'll walk down," I said, placing my hand on Miss Kitty's sun-faded brown hood.

"You need a moment alone with the car, boyo? Maybe say a few words?" Blanc said. I could hear a smirk in the statement.

"Fuck off," I said, shooting him a glare.

He winked at me.

With his dead eye, of course.

"Bray," Blanc said with a wave as he headed back toward the front.

"Lou," replied Bray as he turned toward the car crusher.

I didn't get so much as a fare-thee-well, but I was just happy that I hadn't ended our date together by getting myself shot.

I looked back at the condemned, remembering the times. The good times. Feeling slightly stupid at the emotions I was feeling. And as bad as I felt, this was going to destroy Junior.

We'd spent our lives with nothing. In St. Gabe's, we didn't own a damn thing, or have anything we could claim as ours. Miss Kitty was the first thing Junior possessed of any significance, of any permanence, that said we were free of a system that did its damnedest to bury us as numbered casualties of a class war nobody even knew was being fought. Or if they did, they didn't care.

There was a reason Junior spent fifteen years repairing a car that should have seen a yard like Bray's five years before he even bought it.

He could have gotten himself a different car at any time.

He didn't.

She was as much a part of our crew as I was, as Twitch or Ollie was.

And there I was, putting her in her grave.

I still felt stupid, though.

I unscrewed her stiff antenna, collapsed it, and placed it into the pocket of my sweatshirt. "Sorry," I said.

A thick hand placed gently on my shoulder made me tense. I turned to look at Bray, who I was surprised to find wore an expression that matched my own.

"For what it's worth, I get it."

I nodded, feeling awkwardly grateful for his empathy.

"You got five minutes," he said. "Then I let the dogs out to roam."

Then I had a thought. "You have all those instruments inside. You play?"

Bray shrugged. "A little bit. Mostly a listener. You looking to buy or sell?"

"Neither. Looking for an opinion. You know instruments?"

"Enough to buy 'em from failed musicians. Wouldn't be too good at running pawn if I didn't."

I opened the car door and removed the trumpet case, which I'd almost forgotten was still in the car. Would've made a perfect ending to a perfect day, me not remembering the one piece of possible evidence I had that might keep me and mine out of jail for the rest of our fucking lives. I shuddered at my near-forgetfulness. "Would you look at this trumpet? I want to know if it's anything special."

"Special like what?"

"I don't know. Unusually valuable or something."

"Bring it inside so I can look at it." He led me back to the trailer. When we walked back in, both dogs gave a whimper. "Give it here." He looked at the beat-up case, flipped it over, and gave it a once-over. "Case is nothing special, but let's see what you got. Give you a good price on it, if it's worth anything."

"Maybe." Wouldn't that be a kick in the ass? Sell the freaking thing and make some chicken salad out of the chicken shit I was up to my eyebrows in. "What would a valuable one go for?"

"Well, that depends. Dizzy Gillespie's trumpet sold at an auction twenty years ago for sixty grand." He popped the latches and I held my breath.

Sixty grand. That would be the right number of zeroes for somebody to take another's life over.

Bray turned on a pair of bright work lamps over the drafting table. "If there's some kinda historical significance to it, I won't know until I look at it. See the maker and whatnot. You think it's something like that?"

"I really have no idea." And yet, it seemed ridiculous. How would Byron, playing in a Boston club-level jazz band, acquire himself a trumpet worth that kind of scratch? It didn't make sense.

Bray clicked open the hasps on the case and reached in. The trumpet looked stuck. The whole case lifted when he tried to pull it out. "The hell?" he said. He pulled a flathead screwdriver off the wall.

I didn't like this. Not one bit.

Suddenly having the Irish mob associate with the cops in his pocket and murder dogs in his home didn't seem like my best choice to have appraise the potentially head-stoving-worthy valuable I'd been carrying around.

What could I say? Seemed like a good idea at the time.

Something inside the case made a *click*. Bray's eyebrow shot up, but quickly went back to its at-ease position as he quickly—but not too quickly—closed it again.

The energy of the room changed. Real fucking fast. The dogs knew it too. They immediately started whimpering. The gray mottled pit let out a sharp *woof.*

Bray had seen something in that goddamn trumpet case. Something he didn't want me to see. His fingertips never once left the top of the trumpet case. With complete insincerity, he said, "It's not a bad instrument. I'll give you two hundred for it." He wouldn't look me in the eyes, but kept glancing around me. I took a quick look over to see what he was looking at.

His nightstand.

Want to bet that nightstand wasn't where he kept his ice cream?

And he didn't put the screwdriver back either. If anything, his grip tightened on it.

"Two hundred?" I said, trying to keep the suspicion out of my tone. "That what you think it's worth?"

"Give or take."

"Give or take?"

"Give or take." His eyes flicked from the nightstand and finally connected with mine. I didn't like what I saw in them. I saw me in the trunk of a fucking Buick.

I rolled my neck. "Why don't we try a different give or take?"

"What are you thinking?"

"I'm thinking you give me that screwdriver, or I take it from you and shove it somewhere you're not going to enjoy."

That stopped him. He looked me dead in the eye, mulling his options so hard it nearly made a sound.

"So why don't we do this. I take my trumpet, I don't talk to Blanc and Cade, and we part our ways. You keep on—"

Then he whipped the screwdriver at my head.

It was a hard throw, meant to stick in my brainpan, but it wasn't a good one. It sailed slightly to my left, clunking harmlessly off the wall. But as I predicted, he had a plan if he missed. That plan was in the nightstand. I zigged, making the assumption he would zag.

The dogs went berserk as he charged.

Right at me.

That I was not expecting.

With his thick, oversize skull, he drove himself like an enraged rhino right into my stomach.

He rammed his forehead so deeply into my gut, all the wind violently rushed out of my lungs.

I dropped, wheezing like a balloon with a slow leak.

Bray jumped right back up and went for the nightstand.

I couldn't breathe or stand. He hunched over, opening the drawer. I rolled onto my back and kicked him hard as I could square on the ass. He launched forward and smashed his head into the aluminum trailer wall with a loud *gong*.

While he was stunned, he was far from out. I pulled myself up and worked real hard to get some oxygen back into me.

In the open drawer sat an electrical-taped snubnose.

That fucker was trying to kill me.

Over a motherfucking trumpet.

Despite my innate and burning hatred for the implements themselves, I took the snubby from the drawer and pressed it to his swelling forehead, the gun butt burning in my grip.

"No," was all he said, a trickle of blood gumming his filthy moustache from a sliver cut just under his cheek.

"No?" I screamed in a higher pitch than I thought would come out of me. "NO?" A lot of people had spent the better part of the last year trying to kill me. I had fucking had enough.

Through my eyes, the room was bright, bright red.

The dogs bayed and screeched, no doubt smelling the violence pouring off me.

I popped open the chamber and dumped the bullets onto the floor. Bray relaxed, comfortable with the idea that I was no longer going to seam his forehead with one of the bullets. Instead, I flipped the short barrel in my grip, and with the taped handle, pistol-whipped him to the temple.

He fell to his knees, clutching his head. Blood streamed from between his fingers and he curled fetally on the floor. He still wasn't out. Christ, that guy had a thick forehead. He pushed himself onto all fours and crawled a couple of feet before falling back over.

Slowly, but with purpose, I walked to the trumpet case and threw it open. Inside was…

STILL ONLY A FUCKING TRUMPET.

What the hell had Bray seen in there? I had every intention of happily beating that information out of the bridge troll.

Except while I was making another unsuccessful attempt at figuring out what was so special about a trumpet, Bray was busy crawling.

To the dog cages.

Oh.

Fuck.

Blood covered his face, ran into his mouth. "Fuck you," he said through a tight gore-red smile.

Then he popped the latch.

And screamed the command.

"*Throat.*"

And for my next impression: Jessie Owens.

The dogs exploded from their crates at the exact same moment I ran through—

—yes, through—

—Bray's screen door, my panic and mass tearing it right off the hinges.

Lucky for me, Bray had installed an iron-gated door on the front of his trailer. I slammed shut the heavy door behind me a half second before the first pit's jaws of death clamped down onto an iron bar an inch from my fingers.

You're going to think I'm crazy, but I swear to God, I thought the iron bent under the impact from Fido's skull. The gray pit hit the door behind the second one, and the whole trailer shuddered.

I was so concerned with the dogs that I hadn't noticed the woozy Bray had crawled over to the bullets and gun I'd idiotically thrown to the floor. The first bullet *spaaannng*-ed off the bar next to my face, showering me with sparks. I dropped to the ground and rolled away from the door. The latch held against the pit bulls' assault, but I couldn't be sure for how long.

However, I did know how long it would take for a slug to catch me.

I vaulted over the rail, dropped three feet, tucked the trumpet case under my arm, and ran, ran, ran like two hundred and forty pounds of shit through a goose.

I made it twenty feet before I heard the gated door screeching open. I didn't know if it was the dogs or the hairy beardo with a reloaded gun. I didn't like either option.

The second bullet whizzed past my ear and smacked into the tree directly to my left.

I had the first part of that question answered.

I turned my head away from the shards of bark that flew off the tree and saw the dogs bearing down on me.

I could serpentine through the trees as I worked down the hill, lessening the chances of my skull getting split with a bullet, but increasing those of my getting caught by the dogs and becoming man-flavored Alpo.

Fuck it. I might be able to hold off the dogs. There was no way I could fight a bullet.

I cut to the right sharply, ducking below a dead pine as the second shot shredded the dry wood by my neck. The gray-mottled dog overestimated its charge and ran past me, but not before snapping at my wrist as momentum carried it too far. I zigged back to the left and ran for the line of cars.

Thank God only one of the shitboxes was red, so I bolted toward it and hoped that it was the Omni.

The brown dog came at me from the other side, right out of my blind spot. I shifted my hips at the last possible microsecond and avoided the dog enjoying a full serving of my ass cheek. In doing so, my feet slid out from under me on the icy ground.

Deciding to let my fat ass do the work, I transitioned my inelegant topple into a Macho Man Randy Savage Atomic Elbow onto the dog's thick skull. Half WWE—half Loony Toones, but fuck it. Whatever worked,

The dog yelped and backed off for a moment, my elbow exploded in pain, and I wanted to apologize.

I like dogs.

I really do.

But for some goddamn reason—between Burrito, my own adopted Chihuahua, Pickles, and now these two—they were always trying to kill me. There wasn't any time to feel bad about clobbering the murder dog, though. Its partner had found its footing and was ready to come at me again.

I found myself pleading with the hairy kill machines. "Heel!"

Didn't work.

"Good boy! I like dogs! Please don't kill me!" Didn't work either.

I couldn't remember what Bray's order was for the dogs to stand down.

Wait…

"Stand down!" I yelled.

Both dogs immediately sat on their haunches, but kept growling a low rumble at me. I took a step toward the red car, and both dogs increased the volume of growl, stepping between me and the car. I was boxed in.

Where was Bray?

Then I realized why the shooting had stopped.

A loud grinding metal sound startled all three of us.

Bray had gone back inside the trailer.

And the gate was closing.

The loud noise of the moving chain link took the dogs' attention off me for just long enough.

I ran first for the car, getting a few strides in before I heard the dogs' paws scrabble frantically on the gravel in order to launch themselves back into the chase.

Twenty feet.

Ten feet.

Then the floodlights fired back on, blinding me for just enough time to miss the swath of thick ice that was right in front of me.

My eyes refocused one step too late.

And this was no slippery gravel that I could majestically parlay into a primetime wrestling move.

No siree.

This ice was thick, and wide, and boy-oh-boy was going to hurt.

I hit Mother Nature's Slip'N Slide at top speed. My feet went up and over my head. I spun in the air at an angle of about 112 degrees and came down hard, all the breath knocked clean out of me.

And somehow, that was the luckiest thing that could have happened. Gray dog hit the ice running even harder than I was. If he wasn't trying to turn me inside out with his fangs, the dog's expression of panic and confusion might have been funny as it rocketed past me on the ice, down the hill, and out through the slowly closing gate.

Wheezing, I got to my feet and limped toward the comically tiny car with Omni written above the bumper.

The brown dog leaped for my throat as I reached for the handle. I held up the only thing I had to put in the dog's mouth that wasn't part of my anatomy. The dog's teeth clamped down on the trumpet case with a crunch. He shook his head so violently, something popped in my wrist, but I managed to hang onto the handle of the case.

"Let go, you sonofabitch," I yelled.

The dog went into another violent spasm, trying to wrest the case out of my hand, and I couldn't help but think in the moment how glad I was that it wasn't my throat between those teeth.

With one final pull on both our parts, the handle tore off the case, and one of the latches ripped off in the dog's jaws.

The gray bitch came back around the car, snarling, as I tucked the case under my arm and reached for the door handle.

They had me dead bang. I wasn't going to get in the car with all of my meat still attached to the bones.

Then two bullets smacked into the dirt between us, kicking up snow and stinging chunks of earth right up into the dog's muzzles. The gray dog yipped in pain and surprise and scuttled away behind the other cars.

Bray was back, and his terrible aim had just saved my structural integrity.

Both dogs scattered for a second, giving me barely enough distance to get inside the car. I opened the door and dove in, chucking the murder trumpet onto the passenger seat. I got my door shut just as the gray dog smashed her whole body weight into it. She struck the car with enough force to knock the trumpet case onto the floor all the way over on the other side of the vehicle. Her brother ran around the passenger side as I popped the key into the ignition and prayed that I was in the right car.

The engine roared to life. Well, it felt like a roar. A roar of victory. It was an Omni, however, and the reality was that the engine came to life with a sound like an asthmatic twelve-year-old trying to play a tuba.

I roared with victory.

Then, through some goddamn doggie intuition, the brown hellbeast locked his teeth right onto the handle of the unlocked passenger door, yanking it open.

Fuck it.

I dropped the car into drive and stomped on the gas.

With more gravity and ice to propel it than actual horsepower, the car dropped down the hill toward the closing gate. The passenger door slammed shut, but the dog hung on tight like a streamer on a little girl's bicycle handlebars.

What was left for an opening in the gate didn't have enough room for the car and the dog.

Sorry, Fido.

The impact of dog-to-fence was sickening. I didn't know what part of the dog hit the fence, but it popped him off the side, tearing the door handle off with it. In the rearview, I saw the brown furred assassin flopping end over end behind the car.

Then he got right up and resumed his chase.

What the fuck was up with these dogs?

I yanked the steering wheel hard onto the road with minimal drift.

Both hellhounds gave chase for three blocks before I put enough distance between us for it to break their doggy spirits.

I couldn't believe I'd made it through all that with only a rapidly swelling wrist. It was unbe-fucking-lievable! I wanted to cheer and sing at the top of my lungs. I pounded on the roof of the car with my good hand and whooped at what was undoubtedly a change for the better as far as my fortunes were concerned.

I wanted music, and whiskey, and women. But since I only had the car radio, and a distinct lack of whiskey and women available in the car, I cranked the volume all the way up and let her rip.

Right onto a radio station playing Taylor Swift.

Good God, no.

And the tuner knob was busted.

Why have you forsaken me, oh Father?

The trumpet.

FUCK! THE TRUMPET!

I pulled the car off the road and behind a darkened Sunoco station by the on ramp. I shut the engine off and listened to the engine tick and groan as it cooled in the freezing air. Or maybe that was my heart going bugnuts off the adrenaline dump and terror that the trumpet had been rendered worthless by a goddamn dog.

If those teeth were strong enough to pull a door handle off, there was no telling the damage they might have done to my one possible bargaining chip. I didn't have clue one about how these things were appraised, but I was sure that chew marks would dramatically lower the value of the thing.

The trumpet itself looked undamaged, thank Jesus, Buddha, Allah, and any other god or saint that looked after trumpets. I ran my fingers over the cold brass, feeing for indentations, but found none. Then I rubbed it two more times quickly just to see if a genie would pop out. For all I knew, I was in possession of the magical trumpet from Milo Davis's *Arabian Nights*.

Nope. No genie. But if one had popped out, it wouldn't have been the strangest incident of my week.

What my fingertips did find were a pair of deep fang grooves in the felt right at the point where the clasp had been ripped off. Where the felt met the plastic hardshell, one leftover canine—were all dog teeth canines?—jutted out from the bloody root. Yuck.

It left a pinkie finger-size hole between the board and the velvet. So, of course, I stuck my pinkie finger in it. I was only human.

Then the felt popped up.

As did the lateral half of the trumpet.

That's right. Half.

It wasn't a trumpet in there at all. Somebody had gotten industrious and cleanly cut a trumpet in half, made a small indent in the felt to make it look like there was space underneath, and then kept the bottom half empty.

The felt backing was heavy, covering a metal plate of some kind. I guessed that it was lined with lead, to throw off x-ray machines in airports and the whatnot. Looking from the top, it sure as hell looked like a damn trumpet.

The million-dollar question: what was in the hollow bottom?

Whatever was being so carefully camouflaged was tightly wrapped in what appeared to be strips of black garbage bag, then bound with duct tape. Each brick was three inches deep and three by six inches across the top. Whatever was in there, it sure wasn't going to improve my day.

I pulled out one package, which was snugly placed next to six more, side by side in the case. I tore a corner off the plastic and tore the duct tape along the length with my teeth.

Then I knew what Bray had tried to end me over, what a fake cop was willing to take out three people for. I knew why Byron had wound up on a Revere street corner with his skull staved in.

And boy, was I ever wrong.

What was in there improved my day. A whole fucking lot.

Each packet contained three wrapped bundles of hundred dollar bills.

That added up to…a buttload of money. It was too goddamn cold and I was too goddamn amped up to do the math in the moment.

I started hyperventilating.

I got out of the car and took deep gulps of frosty air as I leaned onto the still-warm hood. Wasn't that what you were supposed to do when you hyperventilated? Breathe or not breathe? I didn't know, but it wasn't helping. I was going to wind up passed out in the parking lot if I didn't figure it out soon.

Then red and blue lights started dancing between the trees along the side of the gas station.

A spotlight soon followed.

Looked like Bray had made a phone call to his cop buddies not long after I'd peeled out.

Then bad got worse when I realized I was quite likely parked behind the Sunoco where Officers R.J. and Stephanie had been playing moisten the nightstick.

I looked back at the money and realized it was also great. Really great.

I held my breath and stuck to the shadow of the building as the police car passed. My instinct to get the car off the road and not just pull over had been the right one. The years in St. Gabe's had served me well. You doing something, anything you didn't want people to see? You went to a place where they wouldn't see you, even if it was in the middle of the night in Bumblefuck, Massachusetts.

The flashing lights passed, then moved toward the exit ramp ahead that I would have been heading for.

The glow from the arcing spotlight slowly moved away. Then they were gone.

I exhaled the breath I'd been holding, and my lungs felt better immediately. So there. Hold breath when hyperventilating. Learned something new every day.

I climbed back into the car and held the money up to my nose and breathed deeply. It smelled like most of the problems in my life taking the first bus out of Boosville.

Of all the contraband that could have been hidden in there, it was the one thing I actually knew what to do with. If it had been bags of coke, or pills, or state secrets, I'd have been screwed.

But what the hell was I thinking?

This was the reason Junior was in lockup. I needed to figure out whose money it was.

Problem was, it could be anybody's money.

Just like it could be mine.

I shook my head.

No.

This amount was the killing kind. If I could find out where it was supposed to end up, or who it was coming *from*, then I'd most likely have a definitive bead on whoever took Byron out.

Mystery solved, me and Junior off our hooks.

Except I had no idea where to go from here.

It was just after 3 a.m. when I made it back to Boston proper. In that car, it was a miracle I made it at all. Every mile or so, the transmission would give a sickly whirr, then catch again. Each time, I found myself gently patting the dashboard and talking to the damn thing.

It was in those moments that I understood Junior's relationship to Miss Kitty.

I hadn't eaten a thing since the diner with Junior, which felt like a decade ago. I got a sack of Mexican goodness from El Triunfo in East Berkeley. While a 3:30 a.m. shrimp and bean burrito might not be the greatest gastrointestinal choice in your country club, it was either that or a microwave barbecue sandwich at Store 24. So don't you fucking judge me.

I paid for my late-night snack with the hundy off the top of the open stack for two reasons.

One: I wanted to make sure that my enthusiasm wasn't going to be cut down by finding out the hard way that I was dragging around stacks of counterfeit bills. The nagging voice in my head that had read too many Ed McBain novels needed to know.

Two: Whoever was the rightful owner of the money could suck my chode. I'd earned at least a burrito in payment for my recovery services. The voice that had read all of John D. Macdonald's Travis McGee books told me so.

The Hispanic kid raised his eyebrow when I handed him the crisp bill, no doubt having seen his share of fake bills during the late hours. He held it up to the light, ran his thumb across the paper, then took out a counterfeit pen and drew a wide X across Benjamin Franklin's face.

He rang in my tab on the register and gave me change.

Sweet bleedin' eyes o' Jeebus, it was all real.

I PARKED IN the municipal lot behind the bar, stuck the burrito under my arm, and grabbed the trumpet case. The Cellar had been closed for two hours, so it was as safe a place as any for me to rest my head. My apartment was still off-limits until I knew who had targeted me there. My first thought had been Summerfield as the obvious suspect, but with all the current goings on, I couldn't be so sure any more. At least The Cellar I could lock down.

I locked the door and turned directly into a flashlight beam shining in my eyes. Instinctively, I threw my hands into the air. The burrito hit the concrete with a wet splat.

"Where have you been?" yelled the man blinding me.

"Goddamn it, Underdog. Look what you did to my burrito."

"I don't care even the slightest about your freaking burrito. I've been looking for you all night."

"Weren't you the one who told me to go out and find a reason not to put me and Junior in jail?" I bent over to collect what remained of what was now a taco salad. "And shut off that fucking light."

"I also told you to stay in touch with me." He shut the Maglite off, then pointed it at my hand. "What is that?"

"It's a trumpet case."

"Why are you carrying a trumpet case? And what are you driving? Where is Junior's car?"

"Any particular order you want me to answer those questions?"

"Do you really want to be a smartass right now, Boo?"

"You really want to be the cop right now? Or are you my friend? Hard to tell nowadays."

Underdog sighed, his long exhalation frozen on the night air. His shoulders slumped back into their submissive position. Like the Hulk in reverse, Brendan Miller the police officer slowly shrunk back into Underdog. Sweet, needy, pliable Underdog.

My burrito-spurred appetite dwindled as guilt washed over me. Second time in two days I'd forced him into submission, when if I was a real friend, I should be doing everything I could to keep him strong. Underdog was a mess—a human trash fire. Brendan Miller was the man I wanted my friend to be.

It made me feel like shit, but I didn't need another cop in my night. I needed Underdog. But if I was the type of guy who needed to knock a man down to where I felt he wasn't an enemy, what did that make me?

I didn't like feeling like a bad friend.

"You know?" Underdog said. "Every day, it gets easier to understand how people might want to shoot you."

As a reminder, the cold was starting to crush my old knee wound with an icy vise. "Listen, can we at least get inside a car and talk?"

"Which brings me to my first question. Where's the Buick?" Underdog opened the door to his sedan, gesturing for me to get in the other side.

"I don't have it." Not the whole truth. I needed to dodge lying where I could. I was bad at it. And the cop in Underdog would sniff it out right away. So I left it at that as I slid into his unmarked police car. I hoped it was the last time I would be getting into one for a long, long time

"Where is it?"

"I don't know."

"You're lying to me, Boo."

Goddammit.

"There's an APB on it, so it'll turn up sooner or later. Why don't you save us both the trouble?"

"I can't."

Underdog rubbed his eyes vigorously. "So, the car that is possibly going to be pivotal in a murder investigation is…what? Missing?"

"Yeah."

"You're supposed to be helping me here, Boo. This does not help. What's in the trumpet case?"

"Something that might help."

Underdog glared at me. Again, it wasn't a full-on pants-on-fire lie, so it must have thrown his radar off. "You want to give it to me?"

"Not yet." *Probably not ever*, said a voice in the back of my brain.

"Should I bother asking where you've been?"

"I wouldn't suggest it."

Underdog closed his eyes and slowly bellowed out his cheeks with a pained exhalation. "I can't help but feel like you're not taking this as seriously as you should, Boo. When they charge Junior—"

"When?"

"When. The homicide guys feel they got a slam dunk. So, when they charge him, they'll be coming for you not long after. You understand that, right?"

"I understand that."

"You also understand that it's worse than just that. Why did Byron have Junior's phone in his pocket?"

"I have no idea. We tussled. Confusion ensued."

"Confusion ensued? That what you're going to say in court?"

"How bad is it looking?"

"Almost as bad as it can get, Boo. They've decided to move forward with this as a hate crime. Your bad got worse."

My suddenly dry throat clicked as I swallowed. "There's no way to prove that one way or the other."

"Well, with Junior referring to the victim casually as 'the faggot' three times during interrogation, I don't think they'll have to try too hard."

"Is it going to help in court that, to Junior, the use of that word is less of a slur than a descriptive?"

Underdog hung his head sadly. "You can get out of my car now."

I opened the door with a sinkhole feeling in my gut, like I was leaving behind a broken piece of our friendship in the car. "If I can figure anything else out…"

"Close the door," said Brendan Miller.

I did.

He drove off, leaving me with nothing but deepening desperation and a cold and dirty burrito.

Fuck me.

I went in through the back, hoping Luke was done for the night. I quietly opened the metal back door, which screeched on the hinges like an attacking Pteranodon.

Luke poked his head around the corner of the basement stairs. "Who's there?" His skinny arms held the mop handle aloft.

"It's me, Luke."

"Oh, Mr. Boo, you gave me a fright. Weird vibes running through here tonight."

"What? What's happening?" Automatically, I went into caveman mode. The Cellar was my cave away from cave. Part of the reason I was good at what I did was that The Cellar really was a home to me, and I was honestly protective of her.

Oh Christ, did I just call The Cellar "her"?

I'd always busted Junior's balls for naming Miss Kitty as such. I'd driven his car for less than a day, and now I was suffering *The Shining*-like symptoms of his personality.

"G.G. said there was a lotta people looking for you tonight. Where were you, by the way? Don't you normally work Sundays?"

"I had errands to run." I opened my burrito wrapper and flopped my tired ass onto a barstool. What was inside looked more like Tijuana slurry than anything edible, but it was all I had. I tore off a piece of mangled tortilla and did my best to mop up the mess.

Luke's face scrunched up. "Don't know that you want to be eating that, Mr. Boo."

I popped the mess into my mouth. Still tasted good. But at that point, a sewer rat might have tasted like foie gras. Luke winced. I went on. "What else?"

Luke snapped his fingers like he'd remembered something. "The girl, works here…Ginny. Don't know what's going on with that young girl, but she was crying something fierce when I came in."

"Wait, she came here? She was still here when you got here?"

"Thought that was strange too. There was some new girl working her tables, and Ginny came in anyway. Just sat at the bar drinkin' like she was trying to hurt herself, drinking with a man with a silly-looking moustache who I'd be willing to bet was not the source of her heartbreak," Luke put a finger under his lower eyelid, "if you catch my drift."

I caught it. "What time?"

"This was around midnight. Came in early tonight. Audrey gave me a call, said the beer compressor was acting up."

I guessed Ginny and Dana had come here for the same reason I had. The Cellar represented the safest place we had. I felt a twinge of guilt for cutting them loose like I did, but I had no idea what else I was supposed to do. Were they the reason an APB got put on the car, or was it the cops digging deeper into Byron's death? Had they cracked? "When did she leave?"

"Dunno. I was working on the compressor. Got back upstairs while Audrey was counting the money. They was gone by then."

"Who else was looking for me?"

"I dunno. G.G. left messages for you upstairs. I know that Brendan came by twice after the doors shut, asking where you were. Ain't he a police officer?"

"Yeah."

Luke's eyes narrowed at me suspiciously. "Anything I need to know or that you'd like to disclose?"

"I got nothing, Luke." Really, I didn't. How I'd managed to make it through this entire day without achieving any knowledge other than a probable motive was beyond me. I'd have to backtrack to Ginny's in the morning. This had been one losing battle of a day.

"Well, I'm done in about fifteen more minutes, so I'll leave you to your thoughts. At least until you want to share 'em." Luke beamed his best grin at me, and I'd be damned if it didn't make me feel a bit better.

With all of the dirty, nasty, ignorant, mean motherfuckers in my life, some of whom were my best friends, there were still people in it like Luke. To step outside myself sometimes made me ashamed of who I was. What I'd made of my life. Luke's simple kindness humbled me. And did so nearly on a nightly basis.

As he went down to finish his cleaning, I poured myself a thick finger and a half of Jim Beam and downed it. The bottle had a finger's worth left in it, so I popped that back too. There was a backup bottle under the bar. I cracked that one open and took a long pull. I wasn't drinking for any reason other than I wanted to get good and ripping drunk.

Things Ginny said had hit me. Without putting words to it, Junior and I, from the time we were at The Home right up until today, we'd fashioned ourselves the anti-bullies. We bullied the bullies without allowing the irony of that existence to seep into our consciousness. Any man should be able to handle his shit—to a degree. If you stepped to one of our friends? If anybody tried to lord themselves physically over someone else on our watch? There were fewer things we found more enjoyable than being a counterweight on the Darwinist scale.

But, somehow, someway, all of that unspoken philosophy had gone out the window over the last couple of days. And it all came down to dick. Ginny made me realize that we'd abandon our protective stance if somebody was gay. Simple as that. And her assumption that this would be the case pissed me off.

Because her assumption was straight-up right on the nose.

I wished I could explain why that was.

I couldn't even discern where my natural alpha male protect-the-tribe instinct stopped kicking in and ran screaming in the other direction. It just did.

Maybe my open mind wasn't quite as open as I'd deluded myself into thinking it was.

Maybe we weren't the knights in shining armor we liked to envision ourselves as. Shit, we were barely serfs in dirty underwear.

By the time I came to the end of my deep, dark musings on the number of things that made me an asshole—new things, anyway—I'd polished off another third of the new bottle.

I heard Luke say good night. I responded, noticing a slur creeping into my pronunciations. I headed toward the back stairs, legs a little wobbly, and made my way up to the office. I would take a few hours sleeping on the desk, and then hit tomorrow fresh. Junior... Where was Junior? Was he still being questioned? How long could they question somebody?

The whiskey sloshed around the burrito in my stomach as my entire body cried out for sleep. I unlocked the office door and threw my jacket on the floor. Flopping into the threadbare desk chair, I saw my burner phone next to Junior's phone—Byron's phone—which he'd left when Underdog walked him out.

I had to stop being so hard on Dog. Simply allowing me to hang on to the phone wasn't the action of a cop. It was the action of a friend.

Both phones' batteries were dead. I fumbled through the lost and found drawer until I found the right chargers amongst the tangle of wires.

I crossed my arms on the desk and lay my head down. I felt every muscle give in to inertia. Before I exhaled, my eyelids slowly drifted down...

Something thumped loudly in the stairwell.

My eyes popped open as I inhaled sharply through my nose.

Blood immediately began surging in my ears as all the old anger flared.

Enough was enough.

I was suddenly and actively murderous.

Enough.

This whole time, I'd been running against a tide, backpedaling. Trying to advance while maintaining a steady retreat.

I wasn't a runner. Fuck that. it went against every natural instinct I had to fight.

Fight or flight, and flight was for pussies.

Boo Malone was going to show whoever was in that stairwell just what a fucking fighter was.

It was time to move this shit forward, fists first.

I pulled the door open hard, screaming my best blue-face-paint-balls-hanging-out-in-a-kilt Highlander war cry. Whoever was coming up those stairs was getting themselves one hell of a surprise along with a face full of whiskey bottle.

Except I was the one who wound up surprised when my war cry was met with a very high-pitched terrified shriek.

I was even more surprised when Ginny stabbed me in the stomach.

My war cry ended with just a loud, "Ow!"

The "ow" was more for the shrill tone emanating from Ginny than the knife, which didn't hurt yet.

But it would. Boy howdy, I was willing to bet my ass on that.

Ginny's mouth fell open as she realized precisely who she'd perforated. "Oh God, Boo! What are you doing here?"

I looked down at my belly.

Yup.

That was a knife handle sticking out of me about three inches to the left of my bellybutton. "The fuck are *you* doing? Did you just stab me?"

Her face blanched. "I didn't know it was you. You scared the piss out of me!" She quickly pulled the blade out of my abdomen. She'd got me right above the hip. I felt the blade skip off the bone as she removed it.

I clamped my hand over my newest wound. Blood quickly seeped between my knuckles. "I don't think you're supposed to pull—"

Oh yeah. There was the pain that had been missing. My abdomen cramped immediately and a white flash exploded before my eyes. The ol' knees buckled and I slumped into the stairwell. "Ow," I reiterated for good measure.

"I'm so sorry!" Ginny's fingertips flittered around my general area, as though unsure whether touching me would make things worse somehow. Or maybe she was just grossed out.

I took a deep breath and pulled myself up by the handrail. "Can I please have that knife?"

She clutched the knife to her chest, my blood running down the blade. "Are you going to stab me?"

"Not right now." I held my hand out. She placed the fruit knife with the green handle into my hand. Small blessing, the knife only had a two-inch blade that the bartenders used to cut limes. Hurt like a bitch, but it probably hadn't filleted anything too important. Thank God the kitchen was locked at night, or she might have cut me in half with a real one off the butcher's block.

"What are you doing here?" I asked.

"I didn't have anywhere else to go, you prick. Remember the body you left on my floor? What are *you* doing here?"

"Same answer. Minus the body." I went back into the office and tried to lift my shirt up, but I couldn't lift my arms without another flare of bright pain. I handed her the knife back. "Would you mind cutting the shirt off of me?"

Ginny grabbed the hem at the bottom of my T-shirt and sawed through the material. Even through my whiskey haze, I could smell the rum coming off her. Once she cut through the thick base, the sharp knife zipped up the first six inches of material.

"Please don't slice me open any more than I already am."

"You want me to help or not?"

"Where's Dana?"

"He's passed out in the equipment room. Which is where we both were sleeping when we heard you clomping around up here. We heard Luke leave and thought..."

Which would explain why Luke didn't know they were still in the building. Since the equipment room was off limits to anyone who wasn't staff, he wouldn't have to clean it as regularly as the high-traffic areas that usually ended up painted with spilled beer and vomit.

She slowly worked the knife up to the neck. "Oh..." she said. "Oh, wow."

I was so wrapped up in my current predicament—what with having been stabbed and all—that I hadn't been thinking about the slasher-movie assortment of scars on my torso. The self-consciousness was bad enough when Blanc got a look at them. Call it whatever the fuck you want, but my body-consciousness skyrocketed when a woman got a look at them. I normally kept them well-hidden, even during intimate moments with the odd young ladies who every now and then chose to fiddle my diddle.

I was a lights-off guy, to put it simply.

I felt myself blushing, my cheeks and neck going hot. "Guess the good news is that my new scar will hardly be noticed amongst the general mess, huh?"

"Dude. What happened to you?"

"Porcupine," I said. "Porcupine with a butterfly knife. Attacked me at a camp site when I was twelve."

Ginny glared at me. "I don't have to help you, you know."

"And I don't need to tell you my fucking life story right now. You stabbed me. I would hope that alone might be enough reason for you to help me."

I took a bottle of vodka off the liquor shelf and cracked the cap.

"At least this is going to hurt you," she said. Adding, "Dick."

She had that right.

This was going to hurt.

And I was a dick.

I poured the vodka directly onto the wound.

And screamed my head off in a tone oddly reminiscent of Whitney Houston after stepping in a bear trap.

Boy howdy.

When the dancing pain-lights fled my vision, I took two clean bar rags from the linens, soaked one in the vodka, covered it with a dry one, and pressed them against the hole. "Duct tape is in the upper right hand drawer."

"Seriously?"

"Just do it."

With a noticeable blear in her eyes, she tore off a long strip of the gray tape and wrapped it around me at an angle. I gritted my teeth as she pulled a second strip tight. That tiny hole hurt more than I wanted to let on.

What little chauvinistic manliness I had remaining didn't want Ginny to feel guilty for the pain I was in.

The pain.

From her stabbing me in the fucking stomach.

MANLINESS!

Ain't that some shit?

I closed my eyes against the hurt and tried to think of England. Except I'd never been to England. I'd never been anywhere. So I found the next best thing and inhaled the pleasant smell of Ginny's perfume and shampoo mingling with the spicy rum wafting off her.

It took a couple seconds after the fourth strip was applied before I realized nothing more was happening. I opened my eyes, and saw Ginny's alcohol-wobbly gaze looking up at me.

It was equal parts terror, apology, and a dash of plain old sexy-time.

I hadn't seen that last look in a while.

As her fingertips pressed against my ribs, where she held the duct tape, I was suddenly aware of the heat coming off of me, coming off of her as she straddled my leg in order to get the tape on me.

Before I could say or do anything about it, she pressed her mouth to mine and kissed me deeply.

Stabbing as foreplay?

Why not?

I wasn't even sure she was particularly attracted to me, but in that moment, all things considered, the act was a "fuck you" to death. Two stabbings and beatings and all of the bad things that had rained down on our heads like so much bird shit pouring from the anus of an angry avian god.

That, and we were hammered.

It was an acceptance of drunken release and animal want. It was a damned good kiss, despite the overwhelming taste of Captain Morgan on her tongue. I pushed all thoughts of pirates out of my head and leaned into her kiss.

She broke off the smooching, grabbed my face and said, "I so fucking hate you, Boo Malone."

Fair enough. She wasn't the first woman to express the sentiment. Kelly had expressed similar vitriol less than twenty-four hours ago. I reached for my sweatshirt. Guess we were done here.

She reached for my belt.

Maybe we weren't done here.

It was the angriest unbuckling of my belt I'd ever experienced. Then I realized that I was angry too. I grabbed her hair hard and planted my own solid whiskey kiss on her mouth. I grabbed Ginny under the ass with my other hand and spun her around, seating her on the edge of my desk, hands reaching for the buttons on her jeans.

She got her hand inside my boxers and gave my junk a good, possessive squeeze. It hurt, but man oh man, it hurt *real* good.

I got her pants to her ankles, then tore her damn panties off.

It was a ferocious fucking. I think she punched me in the face once in the middle there, but it might have been a drunken flail on her part. We fucked the death, the fear, and the fear of death off of us. We fucked because, goddammit, we were alive. And nothing said you were alive like a good, stinky, bruising, sweaty, hair-pulling, ass-slapping, thigh-pounding, possible-face-punching toss in the hay.

Once or twice, my mind flashed to Kelly. And the anger kicked in harder, so I laid into Ginny a little harder as a result.

Okay, maybe three times.

In all fairness, when Ginny wasn't snarling at me, her eyes would wander off on their own, no doubt imagining who she would rather have been with at that moment. But we both made do with the available drunken genitalia in the room.

We finished up and Ginny lifted a leg and pushed me off with a heel under my hip. I was just thankful it wasn't the side she'd stabbed.

The exertion had made the wound bleed though the bar rags, and pink sweat dribbled from under the duct tape.

Then it dawned on me that the last time I'd had sex, which was with Kelly, I'd had a traumatic knee injury. I hoped there wasn't any kind of karmic balance at play. Because Lord knows, I enjoy sex, but I didn't know how much trauma my body could manage in order to facilitate the exchange.

Then the mood got awkward right quick.

Ginny slipped her bra back on, not looking at me, then gave her head a small, almost imperceptible "I can't believe I did that" shake.

If I'd had any self-esteem left, that might have bruised it.

"Uhhh..." I said. "Where's Dana?"

"He's still passed out in the equipment room."

"Oh. Okay, listen..."

She held her hand up and winced, angrily putting her top back on. "No. Please don't make this any weirder than it already is. I don't need platitudes and Hallmark liners right now. I just needed..." She paused, trying to find more elegant words for *to get laid*.

I saved her the effort. "I was going to say that you could crash on the desk if you wanted. It's warmer up here than in the basement."

She gave me a weird look, as though she was a little disappointed I didn't even offer a Hallmark sentiment she'd said she didn't want.

I do not understand women. At all. The end.

She shook her head, tying back her wild hair with a rubber band from my desk. "I'm going back to the equipment room. I just need to close my eyes for a couple hours before we figure out what we're going to do."

"Well, I'm kind of at an impasse."

"No offense, but our 'we' doesn't include you. I think you've done enough."

"Then I hate to break it to you, but you are both part of mine. This is still technically your fault, or have you conveniently forgotten that?"

"Have you forgotten that your psycho friend killed a man in my home?"

"Have you forgotten that my psycho friend possibly saved your life?"

"I am not continuing this conversation until you at least put your pants back on."

Dammit. The strength of my argument might have been damaged by delivering it in my boxers with the pee-hole wide open. I hastily addressed my pants.

Ginny closed her eyes and blew out a rum-soaked breath. "Listen, I'm drunk and exhausted. I need to crash out. We're both in bad places right now. Let's hash it out in the morning."

"Fine." I caught myself before I thanked her for the sex.

She walked down the steps and I looked at the two phones charging on the desk. My burner had almost a dozen messages. The first was from Underdog, telling me we had to talk. Well, that we did. I didn't know how he'd gotten the number, but it was most likely from Junior. The second and third were from Junior, cursing a lot and saying that they hadn't charged him with anything yet. Three more from Underdog. More of the same. More of Junior cursing.

The last was from Twitch.

Yeah. These guys are done. They did an awesome job. Didn't have to shoot anybody, so I guess that's a plus.

Well, wasn't that just ducky.

Place is cleaner than when we got here. I'm, uh, gonna have some beers with them and then I guess I'll go home. They're all right. They gave me a card in case I ever need their services.

Jesus. Nice to hear that Twitch was making new friends.

So I guess I'll go home and I'll find you tomorrow. Peace.

I had no doubt he would find me. I was a little afraid he would.

I looked at Byron's phone and my heart-rate skyrocketed.

There were twenty-four messages showing.

The display only told me the number of messages, not who they were from, or when they were from. I needed to know who was so eager to get in touch with the departed. Especially if any of those messages happened before Byron got himself cooled.

I needed to crack the password.

And I had an ace up my sleeve where technology was concerned.

I needed Ollie.

I rang his phone, but he didn't answer, no doubt still pissed off at us.

When the voice mail beeped, I said, "Ollie, call me back, brother. We need your help."

I took a few more pulls off the whiskey bottle to calm my newly excited brain.

I had something, but the answer was going to be unavailable until the morning, at least.

I closed my eyes and lay my head down with a smile on my face for the first time in days.

Gotcha, fucker.

"WAKE UP." GINNY placed a black coffee next to my head, then handed me a bagel.

"Thanks. What time is it?"

"Ten after one."

Good Christ. The bar was already open. I was hungover, but damn, the sleep felt good. I looked at the burner. No message from Ollie. Guess there was my answer to how pissed off he still was.

"Where's Dana?"

"He's downstairs. Audrey is trying to get some hair of the dog into him.

He's not quite made of the sturdy stuff that we are."

"Keep an eye on him or Audrey is going to jam the entire kennel down his throat."

"If I say he can handle himself, are you gonna say something wiseass?"

"It's a safe bet that I might."

"Then let's leave it at that. How's the uh…" She wiggled a finger at my new hole.

I gave it a quick look. It had stopped bleeding, but was rimmed with a fiery red inflammation. I was going to have to get some anti-bacterial ointment and redress it. Last thing I needed was to add an infection to my list of growing ailments. "Looks dandy," was all I said to her.

"Can I say I'm sorry again?"

"Sure. You made up for it," I said, trying to lighten the air.

"Just…don't," she said, holding a hand up as she turned and walked back down the stairs.

Self-esteem awaaaay!

I shoved a huge chunk of bagel and cream cheese into my mouth and followed Ginny down to the bar. I chased it with a scalding mouthful of Dunkins, which woke me more with the burning than the caffeine.

Dana sat at the bar, looking greener than the Grinch and about half as happy. Audrey was doing her thing, Jack and water in one hand, the other rubbing Dana's back with a motherly love. "Drink it, hon. You'll feel better." She took a gulp of her own beverage, then slid a merciless pint of Bloody Mary toward Dana.

"Gah," Dana replied before turning a half shade greener. With a jade-hued hand, he gamely took a big gulp, shuddered, but held it together.

Burrito scuttled up and down the bar, happily ignoring any and all health codes against fat hairy bags of fur in a food service area. My adopted dog gave me a thousand-yard Chihuahua stare and snarled. I could say he was mad due to my two-day absence, but the mangy prick was probably more concerned that I was there to take him home, away from Mama Audrey.

I sat down next to Dana. Audrey auto-piloted a shot of whiskey onto the bar in front of me. I dumped it into my coffee and took a big sip off the top. "So, let's begin at the begin. When did the shit start hitting the fan with you and Byron?"

He pressed his eyes together tight. "There was no shit. There was no fan. We hooked up over the course of a few months. We went dancing. I went to see his band on Mondays. We hooked up when it was convenient. We weren't looking for anything more than that. Nothing that should have wound up... where we are now."

"Is there anything, anything at all, you could tell me about what he did outside of playing in a band and fucking you?"

His eyes popped all the way open, and he shot me a look of indignation. "Well, that's awful presumptuous."

Ginny shook her head at me, disgusted. "You're such a dick."

"The fuck did I presume now?" I broke off a piece of bagel and put it on the bar for Burrito, who sniffed at it before licking at the cream cheese, giving me the hairy eyeball the whole time.

"How do you know who was fucking who, straight boy?" Dana's lip curled in a sneer.

"I was being metaphorical. He fucked you financially, didn't he?"

Dana and Ginny looked at one another.

"Listen," I said, "we all need to let whatever preconceptions we've got hanging over us go. You've both been pissy with me and Junior because of ours. I'm trying, really trying, to let my issues go. You two need to do the same if we're going to get anywhere here. For starters, could the two of you at least try to treat me like I'm not a flying asshole? 'Cause I'm really trying not to be." I looked to Dana. "I'm sorry if you feel like I was making assumptions."

Dana rolled his eyes. "As am I, then."

"To be fair, your own dog doesn't seem to like you very much," Ginny said, nodding at Burrito.

Burrito bared his crooked teeth at me again with a whistling snarl.

"Okay, if everyone is through crapping on me, can you two get yourselves back to the place where you liked me? Or at least where you liked me enough where you thought I was useful to your cause? I need your help here. Did you want me to say it? I'm saying it. I need your help."

"Was this point before I knew that you and your heterosexual life partner were violent homophobes?" Dana said with a sneer.

"You serious right now?" I said, my blood pressure ticking up a notch.

Ginny put her hand on Dana's forearm. "I don't know how to help you, Boo. I really don't," she said.

"What about you?" I said to Dana.

"What about me?" he said. "I didn't ask for your help in the first place. I didn't want any of this."

"We've all fucked up here, one way or the other," I said. "Least we can do is work together to un-fuck the situation as best we can."

"My only mistake was a poor choice in boyfriend," Dana said.

"Let's not forget your pirating something that belonged to him that led to his death. Let's not forget that, shall we?" I said.

Dana just turned his head from me.

"How about starting with the issues you two had with one another," I said, hearing a pleading in my voice that made me angrier. Blood pressure up another notch.

Dana braced himself with another mouthful of spicy tomato juice and vodka. He gave a pained sigh before he spoke. "Three weeks ago, Byron came back with the band from Europe. They had a couple gigs in Amsterdam and Germany. He came back, dropped some of his stuff at our place, then disappeared on us. After a week, I started getting pissy with him about the money he owed me—which he said he would pay me when he got back."

"I had to cover Dana's rent for the month," Ginny said.

"I didn't even have the rent because of that asshole."

I thought about the amounts of irony in play. How much could the rent have been? A grand? How much did Byron owe Dana? Maybe a couple grand?

The whole time, a fuckload of money sat in the closet. More than any one of us would see over a long stretch of our lives, if ever.

And Byron, schmuck that he was, couldn't get to it. He could have easily given Dana back the money that he owed out of the trumpet case.

But if he paid Dana out of the case, the people who the money belonged to were going to notice. People who were openly willing to kill for that kind of money.

And that could include a lot of people.

It was the Ouroboros of idiocy.

"Think the band might know?" I asked.

"Know what?" Dana said.

I almost blurted out about the money. Maybe I didn't need any more whiskey. But I sure as hell needed the coffee. Hell with it. I took another gulp of my laced brew. "Anything. Anything at all. Anybody who Byron might have pissed off enough—"

Ginny cleared her throat loudly, then darted her eyes past me to the bar.

Out of the corner of my eye, I saw Audrey hovering, her bartender ears tuned into our conversation while she polished the one martini glass behind the bar. The martini glass that hadn't had liquid in it sine 1983.

Christ. There was no way we were going to have this conversation without me accidentally saying something I wasn't supposed to or them saying something Audrey didn't need to be party to.

This was going nowhere. No matter how many times I tried to dig out anything, anything at all that could help, they didn't know a goddamn thing. They just didn't.

All I had left was the band. "You said you saw them on Mondays?"

"They have a regular gig in Cambridge every Monday night at Blue Envy."

"Are they playing tonight?"

"Is today Monday?" Dana said, not bothering to hide his disdain.

"You know, Dana? All that shit about us not helping you because you're gay? That's one thing. Right now, I would choose not to help you simply because you're an asshole."

Ginny stood up. "Okay, boys. We're all tired, hungover, and a lot freaked out. Why don't we all take a deep breath and try to work out what to do?"

"That's what I'm trying to goddamn do here. And his bitchy attitude isn't helping," I said, jabbing a finger at Dana's forehead.

"My bitchy..." Dana said, his voice rising. "My *bitchy* attitude?"

"Watch it," I said.

"Or what? You going to have your little buddy put a bullet—"

I grabbed him by the throat.

"Boo!" Ginny yelled

I heard Audrey, old school as ever, mutter into her Jack and water, "Talk a lot of shit, spit a lot of teeth."

Without a word, I dragged Dana through the bar, down the stairs, and out the back.

Ginny followed, yelling, "Don't hurt him, Boo. Let him go."

I fired a look at her. "We're simply going to have a nice talk."

I slammed him into the door-bar on the back door and pushed him all the way into the parking lot with my hand on his neck.

He let out a soft, pained grunt as I shoved him hard against the dumpster. "Listen up, you little dickhead," I said. "I'm at the point of not giving two shiny fucks anymore. You hear me?"

Dana's eyes were wide, his lips staring to go purple. He tried to say something, but his air was being constricted by the fingers o'mine I had clenched around his trachea.

"If you're understanding me, nod before you pass out."

Dana's chin moved.

"Boo!" Ginny said sternly as she followed us out.

I wheeled to her. "Shut your mouth, Ginny. Little man wants to talk tough? Then let him bring some tough to the table. I have had fucking enough!"

Ginny flinched under my fury.

I'd tried to be nice.

I really had.

"You can both see that, right?" I said.

Ginny nodded.

I felt Dana's chin move atop my fingers in an attempt to nod.

"Good. Now let's get something straight right here. I'm about a day away from my brother being railroaded for a killing he didn't do, and I'm on the fast track to following him right into a jail cell. I am beyond a point of caring about your issues when you're going to be a dick when I have questions for you. Understand?"

Dana nodded again.

"Just so you know exactly where I'm at, I don't give a rat's ass who you fuck, how you fuck them, or whatever goes up, into, or around your anus. What I care about is keeping me and mine out of a cage. What I also care about is the simple fact that you're a goddamn asshole, and no amount of sexuality is gonna influence my opinion deeper one way or the other."

Ginny said softly, but firmly, "Get off of him," and reached for my hand. With equal restraint, I took her in a tight grip by the front of her sweater and held her off at arm's length.

"Almost done," I said. But when I turned back to Dana, I saw the last thing I wanted to see. The look he was giving me had shed any fear that he was going to be hurt by the big bad man.

What I saw was the hatred and sadness of a small man. A small man who got called "faggot" his entire life. There was a shaking defiance in the look, and in my mind, I could imagine the other tormentors he'd faced off with that expression. Every jock who stuffed him into a locker. Every alpha who tried to knock him down simply because he thought he could, or should dominate the small boy who acted like a girl.

I was now in their company in his mind. And now I saw his bitchiness and attitude for what it was—his only weapon in a dangerous fucking world. Especially dangerous when guys like me and mine called him names, slammed him against dumpsters.

He'd been hurt before by other big bad men. I was presenting him with nothing to fear that he hadn't faced over and over again.

I let him go.

Dana sagged against the dumpster, his back sliding down the cold metal until he planted onto his ass, flakes of rust falling into his hair.

I let Ginny go too, and she ran over to Dana to help him back to his feet.

I still felt he was an asshole.

And his moustache was hella stupid.

I wasn't the bad guy here, but I sure as fuck wasn't the hero.

I wiped my hands on the front of my jeans, trying to maintain control though my self-righteousness had slipped into discomfort at being the bully. "So, now that that's done with, I'm gonna tell you what we are going to do. We are going to go back to the bar, you are going to answer my questions. That okay with everyone?"

Ginny tried to immolate me with her eyes. Dana wheezed and nodded.

"Good. Let's go back in. I'm freezing my balls off."

Audrey made a point of not looking at us when we re-entered. "Everything okay?"

"Peaches," I said. "So again," I said to Dana, "Byron's old band is supposed to play tonight?"

He cleared his throat. "Unless they're on the road. Or if they're even able to play. They are missing a trumpet player."

True that.

"What time they go on?"

"Nine-ish?"

It was almost three. I had some time to kill before I could talk to the band. I needed to make things right with Ollie somehow. Other than the band, the cell phone was the only road I had to any place other than IAin'tGotShitsville.

"What are you guys going to do?"

"What can we do?"

"You can go home."

"Can we?" Ginny asked, glaring.

I opened my mouth to answer, but then felt hypocritical for telling them they could. I'd abandoned my apartment right quick after the first assault. And those guys, whoever the hell they were, only left me with the impression that they were there to lay down some hurt on me. Not to end me like Galal Shaughness was there to do. Maybe. "It's all handled. Unless you want to go back to my place."

"Excuse me?" Ginny said, offense in her tone.

My mind raced *What the fuck was her problem now…ohhhhh sheeee-yit.* I held my palms up to her. "Wait, wait, wait—are you thinking that with all that's going on, I'm coming on to you for another round of abuse you call sex?"

Ginny's mouth formed a perfect O of horror and wrath.

Behind me, I heard Audrey spit-take a mouthful of Jack and water.

I went on. "Don't get your panties twisted, sister. Or are they still on the office floor?"

I know.

I shouldn't have said that.

But c'mon. That was a good one.

Either way, I knew it was just about the dickiest thing I could have said the moment the words left my lips—good one or not.

So…whoops.

Dana looked back and forth at the two of us. "Ew," he said softly, finally understanding what had happened while he slept in his alcohol-induced coma.

Ginny gave me a pretty solid right hook to the mouth and stormed out the door.

Dana gasped.

Audrey wheezed.

Burrito yipped and snapped at my fingers.

Dana followed Ginny out the door, off to who knew the hell where.

Audrey handed me a short stack of bar napkins and another shot.

I dipped the napkin into the whiskey and dabbed it against my lip. It burned like hell, but didn't seem to be bleeding too much.

Audrey's eyes were watery with the laughter she was holding in.

"Please don't," was all I said.

And it was all she needed. The dam burst and she spent the next ten minutes guffawing at me. "You got less game than the Special Olympics, Willie."

THE SNOW HAD started falling in thick clumps again, because, you know, fuck me and my life. As strong winds blew sideways, I relished the one advantage the Omni had over Junior's Buick. Unlike Miss Kitty, the shitbox I was currently sitting in had an operational heating system.

Without warning, I was flooded with guilt at my disparaging thoughts toward Junior's old car, and…a little grief?

What the fuck was wrong with me?

Junior was the sentimentalist amongst the two of us. Part of my varying and often self-destructive defense mechanisms was the ability to let go, to separate myself from the painful memories of my past, my childhood.

Junior embraced and expanded on them. Where my apartment and living conditions could be considered Spartan at best, Junior decorated his apartment with collector's totems from the childhood neither one of us had.

One morning, after a particularly epic drinking session, I'd woken up on his couch with all the flavors of hell having an oily orgy in my mouth.

I went into his bathroom to find some toothpaste, mouthwash, anything to banish the unholies from my tongue. What I found instead was a trail of toothpaste on the floor to Junior's bedroom door. Apparently, he'd tried an oral exorcism of his own.

I found Junior on the bed in his boxers, snoring like a water buffalo with emphysema, tube of toothpaste in one hand, the other down the front of his drawers. As I quietly shut down my gag reflex and attempted to remove the toothpaste from his paw, I saw the action figures in bed with him. In this drunkenness, he'd opened a half dozen of his precious in-the-box toys. Duke and Starscream and Magneto had met on the epic battlefield of Junior's single bed. The single bed with the Justice League sheets.

Somewhere in his drunken lizard brain, the twelve-year-old Junior played with the toys that the angry, isolated kid at St. Gabe's never had a chance to own.

The whole tableau made me sad, especially when my first thought was that Starscream wouldn't have had a chance against Magneto.

That thought belonged to the kid in me who never had those toys either.

A small, ghostly hand crept over the side of Junior's bed. The Boy's fingers tried to close over the G.I. Joe figure, but passed through, unable to grasp the playthings.

I know. I really should see a psychologist at some point.

But on the other hand, fuck you.

It was the same emotion that filled me when I thought about that goddamn car.

Junior had infected me with his sentimentality.

And I didn't have the time or patience for sentimentality.

I drove by Ollie's place, hoping he could work what was technologically impossible for me, and crack Byron's phone. I parked the car behind a big pile of snow in a spot that wouldn't have been able to take half of Miss Kitty's girth.

I knocked on Ollie's door and waited, apology ready and my sword positioned to fall on. Nothing.

Through the slatted blinds, I caught a flicker of movement.

"Come on, Ollie," I said to the door. "I'm sorry."

No response.

"We need your help, buddy. We really do. I'm sorry if I made you feel…like you couldn't contribute."

Another flicker of movement.

"Really?" I said to the air. I knocked at the window by the door and tried to peek in when the blind shifted and I found myself face-to-face with an ugly orange tabby with a lazy eye. The tabby seemed as surprised as I was, jumping back and shifting the blinds over behind the couch cushion.

With the cat's help, I could see into the apartment that clearly had no Ollie in it.

Where the hell was he now?

I felt a second of concern before I remembered nobody had any reason to go after Ollie, except to get at me. Amongst our peers, Ollie was as removed from the scene as one could be.

It wasn't like Ollie brought dates to The Cellar.

Far as I knew, Ollie barely dated at all.

Far as I knew.

Jesus. Was I really so disconnected from his life?

I didn't even know he had a cat. Must have been a recent purchase, since the last time we did a boys' day kung fu marathon at his pad, there wasn't a cat.

But the addition of a pet into his life was something I should have known about.

On cue, the cat returned to the sill and pressed his bright ginger fur against the glass. I traced my fingers along his ruffled pelt, feeling his deep purr vibrating on the window.

First animal this week that hadn't tried to eat me.

Felt nice.

But where the hell was Ollie?

CHAPTER 14

BLUE ENVY LOOKED like it was drawing a decent crowd, considering it was Monday and considering the radio was calling for another snowpocalypse to drop within the next twelve hours. And also considering it was jazz.

I wrapped my coat tightly around myself and opened the door to another gust of bone-chilling winter wind. My knee immediately flared up, begging me to get back inside somewhere, preferably a place with a large supply of both whiskey and Bengay. The cold felt good against my stab wound, though, so it wasn't all bad.

I walked over to the doorman.

"Twelve dollars," he said, brows knitted together as he gave me the once-over.

Oh for chrissakes. I gritted my teeth and handed him a twenty.

He wasn't someone I recognized from the circuit, so I couldn't pull the old "club courtesy" angle and skip the door charge. I had twenty-six bucks left in my wallet after the cover, and I cursed myself for not at least pulling another hundred out of the doctored trumpet case. As far as blood money was concerned, fuck 'em. It wasn't the blood of me or mine that was on the floor.

Yet.

Blue Envy wasn't as frou-frou as Raja, but it was still several steps—several staircases—above The Cellar. Lot of dudes around me dressed nicely. And they all smelled nice. I couldn't be sure, since it was my own stank that was filling my senses, but after two days without a shower, and one rough and tumble roll in the sack, I was reasonably sure I was raising a Pigpen-esque cloud of filth.

The bartender wore a vest and sported a pompadour that had more work put into it than an aging starlet's face. "What would you like?"

"Jim Beam and a Bud?"

He hid his disdain fairly well.

Fairly.

He put the drinks in front of me. "Nineteen dollars, please."

I was glad he'd told me the price before I'd taken a sip, otherwise my spit-take might have ruined his fancy haircut. I placed another twenty down. Prick didn't give me change, then had the balls to look at the bar to see if any other bills had sprouted wings and flown their way onto the mahogany.

He sniffed, then went back to making a regiment of bright pink and green martinis that had some sort of fruit salad dangling off the glass.

That should have been my first hint.

I took my booze and walked down to the front by the small curtained stage. There were a couple of tables, but they all had paper tents with *Reserved* written on them in gilt cursive.

There I was, all up in the schmancy again.

I leaned against the wall and waited for the show to begin.

Then I got my first sense.

My internal bouncer alarms gave a light jangle.

All good bouncers, and many bartenders, have a highly tuned sixth sense. Science hasn't proven it, but it's a fact. I've heard it described along the lines of when you were a kid and you walked in the door and knew, just knew, that your parents had been fighting.

That feeling.

You do what I've done long enough, you can read all kinds of shit off people—in their expression, in their posture, in their tone of voice. A good bouncer can walk into a crowded room and not only be able to tell that something heavy is about to hit the fan, but will be able to pinpoint from what direction it was emanating within a second or two.

Junior says it has a smell. Testing his theory, I breathed deeply through my nose, but all I caught was a suissant of dirty balls. Again, those were probably mine.

Then, just as quickly, it passed. It wasn't gone, but it passed, right as the first notes from a stand-up bass thrummed through the loudspeakers. A deep voice announced, "Please give a round of applause for Ellie Confidential and the Brass Balls Band."

Well, at least they were starting the evening. I didn't want to have to sit through opening bands if it was all jazz. That, and I couldn't afford another drink. I'd just wait out the set and chat up a couple of the band members after. Assuming my ball stank didn't clear the room first.

A lone trumpet note carried the opening into "My Funny Valentine." Something warmed in my chest. Not only did I not know that the song was considered jazz, but the old Chet Baker album had been one of my mom's favorites.

The curtains parted, and Veronica Lake's little sister stood center stage. She was the one playing the notes, a trumpet pressed to her full lips. I guess they had a replacement ready to go for Byron. Being a Neanderthal, watching her on the horn nearly instigated a second puberty in me.

Ellie was hot, straight-up.

Then she put down the horn and began singing one of my earliest lullabies with Greta Garbo's voice. Her thickly lashed eyes pressed closed, she breathed the song gently into the microphone. Ellie Confidential had some mad talent.

I closed my eyes too, and let the notes wash over me.

For a moment, only a moment, I was The Boy and he was me, and we were in a warm place inside my childhood. I couldn't tell you how long it had been since music had carried me away so far from the moment.

Man, it was music to fall in love with. My mind drifted to Kelly, to the idea of what we could have been, could have had. The mental image started to float away toward the idea that she'd been playing Hide the Kielbasa with Ian Summerfield, but even that thought was calmed and washed away on the music.

Then the first red flag popped up in my head just as the mush hidden deep inside me was traipsing through a field of daisies. It popped up with such force, I wouldn't be surprised if the whole room heard the *booooiiiiing* inside my head.

I opened my eyes. Yup. There were no women in the room. Toward the front of the stage, couples were slowly dancing to the song.

Guy couples.

Uh-oh. Maybe that dirty-ball souissant wasn't only mine. There were a lot of balls in that room. At least a percentage of them had to be dirty.

Shit.

This wasn't Kansas.

And I was in a room filled with Friends of Dorothy.

Red flag number two billowed magnificently in the winds of my brain as that sixth sense kicked in again. My eyes darted from person to person. My eyes first locked with the Veronica Lake lookalike on the microphone. Her eyes were wide, locked on mine. A note warbled in her throat and she glanced to my right.

I turned and was met with a glare blasting cold hatred from a swollen face—purpled under the eyes, a line of new stitches over the right eyebrow. It took me a second before I could piece together the features under the beating and where the hell I knew them from.

Alex.

Remember him?

Took me a second too.

I'll give you a minute.

...

...

...

...

Time's up. Same for me.

As I remembered the little gay dude who'd caught a savage beating at The Cellar...

...just as the beginnings of an apology were forming in my head...

...somebody grabbed my left arm from behind and wrenched it back. I turned and saw Cornrows from my apartment assault, both meaty hands clenched tight around my wrist.

Rookie mistake, leaving me with one arm open. I clenched my right fist and readied a hook that was going to break his fucking jaw.

Then somebody grabbed my right arm and wrenched it back to meet the other. Fuck. Lineman.

The rookie mistake was mine.

That wrenching of my right arm was the one that hurt, pulling open the tape and my stab wound.

I cried out in the sudden pain before I could even say a word. And any word that might have followed was cut short by the bottle of Grey Goose that walloped me on the face. The thick glass—or my temple—made a loud crack that drew a long and horrified "Oooooh!" from the room.

Bright spots danced before my eyes and my knees buckled. The two goons didn't let me hit the floor, but my falling weight pulled at my side again. The starburst of pain from my perforated belly took my breath away, but was the only thing that kept me conscious.

I didn't think I was going to be so lucky the second time, in more ways than one.

(Here's a Boo Malone Bouncer Fun Fact for ya! Most of the time, the impact from a bottle strike isn't where the damage happens. It's the glass. Say someone whacks you on the skull with a thinner-glassed bottle—Stoli, for instance—it's going to shatter. At which point you've got a shower of glass streaking across your face. Then, what's left attached to the bottleneck carves your face into ribbons. I've seen it. It ain't pretty.)

Through my blurred vision, I could see a long crack along the vodka bottle from the impact on my head. The second shot, when that thick glass shattered, would fillet my face off like a chicken cutlet.

Self-preservation and my rage kicked in.

The room went red.

With a roar, I dropped all my weight down, pulling the goons halfway over with me. I didn't care how many gym muscles you have, two hundred and forty pounds of dead weight is a bitch. They held their grips on my arms.

Good.

I ignored the pain in my side and the motherfucker of a headache that I'd been delivered via French vodka bottle and rolled back, mule-kicking my heel up along the length of my left arm. The bottom of my Timberland blasted Cornrows right under the chin. He was unconscious before he even had a chance to let me go.

I swung the same leg back behind Lineman and swept him at the knees. He pitched forward on top of Alex, and they both went down in a heap. I tried to spring to my feet, but still didn't have my equilibrium back. I saw the exit, had every intention of running for it, but my looped brain decided to turn the floor into a listing boat on the high seas, and I toppled, doing a soft shoe the entire way, until my back slammed against the stage.

In the scheme of things, it wasn't the worst thing that could have happened, tactically. If I had to fight off a bar full of righteously pissed off gay dudes, at least I wasn't going to have to defend my flank.

(And no, I wasn't going for a rimshot there.)

(And no, I wasn't going for one with my use of "rimshot" either.)

I put my fists up and readied myself for an ass-kicking I hoped would only send me to the hospital and not to a slab.

Sometimes being a man meant you just had to take that beating. But I was damn sure going to let these boys know they were in a fight.

Lineman disentangled himself from Alex and stood, reached into the back of his pants, and with a flick of his wrist, opened an extension baton.

This was going to hurt.

Lineman rushed me, the baton raised high.

I put my left arm up to block the baton, and cocked my right to throw a haymaker that would, with a bit of luck, take his head clean off. And then, I hoped, the sight of his bleeding neck stump and disconnected head would be such a shock to the room that it would buy me enough time to scamper out the door and run like a bitch.

As Lineman closed the distance, my mind went through the fastest prayer in history along with the thought that I was a dead man.

Five feet.

One foot.

KER-FUCKA-BLOOEY!

From behind and above me, the weighted bottom of a mike stand arced through the air and blasted Lineman right on the side of the face with devastating force. The bone structure of his face shifted unnaturally to the left, spinning him around as he nosedived to the floor. A pool of blood immediately fanned out from his broken face.

Somebody screamed, and the room fell into chaos.

I looked up and saw the Veronica Lake-alike standing over me like a Viking queen, the mike stand her sword. Through my concussed brain, she looked like Brunhilda come to deliver me to Valhalla. (Did Brunhilda deliver dead souls to Valhalla? Who the fuck knew.)

She tossed her improvised weapon to the side and reached under my shoulder, pulling me up onto the stage. "We're going out the back, buddy," she said.

I planted my other hand on the stage and pushed myself, rolling onto the stage.

Alex still had other ideas, despite his fallen henchmen.

With a yell, he charged us both from stage left, two bottles held high, one in each hand.

Veronica tore the blonde peekaboo hair off her head and tossed it into Alex's face, blinding him with lustrous wigginess. Within the second that Alex's vision was impaired, Ollie followed up with a straight right, square into the wig's part—which happened to line up perfectly with the middle of Alex's face.

Alex wobbled and fell off the stage, landing on one of the bottles. A good dozen shards of glass poked out of his designer suit, blood trickling out of each fresh puncture.

Alex screamed again.

Wait a minute...

OLLIE?

I spun back and looked at the face of one my oldest friends, now recognizable under the carefully applied makeup.

Ollie smiled through his flawless lipstick, breathing heavily. "Still think I'm no good in a fight?"

CHAPTER 15

REMEMBER ALL THAT self-motivational hoodie-doo I said earlier about forward movement? About not backing down and getting all manly and proactive?

Yeah, well, when you had a hundred really pissed gay dudes on your ass… Again, I'm not cracking wise here, but you can see why my basic vernacular got us in trouble in the first place.

So, we ran. We ran like an unwashed wind. I didn't know the layout of the club, but Ollie moved like he did. So I followed him and tried to ignore the sounds of the mob that was forming behind us.

I was still woozy from the bottle shot to the temple, and bounced off the walls as I tried to keep up with my friend who was hauling ass in an evening dress and heels. We ran up a short flight of stairs and Ollie burst out of a fire exit.

Which in turn blared the alarm that alerted the lynch mob to our location.

I heard someone behind us toward the stage yell, "They're going out the back."

We had about ten seconds before they got to us.

Piles of garbage bags and some broken furniture from the club lay in piles. Nothing that could hold the door closed behind us. I planted my feet and held my back to the door as the first body slammed into it. I heard a muffled "ow" as the body hit. The reverberation echoed through all of my injuries, but the door stayed shut.

"The fuck are you doing, Boo?" Ollie hollered.

I reached into my pocket and tossed him the car keys. "Red Omni. In front. Pull it around."

Another, heavier body slammed into the door at my back. My feet skidded in the snow and the door popped open, but slammed back shut behind me. I heard another voice behind the door alert the masses. "Hey! He's back here. We need to get the door open."

Ollie ran for the car. I re-braced my feet and gritted my teeth.

Their pushing resumed.

Warm blood started trickling down my belly from the stab wound.

The door opened an inch.

Sounded like there were at least a dozen guys back there.

Two inches. Three sets of fingers appeared in the crack. Someone yelled, "Here! Here!" A steel pole moved through the opening and began to pry the door at my back.

My boots skidded a little more.

The opening was the width of my fist.

So I spun and threw a haymaker blindly into the gap.

I connected solidly with what felt like an ear. Somebody yelped and I grabbed the pole and yanked it toward me.

The steel pole was mine now, bitches.

I spun off the door, letting it crash open, much to my pursuers' surprise. The returned-to-consciousness Cornrows stood in front of the horde. I brought the pole down in a Samurai chop, whaling the semi-recovered Cornrows right on the collarbone. He screamed and dropped backwards onto the assembled lynch mob. I hurriedly closed the door, dropped the pole, and re-braced it with my faltering body.

Spots of blood began polka-dotting the snow at my feet.

An engine gunned and Ollie spun the Omni around the rear, almost snowplaning it into the building. Not far enough behind him, the couple dudes who were smart enough to take the long route around were in pursuit.

"One!" I heard from the other side of my door.

Uh-oh.

"Two!"

I sidestepped the door.

"THREE!"

I don't know what they were expecting, but no resistance whatsoever wasn't on the list.

A great wave of dudes came tumbling out the door, and once the first one hit the slush and went down, it quickly turned into a Benny Hill routine as they all went ass-over-teakettle on top of each other. I limped down the alley at a brisk waddle as Ollie slammed on the brakes.

The alley was almost too narrow for me to open the goddamn door of the smallest car in North America. I gave both ends of the alley my middle finger and squeezed myself on the passenger side.

Then couldn't open the fucking door.

The door handle was currently being used by Bray's dogs as a chew toy.

I rolled onto the hood, grabbed the windshield well, and yelled, "Drive!"

"Which way?" Ollie looked to both ends at the impending angry gay Malachi Crunch that was about to swarm and beat us to death.

Behind me, I heard the scrape of someone picking up the discarded pole. One would assume to plant it in my skull. I didn't like that option. There were still only a couple of guys coming up the other end.

"Reverse it!" I hollered.

Ollie stomped the gas, and if the engine had had more power in it than a farting weasel, I might have shot off the hood. The handful of guys down the other end quickly decided to push a hasty retreat as the petite car mewled its pitiful roar and charged.

The slower of the bunch dove out of the mouth of the alleyway as the car spat out onto the street. Luckily, the traffic was moving slower than normal in the gusting snow, otherwise we could have easily gotten blasted in the cross-traffic. Instead, amidst a couple of hard swerves and angry horns blaring, Ollie cut the wheel hard and sent the car into a spin on the ice.

When suddenly—centrifugal force, everybody!—I was launched like a scud missile off the hood.

I was in the air long enough to process this thought in its entirety: *Whoa! I'm really flying, here. This is actually kinda cool. Going to hurt a lot when I land, though.*

Then I landed.

And I was right.

I tried to go limp.

I tried to roll with it.

I really did.

Instead, I bounced and skidded on the slick street. I may have passed out for a few seconds. When I came to, the car was next to me, and Ollie was trying to get me to my feet. I saw a ten-foot skidmark of blood that I'd left behind on the macadam. Hell, I was really bleeding hard again.

I fell into the car and Ollie jumped back into the driver's seat as the first rock hit the windshield, spiderwebbing the glass. Ollie put the car into drive, and we made our escape. Only took about half of the blood in me and about a foot of skin, but at least I didn't get any new information or anything.

Sigh…

We headed up toward Allston, and, presumably, my apartment. I pressed my hand against my belly underneath my shirt and coat, the duct tape soaked through and no longer sticking. The point of knife-insertion was alarmingly warm in contrast to the frozen rest of me. My knee didn't hurt yet, but I could feel it swelling under my jeans. There was a hazy spot in my vision on the far corner of my right eye, and I was a little nauseous, no doubt slightly concussed from Alex's attempted vodka bottle lobotomy. And I was still brain-rattled from Ian Summerfield doing his cha-cha on my head the other night.

I was not doing well.

I took my hand out from under my layers. It wasn't pretty. Dark blood stained my fingertips like I'd dipped them in thick red paint.

Ollie's eyes went wide. "Why are you bleeding? What happened? Do you need to go to the hospital? Are...are you duct-taped together?"

"All my life, Ollie. All my life." I tried to smile, while ignoring the distracting fact that my brother was still in full makeup, driving in an evening gown and fuck-me pumps. I immediately closed my eyes against my own mental imagery with association to Ollie wearing fuck-me pumps.

And the fact that he'd kind of given me a chubbie up on that stage.

Goodbye erections! See you in maybe a decade.

Ollie's plucked eyebrows were knit in concern. "I'm not kidding. You look like you're bleeding pretty bad. What happened?" Were his eyebrows always so well groomed? Had I just not noticed under his thick Elvis Costello glasses? The car swerved dangerously every time Ollie tried to get a look at my various cuts, bruises, contusions, and well...holes.

"Please keep your concentration on the icy road, Ollie. Let me worry about bleeding to death."

"Did that happen just now?"

"Nah. Happened at The Cellar."

"Who stabbed you?"

"Ginny."

Ollie shot me another shocked look. "The waitress?" Another swerve.

"Eyes on the road, please," I said, pointing to said road. "And, yep."

"The one with the luscious titties?"

A moment of silence.

And then I laughed. It hurt really fucking bad. Maybe it was the blood loss, the renewed concussion, or a combination of traumatic injuries to my mortal coil, but pieces were coming together. Twenty years late, but they were coming together.

Ollie—all at once the most sensitive amongst us, and the crudest. Always the guy with the most nerdishly inappropriate comments about sex and women—although, to be fair, the large majority of those statements were regarding fictional characters from *Battlestar Galactica* and the Marvel Universe. Always the kid who talked so much over-sexual nonsense that the inevitable conclusion was that he was covering up for his deficiencies with the other sex. That he was trying to impress the boys with a distracting crassness in lieu of actually having ever had his hand on a warm boobie in his life.

Suddenly I realized the reason for Ollie's overzealousness. I knew the exact reason he'd never known the pleasure of cupping said tit.

"Holy, holy shit," I said, seeing a kid I'd known for twenty years, seeing him for the first time—albeit underneath a metric ton of L'Oreal products.

Ollie was keenly aware of my staring, maybe of my seeing him for the first time. Even underneath the makeup, his color rose. His Adam's apple—which should have been a giveaway while he was singing on that that stage, but what are you gonna do?—bobbled up and down. "What?"

"You look very pretty," I said, with a serious attempt at sincerity.

Ollie looked like he was debating for a second whether to start crying or laughing.

I busted out howling again. It was all just so, so hilarious and fucked up.

After a minute, he also broke into a smile, then the deep honking guffaws that he called laughter.

He pulled Junior's new car in front of my house. Hippy Phil, my upstairs neighbor, sat on the front steps, staring up at the thick snowflakes falling around his head with a childlike grin on his face. Between his knuckles, he held a tobacco product the size of a Polish sausage, no doubt filled with Tijuana's finest crop.

That innocent grin fell off his face when he saw the half-dressed drag queen and the beaten and bleeding me limping out of the car.

He had good reason to be nervous. It had been a few months since I'd even come across Phil sitting on the stoop in a cloud of his own making. I was pretty sure he'd been dodging me ever since our last encounter, which had me carjack him and his party van into a high-speed rescue attempt with a fresh bullet hole in my leg. It ended with a flipped van, three cars totaled, and me surrounded by cops in the middle of the street whilst clad only in my tighty-whities.

Good times.

At least the underwear was clean.

Phil looked like he didn't know whether to have himself a good old-fashioned freak out, run for the tree line, or both.

"Hey, Phil," I said.

"Uh…hey, man."

"Ollie, Phil. Phil? Ollie."

Ollie extended his hand to shake, his fingers tipped with nails painted blood-red. "Pleasure."

"Hey," Phil said, blinking rapidly.

I bent over and scooped a handful of snow and pressed it against my stab hole. It hurt for a second, but then felt so, so good. If my life was going to tear me apart one wound at a time, at least Mother Nature was providing me with ice packs everywhere I went.

Phil turned his terrified blinking to my gut. "You okay?"

"Never better." I grinned, then took my hand away, the quickly melting snow veined red with my blood. Then I faceplanted into the snow.

Like ya do.

I WAS COLD, but I was comfortable. I was in a safe place inside my mind, after my body had endured enough and given me the old *fuck you, I'm outta here.*

I felt pressure on my belly hole, a throbbing on my temple where I'd taken the vodka bottle, and my heartbeat in my poor knee. Nothing hurt too badly, but I could feel each and every spot of trauma.

My vision, or what passed for it, was a field of white. I didn't think I was in Heaven, since I didn't believe in it, but saw a Chinese angel smiling at me when I could focus enough on the blurry images floating within the pristine landscape.

My first confused thought was that there had been a mix-up and I'd wound up in the Asian afterlife. That wouldn't be so bad, since as far as my long history of karate movies had taught me, it was a pretty cool destination for warriors. I would be happy in the same eternity as Wong Fei-hung and Bruce Lee.

She handed me something to drink. I expected a golden celestial goblet, but it was only my old *Tom & Jerry* jelly glass. The heavenly nectar also tasted suspiciously like the Goofy Grape Kool-Aid I had in the fridge, but I was so, so thirsty, and didn't feel I should start complaining during my first hours in paradise.

Maybe it was slightly odd that my angel had blue dreadlocks, but fuck it.

I drifted back into the void for a bit before Godzilla's roar brought me back.

I rethought my position on eternity in the Asian afterlife if Godzilla was going to be there too.

I opened my eyes and found myself propped up in my bed, clothed in nothing but my boxers. My sternum was wrapped in clean white gauze. I was weak as shit, but overall felt better than I had in days, banged up to hell, but rested. Shee-yit, I even had morning wood. Yaaay.

My brain was stuffed with tapioca, but I managed to prop myself out of the bed and slowly followed the roar of the King of the Monsters back into reality. Sunlight streamed through the windows.

How long had I been out for? My internal clock couldn't calibrate.

My blue-haired angel sat on the couch in my living room, watching Godzilla fighting Mechagodzilla on my TV. She didn't see me for a second, enraptured by the carnage and the chili burger she was munching on.

"Hey," was all I said. Even that was tough to enunciate through my numbed lips.

"Ohmygod!" She startled, then choked for a second on her burger. Through her wheezing, she said, "You're up."

I had so many questions. But before they could gel inside my pudding-filled mind and scramble their way into my mouth, I saw her gaze drop and her eyes widen.

Oh yeah. My boxers.

And my raging erection.

Lil' Boo had decided to see what was going on, and was just as interested as I was in figuring out who the hell this girl was.

Hooray! Despite my horror at the sexual attraction I felt toward Drag Queen Ollie, I was still able to pop a boner. Victory!

Then the memory of Drag Queen Ollie made my erection disappear faster than a hot dog at fat camp.

"Excuse me," was all I said. Then I worked my way back down the hallway to my bedroom. I tucked Lil' Boo into a pair of black Levi's and slowly put a T-shirt on over the bandages. That hurt a little bit. Whatever had been keeping the pain at bay was receding, and I felt a pull at my wound. Had somebody stitched me up? Sure as hell felt like it, but I didn't want to unwrap myself to check.

I heard the front door opening and grabbed the aluminum baseball bat propped next to my closet door. I stood in my best Big Papi stance, ready to knock the head of my next unexpected visitor over the Green Monster.

I heard Ollie say, "He's up?"

I put the bat back down, a little disappointed that the first time I was ready for an attack wasn't going to be fulfilled with triumphant bat-swinging and possibly a witty catchphrase or two.

Ollie and Phil were carrying a box of Dunkin Donuts and a cardboard tray of coffees. "Figured we'd grab some supplies if we were going to be battening down the hatches." Ollie had removed all his makeup, and was dressed in clothes I could only assume he'd borrowed from Phil. I could still picture him singing jazz standards in full Veronica Lake drag, but not in a patchouli-soaked rainbow Phish shirt.

"What happened?" I asked

"Uh, you passed out," Ollie said.

"Got that. Then what? Who is this?"

My Chinese angel stood and extended her hand. "Sophie. Figured you should know my name, since I've already seen your dick."

"What?" said Phil, a light distress in his tone. Well, that explained a bit about where she'd come from.

"It was an accident," I said.

"He didn't know I was here. He walked out in his boxers."

"Oh, okay," Phil said. Still unhappy with the events, but eased by the explanation.

"He had a big boner poking out." Sophie smiled at me and gave me a thumbs-up. Flattering, but a little weird.

And Phil's distress was back.

I cleared my throat, wondering if I should thank her for the thumbs-up. "I think we can dismiss with the full descriptive. Who patched me up?"

"Me again." Sophie wiggled her fingers happily at me. "Pre-med at BC. Was kind of cool getting some real-word application for my classwork. It's a little different from stitching up a dead piglet."

"Always glad to help the cause of education," I said through lips that wobbled like gummi worms glued to my face. "Just how doped up am I?" I took another sip of Kool-Aid and managed not to dribble the warm sugar water all over myself.

"You're pretty doped up," Sophie said. "About eighty milligrams of Oxycodone, ground up into the Kool-Aid. Which made the fact that you even could get a boner that much more impressive."

I put the Kool-Aid back down. "Can we please stop talking about my boner?"

"Please?" said Phil.

"Also my vote," Ollie said.

"Well, I'm glad we're all in agreement on my dick," I said. "Moving on, can somebody also get me something to drink that isn't a Jonestown Refresher?"

Ollie took a bottle of spring water from the bag and handed it to me. "I'll take one of those donuts too."

Ollie opened the box, and I plucked a Boston Crème out of the mix. Ollie said, "I didn't know if bringing you to a hospital was the best idea. Phil here got on the horn to Sophie, and took care of it the best we could."

For all I knew, the entirety of the Boston Police Department was hunting both the deceased Buick and my ass. The only thing that might have kept them from my doorstep was the storm raging outside. "Yeah. Things are sticky right now."

Ollie shoved half a bear claw into his mouth. "Where's Junior? I tried to call him, but he's not picking up. It's going straight to voice mail."

"Cops got him."

He stopped chewing. "The hell for?"

"Murder."

This time, he inhaled a good chunk, coughing and wheezing. Phil whacked him on the back. Sophie got excited. "Ooh!" she said. "Can I give you the Heimlich?"

"I'm okay," Ollie wheezed. "Liquid." He grabbed the first thing nearby, which was the laced Kool-Aid.

"Ollie, you might want to find something else to drin—never mind." He took a big belt before I could stop him.

He looked at the cup. "Aw crap. This is going to fuck me up, isn't it?"

"Oh yeah," Sophie said, nodding with a Cheshire smile. "You ever taken that stuff before?"

"No," Ollie said, staring into the glass.

"You'll feel it in about ten minutes."

"Just enjoy the ride, man," Phil said, bobbing his head with a grin, ever the goddamn hippy.

"I didn't want a ride," Ollie said to me.

"Well, you're getting one," Sophie said, giving Ollie the same thumbs-up she'd given my boner. Which just made it all a little weirder.

"Okay, then," I said. "While I'm immensely grateful to all involved for not letting me die in the snow, Ollie and I need to discuss some matters."

"Like your friend getting arrested for murder?" Sophie said, fascinated.

"That he didn't commit. And as far as I know, he hasn't been charged yet."

"Who did he not murder, then?"

It was then that I noticed Sophie's pinpoint pupils. If I had to guess, she'd given the Oxy a test run of her own. "Everyone on earth. That's who he didn't murder."

"Whoa," she said.

"C'mon," said Phil, noticeably eager to remove himself from his stabbed neighbor, the neighbor's recently-in-drag friend, murder conversation, and the recent boner sighting.

"Can we borrow this DVD?" Sophie said, pointing to Godzilla.

"Sure," I said.

Once they had vacated, I gingerly lowered myself to the couch out of habit and anticipation, more than because of any pain I was in. The dope was doing its job.

Ollie sat in my ratty chair and looked at his hands.

"Where do you want to begin?" Ollie asked.

I decided to go right after the elephant in the room. "You gay, Ollie?"

"Yup," he said, staring out the window at the blinding snowstorm.

"Huh," I said, letting it sink in for a moment. It didn't take too long, since I think there was a part of my subconscious that may have already suspected, and the, you know, "dressed in drag at the gay club" hint. "There any reason you've kept that to yourself all these years?"

Ollie looked back to me with incredulity. "You honestly asking me that?"

"Half and half. You don't think it's something we could have handled?"

"You? Probably. Twitch, possibly." He stopped there.

"Junior—"

He cut me off. "No fucking way."

I sighed. He wasn't wrong. I thought. I didn't know. I tapped out a cigarette from my pack while I thought about the next thing I was going to say. "He doesn't hate you. You're family. I don't think he could."

"You don't think he could? Almost everything negative in his lingo relates back to something I either am, enjoy, and do. Every prick at the bar is a 'cocksucker.' Every time he has a bad day, he 'took one up the ass.' Everything and everyone he considers to be less than living up to his own scale of masculinity is either 'faggy' or just 'a faggot.'"

He had me there. I'd never put too much thought into his insensitive vernacular, since none of it applied directly to me.

"It's not personal. It's never personal," I said.

"It is. It's just that you guys never knew it was."

"We never knew because you didn't tell us."

"And now we're talking in a circle." Ollie chewed on a thumbnail. A thumbnail that I couldn't forget had recently been polished red.

Looked like I still had some road to travel before I didn't deserve every word Ollie said. "Does it help you knowing that we're not consciously ragging on gay people when we use those words? I'm not tearing down Oedipus when I call someone a motherfucker."

"Seriously? That's worse."

"How is that worse?"

"Because it's not conscious. Every time, you're subconsciously and habitually thinking of me as a second-class citizen. And the dismissal of my hurt as something I should just 'get over' is also personal. Whether you realize it or not, you guys are always using me and who I am to describe something rotten."

"I'm sorry." It was all I had left to say.

"Will Junior be? And can either one of you at least try to change your colorful descriptives?"

"Fuck it. I'm a creative guy. I've been meaning to get more innovative with my cursing anyway. How do the terms twatwaffle, shitblimp, and cockpickle sit with you?"

Ollie squinted. "Cockpickle?"

"Cockpickle."

"I feel like cockpickle should offend me, but have no idea why."

"C'mon man. You gotta give me cockpickle."

"I think I now know why it's offensive."

"Fair enough." I ground my cigarette out in the ashtray.

"Couldn't help but notice that you haven't expressed any thoughts about how Junior might handle this information."

"You know Junior."

"I do. And I also know that something in him got twisted after the whole incident with Zach Bingham."

Jesus. Zach Bingham.

For me, Zach was just another story. Just a few brush strokes in an enormous painting filled with similar depictions of anarchy and chaos. But that painting's frame had been getting smaller all week, and now, all I could see was that one day, the one incident that had a hell of a lot more impact on my family than I'd ever realized.

Now that I too was looking at that big picture through the small frame, I could not only understand how things had changed for Junior from that point on, but how it changed everything for Ollie too. Changed how he related to Junior, a man who he was supposed to think of as family. And who was supposed to feel the same for him.

What was there that I could say? That I could do? We were creatures made up of our wounds. All of us. Some of them you walked away from. Others left you with a limp. Others left you with pain you woke up with every day. But if the pain wasn't yours, you might never notice how much it hurt the person across from you.

"I don't know what to say."

Ollie thought about it for a minute, picking at a chocolate glazed the whole time. "Don't say anything."

"I won't."

Ollie looked at me over the glasses he was no longer wearing. It was just a look he gave so many times that it was automatic, glasses or not.

I'd never seen the kid in contacts before. Never even knew he had them.

That was the least of things that I didn't know about one of my closest friends.

"Can I say I'm sorry?" I said.

Ollie closed his eyes. "That counts as saying something."

"Well, I'm sorry."

"For what?"

"For things I might have said over the last twenty or so years. I'm sorry that made you feel like you had to hide yourself from me...from us."

Ollie's face went red with anger. "Now *that's* the most insulting thing you could have said."

"What? How?"

"You fucking assume that I'm not who I am. That 'Ollie' has been a construct to keep myself safe from you all these years. I'm still me, Boo. There's nothing, no goddamn thing about who I am that I've kept hidden from you guys. Nothing except one detail that shouldn't make a difference one way or the other because it's never affected you one way or the other until this fucking afternoon."

I had nothing. He was right.

"Can I say I'm sorry for saying that?"

Ollie rolled his eyes. "I can't believe you keep talking."

"I won't," I said again. "But you should."

Ollie didn't say anything.

"Can we start with anything you might know about Byron Walsh?" I reached for my smokes again, and lances of pain shot through me before I even made it a third of the way.

Ollie shook his head, confused. "What does he have to do with anything?"

"He's dead. Junior's being accused of doing the deed. Can you hand me those?" I pointed to my Parliaments and my lighter.

Ollie's mouth fell open as he handed them to me. "How did...what...?"

"It's a long story that I promise to fill in the blanks on later."

"When were you going to tell me that?"

"Sooner than later? Anything you know about the guy that can help me maybe find the real guy who did?"

"I didn't know him."

The hell? "Wasn't he in your band?" I lit a smoke and inhaled deeply.

"Not really. I just replaced him after the other guys kicked him out. He *was* Ellie Confidential. Last night was my first gig. And undoubtedly my last."

"Why'd he get kicked out?"

Ollie shrugged. "Never asked. But from what I could glean from conversations the other guys had, he was supposedly into some really shady stuff."

I tucked that into my *No Shit* file. "Think any of the other band members might be able to shine a light on that shadiness?"

"Maybe. But I don't think they'll be eager to talk to you after last night. I think you broke Nathan's jaw in the melee."

"Who's Nathan?"

"The bass player."

"Shit."

"Yeah."

"Sorry I fucked up your gig." Damn, I had a lot of sorrys to drop at Ollie's feet, didn't I?

Ollie shrugged, but I could see he was really bummed out about it.

"You were seriously great," I said. "I'd like to see you perform again sometime."

A tiny, proud smile crept across Ollie's lips. "No kidding?"

"No kidding. I promise not to fuck up your next band too."

"Please don't."

Then the blue and red lights flared through the snow, illuminating my living room through the gloom and driving blizzard.

Fuck.

"They here for you?" Ollie asked.

"Good chance they are." The thick flakes had accumulated over the window. I saw a lone figure walking from the car.

Ollie stood. "What are we going to do?"

I tossed Ollie the keys to the Omni. "You lay low. Can you crack a cell phone password?"

"Shouldn't be a problem."

"You sure? It's an iPhone. Freaking F.B.I. took months on that shit, and I need it yesterday.

Ollie smiled at me, his upper lip curling towards a sneer, but the old fire back in his eyes. The fire that that could burn the world down when we needed each other. "I look like the fucking F.B.I. to you?"

That's my boy.

"In the office at the Cellar, there's a cell that I need the numbers off of, messages too. Audrey has keys."

The doorbell rang.

"I can access the records for incoming and outgoing calls faster than I can crack the phone," Ollie said.

"Do whatever you can. Get it to Underdog."

The polite doorbell ring turned into an insistent pounding on the door.

I grabbed my coat. Just in case. Then I realized I had no idea why they were here. Was I only going to get questioned or was I about to be straight-up charged with Byron's murder? Were they there for the riot at the club that I'd inadvertently been a catalyst of, and the dozen or so assaults that had happened as a result?

Oh yeah, Galal Shaughness too. Almost forgot about that guy.

Jesus, there were a lot of potential reasons I was about to get walked away in handcuffs.

I girded myself against all of them as I opened the door.

I wasn't, however, girded against the snow-covered Junior standing in the doorway.

"What's up, faggots!" he yelled.

Of course he did.

CHAPTER 16

"Thanks, Officers," Junior said, waving to the departing police car. The officer on our side gave Junior a halfhearted thumbs-up as they pulled away slowly, tires skidding in the slush.

"Holy hell, it's cold," Junior said, pushing his way past me into the apartment.

Between the shock of his sudden appearance and the painkillers, the bajillion or so questions that immediately crowded to the front of my mouth all tripped over each other and fell in a sprawl at the tip of my tongue. What came out was, "I don't know what's happening."

"Ollie!" Junior said, arms wide. What with the conversation we were just having, I saw Ollie's shoulders tense under Junior's smothering bro-hug. "Jesus, did I interrupt a circle jerk or something?"

"What?" I said.

"What?" Junior said, a stupid grin plastered on his mug. Then he started really laughing hard. "What the fuck are you wearing, Ollie?" he said, waving a hand over Ollie's horrible, horrible tie-dye.

"I fell in the fucking snow. My shit got all wet. Gigantor over there didn't have any clothes to fit me, so I borrowed from upstairs," Ollie said without missing a beat.

I was a little astonished at how easily, how quickly he'd crafted a lie. Guess when you've had to do it your whole life…

"Jesus," Junior said. "You look like a trannie Mothra."

I started coughing.

Ollie shot me a look that said, *Are you fucking kidding me?*

For Christ's sake, were we always this bad?

"And where are your glasses?" Junior asked Ollie.

"I'm uh…trying contacts out."

Junior pursed his lips. "Not bad. You look twenty percent less of a dork."

I cut in. "What the hell happened? How are you here?" I said.

"Detectives kept me as long as they could without charging me. End of the day, I kept my mouth shut apart from telling them that we didn't know what happened to the homo after we dropped him at the beach."

I felt the burn of the words, knowing that what I was feeling was only a tenth of the intensity with which Ollie'd felt them for the last two decades. But for the first time in my life, I felt them.

Ollie, like he always had, didn't react at all.

"So with heavy hearts and a lack of evidence on their side, they had to cut me loose. Ooh, donuts." Junior shoved half a coconut donut into his mouth.

"But why are you here. Specifically?"

Junior held up a finger while he chewed furiously through the mouthful. "Where was I supposed to go? You have my car." Flakes of coconut flew from his mouth. "Which reminds me, what the fuck did you do with it? They kept trying to get me to talk smack about you, telling me that once they got their hands on it, they would have both our asses."

My mind raced for a plausible answer without full-on lying. "With everything that's happened, I figured it might not be the best idea to tool around in Miss Kitty."

"Very smart, my brother. Very smart. Please don't tell me that you traded it in for that Omni in front." Junior stuffed the rest of the donut in his mouth.

"Yeah…that."

A pause.

My heart skipped.

Then Junior burst out laughing so hard chunks of half-chewed dough came flying out under the force of his guffaws. "But seriously, we're still deeply screwed over here. Just because they didn't have enough dirt to bury our asses right now don't mean they're not looking for a backhoe. What do we got?"

"And please start from the beginning. I'm very confused right now," Ollie said.

With everything that had happened, Ollie still didn't know the first thing about the events that had led us to this point.

I laid it out the best I could, leaving out some points that weren't necessarily an important part of the narrative.

I didn't mention anything about the execution of one Galal Shaughness. I figured if that came back to bite us on the ass, I could at least spare the two of them from having to lie about their knowledge.

I left out the execution of Miss Kitty. That way another murder could be excised from the narrative: my own.

What I gave Ollie were the assaults, both Byron's and my own, then brought them both up to date on the fuckload of money in the false trumpet case.

I noticed Junior's bug-eyes and…was he panting?

"How much money did you say was in there?" he said softly.

"Not sure. I didn't give it a full count."

"Estimate me."

"Over a hundred G. At least."

"Mexico."

"What?"

"Hold on." Junior took off his jacket, tossed it into my bedroom, and shut the door. Then he went into the bathroom. "I haven't taken a comfortable crap in two days. You nearly made me shart my drawers. Let me take care of this before we continue."

"The explanation was unnecessary," I said.

"Was it, Boo? Was it?" Junior flipped me off and shut the bathroom door just as he ripped a long and tremulous fart.

"You okay?" I said quietly to Ollie.

"Yeah. I'm fine."

"You don't look fine."

"Even removing my sudden and unexpected outing, this is all a lot to process and swallow." The toilet flushed, and Ollie lowered his voice. "And if you make a gay joke right now, I'm going to punch you in your stab wound."

"Stab wound?" Junior said, wiping his hands on the front of his jeans. "You got stabbed?"

"By Ginny," Ollie said.

"Why the fuck did Ginny stab you?"

"He stabbed her too," Ollie said, wiggling the eyebrows of his hastily re-applied overreaching hetero-male façade.

I slowly gave Ollie my deadliest stink eye. "Thanks, Ollie."

Junior's jaw dropped. "You banged Ginny?"

"Hey! None of this has anything to do with anything right now!"

"Other than the fact that she stabbed you."

"That was an accident."

"Oh, yeah," Junior said. "She accidentally stabbed you after she banged you. I'm gonna go ahead and assume the banging was also accidental."

"She stabbed me first."

That shut them up.

For about six seconds.

"Kinky," Junior said.

"Yeah," Ollie said. "Why does that make it better somehow?"

"Wait. Why was it worse? Don't answer that."

"So we can count her out for Mexico, then."

"The fuck are you talking about Mexico?"

"Let's pick up Miss Kitty, grab the loot, and drive straight the fuck to Tijuana."

"You don't care at all that it's not our money? You don't care that people are getting killed for it?" Even as I somehow found myself on the high road, I couldn't help but think about a beach and piña coladas and sunshine. Away from junkie bandleaders, dead button men, living button men, Euro-trash drug dealer club owners, and the foot of snow outside the window.

Man, it sounded good.

"First off," Junior said, "if we got the money, it's our money as far as I'm concerned." He notched off a finger on his hand. "Secondly, there's a great big pile of fucks I don't give about whose money it is or how butthurt they wind up over us spending it on tacos." He notched off another finger. "Thirdly, even if we find out who it belongs to, there's no guarantee that we're gonna be able to prove that we didn't do it. We still have a better than even shot at going down for this, either way."

"So…"

"So, fourthly, gimme the loot, gimme the loot!" Junior said.

"Please don't."

"Gimme the loot, gimme the loot!" Oh god. Then he started to dance a little.

Kill me.

"I'm not telling you where the money is," I said.

"Dick."

I went up the stairs to Phil's apartment and rapped on his door.

Sophie opened the door, naked but for a tiny pair of pink panties. "Yo." A thick cloud of Class B smoke smacked me right in the sinuses.

"Uh…yo." I looked up toward the ceiling. "You always open the door like that?"

"Why, you going to knock more often?"

Okay. The weirdness kept getting weirder. And a whole lot more uncomfortable. My eyes drifted down to hers. Then back to her boobies.

Hey, I tried.

Then, with an effort that nearly gave me a hernia underneath my eyeballs, I made eye contact again.

She gave me what I have only heard described as a coquettish smile. Would have helped if I had any idea what coquettish meant. "Phil still up here?"

"Yeah. He's taking a shit."

Ollie had hid his sexuality for twenty years, but in my world, it was perfectly okay for people to discuss their bowel movements. Twice in a half hour. Really? This was my reality?

A toilet flushed, and Phil hurriedly made his way into the hall wearing a loose blue-and-white kimono. "Dammit. Why did you have to tell him that?"

Sophie put her hands on her hips and adopted an impudent stance. "Is that or is that not what you were doing?"

"That's not the point!"

"Well, I think it's part of a point."

"Excuse me," I said.

"I don't need anybody knowing what I'm doing in the bathroom," Phil said.

"Why are you so embarrassed by your body?" Sophie asked, arms wide to display her own naked glory.

Somehow, Phil was getting out-hippy-ed. "Excuse me," I said with more volume.

"And you're freaking naked!" Phil finally noticed.

"Oh, now you're embarrassed by my body too?"

"*Phil!*" I yelled.

"One minute, Boo," he said, then turned back to Sophie. "Just because I don't want to share your body with my neighbors doesn't mean I'm embarrassed by it."

"Oh, now my body is yours to decide who I get to share it with."

Ouch. This was turning into a bloodbath for poor Phil. "Sorry. Can I just grab those van keys?"

Without thinking about whether or not handing me the keys to his van was a good idea—and to be perfectly honest, it wasn't—Phil plucked the key ring from the hook by the door and handed them to me.

"Thanks, buddy," I said, and ran down the stairs. "Let's go guys. Quick, quick, quick, before Phil comes to his senses."

Junior and Ollie put their coats back on and hustled out the door as I started the van. They hopped in the back just as I heard Phil's window open. Apparently sense had cut through both his irritation with Sophie's generous nudity and his high. "Uh, Boo?" he yelled from the sill.

"Thanks, Phil!" I said, waving up to him.

"Where are you taking my car?"

"Owe you one, Phil," I yelled as I drove slowly away in the thick unplowed snow. I knew there was no way the Omni would make it through the storm. One wrong sideways gust of wind could knock that clown car over.

"Boo? Where are you taking my car?" Phil sounded sad the second time he asked.

I gave him back a complicated series of broad mimes to indicate that I couldn't hear him, but added a sunny smile and wave as we turned the corner.

"So what's the plan, Stan?" Junior asked.

"First off, we need to get the cell phone cracked, see who that asshole was calling. Gonna pick it up at The Cellar, and drop off Ollie at his place."

"Yeah, been meaning to ask. Thought we were keeping you out of this, Ollie. How in the hell you wind up back in the mix again?"

Ollie looked to me.

"I needed him to get the phone info." I said a bit too hurriedly. I was not nearly as good as Ollie was at both the speed and casual nature of the lying. Even though what I said was mostly true, it came out in a panic. "Unless you think you can crack it."

"Maybe with a hammer," Junior said.

"Different kind of cracking, brudda."

"Huh. Okay. Where's Twitch?"

"Yeah, where is Twitch?" Ollie was more than happy to take the line of questioning off himself.

"That I do not know," I said. Although I was beginning to wonder.

The streets were mostly empty, huge windblown drifts on the south side of Comm Ave. held the few cars into one slow lane.

"What kind of phone am I looking at again?" Ollie asked.

"iPhone," I said. "Same as Junior's."

Ollie chewed on his lip. "So, once I get in there, I'm going to go ahead and look for any calls on the phone to either Blue Envy or Raja. If we're lucky, Summerfield himself might have left a voice mail, but there will be at least a call log. Maybe I can hack the provider faster than I can crack the phone."

The car in front of me started to fishtail on the slick road. I slowed down even more, but felt the van's tires start to shift on the ice. Man, the roads were bad.

Wait…

What the fuck had Ollie said?

"What did you just say?" I said.

"Didn't we discuss this already?" Ollie said.

"No! What the hell are you talking about?"

"I thought that was why you were at Blue Envy in the first place. I mean, why we went there." Ollie and I were already starting to stumble over the poorly constructed web of lies we'd only begun to build.

Junior blinked at us. "What in blue blazes are either one of you talking about?"

"I don't know!" I said, a bit louder than was appropriate. "What does Summerfield have to do with any of this?"

"He owns Blue Envy."

Boom.

The sudden piece of the puzzle jarred me so hard that I almost lost control of the van. We skidded toward the median.

"Heyhey*hey*!" Junior yelled.

I got the car back under control. "Why didn't this little chestnut come up already?"

"I don't know," Ollie said. "I guess I was assuming we were on the same page."

"I don't know that bar," Junior said.

"Jazz club," I said quickly. I turned back to Ollie. "I went to Blue Envy to talk to Byron's band, to see what they knew."

"Why am I three steps ahead of you here?" Ollie said.

I shot him a look for an answer. I had one, but I was sure Ollie didn't want Junior to hear it yet. Then the weight of all we'd done, seen, and been through these past couple of days hit me like a thunderbolt. Almost all of which could have been eliminated had I not cut Ollie out in the first place.

Holy Hell.

Ollie went on. "The guys who grabbed you are the bar security. The guy who popped you with the bottle is the club manager. They all work for Summerfield. I thought that was why they attacked you in the first place."

"You got attacked again?" Junior said.

"I...I'm really goddamn confused right now. Did those guys...are they IronClad Security?"

"I don't know," Ollie said. "I know they work at that bar all the time. I figured, once you told me about the money, that it was somehow connected to Summerfield. That guy—the one who got killed..." Ollie was getting better at the playing-dumb game.

"Byron."

"Yeah, Byron. Didn't you say all this happened after he came back from Amsterdam?"

"Yeah."

"Lot of designer drug traffic coming in and out of The Netherlands. Maybe this guy was a courier."

"As well as a jazz musician," I said. "Makes a fine cover."

"And also a douche," Junior said. "But that don't make no sense. Why would he have money and not product? That seems like the logistical way for it to work here."

Had Junior just said logistical? I was pretty sure he meant logical. I went on. "Either way, it would make sense that it ties in somehow. Maybe something zigged when it was supposed to zag over in Europe and the deal didn't happen, or Byron got cold feet. Something."

"Something doesn't make sense," Ollie said. "But it's a direction to look when I open the phone."

"My head hurts," said Junior.

Then I was warm. Warm in my heart. For the first time in my life, I understood musicals. Didn't know if it was the drugs or that I'd just been handed Summerfield's ass on a platter, but suddenly I knew why people could break out into song.

"Fly Me to the Moon" was screaming in my head at a volume of eleven.

This.

This was joy.

We got the rare space right in front of The Cellar, because, you know, awesomeness. I parked, then leapt out the door with a joyous whoop.

"He's happy," Ollie said.

"Oh yeah," Junior said. "Nothing would make that man happier than putting it to that limey prick."

"What's your beef with Summerfield, Boo?" Ollie asked

"He's fucking my ex-girlfriend!" I said, clapping Ollie on his shoulders.

"She was never your girlfriend, you deluded douchecanoe," Junior said flatly.

"Shut up, Junior!" I said. "I think I'm going to do a snow angel. You guys! Do a snow angel with me!"

"You're freaking me out, man," Junior said.

"It's the drugs," Ollie said. "But I'll do a snow angel."

"Please don't," Junior said.

"Meh," Ollie said. "I'm a little doped too,"

"I shouldn't have been driving!" I said.

"I'm going inside," Junior said. "You two Marys can come talk to me when you finish doing your snow ballet."

"That's somewhat hurtful," Ollie said to me after the door closed behind Junior.

"I know, brother. We're gonna work on that."

Then we made snow angels.

THE CELLAR WAS as empty as one would assume during a blizzard. There was a trio in the darkened back corner huddled over their drinks. Audrey sat at the end of the bar watching some George Clooney movie on her laptop, idly feeding Burrito olives as he sat on the bar. Flogging Molly's "Another Bag of Bricks" blared through the speakers.

My beloved pooch looked up and gave me a snaggletoothed snarl when he saw me, ready as always.

I slipped a dollar into the jukebox and tapped in the numbers for Hank the Third's "Pills I Took."

As the twanging guitar filled the room, I snatched Burrito's fat Chihuahua ass off the bar and did my best two-step along the bar with him. Two steps into my two-step, Burrito went absolutely apoplectic in my grasp, nearly squirting from my fingers like a watermelon seed. I dropped him to the floor, and he blobbled away back to Audrey. If he'd had the ability to spit on my boots, I was sure he would have. And yes, I said blobbled. It's the only word to describe the way that tubby prick moved.

Having lost my dance partner, I broke into an impromptu do-si-do with Ollie.

"Okay, lines are being crossed," Junior said.

"Are you on drugs right now?" Audrey asked.

"Little bit," I said. But I was pretty sure they were starting to wear off. Pain was working its way back into my various nooks and crannies.

Audrey waved and then dropped a sheaf of papers on the bar. "Everybody and their grandmother has been trying to find you."

I stopped to flip through the messages. The first couple were from Junior while he was in the precinct. Then Underdog, Underdog, G.G. making several and increasingly violent threats against my anatomy for the consecutive nights of work he'd been forced into. Some detective whose name I didn't know. Underdog.

Then one from Ian Summerfield.

Well, lookie, lookie.

"What did this guy say?" I held up the yellow receipt paper to Audrey.

"Is he English?"

"He is."

"Ooh. I love that accent."

"Great. What did he want?"

"He would like you to call him when you have the chance," Audrey said in a terrible Brit accent, fluttering her eyelashes. "Very polite. Like getting a call from Doctor Who."

And my afternoon just got even more interesting.

I looked at Audrey's laptop. "Ollie."

"Yeah?"

"Can you crack the phone on that? I don't think we can drive any more in that storm right now."

"Maybe." Ollie pointed at the computer. "May I?" he said to Audrey.

"Sure, hon," she said, turning the screen toward him.

Ollie focused on the computer like a laser beam. His fingers flew across the screen, tappity-tapping on the keyboard. "Might take a while, but I can do it. I don't have any of the programs that I have on my computer, but I can download them. How's the Wi-Fi in here?"

I shrugged.

"It blows, but it works," Audrey said.

"Let me see what I can do," he said. Ollie cracked his knuckles, readjusted the thick glasses on his face that weren't there anymore, nearly poking himself in the eye. Then, mostly to himself, he said, "I'm fucking MacGuyver," and began quietly humming the *Mission Impossible* theme as he typed.

"What can I do?" Twitch said.

I almost jumped out of my skin. "How the fuck do you keep doing that?" I yelled. "*Why* the fuck do you keep doing that?"

"So-rry," he said. "I've been sitting in the back the whole time, you unobservant prick."

I looked back to the one table with people at it and then noticed that the other two occupants at the table were the cleanup guys from Ginny's apartment. They both held up their half-empty Coronas in salute to me.

"You're still hanging with those guys?" I asked.

"What the hell else was I going to do but come back here and wait for your ass to re-appear? Benito and Manny were as bored as I was, so I figured we'd have some beers."

"Let me go get the phone," I said to Ollie. He just gave me a cursory nod, never taking his eyes off the computer screen.

I held the scrap of paper with Summerfield's number on it as I took the stairs two at a time. I ran the potential conversation through my head, saying the lines out loud as I opened the office door. "Missing something, fucko? You lose something, asshat?" I couldn't decide.

Grabbing the cell phone off the office desk, I took a quick peek behind the bottles of Dry Sack. As predicted, not even the dust had been disturbed around the trumpet case.

"I think I have something of yours. You got something of mine, Mr. Bean."

Was that too much? How could I parlay this into him cutting Kelly loose? Was that messed up? It started to feel like it was. Like *I* was. Meh. Screw it. This might actually be fun, even if it was in the most emotionally immature, potentially deadly way. Still fun.

I heard the bar phone ring as I went down the stairs.

"BOO!" Audrey bellowed, nearly rattling the lead paint off the walls.

"Coming," I yelled back.

As I rounded the hallway, she covered the mouthpiece and grinned. "It's the man who sounds like Hugh Grant," she said.

Record scratch.

Everybody's eyebrows shot up.

I sniffed, rolled my neck, and took the phone.

Game on, bitch.

"Listen up, Summerfield—"

"No, you listen up, Malone. You got something of mine."

"Yeah, well—" Two lines in and the conversation was already running away from my fantasized narrative. That was supposed to be my line. Well, one of them, anyway.

"Well, nothing. I'm not mucking about with you and yours anymore."

"Wait…what?"

"You got something I want back. I got something of yours that you might want back."

Shit. That was also supposed to be my line.

Waitaminnit… That sounded like a threat. He wasn't supposed to be threatening me.

The breath caught inside my chest. The line was silent.

"You still there, mate?"

"I'm still here," I said through a clenched jaw.

Junior saw my expression. He held his hands out. "What?" he whispered.

I shook my head.

"Good," Summerfield said. "I want you to listen very carefully to me." Then the sound of deep puffing came over the earpiece. "You hear that? That's the sound of me puffing a cigar that's more valuable than your whole bloody life." A couple more puffs.

A deep sickness cramped my gut.

"There," he said, "got that cherry nice and hot."

I could hear a woman crying softly.

Then the ripping of cloth.

And a screaming muffled cry.

And the world exploded red.

"Can't help but notice the silence, Mr. Malone. You still there?"

"Yeah," I croaked.

"That was a preview. I didn't even burn this little bitch. But I came close. Oh. So. Close. Next time, I'm going to grind out this fabulous cigar right on her nipple. Then I'm going to light another one and burn off her other nipple."

The plastic of the phone case creaked in my grip.

Summerfield went on. "Bring me what's mine in the hour, and we can prevent what's yours from getting her lovely tits blemished. Because when I'm done with them, I move my lovely cigar to her eyes. Then the two of you can take a romantic stroll to the ASPCA to pick out a dog to lead her around for the short time I allow you both to continue breathing."

I tried to speak, but couldn't. How did he know? Guess he did his due diligence on me as well.

The rage...

The rage had me tight.

What was left of my sensible brain pleaded with me to not immediately charge into Raja and tear the skin from Summerfield's corpse-to-be.

He had me right where he wanted me.

Because he had Kelly.

And he was going to hurt her.

To hurt me.

"Hullloooo? Am I talking to myself?"

"No," I said.

"Be here in an hour. Are we clear, mate?"

"We're clear," I said, the words choking me.

"Excellent. See you soon, mate." Then he hung up.

I placed the bar phone on the bar gently, with a hand shaking like I was stroking out. I could feel every heartbeat pulsing through me.

"Boo?" Junior said. "What the hell did he say?"

I couldn't talk.

It was happening again.

I'd cut Kelly loose because bad things happened to the women I loved.

They died.

They died badly.

I couldn't handle the same happening to her. Couldn't disconnect from the mythology of my history.

I'd cut her loose so she would be safe.

It didn't matter.

She was going to get killed.

Because of me.

It was happening again.

My knees went weak, and I crumpled halfway to the floor, catching one arm on the bar, Junior grabbing the other as I fell. "Boo! What the fuck is happening?"

"He's got Kelly," I said, feeling the vomit rising with the air I needed to even say the words.

"Oh, oh goddamn," Junior said.

I stumbled to the door, bursting out into the blinding storm. I dropped to my hands and knees and puked into the pristine snow until nothing but yellow bile poured out of me.

Through the howling snow, a diminutive figure walked toward me. Even inside the whiteout storm, I could see The Boy clearly as he approached. The flecks of ice danced through him, swirling inside his tiny scarred form.

He dropped to his knees and faced me.

I stared into his eyes.

My eyes.

His mouth moved, but no words came out.

I knew what he was saying.

Save her.

I could.

Could I?

I had to.

Freezing tears rolled down the cheeks filled with wind-whispering snowflakes as he reached a ghostly hand to touch my face.

Save her.

"Then let's stop with the fucking puking and get to it," Junior said from behind me, his voice an enraged grumble.

I turned and saw Junior, Twitch, and Ollie in the doorway.

I hadn't realized I'd said the words out loud.

My brothers stood there.

The Boy was gone.

My brothers.

My family.

Avengers assemble, motherfuckers.

CHAPTER 17

OLLIE WAS STAYING at the bar and opening that goddamn phone. It was all we had to potentially tie Byron to Summerfield. I hoped to hell there was something that would at least take the heat off me and Junior for his death. If reasonable doubt was all we could get, then reasonable doubt was what we'd have to settle for.

I walked Twitch up to the office and poured us both a couple of fingers of Jim Beam.

Twitch didn't drink, but he was game enough to take a timid sip, wincing as he did so. "You've never poured me a drink before."

I threw mine back, letting the physical burn match the anger churning inside me. Everything was fire, everything burning under my fingertips. I wanted to rage. I wanted to tear the world down. But I knew that letting my natural instinct to Hulk the fuck out would not only get me killed, but Kelly too.

Maybe I was growing up.

Still felt like we were all going to get killed anyway.

"So, Manny and Benito are hip to take this fucker down with us, John Woo-style. If you know a place where we can buy a shitload of doves, we're good."

"I'm going in alone," I said.

"Fuck that," Twitch said, shaking his head. "No. *Fuck* no."

"I need you guys behind me."

"I'm confused now."

"This guy has me by the balls here."

"Uh-huh," Twitch said. "I got that."

"Which is why this is mine, and mine only to handle."

"I'm still not following." His eyeball twitched in confusion.

I bit the inside of my cheek "I don't see me walking out. If I can get Kelly out, fine. But I don't see where this ends any way except with me in a ditch."

"So we blaze in there. Shoot anything that doesn't have tits. What's the problem?"

"Are we the Avengers?"

Twitch smiled. "Fucking A."

"Then avenge my ass if I'm not back here with Kelly."

"But..."

"If I don't come back, then burn it. Burn it all down. You guys are my contingency plan."

Twitch's eyes lit up at the prospect of unleashing the Biblical-level of violence that I knew he was capable of. "I both like and really don't like that part of your scenario. Don't get me wrong. I'm more than happy to follow through on my part of the plan. But that still doesn't change the fact that *your* plan is hella stoopid."

"I'm not going to argue with you on that. If I can get Kelly out, just hand the money over and walk away, I'm going to. I have to try that first. I can't risk her getting killed."

"But you can risk getting yourself killed."

"Yep. Like we do."

"Like we do." Twitch popped the rest of his shot, coughed, then squinted back tears.

"You okay?"

"Good as I'm going to be," he said. "Junior is okay with this?"

"He's gonna have to be." But boy howdy, he wasn't going to be.

"Manny and Benito are going to be disappointed."

"They'll get over it, I'm sure."

Then, unexpectedly, Twitch threw his arms around me in a bear hug, face pressed against my chest. "Sorry."

"No, man. Maybe we should hug more. We can still be macho and hug, right?"

"Ollie would like that." Then he snickered.

I stared at him. Something dinged in my brain. It was no different than the thousands of cracks we'd made over the years about each other's sexuality and masculinity.

But because of the recent events, I heard what Twitch was saying for the first time.

"What?" Twitch said, noticing the change in my face.

"Why did you say that?"

Twitch shrugged. "I dunno. Because he's gay? And we always make gay jokes about Ollie."

I felt my jaw drop nearly through the floor. "You knew?"

Twitch's eyes went wide. "You didn't?"

I had nothing. "How long have you known?"

Twitch paused, eyes narrowing as he tried to assess whether or not I was messing with him. "Uh, since I met him? Please don't tell me that you're just figuring this out now."

"Did he tell you?"

"We never had a conversation about it. I think it's pretty clear."

Well, maybe for some of us.

Twitch scrunched his face up. "Did he *have* to tell you?"

"In a way."

"So lemme get this straight. For the last twenty years, you thought that all my fucking with him for being gay was…" He stopped. "Oh, shit. So when Junior makes all those cracks…"

I finished the sentence for him. "He wasn't meaning to be a dick."

"You think."

"Pretty sure. Me and Junior thought you were busting his balls. Like we do."

"And I'm the only one who knew?" Twitch said. "You gotta be kidding me."

"Did Ollie know you knew?"

Twitch opened his mouth to answer, then paused. "Oh shit. He just thinks we're assholes."

"To be fair, some of us *were* just being assholes."

Twitch shook his head. "There is the probability that Junior might really be one…y'know, where this is concerned." Twitch whistled as he stuck his index finger into his closed fist. Then he pointed at said fist. "In this instance, the hand represents a dude's butt."

"I get it," I said. "I'm gonna have a talk with him about it."

"Thought you probably weren't coming back later."

"Oh yeah. That." I clapped my hands together. "Anyhoo, I'm going to get myself together and head over to Raja."

"Okay. I'll talk to the boys. How long you want us to wait before we storm the castle?"

I grabbed Twitch by the back of his neck and looked him dead in the eyes. "If I'm not back by the time the sun comes up, it's the last sunrise I want that motherfucker to see."

Twitch's eye made with a happy little jumping jack. "Done." Twitch walked back downstairs to break the news to his new besties.

I slid the trumpet case out from behind the Dry Sack and opened it.

Damn, that was a lot of money.

I sighed and opened the desk drawer where we kept the rolls of duct tape and what remained of the first aid kit. As I started redressing my wound before battle, I got an idea.

Maybe not the greatest idea.

But an idea.

I WALKED BACK down the stairs, all bundled up and ready to roll.

"Ollie. How you doing on that phone?"

Ollie didn't look up from the screen. He was in his zone. "I'm pretty close to hacking the provider's website, at which point I'll at least have a list of recent calls. I have the programs uploaded. All I have to do then is run the numbers through the IOS."

I had no idea what IOS meant, so I just said, "Rock on."

Ollie gave me the devil horn fingers.

"Junior, soon as he opens that thing, get Underdog here and give him all of whatever we get."

"Nah. Twitch can do that."

Twitch raised his hand. "I don't think I should be the guy dealing with the cops."

I opened my palm at Twitch. "See? You have to do it. I gotta go." I turned and headed to the door.

"Hey, hold on a sec. Let me get my coat," Junior said.

"I gotta do this solo."

"Nah. That's not gonna happen," he said, buttoning up his pea coat.

"Don't fight me on this, Junior. I need you guys to—"

"I'm not fighting with you. I'm just coming with." Junior finished his plastic cup of wine in three huge gulps, then burped. "If you want to fight about it, feel free. I'm still going."

"Dammit." I looked at Audrey, who was still blissfully unaware of what was about to go down. Granted, the activities so far—what with my vomiting, injuries, and general air of pain and violence—were nothing unusual for The Cellar.

"Are you taking my schnoogums home with you tonight?" She scratched

Burrito behind the ears. Burrito happily leaned into her fingernails and purred.

Yes, purred.

My dog is fucking weird.

"You mind another night? Or two?" I asked.

"Of course not!" she said. "You hear that, Buwwito! You're going to stay with Grammy Audrey some more."

Burrito yipped in Chihuahuan glee, his tiny tail whipping the air.

I decided to head out before her baby talk left me with type-2 diabetes. Because I needed that on top of everything and everyone else that was going to try to kill me in the next hour. "Time?"

"We got eleven minutes," Junior said. "Take note that I said 'we' not 'you.'"

"Noted, fuckhole."

"Let's go, then, cheesedick."

"Okay, twatwaffle."

"Twatwaffle?" Junior scrunched his face. "The hell is a twatwaffle?"

"Never mind…"

THE STORM WAS still in whiteout, with the gusts lashing our faces. Junior and I had to yell in order to hear each other over the screaming wind. "I can't believe you thought I wasn't coming along," Junior yelled. "Were you just going to walk on me?"

"First chance I get, I'm taking him down, out if I can. The second I'm close enough, I'm ripping his fucking throat out."

"Okay. I got no problem with that. What's your point?"

"His boys are probably going to beat me to death once that happens. If I'm lucky, I'll get a bullet."

"So it's a suicide mission. This ain't our first one, frankly." Junior slipped, his feet sliding willy-nilly before he caught himself on a parking meter. "Fuck! Save them the trouble if we break our necks walking over there. I'm gonna ask again, what's your point?"

"I'd rather not have your death on my hands, but you seem determined to have it your way."

"Meh. What else did I have planned for the day? Let's do this, Sundance!"

I tried to explain why Butch and Sundance was a terrible fucking appropriation, but another gust of wind blew what felt like an entire snowball down my throat. Then I realized that for the first time, his usage was appropriate considering the circumstances.

It kinda sucked to realize that.

We turned onto Lansdowne and stood for a moment in front of the large double doors at the entrance to Raja. The place was locked tight, but there was an intercom to the left of the ornate metal gate.

Junior took a knee, stretching for his toes as I reached for the buzzer.

I stopped just short of hitting the button. "The hell are you doing?"

"Loosening up my quads. Making sure my laces are tight. Shit gets real, I don't wanna trip on a shoelace or get a cramp."

Wasn't a bad idea, that. I began my own slow calisthenics, glad that no passing cars would see our ridiculous warm-up. Once my blood started flowing, that's when the guilt hit me. Especially when the item in my pocket poked me in the ribs while I did my trunk twists. "I gotta tell you something, Junior."

"Now? Can you tell me inside, where I'm not freezing my balls off?"

"In the event we both get shot in the head the second we walk in the door, I think it's best that we talk now."

"Oh, for fuck's sake," he said, blowing into his mittens. "What is it?"

"Miss Kitty is gone."

Junior blinked at me. "What are you talking about?"

"I had to scrap her." Did I just call the goddamn car "her"? "I couldn't take the chance that the car was going to be more evidence to bury us with." Mostly true.

Junior blinked at me again.

"I saved you this." I fumbled in my pocket and brought out the antenna. I placed it in both his mittens like I was handing him a holy relic.

He stared at it a second. I couldn't tell if there were tears in his eyes, since they would have frozen instantly anyway.

"I'm sorry," I said, the guilt knotting my stomach. "Say something."

Junior flicked his wrist, extending the antenna. Then he started viciously whipping my legs with it.

"You son of a *bitch*!" he yelled. "How could you do that to Miss Kitty?"

"I, *ow*, didn't do it, *fuck*, for the fun of it!" The thrashing antenna hurt even more than it normally would, what with my shin being half frostbitten.

"I loved that car, Boo! How? How could you do that?"

"I thought it, *shit*, needed to, *fucking ow*, happen! Dammit, dude. Cut it out!"

Junior stopped flaying the skin off my legs, and I stopped the ridiculous dance I was doing as I tried to halfheartedly avoid the blows I knew I deserved. "You lousy fuck," he said sadly.

"Noted," I said, rubbing at the intense stinging on my legs. "Save some for the guys inside, though, will ya?"

"Why are you telling me this now? You're the kind of prick who takes a girl to the fancy restaurant to break up with her!"

"Because we're probably going to fucking die here, Junior. I didn't want to take that to my grave."

Junior shook it off, retracted the antenna, then gave it a kiss before he put it in the pocket of his coat.

That kiss was one of the saddest things I'd ever seen.

"We good?" I asked.

"No. No, we are not good. You killed my car. But we will discuss this at another time."

At least he was still operating under the notion that there would be another time. Unless he planned on hounding me with the issue into the afterlife—which wouldn't surprise me in the least.

I pressed the doorbell by the club's entrance. I couldn't hear the ring, but a buzzing sounded along with a click. As I opened the door, the flood of warm air melted the snowflakes on my face and coat.

We got two steps in before the gun was placed against the back of my neck.

"Surprise," said Marcus. "Junior?"

"Yeah." Junior's face immediately shifted into war mode.

"Kindly walk in front of Boo, here." I could hear the smile on his face.

"This isn't a great way to start a negotiation," I said. Although I couldn't look at him, I could hear by his high nasal tone that his schnozz was still taped good and tight after I'd given it a horsey ride on my kneecap.

"Unh-unh," Marcus said. "See, that's where you've been wrong about what's about to go down here. Ain't shit about to be negotiated."

Junior went, "*Wanh wanh, wanh wanh wanh wanh.*" A pretty good impersonation of both Marcus and Charlie Brown's teacher. Junior snickered through his nose at his own impression.

I giggled, then got mad that I did. That fucker—couldn't we do anything seriously?

Marcus cleared his throat, hard. "This isn't a negotiation. It never—"

"*Wanh.*"

Another giggle.

I snorted.

Marcus said, "It never was. You're going to give us what we want."

"*Wanh wanh.*"

Then we both lost it, making it worse by trying really hard not to lose it.

"Hey," Marcus yelled. "I am holding a fucking gun at your head here!"

"Yeah, meant to mention that," I said. "You working guns now? Wasn't this a part of the whole 'who's a pussy' debate we just went through a couple days ago?"

"Because this makes you a pussy, you know," Junior said.

"I'm moving up in the world, Malone. Doing some critical work for Mr. Summerfield now. Need some serious hardware to back that up. Start walking."

"I'm not walking with a gun to the back of my head." I dusted the snow from the front of my jacket all over the expensive carpeting at Raja. Maybe gave it a water stain. That'd learn 'em. Fight the power.

"You messing with me?" Marcus said, his voice rising a notch. Poor Marcus. I bet he had a really cool scenario in his imagination that was supposed to go down. And there I was, fucking it all up again being a dick about things.

"You know where the money is?" I asked him over my shoulder. It was then that I noticed he was wearing one of those NBA-style hard plastic nose guards. Guess I really broke his face up good.

"You didn't bring it?" Marcus said incredulously.

"I'm not as stupid as you and your boss think I am."

Junior looked me up and down. "Yeah. I didn't know that either. Feel like I should have noticed you weren't carrying a goddamn trumpet case. You think you could have mentioned that part of your plan?"

"We didn't discuss any plan. You weren't part of this plan. You insisted on tagging along."

"Are you fucking kidding me?" said Marcus. "Again, I am holding a gun here."

"And you're going to either put it down or shoot me, "I said. "Then you can explain to Summerfield why you put a bullet into the only man who knows where his money is."

Marcus just stood there, the gun pressing harder under my ear.

"And you don't even know how to properly use that thing," I said. "I'd rather not have you catch your foot on one of these fancy-ass curtains and accidentally blow the top of my head off."

"The fuck you talking about?"

"First off, you never stand this close to someone and press a gun against their head unless you intend on shooting them."

Marcus sighed. "I promise I will not accidentally shoot you."

"Not that at all. Bullets move fast. That's the point. You stand this close, you're giving up the advantage that distance and speed would give..." I took one step back, the gun slipping past my ear, then harmlessly parallel to my face.

Before he could react, I grabbed his arm by the wrist and bent at the waist, throwing all my upper body weight into it. His shoulder popped and he shrieked, squeezing off two shots before he was airborne and upside down.

When he landed, I knelt on his wrist and drove my elbow down straight into his noseguard. The molded plastic shattered and his eyes rolled up.

I drew back for another shot, but Junior soccer-kicked him to the temple with his Docs.

The gun clattered when it hit the floor. I grabbed it and pointed it at Marcus's chest.

From a distance.

"Holy fuck, Bruce Lee! That was awesome!" Junior said, fist-bumping me. "The hell you learn to do that?"

"YMCA class, bitch," I said to Marcus, and spat on his face.

Marcus groaned and rolled to his side, clutching his head.

"Now stand up and lead the way," I said.

Legs still wobbly, Marcus stumbled as he tried to stand. He caught himself on the armrest of a velvet couch, and snarled at me. "You are a fucking dead man, Malone. You're not walking out of here. No way."

"Guy talks a lot of smack for somebody who just lost a tooth," Junior said.

Marcus reached into his mouth, his finger finding the gap where his lower incisor used to be. His eyes flared with rage, but it was quickly extinguished by the barrel I was holding on him.

"Drop it!" came a voice I wasn't expecting or happy to hear. Alex parted the curtains that led to the main bar. With him were my old buddies, Cornrows and Lineman.

They all had guns pointed at me.

"See, Marcus?" I said. "These guys know how to hold a gun." I opened my grip and let the gun dangle by the trigger guard.

Marcus grabbed a heavy iron lamp off the table and got ready to swing it into my temple.

"Quit it, Marcus. You've already fucked this up enough," Alex said.

"Yeah, Marcus," Junior said, waggling his finger.

Marcus bellowed and threw the lamp to the floor with a sound thump.

"Don't worry. They keep this up, and you'll get your opportunity," Alex said.

"Don't know if that's such a good idea," Junior said. "He's had chances already, and look how that's turned out."

"Where's Summerfield?" I said.

"He'll be with us in a moment."

"Where's the girl? Where's Kelly?"

Alex's eyebrow went up. "All of your questions will be answered in a minute. Please walk with us. Boys, put the guns down."

Cornrows and Lineman looked at each other warily, but lowered their guns as told. They were even more bandaged up than Marcus was. Cornrows had his non-gun-bearing arm in a sling and Lineman had a lump on the side of his jaw that looked like he'd taken a hook from Tyson in his prime.

"Whoa. What happened to those guys?" Junior asked me.

"That was me."

"Nice! You did some damage while I was away."

"Didn't feel like it at the time, but I guess I did."

We fist-bumped again.

Alex and the goon trio led us up a wide carpeted stairwell to a glass door. Curtained, of course. What was with all the curtains? Every time a goddamn curtain opened in this bar, I didn't like what was on the other side. Affixed to the wall was a small brass plaque that read *VIP* in elegant cursive.

Lineman opened the door to a long room with a wide oak table in the middle. On the far end was a bar filled with top-shelf liquor. Six bar stools in slipcovers lined the short bar. Even the damn chairs in the place were curtained. "I'll take a Pappy Van Winkle, neat," I said to Marcus.

"Fuck you," he said.

"Well, there goes his tip," Junior said.

"We should speak to the manager," I said.

We were almost hit with another fit of giggles when, from under one of the barstool slipcovers, a whimper. The chair was turned toward the bar, so I didn't notice that the cover was also draped over what appeared to be a person sitting on the barstool.

The room burned red. Acid pumped into my heart and every muscle went into nitro mode.

Junior grabbed my forearm. "Don't," was all he said. "Not yet."

I slowly walked toward her.

"Sit down," Cornrows said.

I kept walking. "Shoot me," I said.

From the corner of my eye, I saw all three of the goons give each other looks, but none of them moved to stop me, and none of them shot me.

I crouched in front of the chair and turned it toward me. Another frightened whimper. Gently, I lifted the thin plastic off Ginny, her eyes terrified and red-rimmed.

What?

I didn't know which one of us wore the bigger look of surprise, but hers quickly turned to fury as she started to kick her legs at me, her curses at my general existence barely muffled by the duct tape over her mouth.

I rolled back, her foot missing my chin by an inch.

From the other end of the room, Junior said, "All right. Now I'm confused."

I jumped up, trying to maintain composure. "What is she doing here?"

Marcus looked at me, now also puzzled. "Who the hell did you think was here?"

"Where's Kelly?" I asked.

"This Kelly?" asked a BBC-accented voice. Ian Summerfield walked into the room from a door that was flush with the wall on the far end of the short bar. I didn't even know the door was there. I guess VIP's needed to be sneaky.

"You know fucking well and good—" I stopped short as my heart leapt out of my chest, ran behind me, and gave me an emotional wedgie.

Summerfield led a visibly concerned and confused Kelly into the room, his hand roughly gripping her upper arm.

Plainly not a hostage of any goddamn kind.

Or at least she wasn't until I opened my goddamn mouth.

There were a couple of weighted seconds of silence…

…before Junior absolutely lost his shit laughing.

CHAPTER 18

JUNIOR WAS NEVER going to let me live this one down. It was a small blessing that our life expectancy was topping out at only another fifteen to twenty minutes.

Junior was now screaming with laughter, his face as red as his hair, fist pounding on the table.

Everyone looked at each other and Junior uncomfortably.

Summerfield pointed at Junior. "Can he stop that please?"

"I can't!" Junior squealed, then fell into huge whooping coughs. "Water," he wheezed.

Summerfield let go of Kelly's bicep and gave her a little shove towards the bar. "Will someone please get him some fucking water," he said, staring at his goons.

Alex went behind the bar and filled a pint glass from the soda gun.

"Thank you," Junior said, chugging the water before wiping his wet mouth and eyes on his sleeve. "Oh God." Junior looked at me through laughter-teared eyes. "You really screwed the pooch on this one."

That I had. This was nothing new.

I couldn't read Kelly's face. She maintained a certain amount of stoniness, but her eyes darted around the room, as confused as I was. Before I could catch the words coming out of my mouth, I said to her, "What are you doing?"

Her eyebrows pulled down angrily at me. "What are *you* doing?"

"I thought I was coming here to rescue you."

"From what? My job?"

"Your what?" My confusion was getting worse.

"I work here. I'm the event coordinator for Ian's bars."

Summerfield held up a finger. "So. You two know each other how?"

Junior, mouth full of water, made a fist and a finger. Then he vigorously and repeatedly jammed said finger into his fist, but instead of Twitch's reference, the fist represented...

...why the fuck am I explaining this?

"Ew," said Summerfield.

"Who is that?" Kelly said, pointing behind me to Ginny.

"That's Ginny. She works at The Cellar," Junior said.

"So it's her you're here to rescue," Kelly said, lowering her gaze at me.

"I didn't know she was here. I thought she was you."

Then it was Ginny's turn to give me a death stare.

Well, none of this was coming out right. Not one bit right. All I could do was look back at Ginny and grimace at her apologetically. "Sorry," I said.

"Why would she be here? Why would you think I was her?" Kelly asked.

"They 'had relations' the other day," Junior said, air quoting himself.

Ginny yelled and snarled something angry from behind the tape.

Kelly's face went redder. And I'd be lying if I said it didn't give me some satisfaction to see.

"Please shut up, Junior," I said.

"It's the truth."

"Can we discuss this later?" I said.

"Like we're going to discuss Miss Kitty later?" Junior said, hurt in his voice.

"Miss Kitty?" Summerfield asked, his own confusion deepening. "Who is she?"

"Nobody," I said.

"Don't say that," Junior said through clenched teeth. "She wasn't nobody to me."

I looked around the room for some help, but had no idea who could offer assistance in this utterly ridiculous development. The whole situation had gone fuckadoodle.

"Let's just settle all this first," I said, waving my hand at the guns, the duct-taped Ginny, the frightened and miffed Kelly and the rest of the room in general.

"No," he said, starting to exhibit more than a little pissed off intent behind his words. "You've been bitching and moaning about this broad for months now, " he said, pointing his mitten at Kelly. "Get this out and over with so we can all move on with our fucking lives."

Kelly was boring holes in me with her eyes as she flicked her gaze back and forth from Ginny to me. Really? Was she judging me here? I cut her off as she opened her mouth to say something.

"You," I said to Kelly, "do not get to form an opinion here. At least I'm not fucking a goddamn Euro-trash drug dealer, am I?"

The mouth that had started opening to speak, simply fell the rest of the way down in shock. "Oh my God. You're serious?" Kelly said.

Frankly, I was a little stunned at myself for saying it. It had just come out.

"Really?" Summerfield said. "Are you? Oh my god. He's completely serious right now, isn't he?"

Despite the voice in my head telling me that it was time to stop embarrassing myself, I felt the need to go on. "Goddamn right," I said. "Sorry if my terms offend you, but if the Euro-trash drug dealer shoe fits, wear it."

"Oh, Jesus," Kelly said, closing her eyes.

"I'm *gay*, you twat," Summerfield yelled at me. "Are you fucking thick?"

Aw, shit…

I guess I was.

The uncomfortable silence was broken by Junior's explosion

of laughter. "Oh my GAAAAHD!" he shrieked. "I'm gonna puke! *WAAAAAAHAHAHAHAHAHA!*" Then he had himself a good couple of wheezing coughs before he was able to squeak out, "Everybody is fucking gay!"

"Excuse me," yelled Summerfield. "What the bloody hell is happening? Did you all suddenly forget what we're doing here? That there are several men here with guns to shoot you with?"

Oh yeah. That. "Well," I said, "clearly we've lost the narrative thread within this situation."

"Clearly," Summerfield said, pinching the bridge of his nose.

"Let's start with you letting Ginny go. She's a lot less involved here than you think."

Summerfield shook his head in disbelief. "Give me my goddamn drugs you stole, then, and only then, can we discuss letting any of you go."

"I don't have any drugs. I have a whole lot of your money, though."

Summerfield rolled his eyes, his exasperation growing with every word that came out of my mouth. "So Byron never even got the pills. That cunt was planning on taking my money from the get-go."

"Look, I have no idea what, if any, plan he had. We were—"

Summerfield cut me off by pulling a chrome-plated .32 from inside of his coat. "You pricks were thinking you'd kill my courier and run with my product and/or money. Why?"

"That's not—"

"Was it because of her?" Summerfield pointed the gun at Kelly's face. Kelly gasped and stepped back until she was against the bar.

My heart cramped excruciatingly.

Summerfield's face was getting redder with each word. I couldn't tell if it was his blood pressure or mine that was making it change colors.

He went on. "You were going to try to take me down a fucking peg because of your...whatever she was to you?" Summerfield took a step closer to Kelly. "Or were you involved with this from the start?"

Kelly backed to the wall, blinking rapidly. "Ian, I swear—"

"You better swear, you deceitful bitch. Because I'm not the kind of man who believes in coincidences."

"Hey, hey!" I yelled, hands held up. I was too far away to jump in front of the gun if need be. "Listen, you got this whole situation ass-backward. We didn't rob your fucking courier." My hands were up, pleading. My heart pounded in my chest, blood rushing in my ears.

I was fucking terrified. I could hear it in my own voice.

It was all happening again.

It was going to be my fault.

"We didn't kill your courier. He was harassing my co-worker over there, and all we wanted to do was get him to back off. Everything else was incidental. You have all the cards right now. We have no reason to lie to you about this."

"Other than to save your own asses and making me feel like a right cunt in the meantime for trusting this *bitch*." He jabbed the gun in the air at Kelly's face. She flinched and cried out.

"*I'm* swearing to you. She's not involved other than the pure coincidence of it all."

"Then how did you get my money? How did you even know about my money?"

"The dumbass left it at her house," I said, pointing back at Ginny. "He had it in a hollow trumpet case. Until yesterday, I thought I was carrying a fucking trumpet."

"You're joking."

I sighed under the weight of my own stupidity. "Wish I was. Didn't even know it was yours. At this point, I don't give two shits about anything other than clearing this plate."

"Start by giving me my fucking money!"

"I…uh…didn't bring it."

Summerfield lowered the gun and slumped into one of the plush chairs, beaten down by my nincompoopery. "Why didn't you bring the money?"

"Because I didn't think that any of us were going to walk out of here once you had the money. You made your point. You can get to me and mine. I was planning on walking out with who I thought was her," I said, gesturing to Kelly. "Then I was going to send back an uninvolved third party with your cash."

"What, were you going to FedEx it to me overnight?"

I didn't reply. That was exactly what I was going to do. It hadn't seemed so stupid until he put it that way.

"Oh Christ," Summerfield said, realizing the same.

"Wait a minute," Junior chimed in, raising his hand like he was in the first grade. "Beyond the clusterfuck already laid out before us here, we didn't kill Byron. You're saying you didn't either. So, then, who did?"

That was a damned good question.

Summerfield, with a strained look, stood from his chair and walked to the bar. He took a tiny key from his pocket and opened a small decorative safe above the wine glasses. "I don't want to kill anybody." From the safe, he brought out a decanter of ridiculously expensive-looking cognac. "I didn't kill Byron, nor did I attempt to make it look like you two did. You two boneheads managed to do that all on your own." He poured a good four fingers into a snifter and downed it with a thick cough at the end. "Killing people brings business to a halt. Makes the police take notice of you, no matter how much you pay them to stay out of your endeavors."

"That why you sent your man to kill everybody at Ginny's house?" I said.

Just when I thought I couldn't get Summerfield or myself any more confused, he said, "What are you talking about now?"

"Galal Shaughness."

"*Who the fuck is that?*"

"Seriously?"

"Seriously. I have no idea who that is. And I'm pretty sure that Galal Shaughness is precisely the kind of name I would remember if it came across my desk."

He had me there.

"Well, then, this all points to a third party dicking with the both of us," I said.

"I don't care anymore. Just get me my money. Byron is dead. You're not in jail for killing Byron, so you have that. I didn't kill him. So we have that too."

"What's your point?" Junior said. "I lost both of you five minutes ago."

"My point is that I'm sick of all of this. So why don't we apply Occam's Razor to this scenario."

Junior stood up. "You wanna settle this with a knife fight? Let's do it, fucko!"

Summerfield looked at me. "Is he…what?" Summerfield opened his arms wide, hoping someone would assist Junior.

"It's not a real razor, Junior," I said.

"Oh," Junior said, sitting back down. "Go on."

Summerfield shook the stupid out of his head and went on. "Occam's Razor is a principle of simplicity. Whether or not there is a conspiratorial third hand in play with all of this, you have my money, and I have your…" he looked over at Kelly and Ginny "…whatever your relationship to those two is."

"So we're at an impasse," I said.

"No, we're not. The threat still stands. I am going to shoot one of them in the stomach in ten minutes unless you bring me my money. Ten minutes later, I shoot the other one. I want my goddamn money."

"Thought you didn't want to kill anybody," Junior said.

"I'm going to make an exception with you lot. Enough is enough."

"That's not—" Ollie's phone started blaring "The Imperial March" in my coat pocket. "Hold on a sec."

"Make it quick, please."

I fumbled in the pocket and pulled out Ollie's cell. I swiped the screen, and it automatically opened to the text messages Ollie had sent.

And everything fell into place.

CHAPTER 19

"What?" Junior said, reading me like a book. A book with lots of pictures, if we were going to be honest.

I slid the phone across the desk to him. He picked it up and squinted. Then his face broke into a mask of horror. "Oh, hell no! You couldn't have warned me first?" He slammed the phone face-down onto the oak and slid it roughly back to me. "Gross, dude."

"What is it now?" Summerfield said with a sigh.

I slid the phone in his direction. He picked up the cell, and his face immediately darkened at what he saw. Unlike Junior, he scrolled up at the series of messages…

…and pictures.

Summerfield placed the phone down gently and slowly lifted his eyes to Marcus.

Marcus started to stand, a sickly expression and pallor visible even under his cracked noseguard and busted face. "Mr. Summerfield…" was all he said before the three bullets smacked into his chest.

The slugs burst out of Marcus's back and shattered the glass overlooking the dance floor. He toppled through the frame and dropped the thirty feet to the parquet, his neck crunching loudly as he hit the floor with the back of his head.

Kelly screamed. Junior dove to the side. Cornrows' and the Lineman's eyes bugged out. Ginny shrieked underneath the tape. Alex fainted.

"Well, that answers that," Summerfield said, opening his coat and putting the gun back into his shoulder holster. "And now you know that I'm not fucking around anymore."

Everybody was motionless, silent in the impact of Marcus's straight-up execution. I still had questions. He sure as hell couldn't ask them now. The who-what-where-when and why had died along with Marcus. I guess all the answers that Summerfield required were in the phone.

The photos of Marcus and Byron *in flagrante delicto*. Or to put it in terms Junior would understand, *dicks ahoy!*

Peppered between the pictures were the desperate and threatening texts. Warnings about what Byron would do with the graphic photos if Marcus didn't help him. Help him with what was still a question, but it wasn't too hard to connect the most obvious dots. Byron wanted Marcus on his side, one way or the other. What he got was his head caved in. Both of their heads.

I was doing a lot of assuming, since the brain from which the details could be extracted was slowly leaking out of an ear onto a dance floor.

"You two," Summerfield said to his now ashen-faced goons, waving a hand toward Alex, "put him downstairs on a bloody couch or someplace where I'm not going to trip over him. Then clean that mess up."

The two looked at each other. This was clearly more than they had signed on for. If they were anything like me and Junior, they'd simply taken a gig, nothing more. A little muscle work, a little threatening. But from their expressions, it was clear they were in conflict about what to do next.

"The cleaning supplies are in the basement closet next to the walk-in," Summerfield said.

They were two guns against one.

They could choose to end it right there.

I tried as hard as I could with my mental powers to convince them to come around to our side.

"You got it, boss," Cornrows said. The two walked out of the VIP lounge, each shooting me a solid glare as they exited.

Dammit.

So much for my mental powers. Maybe I shouldn't have kicked the crap out of them quite so much in our previous encounters.

"Let's make this fun for you, Mr. Malone," Summerfield said, taking his gun back out and waving it languorously between Kelly and Ginny. "I'm going to let you choose which one of these women I shoot in the stomach."

Ginny's eyes went wide.

Kelly glared at me with more anger than fear. Fear was there, though. A lot of it.

The hell was she glaring at me for?

"I came here for you. I just want you to know that," I said to her.

Kelly looked back to me. "I'm not sure this is the time or place." She scrunched up her face in an exaggeration of thought. "No. Scratch that. I'm positive this isn't the time or place."

Hell. I tried.

Junior chimed in before I could respond. "Wait a minute. I have some questions before we go get your money."

Oh, dear Christ.

Junior held up a finger. "Let's say we go get your loot, and hand it over to you. You gonna let us go? Just like that?"

Summerfield mulled over the question for a second. I didn't like the options he was considering. "Yes."

"Now, how does that make sense?" Junior asked.

"Excuse me?" Summerfield said.

"I mean," Junior said. "What's to stop us at this point from calling the cops once we're gone? There's no way the mess you've left with Marcus's body is going to be cleaned up by the time they get here."

"Junior..." I said.

"Hang on, Boo," he said. "I mean, what sort of guarantee do you have that we're not going to get on the horn to the peedee the second we're outside? They'll have you for murder, at least. With the other witnesses, you've got kidnapping," Junior counted off the offenses on his fingers, "assault, menacing, felonious haberdashery..."

Summerfield looked at me.

I hoped Junior was going somewhere with this. Otherwise, he was just handing Summerfield every reason he'd need to drop our ground-up corpses into the Atlantic.

"And I'm willing to bet that your nice and shiny club has all kinds of highly illegal goodies hidden in clever places. Am I right?" Junior lowered his face and smiled in a way that I was sure he thought was Clooney-esque. "Amirite, Ian?"

"You're not helping, Junior," I said.

"Oh, but I am." Junior stood at the end of the long table, fingers crooked in the lapel of his pea coat like he was the hardcore version of Atticus Finch. "I'm stalling."

"Uh...why?" I said.

"Stupid weather. Traffic is a bitch, I'm figuring."

A crashing boom echoed through the empty club.

Summerfield raised his gun, unsure where to point it. "What the fuck is that?"

"Put the gun down, ya big scrote," Junior said. "That there is the motherfucking feds."

Summerfield's eyes went into panic mode.

From the club's entrance, the sound of metal doors being rammed reverberated through the cavernous nightclub. Voices yelled, "On the floor! On the floor!" I guessed that Cornrows and Lineman would be getting on the floor toot sweet.

Junior grinned his widest, most irritating smirk. "This a bad time to tell everybody that I'm wearing a wire?"

Every mouth in the room fell open at the exact same moment. Even Ginny managed a low-hanging chin underneath the duct tape.

"Why didn't you tell me this?" I said.

"I didn't want you to judge me," Junior said.

Through the broken mirrored glass, I saw a half dozen SWAT dudes storming the club, automatic weapons raised and scanning the room. "Up here," I said, raising my arms, for the first time in my life, deliriously happy to see men with guns.

I turned back to the room. "I think everybody should raise their hands and drop any weapons, if they have them."

Junior and Kelly both held their hands high.

Ginny mumble-grumbled more of what were undoubtedly colorful damnations of both me and future generations of the Malone bloodline. "You're excused, Ginny."

"Uh, Boo?" Junior said, lifting his head toward Summerfield.

Oh shit.

He hadn't dropped his gun.

He'd gone ash-white and his breathing was ragged, panting.

Junior lowered his hands.

I lowered mine.

Remember that sixth sense I was talking about?

Summerfield was about to do something really, really bad.

He raised the gun at Junior's chest and fired.

CHAPTER 20

As Summerfield's hand came up, I reacted, dipping my shoulder low under the big table and flipping it up between us. The first shot hit right in the spot where it would have nailed Junior in the sternum. The thick wood splintered on our side of the table, but held. Thank God for Summerfield's sense of opulence. Any table at The Cellar would have exploded and burst into flames.

The second and third bullets hit the table by my leg and an inch from my nose.

"*Fuck*," Junior yelled, clutching his face. He'd been hit with the hot splinters popping off the table's underside. "I can't fucking see!"

Then I heard the hidden door next to the bar slam shut.

I poked my head up. No Summerfield. He'd made a run for it.

Ginny was bouncing up and down in her chair.

"Are you okay? Are you hit?"

Through her terrified sobs, she shook her head no.

"Kelly?"

No response.

"Kelly!"

I scanned the floor of the room through the haze of gunpowder smoke and wood dust.

She wasn't on the floor.

She wasn't in the room.

Summerfield had taken her.

And in that moment.

In that realization.

I went into beast mode.

I didn't know where the release was on our side of the room for the hidden door.

Didn't matter.

I charged the door in a fury, throwing my full weight against it. The door gave a fraction. I threw myself at it again. Something cracked. It might have been wood, might have been something inside my skeletal structure.

I wasn't feeling a goddamn thing any more.

There wasn't going to be any pain.

Not for me.

But somebody else sure as shit was getting some.

Third time I hit it, I came crashing through the door like a cannonball, the wood thankfully thinner than that of the table. The secret entry/exit led to a concrete stairwell going up and down. I knew that these clubs could be a labyrinth of hallways, connecting offices to buildings and other clubs.

I had no idea which way they'd gone.

I could hear footsteps, and Kelly pleading, but couldn't determine from the echoes which direction they were coming from.

Then I heard Kelly yell, "Down here! He has a gun."

She must have thought the door smashing was the Feds coming through, ready to save the day like the disciplined professionals they were.

Then I heard a dull, slapping impact, and Kelly grunt.

I couldn't wait for the Feds. She'd have to settle for little ol' me.

I charged down the stairs two, three at a time.

I took one step too many, and heard my knee pop. It didn't hurt, but I couldn't put weight on it any more. I half dragged myself down the remaining two flights and burst out the door into an underground parking garage.

Summerfield was trying to move Kelly into the passenger seat of his Lexus, a thin line of blood dribbling from the hairline over her swelling eye, a souvenir from where it looked like he'd pistol whipped her. She was putting up some resistance, but clearly aware of the gun still in his hand.

The garage exploded in all the red tones of Hell itself. I howled and charged him like an enraged gorilla.

He wasn't moving in slo-mo like the movies would have you believe. But he wasn't moving quite as quickly as the furious two hundred forty pounds of me.

Every bone in my hand crunched with the intensity of the fist I clenched. Then I threw a haymaker with murderous intentions.

And then missed. By a lot. Again.

In the time it took me to close the distance between us, he dropped Kelly to the ground, ducked under my fist, and brought his knee up at the same time.

Oh yeah. He was really good at kung fu and all that jazz.

And remember what I said about how much I hated jazz?

I impaled myself on his knee so deeply, I think his kneecap went through my belly and bounced off my spine. All the wind rushed from my lungs and momentum drove me past him and into the car door. He threw a lightning fast elbow to my cheek, and I saw stars.

I still had enough sense in me to grab his gun hand and slam his wrist onto the doorframe, the gun slipping from his sweaty grasp, clattering along the trunk and falling to the ground.

The gun out of play, I smashed my forearm into his face.

Once.

His nose popped.

Twice.

His head snapped back.

Three times.

Two of his teeth came away, embedded into my wrist meat.

Then I got greedy and went for four.

As I drew back, he knife-handed me to the throat and my windpipe slammed shut. I stumbled backward and fell over Kelly's legs. She was trying to crawl away, having regained at least that much of her senses.

I couldn't breathe, and instinctively clutched my neck as I stood.

With the space between us that he needed, Summerfield leapt into a Superman punch, connecting it to my eyebrow. The garage shuttered into blackness for a microsecond, and I was on my ass.

Summerfield turned his back to me.

Exactly like the last time he'd kicked me in the face.

With me in a sitting position, that kick would snap my neck like a stale pretzel stick.

So I pitched myself forward before he could start his whirlwind of death and sunk my teeth right into the back of his knee.

Ian screamed as I felt his flesh tear and tendons popping underneath my chompers.

He smashed a spinning elbow onto the crown of my skull and I fell, the world blinking out again. Just for a second. I think my face smacking the icy concrete was what woke me back up.

That second was all he needed.

When the blackness flashed back to light, Ian had a sawed-off shotgun in his hands, pulled from the floor of the car's backseat.

Kelly had lifted herself up, sliding back to the wall, a hand clutching the inside of her thigh.

I could barely lift my head to look my own death in the eye.

There was no way I could get to Summerfield. I couldn't stand. I couldn't even take in a final breath.

I was going to die on my hands and knees like a fucking animal.

Summerfield lifted the gun toward me, his face a bloody mask of murderous fury.

Kelly's hand came away from her leg. In it was a small pistol. As her hand lifted the skirt, it was just enough to see the small holster on her thigh.

"Federal agent!" Kelly yelled at Summerfield like Xena, Warrior Princess. "Drop your weapon."

Wow.

Hadn't seen that coming.

Neither had Summerfield.

I wish I had the words to describe his expression. I really do. It was amazeballs. Best I could compare it to was face of someone who just sat on a cactus. And then that cactus went *all* the way up inside him.

That was what he looked like.

Then he shot me in the sternum. The shotgun blast lifted me off my feet and sent me tumbling end-over-end until I hit the cold concrete wall of the parking garage. Once kinetic energy stopped fucking with me, the pain hit pretty fast.

Sweet bleeding eyes o' Jesus, it hit fast.

And hard.

Kelly shot Summerfield on the collarbone.

Summerfield turned and tried to lift the shotgun toward Kelly.

Kelly shot him in the face before he could.

Ian's brains popped out the back of his skull. He dropped to the ground, most of his face twisted around the new hole where his nose used to be.

Kelly ran over to me. "Boo!"

I couldn't say anything. It was hard enough getting breath from the karate chop to my throat. The shotgun blast to the chest wasn't doing my communication skills any favors.

I wanted to tell her it was going to be all right, but couldn't.

Good Christ, everything hurt. Endorphins and adrenaline could only do so much, in the end.

She knelt over me, tears running down her face. I could hear footsteps echoing down the stairs, the authoritative voices of the Feds bouncing off the stairwells.

"I need an ambulance down here!" she screamed as she tore my shirt open.

With an immense effort, I sat up and painfully inhaled a small lungful of air. Enough to say, "Hey, I liked that shirt."

Kelly's eyes flew open when she saw the bundles of money that I'd duct-taped underneath my now-ruined shirt.

Just in case.

Bundles thick enough to have stopped most of the point-blank-range buckshot. Well, stopped them from cutting me in half. As I sat up, trying to maintain cool, I could feel my newly broken ribs shift, and fresh hell erupted upon my nervous system. "Always knew you'd tear my clothes off again some day," I wheezed.

Then, for the second time that week, I fainted.

Just like all us tough guys do.

But I was pretty happy with the line I went out with. So I had that going for me.

CHAPTER 21

WANT TO KNOW what the world's worst alarm clock is?

Sirens. Dozens and dozens of sirens. Specifically, blaring from the multitude of fire engines, police cars, and ambulances that appeared to take up every square foot of Lansdowne Street and most of Brookline Ave.

I came to with the cold sensation of the shears that were cutting through the thick gray tape of my makeshift—and unintentional—bulletproof vest. The pressure against my ribs was incredibly painful, but the pain meant that I was alive.

"Morning, princess," Junior said, sitting to the side of the ambulance's interior. The left side of his face was bandaged up over the eye, pinpricks of blood dotting through the gauze.

"If you start singing *Phantom of the Opera*, I'm going to punch you in the throat," I croaked.

"Meh," he said, touching a hand to the bandages. "Not like this can make me any uglier."

"True that."

The shears made it to the top of the tape, popping open the vest that was also keeping my disassembled ribs in place.

The agony was sudden and ridiculous.

Immediately, I started throwing up. I turned my head and unleashed onto the floor of the ambulance, the turning making the pain even worse.

Just as Kelly poked her head into the back of the ambulance.

Perfect timing.

"Painkillers, please," I said to the EMT.

He drew a syringe as I wiped my mouth and looked at Kelly. She held a compress to her head, the lid already swollen shut over her pretty blue eye.

"Hey," I said.

"Hey," she said.

"I'm gonna take a walk," Junior said. "I can't sit here and watch you two make goo-goo eyes."

Kelly rolled the one eye I could see.

The EMT stuck the syringe into my IV bag, and the pain almost immediately started to numb.

Kelly and I looked at each other a little longer before either one of us spoke. I ran my sandpapery tongue over numbing lips.

"So. You're a Fed," I said. Might as well get right to the point.

"Yeah," she said, chewing on her bottom lip. Might have been the morphine, but I immediately wanted to kiss that lip.

"You asshole!" shrieked Twitch, poking his head out from the other side.

"Hey, Twitch," I said.

"There was gunplay, Boo. Fucking gunplay! And you left me at the goddamn bar."

"Sorry 'bout that. I was kinda hoping it wasn't going to come down to that."

Twitch angrily pointed a finger at me while his eye made spastic accusations. "But it did. Do you have any idea how disappointed Benito and Manny are?"

"You remember Kelly, right?" I said.

"Hey, Twitch," she said.

"Hey."

"You know she's a Fed?" I said.

"Really?" Twitch's finger came down.

"Really," she said with a smile.

"Later," Twitch said, and was gone in the space of a blink.

"Nice to see him again," Kelly said.

"So, back to this whole 'you're a Fed' thing. How long's that been going on for?"

"Long time," she said, pulling a tight grin across her face.

The EMT climbed out the back. "We're ready to roll. You gonna ride with us?"

"If that's okay," she said.

"Fine by me," he said, shutting the doors.

I looked back to Kelly. "So you were a Fed when we…uh…"

"Yeah."

I felt the ambulance slowly navigate the congested mess of vehicles, siren turned to blazing. I closed my eyes against the sense memory from decades ago, to the last time I was in a speeding ambulance after being shot in the chest.

That was the worst day of my life.

I lost everything that day when I was eight years old.

This one, while not the greatest day I'd had, left everyone I cared about alive.

I was going to chalk that up as a win.

The hospital was a mad rush of doctors, cops, and Feds, all pretty much yelling at each other, then me and Junior, then each other again. All were jockeying for answers to what no doubt was going to be a logistical mess for everyone involved.

At least they put Junior and me in the same room while we waited for our various diagnoses and related treatments.

And there were a lot of them.

Where to begin this conversation with Junior? Fuck it. Full steam ahead. "So, you want to tell me about the wire?"

"Sure. Cops were up my ass for about six hours before a couple of guys in suits came in and started yapping at me. That was when I knew shit had gone weird."

"Okay. Then what?"

Junior picked at his bandages.

"Don't do that," I said.

"Shit itches," he grumbled.

"I'm not the guy you want to complain to right now," I said, waving a hand over my shattered and blood-spattered self. "Go on."

"Where was I?"

"Shit had gone weird."

"Oh, yeah. They figured pretty quick that you and me weren't involved in doing any kind of hitter work for Summerfield."

"How'd they do that?"

"My phone. Dumbass Byron called Raja, Summerfield's personal number, and IronClad security. Either to threaten them or asking for a ride. I don't know."

"How did that clear us?"

"Didn't, exactly. But they tracked his phone and it was with us. They figured out a rough timetable for when he died, and we were already back at Ginny's."

"Pretty thin."

"True dat. And they still didn't know exactly who did do it."

"So you agreed to wear a wire."

"Not yet. Dammit, dude. Let me finish."

"Fine."

"Feds have been keeping tabs on Summerfield and his crew for a while. They had a lot of suspicions, but nothing solid. They thought they finally had something when Byron came back from France."

"Amsterdam."

"Same thing."

"Actually, not even close."

"I can stop talking here." Junior pulled a couple bottles of Bud from his coat and popped them on the stainless steel bench next to the bed.

"Where did you get those?" I asked.

"Pinched 'em from the fridge at Raja."

He handed me one. It was warmer than I normally took my beer, but I was in no position to complain. "Well done."

"I have my moments."

"Go on."

"Oh yeah. Where was I again?"

"You agreed to wear a wire? Byron in Amsterdam?"

"Mmm, yeah." He took a big swig and wiped the foam off his lip. "Problem was, Byron didn't do what he was supposed to do. He came back with the money he left with and not the pills, powder, whatever the fuck he was supposed to get. They still could have pulled some IRS or Customs charge, but that wasn't what they wanted."

"Okay. So how did you end up wired in all that?"

"I volunteered."

"Why?"

Junior shrugged and took another gulp of warm suds. "Because fuck that guy."

As good a reason as any.

Junior went on. "But then I started to feel bad, because, you know, snitches get stitches. Also, I didn't know much more than you did. Far as anybody else knew, Summerfield did have Byron killed and was trying to make it look like we popped his ass. Cops seemed to think that he decided to take advantage of the situation that we set up by kicking his ass in the first place."

I thought about all of it. Summerfield hadn't taken advantage, but Marcus sure did.

We were never going to know now about his reasons. Maybe he was the one who convinced Byron to walk with the money in the first place. Maybe he planned on punching Byron's ticket either way. Maybe Byron was the one who got greedy and decided to rope his secret hook-up into making it look like something it wasn't. They weren't the important questions, but they were the ones that we weren't ever going to get the answers to.

Was Marcus so ashamed of his sexual needs that he would kill to keep them a secret? Was it a tough guy thing? I thought about 4DC Security and Junior and me—running our own fiefdom tucked into the smallest corner of the security world. What would happen if one of us came to the realization that we were gay? All of the possible outcomes weren't positive.

It was bullshit of course. Who you fucked had no bearing on how tough you were.

But I wasn't ever going to have to face that. What I had to do instead, was face the people I'd hurt. Whether or not we'd meant to, the shit we'd casually said had contributed to Ollie and even Marcus feeling the need to conceal themselves. Marcus to the point of killing.

That was fucked up.

But then again, so was I.

We all were.

But I could try to be better, couldn't I? What was the point of any of it if we weren't at least trying?

Then I remembered something odd. Not enough that it should have even returned to the forefront of my mind, but once I started revisiting every decision I'd made, every second of the last week, this almost unnoticed detail kept sticking its tongue out at me.

I looked at Junior. "You took off your coat at my house."

"The wire was laced through the lining. You started talking about money. Didn't particularly want the Fibbies hearing about that."

"Thanks for that. I think."

"Hell, brudda. We were already well screwed. I didn't want you to hand those pricks more weight to throw around our shoulders."

"You could have told me."

"Yeah, but I was also hoping that you would say some stupid shit that I could get on tape. That would have been fucking hilarious."

Yeah. Hilarious. Thank the gods I wasn't feeling up to discussing the death of Galal Shaughness.

I guess in the end we all wound up with secrets we had to carry.

Junior and I sat there quietly for a minute, drinking our beers, feeling a gulf between us deeper than any time before in our lives. Secrets we'd kept. Secrets we'd have to keep.

"I'm really sorry about Miss Kitty," I said.

"Yeah," Junior said as he stood and put his coat on. "So am I. Sorry about this too."

"About what?"

In one fluid motion, Junior whipped out the antenna and whipped it down hard onto my shins. I sat up too fast, my ribs grinding together, and almost blacked out from the pain.

I clutched my side with one hand, while trying to save my legs with the other.

But Junior was one and done, putting the antenna that I was starting to regret saving for him back into his pocket.

"We done?" I wheezed.

"We done," he said. "How much longer you going to be in here?"

"They said another night for observation."

"Okay. See you tomorrow. I'll bring donuts and beer."

"You giving me a ride home?"

Junior reached into his pocket again.

"Never mind," I said.

"Still not funny. Not yet."

"I'll give it time."

"You do that. Love ya, brudda."

"Love you too, cupcake."

Then he was gone, leaving me alone with my thoughts, guilt, and confusion. I was no stranger to the trio, but they were usually no more than static in the background of my normal ponderings.

I felt a momentary pang for Marcus, not dissimilar from the one I did for Ollie. Much as I hated the guy, Marcus was a tough bastard, had clawed his way to running the top security firm in Boston. But one loose tongue and that house of cards could have come crashing down.

Fucking image. People dead over a fucking image.

Then the pang for Marcus went away. He made his bed, he took the life. And at the end of the day, the guy was a Grade-A asshole. Normally, I'd have said fuck him, but under the current circumstances, I'd just say to hell with him.

I didn't know if that qualified as personal growth, but I'd take what I could get.

Then I thought back to Ollie, hiding important parts of who he was from the only family he had, the people who loved him more than anybody on the planet, simply because he feared that they wouldn't love, couldn't love the truth. They weren't the most important pieces of what made Ollie who he was, but we'd never seen the whole Ollie. And that hurt my heart.

But no matter what, it never stopped him from being our brother, even when he lived with the fear that our brotherhood, our family, our love for each other would be damaged or destroyed by the simple fact of his nature. It never stopped him from loving us.

I don't care what anybody says.

That's what toughness is.

That was as tough as it fucking got.

And that's what a true family is.

CHAPTER 22

CONVERSATION AFTER CONVERSATION with all kinds of law enforcement.

First it was a briefing with the Feds.

Then the Boston police.

Then the freaking ATF.

Then we were both released with the promise that there would be more to come.

No doubt.

Junior went back to work. He had some new scars on his ugly face, but there was no real damage to his eye. I think he was a little sad about that, muttering once or twice about how cool he'd look in an eyepatch.

We gave G.G. a well-deserved vacation and a bonus.

All the various forces of several federal agencies came down like the hammer of God on Ian Summerfield's holdings. We saw Alex being led into and out of a few courthouses on the news. Assets were seized, the empire crumbled. IronClad Security was gone, and more than a few of their former employees came to me and 4DC looking for work.

All returned to normal, or as normal as our world ever got.

I couldn't work for at least another three weeks. My leg got re-braced, my stitches were re-stitched, and my ribs healed slowly and painfully.

Not that I didn't spend all my time at The Cellar anyway. After all, that was where the booze was. Certain elements of my darker nature had reaffixed their grips on my every day.

I thought about secrets.

All the time.

This may sound shocking, but I had trust issues.

Take a minute.

I was questioning…well, everything. Some secrets are born screaming into the light, others we keep to the grave. I had to let some of mine go. I had to.

I just couldn't.

I had to get comfortable with the fact that I had as many secrets in my closet as anybody else.

So I drank away my physical pains and the self-doubts that always creeped around, but had recently picked up the pace.

There were repercussions to that too. The first of which was that Audrey made me remove all the Tom Waits albums out of the jukebox. One more busy night interrupted with a heart-rending ballad, and she was going to stick her corkscrew in my ears first, then her own.

I was deep into another Sunday afternoon drunk, idly watching the Patriots game, when I saw Audrey's wide face beam happily, her joyous "Hey!" rattling the glasses. She lumbered around the bar to put Kelly into an uncomfortable bear hug. Uncomfortable for Kelly, anyway, what with her blood-rush reddened face and her shoes dangling three inches off the floor.

"Where have you been, sweetie? So nice to see you. You're not here to see this meatball, are you?" Audrey said, tilting her head in my direction.

"I don't think she can answer you, Audrey," I said.

"Huh?"

"Not sure she can breathe right now."

Audrey released Kelly from her Bigfoot death hug, and Kelly dropped back to the floor, trying gamely to hide the wheezing. "Actually, I am," she said, looking to me as she smoothed her newly wrinkled black blazer. "Do you have a few minutes?"

"You're dressed like you're here in an official capacity."

Kelly's eyebrows pulled downward, but only for a second.

Audrey looked confused. "What does that mean?"

Secrets. Again.

And I'd reflexively opened with a dick move. I moved to cover it. "It's Sunday, Audrey. Look at that suit. She looks like she's going to work at the courthouse."

Audrey sniffed. "She's got some fashion sense, you raggedy bum." Audrey smoothed the fabric on Kelly's shoulders with her thick hands. "Don't you listen to him, honey."

"You want to talk here?" I asked.

"Can you come with me for a bit?" The words were ominous, but the tone wasn't.

"Sure. I'll be back, Audrey."

"Okay, hon. I'll put your beer on the ice," she said, putting my Bud bottle into the cooler bin. As Kelly led me to the door and I buttoned up my coat, Audrey, forever the mama hen, smiled at me and wiggled her eyebrows.

If only.

The small talk on the drive was even more painful than my ribs.

"How are you feeling?" she asked.

As loaded a question as any.

I wanted to say that I felt like a meat-filled piñata. I wanted to say that I was feeling like a guilt-filled donut sprinkled with confusion and angst and paranoia and regrets.

Instead, I lied and just said,"Better."

After fifteen more minutes of silent awkwardness, we pulled into the garage at One Center Plaza and the FBI field office.

"I'm starting to lose hope that you're taking me out for a romantic brunch," I joked awkwardly.

"Maybe after."

"For reals?"

"Not really."

Dammit.

Through the first door, to the metal detector, where a Republican-looking wooly mammoth in a suit confiscated the brass knuckles that I'd taken to carrying in my coat. The old "better to have it and not need it." I forgot I had them, and the mammoth was none too pleased at the discovery.

An additional pat-down and two checkpoints with ID checks later, and we walked through the FBI office, staffed barebones on the Sunday afternoon. That didn't stop the few suits who were peppering the space from shooting me glances and glares as we passed, each one pegging me for future reference and not trying to hide that they were.

I didn't like that. Not one bit.

Kelly opened the door to what was obviously not an office but an interrogation room. "Can I get you anything?" she said, a newly officious tone in her voice now that we were in the offices.

"Coffee'd be great."

"Make yourself comfortable. I'll be right back."

"How could I not?" I said, gesturing to the white painted walls, the metal desk and chair, the video camera mounted to the ceiling.

She rolled her baby blues as she walked out, but she was fighting against the smile that my wit, under other circumstances, would have brought out. Maybe.

Least I think it would have.

What the hell did I know anymore?

But like the good old days, I gave her butt a tight eyeballing as she exited.

I was still me, despite it all.

I waited a few seconds, then tried the door. It was unlocked, so there was that. An agent with a white military flattop and a gray suit was passing the door when it opened. He gave me a quizzical glance as I popped my head into the hallway.

"Wait a minute…this isn't Narnia," I said to him as I shut the door again.

I sat down in the incredibly uncomfortable chair as Kelly came back with two steaming cups in Styrofoam, placing one in front of me. I took a sip. Not bad.

"One sugar, just a touch of milk, right?"

"You remembered."

"We have it all on file," she said with a sly smirk that hinted she was only half joking. She opened her leather messenger bag and placed a yellow pad and pens to her right and a small digital recorder to her left. She pressed the record button and began. "January the second, two fourteen p.m., follow-up interview with William Malone regarding case number 12BC44." She scribbled onto the pad and slid it to me.

Cameras aren't on. Feel free to play dumb.

I wrote underneath that as she continued. "It is noted for the record that Mr. Malone, also known as 'Boo,' is here of his own volition and any information that he offers up in assistance to this investigation is given freely and of his own accord."

I slid the notebook back to her.

Kinda my natural state, but OK.

Then underneath that:

Faaaaaaart.

Which made her turn three shades of purple as she tried to keep it together. She shook her head and shot me a glare with lips pursed tighter than a frog's butt.

I covered my own smile with my hand. Maybe it was just me, but man, even in the circumstances we were in, I wanted to pull her over the table and plant a kiss on her mouth. Hard. "How can I help you today, Agent…"

She paused. "Agent Regan."

"Huh," was all I said. Another goddamn secret. She'd introduced herself to me as Kelly Reese when we'd met, and since then, I'd had no reason to doubt that I at least had her damn name right. "Okay, Agent *Regan*. How can I help you?"

"Are you familiar with the name Galal Shaughness?"

Whoopsie.

I shifted in my seat and winced. No way she didn't notice my reaction.

"Are you all right?"

I grabbed my side. "Ribs. These chairs aren't exactly Barcaloungers."

"I'll try to make this quick. Are you familiar with the name?"

"That a brand of Irish babaganoush?"

"Not exactly."

"Syrian whiskey?"

"He works for a subsidiary of IronClad Security, doing club security. He's also reputed to be working for one John 'The Butcher' Bass out of New York City."

"Nope." Didn't know that name, at least. Kind of glad I didn't with a nickname like that.

"Our field office in Manhattan sent us an alert that he might be on his way to Boston at the behest of Marcus Beauchamp."

"Don't know the guy. Maybe Marcus was short-handed on staff since he and his were too busy chasing me and mine around with all these shenanigans."

"That's possible, but not likely, considering the work he has allegedly performed for Jonathan Bass."

"Either way, never heard of the guy. Should I be concerned?"

"He hasn't shown his face yet, but here's a picture, should he attempt to contact you in any way."

She handed me a printout of an old mugshot and I looked into the eyes of the man whose body I'd stuffed into Miss Kitty's trunk. "I'll keep my eyes open." I handed her back the paper.

"At the time of the incident, you had a large amount of cash taped to your body, money that allegedly belonged to Ian Summerfield."

"Allegedly."

"A large amount of that money was destroyed when Mr. Summerfield shot you in the chest with a shotgun."

"That is less alleged."

"We were able to reconstruct a portion of the cash, and the amount that you had taped to yourself was approximately seventy-four thousand dollars."

"If you say so."

"You didn't count it?"

"I didn't care. Wasn't mine." I took a long sip of my coffee.

"Reportedly, and according to numbers that I myself heard stated from Mr. Summerfield, the missing number was closer to a hundred and twenty thousand."

"If you say so. I had seventy-four."

"Is there any way that you can account for the disparity between those two numbers?"

I frowned and shook my head. "Nope. The money wasn't in my possession the entire time. Maybe Byron squirreled away or spent a portion of the money before I wound up with it."

"Byron?"

"Byron Walsh. The original employee of Mr. Summerfield who caused all of the aforementioned shenanigans."

Kelly's fingers traced over the notepad again, hovering close to the words "play dumb." "Are you sure? Possession of this money could lead to charges of not only larceny, but obstruction in a federal case."

I wasn't sure if she was trying to throw me another signal. I went with what was natural anyway. "Got no answers for you, Agent Regan."

"Thank you for your time, Mr. Malone. There may be follow-up questions from either myself or another agent at your convenience."

"Okey dokey, artichokey."

She threw her pen at me.

"This concludes the interview regarding case number 12BC44. Time is marked at two twenty in the p.m." She shut off the recorder.

"Regan?" I said. "Agent Regan?"

"Please don't."

"What was going on when you were…when we were—"

"I was working." She began placing her items back into the leather bag. "I couldn't say anything."

"You were investigating Donnelly?"

"And Barnes. Mostly Barnes. Best way to get next to Barnes was to get into Donnelly's offices and campaign. He was tied into things other than politics and police work."

All of which I found out about a little too late, but found out about nonetheless.

"And I was…"

Yeah. I said that.

Sigh.

Kelly tilted her head and smiled sadly. "You were fun. And a good guy. And potentially a lot of trouble for me. I'm a Federal agent, Boo. But I'm still a person who can like people."

"I get that."

"Once it all imploded, I wanted to tell you everything, even though I knew I shouldn't. So when you shut me out, you made it easier for me not to."

I'd shut her out because I didn't want to see another woman I'd loved hurt or killed. "So what now? Can I buy you lunch? Dinner? A trip to Vegas?"

"Can you suddenly afford a trip to Vegas?" she asked, eyebrow arched.

"Oh yeah," I said with a big grin and exaggerated nodding. "I mean…nooo."

She squeezed her eyes shut tightly. "Forget I asked that."

"So…"

"I'm being transferred out of Boston tomorrow. Clearly my status as an undercover has been severely compromised."

"Guess it has."

Kelly stood and started packing the materials into her professional-looking leather valise. "Can I ask you a personal question?"

"Why not?"

"Did you ever look up Emily?"

And the blade sank into my heart. "Thought that was you."

After the whole Donnelly family drama, someone had left me a packet of information at The Cellar regarding the whereabouts of my sister, Emily—the information that Jack Donnelly had dangled in front of me like a carrot.

Problem was, after twenty plus years of State separation, I was pretty sure she was better off without me. I'd buried that dream, the idea of a blood family, and tried every day not to think about it. I failed most days, but the sharpest edges of the hurt had been dulled over the last months.

I swallowed hard and thought about what to say in response.

Kelly read my expression well. "I'm sorry. It's none of my business."

"No…no," I said, a sick feeling in my gut. "It's okay."

"You burned it, the envelope, didn't you?"

My eyebrows shot up. How the fuck could she know that?

Once again, she read me like a book with lots of pictures. "I saw the fire department report that came in the night after I slid the information under the office door."

Oh yeah. She was a Fed. That was how. "Yeah," was all I said.

"If you ever want that information, Boo, just ask me, okay? But promise me that you won't burn down the bar again if I give it to you."

"Deal," I said. I was trying to come up with more than one word at a clip, but the parts inside that processed emotions had gone haywire. Those parts that all us tough guys thought we'd carved out with broken beer bottles before puberty.

"I'm serious. You're a good man, Boo Malone. She deserves to know you."

I bit my lip and nodded. "Noted," I said, even if I didn't believe wholeheartedly in Kelly's asesment.

Kelly took a deep breath and blew it upward, making an unruly curl jump along her brow. "Okay, then. You're free to go, Boo, unless *you* have any questions?"

"One more."

"Okay."

"Your name even Kelly?"

She gave me a Cheshire smile. "Nice knowing you, Boo Malone," she said, giving me a long, slow kiss on the cheek before she put her hand on the door handle.

Fuck that noise.

I grabbed her hand, pulled her to me, and planted the King Kong of romantic kisses right on her beautiful mouth. She tensed for a moment, then grabbed the back of my head and really dug into my hair.

Fireworks detonated behind my eyes as I let her go.

Then I let her go.

"Goodbye, whoever the hell you are," I said.

And she walked out.

I had to wait a minute for my boner to go away before I followed suit.

I WENT BACK to The Cellar and drank some more. I kept myself together, though. For the first time in a long time, I just wanted to drink, not necessarily get drunk. Mostly, I didn't want to be alone. Mitch and Junior kept the peace, Mitch particularly thrilled to be back in the mix. He was grinning from ear to ear the whole night. I'd given him a call once G.G.'s threats of both quitting and hurting me took on tones of truth.

We needed staff.

Mitch needed some dignity back.

Hell, we all did.

I found myself looking to the door every time a brunette walked in, hoping. But, this being The Cellar, a few of those long curly-haired brunettes were dudes.

Audrey kept the whiskey in front of me, and I kept my thoughts as quiet as I could.

Junior seemed to have regained a certain amount of spring to his step. He was on the path to recovery. I was on the path to…what?

Who knows?

Ginny came on her shift at seven, gave me a weird half-smile, half-wince when she walked in. I tipped my scally cap at her and winked, but it all felt automatic and hollow.

Just after nine, the band started their set, moving most of the upstairs business down into the dank pit where the stage resided. They left behind tables of empty glasses, dirty napkins. Ginny scrambled to clear them off for the next round of customers. I decided to get off my self-pitying ass and give her a hand. I met her at the large double table at the back and started wiping condensation off the tabletop with the leftover napkins.

"I got it," she said softly. Might have been the only thing Ginny had said to me softly in the entirety of the time I'd known her.

"Meh, got nothing else to do," I said.

We both reached for the same pint at the same time, my hand falling on top of hers. She pulled her hand back as if my fingers had sprouted teeth and sunk them into her flesh. With a choked sigh, she turned and walked into the ladies' room.

The one goddamn place I couldn't follow her in the entire bar. From outside the thin door, I could hear her sobbing.

I'm not good with emotional women.

In all honestly—and it should be pretty clear by this point—I'm not great with women in general. At all.

Emotionally distraught was at the top of the Shit About Women That I'm Unable To Deal With scale.

"Uh…Ginny?" I said to the door.

"Go away, Boo."

Yep. Definitely crying. Could this be about our not-so-daring rescue? Maybe I shouldn't have mentioned the fact that we weren't, in fact, there to save her.

That might have been a tactical error on my part.

Maybe our hook-up was more to her than it was to me. Honestly, I'd always thought she kind of hated me. Well, maybe not hated. She at least liked me enough for a drunken, angry pickle tickle.

More female complexity that I wasn't ever going to wrap my mind around, it would seem.

Enough already. I walked into No Man's Land.

Ginny leaned over the bathroom sink, wiping away thick runnels of tears from her cheeks. "Fuck *off*, Boo."

"Listen, we gotta talk."

"There's nothing to talk about."

"Will you take a second? Come up to the office."

"Oh my God," she said. "Are you trying to have sex with me again?"

"No!" I said a bit too strenuously. "No. It's a little more private than it is in here. I'd like to talk to you."

Behind me, the door opened and a thick goth broad yelled. "Get outta here, dude!"

"Give me a minute!"

"Fuck it. I'm getting the bouncer." She stormed off to sic my coworker on me. "Hey," I hear her call to the door.

"Just talk to me. This is starting to get awkward."

"You're making it awkward!"

Mitch opened the door with a slam. "The hell you doing in the—Boo?"

"I need a minute, Mitch."

Mitch frowned. "There's not a better place you can do this?"

"I'm trying to."

"I gotta piss," yelled the goth broad.

"Fine!" Ginny yelled, pushing me out of the way and bumping past Mitch. "Fucking hate you, Boo."

Gothie La Rue raised her eyebrows suspiciously at me.

Mitch also had a face.

"What?"

Mitch twirled the toothpick between his teeth. "In my experience, when a woman says she hates you, the opposite is true."

"I dunno," Gothie said. "That sounded like she meant it."

"On the other hand," Mitch said, "I've been married three times."

"You guys suck," Gothie said. "Now can you please fuck off and get out of the ladies' room?"

I walked into the office. Ginny sat in the chair, attempting to re-apply her makeup with a small pocket mirror, but I could see her hands shaking even at ten paces.

On my slow walk up the stairs, I'd thought about all the possible responses I might have to whatever she was going to say. I wasn't going to say I regretted having sex with her, but my heart wasn't in a place she might want it to be. For reasons even beyond me, I was still carrying a torch for Anonymous Regan. It felt like I would continue down that pathetic walkway for a good long time. It wasn't necessarily fair to Ginny, but it was the truth.

"Talk to me," I said

Angrily, she threw down her mascara pen, where it bounced off the desk and rolled to the floor. "I can't sleep. I can't eat."

Jesus, it was worse than I thought.

"And I can't believe I had sex with you. Ugh."

And ego deflation in three...two...one...

Gone.

I reached for a bottle of Beam, cracked it open, and poured a thick dollop into the semi-dirty coffee cup. This was going to require more alcohol than I thought I'd be doing this evening. "Uh...sorry?"

Ginny took the coffee cup from my hand and polished the remaining fingers, then held it out to me for more. "No. I don't blame you. I mean, I do."

I poured her another two inches of bourbon. "Lost me there."

"We killed a man, Boo. A man lost his life in my apartment. Whether or not he meant to kill all of us, we killed him. And I don't know if that was the end of it."

"I'm pretty sure it is."

"Pretty sure? *Pretty sure?*"

"You don't have to yell."

"Don't I? I've been watching you sitting at the bar, Junior at the door. You guys act like nothing happened."

"Yeah. About that. Junior doesn't know about what happened at your apartment."

"I thought you told your girlfriend everything."

"I think that the fewer people who know about what went down there, the better off we're all going to be."

"That's just it. I call my mom back in Nova Scotia, and she hears me breaking down. She wants me to come home, and I can't even tell her why I'm crying so I make up some lie that she can hear in my voice seven hundred miles away. She doesn't want me to stay in Boston anymore. I don't want to stay here anymore."

"Then why don't you leave?"

"You think it's easy to leave? I have an apartment that I have to go back to every night, alone. And I spend the whole time afraid that someone is going to break in, or that they'll at least be polite enough to knock on the door and then stab me to death when I open it. I'm terrified here, but I can't afford to leave. Dana is gone. He up and left me, moved back to Oregon, leaving me with a lease I can barely afford and a job with a dickhead that I fucked..." She waved an open hand in my direction.

Ouch.

She took another drink. "I'm sorry. That wasn't fair." She sniffed at the mug. "Ugh. Take this away from me. I drink enough of this and sleeping with you is going to seem like a good idea again."

Did I say "ouch" already? I did, didn't I?

"And I want to go home, but I'm a grown-ass woman, and I don't want to ask my mother for money. I want to be able to handle what I saw. I want to be able to say 'Fuck that guy' for trying to kill us. But I can't. I go home, where I'm supposed to feel the safest, and I don't. I just want to go home, Boo. Oh, God…" The dam broke, and Ginny covered her face and began sobbing, her shoulders shaking.

I kept my mouth shut and let her rip. There was nothing I could really say to her.

But there was something I could do.

I reached behind the Dry Sack bottles to the paper lunch bag I had tucked back there. I stuck my hand in and pulled out one of the thick stacks that I had been unable to fit along my sternum when I'd duct-taped the rest to me.

Part of my contingency plan was to pay off Summerfield a little bit up front, and the rest later, if circumstances directed the day that way.

Turned out different, though, didn't it?

I dropped the stack onto Ginny's lap. "Go home," I said.

Ginny stared at the money on her lap, snuffled loudly once through her nose, and said, "What the fu—"

"Shut up," I said. "Don't say another word. Don't ask any questions. You just quit. Go back to your apartment, pack up and go home. You hear me?"

Ginny stood and looked me in the eyes, more tears racing down her face.

This time, though, they weren't from misery.

She leaned forward and closed her eyes.

Why not?

I gently placed my mouth on hers. I was already one for one on the day. Why the hell not?

She pulled back.

"Ugh. Dude, I was going for your cheek," she said, wiping her mouth.

Aaaaand fail. "Sorry. I wasn't completely positive about what was happening there."

"It wasn't that."

"My bad."

"Wow. You almost pulled off a real moment there where I wasn't going to walk out of here thinking you were a dickhole."

"Ruined that, didn't I?"

"Only most of it. What the hell." This time she grabbed me and pulled me into a kiss. Her hand squeezed the front of my jeans as she bit into my lower lip.

Then just like that, she broke away and walked to the door. "Little something to remember me by," she said with a sad…and evil smile. Then she was gone.

And for the second time that day, I was left with and erection and solitude.

I took a deep breath and tried to shake it off. Blue balls is a terrible parting gift, in case you were wondering.

AUDREY WAS FRANTIC on the bar and on the floor by the time I limped my way back downstairs. "Where did Ginny go?"

"She quit," I said with a smile.

"What? I can't handle the floor and the bar, Boo."

"I got you, Audrey. I'll clear the floor. You take care of the bar."

"Oh that's just great. Ugliest Waitress In Boston can be our new slogan." Audrey haw-hawed at her own joke. "This is your fault, isn't it?"

"Yeah," I said. "It is." Then I smiled. And I kept on smiling the rest of the night.

ENCORE

A COUPLE MORE months passed.

I healed up as well as I was going to.

The city defrosted.

Twitch decided to talk to me again.

All was pretty much back to same shit, different day.

We decided to have a boys' night like we used to back in the day when we were all fresh out of The Home, none of us with much to speak of job-wise or money-wise. Every Sunday, we'd get together, eat too much bad pizza, and watch kung fu movies. Back then, family was enough to get us through those worst days.

It was one of the ways we made the time for each other as we grew up and away from The Home. It was the way that we made sure we never grew too far away from each other.

We were all meeting up at Ollie's place at seven. He had the best hook-up. Me and Junior were bringing the pizza and beer; Twitch would cull his immense Hong Kong movie collection.

Junior picked me up in the Omni, which he had adopted into his lifestyle and, in his own inimitable fashion, named Charlie—after the Charlie in the Box from the animated Rudolph special. He said the car belonged on The Island of Misfit Toys. But like the few things in our lives that we could call our own, Junior had made it his.

Hell, we all belonged on the Island of Misfit Toys.

We walked into Ollie's apartment, with all of the tech equipment lining every shelf on every wall. His place looked like a Radio Shack exploded, but damn if little brother couldn't hook up one hell of a surround sound.

Ollie re-arranged the clutter in a way that seemed orderly, but still looked like clutter to my eyes. In the newly formed space, I lay down the pizza while Junior walked off to put the beers in the fridge. Ollie's cat lay itself on top on the pizza box and began purring as he soaked in the warmth.

"Who's that?" I asked.

"That's Gaucho," Ollie said. "Got him from the shelter a couple months back."

Another orphan.

Just like the rest of us.

He nuzzled my fingers as I stroked him under the chin. "Where's Twitch?"

"He's going to be late," Ollie said. "Said the T is a mess."

I saw a pained expression on Ollie's face, anxious. He looked toward the kitchen. "What's up?" I asked.

"You think you could step out for a few minutes?"

"I could. Everything okay?"

Ollie chewed his thumbnail. "I think…I think it's time I talked to Junior."

"You sure?"

"Yeah."

"Junior!" I yelled at the kitchen.

I heard a clatter of bottles rolling out of a refrigerator. "Goddammit, Boo. The fuck you yelling for?"

"I'm going to step to Dunkins. You want anything?"

"Yeah. Gimme a regular-regular."

"Got it. You want anything, Ollie?"

"More courage than I think I have?" he said, glancing at the kitchen again.

"Milk and sugar in that?" I asked.

Ollie didn't laugh.

I clapped a hand onto his shoulder and squeezed. "He'll be fine."

"You sure about that?"

I heard a bottle smash onto the kitchen tile and Ollie jumped a little. "Sorry!" Junior yelled.

Ollie looked at me.

"You sure?" I said.

"I am," he said, nodding and taking a steeling breath.

"Ollie! Where are your paper towels?" Junior yelled.

"Hold on," Ollie said.

I walked out the door and turned left toward the Dunkins. I tried not to think too hard about what might happen. I knew Junior loved Ollie like family, like we all did, but was family enough for him, for any of us, against a lifetime of fear and deep-seated prejudices?

I hoped it was.

I walked slowly, giving the boys time to hash out what needed hashing. I ordered myself a coffee and a glazed donut, munching on it slowly, taking my time. I was anxious to get back. I didn't think Ollie needed me there, in fact, I felt the opposite. I just...I didn't know how Junior would take it.

It was him I was worried about.

Strange that.

As far as I knew, Ollie had come to a kind of terms with living two lives. I hoped so. Otherwise, it meant that it had been gradually eating away at him for a couple decades.

I didn't know.

I was afraid to ask.

But what I did know was that he'd broken the terms he'd chosen for himself to step in and save my ass at Blue Envy. He could have run for the hills, kept his lives separate, and hoped for the best.

But that wasn't what brothers did.

And I also knew that whatever choices he'd made, for the best or worst of it, he was now making the decision to just live in one world.

I was sure that decision was a scary fucking one to have to make.

But I knew my brother was tough enough.

Through the window, I saw Twitch walking briskly down the street, a half dozen DVDs clutched under his arm. I ran out the door. "Yo, Twitch!"

Twitch stopped walking and looked up and down the street until he saw me. "What are you doing there?"

"Come here!"

"We're already late," he yelled. If there was one thing Twitch was obsessive about, it was punctuality. Okay, Twitch was obsessive about a lot of things, but the dude hated being late.

"Will you please come over here so I can stop yelling at you across the freakin' street?"

Twitch shrugged. "Sure!" he yelled back. He crossed the street hurriedly. "Where's Junior?"

"He and Ollie are having a talk."

Twitch's eye beat a quick samba routine. "Oh, snap. THE talk?"

"The talk."

"Whoa."

"Yeah."

Twitch broke away, running for Ollie's door in a dead sprint.

I was not expecting that.

I gave chase.

"For fuck's sake, Twitch. Give them a minute."

"No!" he yelled over his shoulder to me.

Little fucker was faster than I thought he was, although being faster than me was a pretty low bar to set.

I caught up to him a moment after he reached Ollie's door.

"You hear that?" he said.

"What?" I couldn't hear anything.

"The silence. Don't like it."

"We're outside. They can't hear us either."

His eyelid fluttered. "Junior's going to flip."

"We don't know that."

Then, clear as a bell, we heard Junior say, "No. No fucking way."

Dammit.

Then more silence.

"I want to go in there," Twitch said, his eye switching from spasm all the way up to vibrate.

"No. We have to let Ollie handle this on his own. He's a big boy."

"Junior is bigger."

I glared at him.

"Wow. That was a really shitty thing I just said."

It was, but I'd have been lying if the thought hadn't crossed my mind. These were deep, deep fears and scars that were going to be tested. Nobody ever knew what a reaction was going to be when pieces got pulled out in psychological Jenga.

"I'm gonna go back to Dunkins. I told Junior I'd get him a coffee. When we get back here, we'll see what's happening." It felt like we were killing time. Because we were. The two of us were on pins and goddamn needles.

"Fine," Twitch said. "But when we get back, we go in."

"I'm with you."

Twitch walked with me to get the coffee, but he kept looking back over his shoulder at Ollie's door.

We got the coffee and a couple extra donuts for good measure. A few yards from Ollie's, the door opened. Out walked Junior, shaking his head.

Was he leaving?

No, he pulled out a cigarette and lit it with a match.

Ollie and I stopped.

Junior's face was a hard, unreadable mask.

I handed him his coffee. "Thanks," he mumbled, breathing out a cloud of menthol smoke.

"You all right?" I asked.

"You two knew?"

I nodded.

Twitch's eye somersaulted.

"You guys think I'm a fucking idiot?"

I pulled out a cigarette of my own and flared my Zippo. "Honestly? I only found out recently, and it was by accident. I'd have never figured it out otherwise."

Twitch shrugged. "I've known just about forever. I assumed you two boneheads did too. So I guess my answer to that would be yes? I do think you both are fucking idiots."

Then the door opened up and Ollie came out into the cold. "Oh, you guys are back. I was going to see if you were still at Dunks. Why the hell are we all standing here freezing our asses off?"

Junior looked at Ollie, at his little brother, and I saw the shame carved into every crease of Junior's plug-ugly bulldog face. In each line, I saw the realization of every casual remark, every loose word of thrown-off hate that had worked its way over Ollie's spirit like paper cuts.

I'd never seen Junior sadder than in that moment.

I also saw the love he had. That we all had for each other.

We walked back inside. Ollie was business as usual, like it wasn't no big thang. "Whaddaya got, Twitch?"

"Oh!" Twitch said. "I got *Kung-Fu Hustle, Eastern Heroes*—"

"Nice," said Ollie.

"Hey," Junior said to Ollie.

"Yeah?"

"I'm sorry, brother."

"It's okay," Ollie said

Junior shook his head. "No. I want these chuckleheads to hear me say it. I'm sorry."

"I heard you," Ollie said, but despite his casual tone, I saw him swallow a lump.

Then Junior grabbed Ollie in a bear hug and planted a huge sloppy wet kiss on his cheek. "*Mmmmmm WAH!*"

Ollie screamed, and extracted himself from Junior's affection. "Aw, gross," Ollie said. He wiped the slobber off his cheek and shook his head. "Faggot…" he added.

With a smile a mile wide.

ACKNOWLEDGEMENTS

First and foremost, I have to thank the World's Most Patient Agent, Stacia Decker. Her support and patience mean more to me than I can ever express, and she's stuck with my ass through many a headache that I've caused her. She is fierce and tireless and puts up with more than any agent should have to.

Then thanks go to Jason Pinter at Polis Books for being the only man in the entirety of American publishing to have the balls to publish a book like this one, what with it's potential to irritate all sides of the social spectrum while trying hamfistedly to make a point. Mmmmm…ham.

Can't forget Allison Glasgow—the first person to read any words that I write. Her editorial eye is the best I've ever seen, and she makes me a better writer with every cruel, cruel swipe of her red pen. And believe-you-me, she swipes like a motherfucker.

Thanks to the writing community at large—without the support of those around me, I wouldn't be able to find the joy for what I do as easily within an industry that can be so crushing. And it has tried to crush me, over and over. Don't let anyone tell you that writing is lonely. Without their encouragement, support, and presence, I wouldn't have some of the best friends in my life. There are too many good people and great writers to list, and I'd live in terror if I forgot one of them. Instead, I'm going to just say "Thank You" and move on with my day. You know good and goddamn well who you are.

And thanks of course go to you for being a reader. Otherwise, why do any of this shit?

Last, but not least, all my love to my partner-in- crime and best friend Sam. Someday you'll get to read these words, my little man. And I hope that when you do, you'll be as proud of your daddy as you make me every day.

Every day.

ABOUT THE AUTHOR

Todd Robinson is the creator and chief editor of the multi-award-winning crime fiction magazine *Thuglit*. His short fiction has appeared in *Blood and Tacos, Plots With Guns, Needle Magazine, Shotgun Honey, Strange, Weird, and Wonderful, Out of the Gutter, Pulp Pusher, Grift, Demolition Magazine,* and *CrimeFactory.* His writing has been nominated for a Derringer Award, shortlisted for Best American Mystery Stories, and selected for Writers Digest's Year's Best Writing 2003, and it won the inaugural Bullet Award in June 2011. His first novel featuring Boo and Junior, *The Hard Bounce,* was nominated for the Anthony Award. He lives in Queens, NY. Follow him at @BigDaddyThug.